THE WORLD WE WISH

—A Novel

The Sequel to Of Course They Knew, Of Course They...

Brick Tower Press
Habent Sua Fata Libelli

Brick Tower Press
Manhanset House
Shelter Island Hts., New York 11965-0342
Tel: 212-427-7139
bricktower@aol.com • www.BrickTowerPress.com

Library of Congress Cataloging-in-Publication Data
Moody, John.
the world we wish
p. cm.
     1. Fiction—Thriller. 2. Fiction—Thriller—Suspense.
     3. Fiction— 4. United States—Fiction
     Fiction, I. Title.
ISBN: 978-1-883283-74-2, Hardcover 978-1-59019-004-3, Trade Paper

September 2022

THE

WORLD

WE

WISH

—A Novel

The Sequel to *Of Course They Knew, Of Course They...*

John Moody

To Jim and John
Readers, Critics, Believers.

Also by John Moody:

Of Course They Knew, Of Course They...
Co-author of *The Priest Who Had to Die*
author of *Moscow Magician*, a novel,
Pope John Paul II, a biography, and *Kiss It Good-bye*, a
nonfiction love letter to baseball of a bygone era.

Table of Contents

Chapter 1
Click-click

After a month, he could distinguish the shouts of terror about what was going to happen, from those of actual physical pain being inflicted during the torture sessions. The former was usually an ascending scale of notes from high in the throat that climbed, quieted, then began again. The latter were ragged exhalations of oxygen powered by unknown forces beyond, beneath, really, human control.

It had taken him a few days to comprehend the difference, and once he did, he immediately began calculating whether or not they could be reproduced, exactly, perfectly, artificially. The difference between man-made sounds, and artificially produced ones is mainly one of quality. Artificial was better, but he had known that for many years. Before he had become powerful, before he decided the fates of tens of millions, and, more recently, before he had been disgraced and banished to this land of woe.

Wo.

He remembered Wo, or at least thought he did. A pretentious, slimy power-grabbing official from the Cyberspace Administration of China. Wo gave self-important lectures about the duties of citizens to use digital information only as the Party permitted it to be used. Which meant, not coincidentally, to please and promote the Party. His habit of presenting other people's ideas as his own had been his downfall.

Stupid. He closed his eyes, shook his head sharply, castigated himself. Why was he thinking about that silly remnant of the past? Only because he spoke fluent English and could recognize and appreciate the homonym. Woe. Wo. Probably fewer than ten million people in China would understand that. Six one-hundredths of the population. He nodded in satisfaction, but he was careful not to let his face express any emotion. He knew he was being watched. He knew because he had invented the monitoring system that was being used on him. And everyone else. Irony. Just one letter different from iron, which he could hear thudding against flesh in the other room. English, like Mandarin, had too many similar-sounding words.

He waited for the cry of pain that usually followed a metal-bar beating, but none came. Then he realized: they have stuffed the prisoner's mouth with rice and taped the lips shut. To shout, one needed to inhale. And if the unfortunate prisoner inhaled orally, the rice would cascade into his – or her, mustn't be sexist – throat and cause suffocation. Thus, the prisoner, made aware of this before the torture began, would decide his/her fate: bear unbearable pain in silence, or commit suicide. At least, he thought sardonically, the prisoner would not die on an empty stomach, as so many others did.

Another thud, and the sound of two people laughing. One male, one female. Usually, the female torturer began the session, and when the prisoner had nearly fainted from the pain, the male would take over, with much, much harder strokes of the iron bar. Once the unconscious prisoner was shocked awake with ice water and an electric prod inserted into the ear, the woman would take over again.

For Hui Jen-Sho, the nearby sessions of abuse of the body and depredation of the spirit were mostly a scholastic exercise. Hearing them only, never seeing them, allowed him to deal with them on an intellectual, rather than a physical level. Never show emotion, he told himself for the thousandth time. Emotion betrays us, as he knew better than most. Another advantage of Artificial Intelligence. It has no emotions. At least not yet. He smiled bitterly, something he almost never allowed himself to do. Not with the ever-watching cameras overhead.

Click-click. From another room, not the one where the beating was taking place, he heard the distinct sound. Click-click. He knew by now that this was the sound made by an electric stun gun being charged. As he had anticipated, the next sound was a high-pitched discharge of fierce energy being transferred from the gun to some part – usually the genitals or nipples – of the prisoner. This time, the shriek of pain filled the room and Hui's head. No rice for that one. The voltage of the stun gun could be regulated. But often, the torturers used it at full force, sometimes killing the prisoner outright, most often causing only a blackout, so that it would be resumed when the unfortunate sufferer was injected in the heart with adrenaline, and chemically bolted awake to the prospect of more misery.

Without letting his eyes close, or his lips compress, Hui sighed. It would be another night of screams, terror, and torment. And all he could do was close his ears and his heart, and wait for morning. Mourning. Morning.

Hui had no fear that he would be subjected to torture. At least not the kind taking place around him. He had been introduced to the institute's staff as *mingshi*, an honored teacher, who had been sent to Lop to observe and advise on the re-education of the institute's students, as they were officially called. The three untruths in that one sentence summed up Hui's current existence. He was anything but a teacher, Lop was certainly not an institute, and the torture victims he heard around him were indeed students, but here, they learned only of pain.

Hui possessed one of the few calendars permitted at Vocational Education and Training Center #54. Its masters had determined that students would succumb to despair and become more cooperative if they had no easy way to measure how long they had been here. Most never felt the sunshine or saw the moon bathing the vast plains around them. To them, the world consisted of four windowless walls, a ceiling, a dirt floor, and never-ending cruelty.

Hui knew how long he had been here. Six months ago, four armed policemen had burst into his office at the Institute for Artificial Intelligence Research in Wuhan, and roughly ordered him to accompany them. Though not handcuffed, he was gripped tightly by two of the policemen, each one holding an elbow, as he passed through the hallways, an object of frank confusion to the researchers he had brought into the modest but highly efficient building.

Hui Jen-Sho was the founder, director and resident genius of the Institute, China's leading AI researcher and program designer. He was also –at least, he thought he still was – a Colonel in the People's Liberation Army, one of its more decorated officers considering that he had never fired a weapon in battle or killed an enemy of his homeland. Not with his hands, anyway. And now, *he* was being treated as an enemy of the homeland, exiled to this hellhole where intelligence – artificial or any other kind – was evidence of disloyalty to the Communist Party of China.

He – Hui – disloyal? What nonsense. He had done more to put China at the forefront of AI than any other person. The Party owed *him* gratitude, not the other way around. He had devised the strategy to shift blame for the virus created by China that had swept through the world like a diseased hurricane in 2020, a virus that had killed at least three million people, shut down entire national economies, destroyed families, and, best of all, advanced China to its pre-eminent place among global superpowers. The United States, China's archenemy, had surrendered its status as world leader because of the virus, and China had escaped blame for creating the disease, and intentionally spreading it to every corner of the planet.

Hui had formulated and disseminated the strategy among the Party's decision makers. It had been met at first with skepticism by some – the same brain-dead bureaucrats who later claimed a share of responsibility for its success beyond anyone's imagination. Hui shared credit with whoever wanted it. He knew his name was on everyone's lips. It was he – Hui – who had devised and directed *Da huangyan* – The Big Lie –and it had worked. China had infected the entire world not just with a virus, but with fear, withdrawal, suspicion. The European Union – those twenty-seven spineless states that thought they could challenge the United States and China in economic and political leadership by banding together – had instead turned on each other when the virus struck. Borders had been closed. EU passports were worthless for travel. Families were separated. Old people were left to die alone in their nursing homes. Accusations of incompetence flew across the continent. The European Union shed tears as though it were the European Onion.

America's response to the pandemic – which China had insisted be called coronavirus, not Chinese Flu or Wuhan Virus – was in keeping with its shattered pride and notion of superiority. Trump, who was president when it mushroomed, pretended it was no more serious than the flu. Then Biden, everyone's favorite forgetful great-uncle, told everyone to wear a mask, stay six feet apart and get vaccinated by taking injections of a substance whose contents few people, except doctors, could comprehend. This naturally led to conspiracy theories.

Black Americans said they didn't trust anything created by whites. Conservatives in states like Texas and Florida said they wouldn't be bullied by Washington. Young people in their twenties, most of them out of their parents' control, though still dependent financially, believed they were invulnerable and would take their chances. A life-saving vaccine became a political football, and Hui had heard how much Americans love football.

Even here in Lop, in disgrace, in earshot of heinous twenty-four-hour-a-day torture, without access to the information that had always been at his disposal, Hui knew the next steps that should be taken to secure and enhance China's position. But to whom could he now offer these ideas, two thousand miles from Beijing?

China had used brutal means to quarantine and isolate anyone showing symptoms of the virus. Apartment dwellers whose sneezing or coughing had been overheard by neighbors were reported, and police and "civic duty" squads showed up at their homes, nailed boards across their doors, or soldered them shut, and warned them of dire consequences if they tried to leave. The fact that some residents did not have sufficient food to survive being sealed into their apartment-crypts was not the Party's problem. They would have died anyway, probably. Their lucky spirits – *xingyun jingling* – had simply deserted them, just as the Party had. Even spirits knew enough to follow the Party's wishes.

Hui, from the confines of his Institute, ordered his subordinates to create matrixes to predict pockets of resistance to the Party's handling of the pandemic and to map out the strategy that would blunt unflattering reactions to it from the outside. Because the rest of the world was too busy trying to escape the virus themselves, little international attention was paid to China's inhumane treatment of its people. Hui's AI blueprint, known at the Institute as "Hui Thought," became Party dogma and was transformed into "Xi Thought." Allowing the General Secretary and Chairman of the Chinese Communist Party to take credit did Hui no harm with its rulers.

No, what had brought Hui to Lop, to this hell house, to this humiliation, had been his emotions. He had allowed himself to care about someone, to share his vision with someone, to – the word did not come easily – love someone.

A young American. It was a mistake, as all emotions are, and he had paid a dreadful price for letting his emotional armor be pierced. Far better to remain rigid and in control than to descend into this ignominy. Only one prospect kept him sane.

Revenge.

Chapter 2
Friends and Neighbors

China has a 47-mile border of mistrust with Afghanistan. The so-called Wakhan Corridor is the northernmost territory of Afghanistan, at the end of the Wakhan Corridor and next to Chalachigu Valley. The border is crossed by mountain passes, the Wakhjir Pass in the south and Tegermansu Pass in the north.

The time on the Chinese side of the border is three and a half hours ahead of the Afghan side. Chinese like to say it is also five hundred years ahead of the Islamic side, which, since Afghanistan was given away by the American President, is controlled by those scoundrels called the Taliban.

Once a key passageway on the fabled Silk Road, the border was agreed to between Britain and China in 1895 as part of what historians call The Great Game, the name coming from the belief that the once-powerful British Empire had the right to demarcate those parts of the world inhabited by lesser beings.

Throughout the years, Wakhjir Pass was used as a corridor for smuggling drugs, the one product with which Afghans have learned to turn a profit. When drug runners are captured on the Chinese side, they are thrown into facilities known as Black Holes. The only way to survive the Black Holes is to buy freedom by paying ransom, which most of the smugglers are unable to do. In *extremis*, they beg their families to provide enough goods or cash to purchase their freedom. Guards at the Black Holes often become wealthy because of these transactions.

Since the Taliban recaptured Afghanistan in 2021, however, China has reinforced its border at the Wakhjir Pass, cleared the Black Holes of prisoners by exterminating them, and executed anyone who comes uninvited within five miles of the Chinese side of the crossing.

Because Afghanistan is populated by Muslims. And Muslims, no matter how backward, depraved and useless they might be viewed by China, are one of the few groups that the Communist Party fears. That is because the border pass opens onto Xinjiang province, and that is the home of millions of Chinese Muslims, many of whom call themselves Uyghurs.

And that is why Hui Jen-Sho finds himself assigned to a so-called re-education facility in the depressed and depressing Lop County, listening to Uyghurs being tortured as the main course of their re-education and introduction to Socialism with Chinese Characteristics, *Zhongguo tese shehui zhuyi*. It is the mainstay of the philosophy imposed upon China by Xi Jinping, the Party's and the country's ultimate leader, demi-god, arbiter of all, master of the world, whether the world knows and likes it or not.

He – Hui – is not, he keeps telling himself, a prisoner. He is here because the Party has decided to employ Artificial Intelligence to estimate, detect and eliminate any attitudes or hidden thoughts that do not recognize the Party's authority. And no one in China knows more about AI than Hui. It is, he tells himself, an honor to be selected for this work, since it was decided and ordered directly by Xi, though of course, there were several layers between the General Secretary's dictate and Hui's sudden and forced removal from his Institute in Wuhan and transport to Xinjiang province.

It is an honor to serve the Party. This is the message drilled, sometimes literally, with electric motors and sharp metal bits, into the Uyghurs who are incarcerated in the re-education center. It is the same message Hui must keep telling himself, to maintain his sanity.

Hui knows that he is here because he allowed himself to be made a fool of. To loosen, just one time, his iron-clad self-control. To take the risk, one which now seems insane, of trusting another human, instead of relying on his mastery of AI, which was infinitely superior to so-called human intellect. Hui's hubris, he thought to himself, admitting silently that it was his – Hui's – intelligence that was artificial, so infinitely inferior to the advanced algorithms he had written, commissioned, and promoted for years.

He was not merely one of China's greatest experts on AI, but also one of its valued exports. He traveled the world, preaching the superiority of China's AI research. He was received by scientists, politicians, doctors, professors on every continent, all of them eager to learn what he – Hui – knew about the potential for mating minds with machines. He portrayed himself as a professor. Of course, his real title, the one that mattered, was Colonel of the PLA. But he enjoyed being fitted for, and wearing $2,000 suits, gold cufflinks, British-crafted shoes, and Burberry mackintoshes.

It was in this disguise that he came upon a young American named Henry, an unemployed 23-year-old from New Jersey who sat in on one of Hui's lectures on AI and later sent him a fawning email. Since direct contact with American citizens was discouraged not just by the U.S. but also by his own government, Hui decided to take advantage of a situation that, he could always explain if questioned, was not of his making. Their meeting, monitored by a Party spy implanted in the PLA, gave Hui the idea of inviting Henry to Wuhan on the pretext of studying AI at Hui's renowned Institute. It would, he convinced the Party ideologists, be a good experiment to see if an American, especially a young and intelligent one like Henry, could be converted from the decaying American model of democracy into a useful adherent of *Zhongguo tese shehui zhuyi*.

Henry accepted the offer, moved to Wuhan, and within a year, became Hui's main source of information about the United States, specifically its weaknesses. Hui fed the data he collected from Henry into his AI programs, which produced a series of brilliant strategies for undermining the U.S., especially during its fretful first year of confronting the virus that Chinese virologists had created, and lost control of, in Wuhan.

Then Henry's Mother in America contracted the virus, and Henry asked Hui to let him go see her. Hui refused, so Henry escaped without Hui's permission and flew home. Xi, the country's strongman, learned of the incident and blamed Hui for letting such a valuable propaganda prospect elude him. And condemned Hui to an indefinite future among the Uyghurs, as they were being re-educated, here in Xinjiang.

So no, not a prisoner. But neither was Hui free.

Now, in the dark early hours of a new day, the sounds of suffering coming through the wall were more like a perverted Gregorian chant, broadcasting chronic pain with no relief in sight, not even the relief of a torturer's momentary fatigue. Hui recognized it: a student being re-educated had been suspended by chains from a hook in the ceiling. This was a punishment, not homework. It could last for days. The mental effects were worse than the physical ones, if such a thing was possible. Hopelessness overcame determination quickly. Not knowing when, or if, it would end was its own form of pain. Hui understood this, since his own situation was quite similar.

The room where he slept was austere, but nothing like the muck, vomit and excreta-filled cells where the Uyghurs passed their time when they were not working or being tormented. His bed was comfortable, if narrow. He had Wi-Fi, since he might be receiving information about his Institute's projects at any time, and was expected to respond promptly.

He had been allowed to keep his Huawei smartphone, a Nokia laptop, and a Kindle that he had purchased in America but could only read the books he had downloaded while an ocean away. He had voluntarily closed his TikTok account after his removal from the Institute, to avoid trying to decide how to answer questions. He ate, usually alone, the same food prepared for the top-tier of the training center's officials. It was nourishing and numbingly boring. He could purchase *baiju*, the strong rice liquor that produced unconsciousness and morning-after head throbbing. He dressed in a PLA uniform with no rank on its sleeves or chest. During the days, he had access to a small but adequate laboratory filled with computers, data processors, video screens and a one-way connection to his former Institute in Wuhan. He could send raw information obtained from the Training Center to be analyzed. He did not know who saw it, analyzed it, or how it was used.

All in all, he was incredibly lucky.

And miserable.

To say he was being underutilized was an understatement of Ming-dynasty proportion. Hui had proven himself a genius, a loyal Party member, a credit to the PLA, and a star representative of Xi's

China to the rest of the world. The defection of the American youth, Henry, had occurred without Hui's knowledge and was due to the lies and cunning of one of Hui's nemeses in the Cyberspace Administration of China. The CAC was charged with monitoring, controlling and censoring communications throughout the country. It employed thousands of snoops to read emails, texts and tweets, to listen to phone conversations and WeChat video calls, to prevent websites from presenting information that did not align with the Party's interests. Hui used his Institute to one-up the CAC and gain control of China's outgoing communications with the rest of the world. Artificial Intelligence could not only flag problematic material – written, spoken, whispered or sung – but it could predict from where such treasonous thought might come and intercept it before it went out.

And these Uyghurs, with whom Hui found himself trapped, were certainly traitors of the highest magnitude.

Their main failing was that they were not Han Chinese, the ethnic group that makes up 92 percent of the population. The Han were pure Chinese, unsullied by bloodlines outside their homeland. One of Hui's most satisfying memories was watching the United States handle "diversity." Whites, blacks, Latinos, a smattering of Asians – all the ethnic groups clamoring for recognition, demanding that America become more like them, more like the places from which they had arrived. Diversity makes us stronger, Americans were assured, tried to reassure themselves. It was like insisting that pouring more water into a cup of tea made the tea stronger. Logic would not accept it, but Americans had been cowed into embracing it.

Not here, thought Hui. The Uyghurs were described as a Turkic people. Whatever that meant. Your roots are in Turkey? Please, feel free to move to Istanbul. See what kind of reception you get there. But don't cause trouble here.

They didn't listen. Xinjiang had been part of China since the mid-18th century, and its residents had the honor of being called Chinese. But these Uyghurs, who were concentrated in Xinjiang, refused to accept their status. In 1933, they declared, unlawfully, an East Turkestan Republic, which was allowed to fester only because the newly organized Soviet Union – China's arch enemy among communist lands – recognized it and warned China not to intervene. That lasted only until 1949, when the Soviet Union, depleted and desperate after World War II, gave its consent for China to absorb Xinjiang. Mao Zedong knew what needed to be done. He sent tens of thousands of Han Chinese to live in Xinjiang, in the hope they would civilize the Turkic barbarians, convince them to abandon the stupid rites of Islam and instead worship, as they did, the Party.

The Uyghurs repaid Mao's kindness by declaring themselves independent and refusing to let their children be educated in Mandarin. Instead, they spoke a Turkish dialect that sounded roughly like a dog choking up an animal it had just swallowed. By the 1990s, the Uyghurs grew so bold as to detonate bombs on buses, killing and injuring dozens. The government responded by rounding up and executing anyone suspected of disloyalty. Deprived of bomb-making materials, the Uyghurs attacked Han Chinese living among them with knives and syringes stolen from medical facilities.

The attacks on the World Trade Center in New York and the Pentagon in Washington gave the Party the excuse it needed to crush dissent. It declared that the Uyghurs, since they are overwhelmingly Muslim, were potential terrorists. When Western countries including the United States, condemned the roundup and incarceration of tens of thousands of Uyghurs, the government in Beijing asked them to explain what they were doing in Afghanistan. Protecting ourselves from terrorists came the reply. So are we, said China. We are part of the global war on terror.

The Uyghurs made it easy for Beijing to step up the persecution. Uyghurs were found guilty of perpetrating terrorist attacks in 2009, 2013 and 2014. At that point, a decision was made at the highest Party level. The Uyghurs do not wish to become Chinese? Very well then, there can be no more Uyghurs. And so began the campaign to erase Uyghurs from existence. The Party called its solution re-education, or protective custody, or training. The solution was, in fact, a slow-motion execution chamber.

Where Hui now spent his days amid the shrieks, his nights drowning in unheard moans for mercy.

But this night, this night of all nights, he heard another noise, neither of pain nor terror. He heard a soft ding, which meant that he had a new email in his inbox.

Chapter 3
Tanteeth

"Problem needs fixing," said the email. "Secure line only." It was signed in Latin letters, "MLC."

Ma-lin Cho was a lieutenant in the PLA. She had worked with Hui at the Institute, out of uniform, under the guise of an English translator, and had been instrumental in developing the young American Henry's talents and directing his transfer of information about America and its weaknesses into Hui's algorithms. Anyone who saw her was immediately entranced. Ma-lin Cho was ravishingly beautiful. Her long black hair was bundled into a neat bun when she was in uniform. When she wore non-military clothes, or no clothes, the hair slinked down past her shoulders and framed a face and eyes that drew men's souls into them.

What was less obvious, in fact, known to only a few people, was that her best friend, with whom she had grown up in London while their fathers worked at the Chinese embassy, had gone on to become Xi Jinping's second wife. It was a distinction that Ma-lin used with the utmost discretion, waiting to be summoned for a conversation by one of Xi's many, many guards and protectors.

Ma-lin's email style was brusque, but for a reason. Knowing that your electronic communications may be pored over by the Cyber Administration encouraged both brevity and opacity. And Hui, who was also wary of prying eyes and ears, knew that if the Party wished to contact him, it would provide a secure means of communication. Hui left his laptop on for the rest of the night, but there were no further messages.

Soon after dawn, as he was finishing his boring breakfast and tepid tea, an officer of the facility's guard detail approached him. "Would you come with me, please?" he said.

Hui nodded. He did not expect to be saluted or greeted by his rank. The guards were not sure who he was, only that he was here to work with the "students" at the re-education facility. For the most part, Hui was left alone, which was fine with him, though it added to his loneliness. No! There is no such thing as loneliness, he told himself silently. That is a weakness and weakness is unacceptable.

Outside the barracks a large black car sat, its engine purring, its dark windows impenetrable. Hui recognized it as a Hongqi L5, used by mid-level Party functionaries, usually chauffeur driven. The guard escorted Hui to the vehicle, opened the rear passenger door for him, closed it once he got in. Sitting next to him was a wizened woman in the uniform of a PLA Colonel, the same rank that Hui held, or thought he still held.

"Colonel," she said, as one might greet a next-door neighbor, neither deferential nor demeaning. Hui waited, a game at which he was unrivaled. "There is a call for you. Excuse me." She handed Hui an unbranded black cell phone, got out of her side of the car, and closed the door. The driver also got out and closed his door.

"Yes," he said calmly.

"No need for introductions," said a thin voice that sounded like it came from the moon. Hui recognized it instantly. General Deng-tal, who had taken over leadership of the AI Institute – his Institute! – after Hui was removed for letting the American escape from China. Deng-tal, the woman who had masqueraded as Hui's assistant for more than a year, really to keep tabs on him and what went on there. Deng-tal, who the American youth had nicknamed Tanteeth because, well, the nickname was its own explanation. Her teeth were permanently stained the color of a puppy's excrement. Her facial skin was a perfect match. And if those physical characteristics were not her fault, she added to the displeasing picture of herself by wearing wire-rim glasses of exactly the same color as her teeth and face.

It had to be admitted though, that General Deng-tal was a talented, merciless infighter in the steel-cage match that described everyday life in the Chinese Communist Party. That she also had a keen military mind and was a woman (just barely, Hui thought) made her a good ally to have, and a dangerous enemy.

She and Hui, whom she outranked, were now firmly entrenched as enemies, and so Hui recognized that everything he said or did would be cast in the worst light. Caution, prudence, he said to himself.

"General," he said to Tanteeth.

"The Party requires your assistance."

You require my assistance, he thought to himself, but instead replied, "Of course."

"Lieutenant Cho will arrive tomorrow with two AI experts to consult with you."

"Of course." Why not just bring me to Wuhan, Hui thought, but did not ask. He tried not to ask questions to which he did not have answers. It was a policy that had served him well. Until his downfall, that is, when he did not have any answers.

"Good-bye."

"Good-bye." Hui disconnected the phone. Tapped on the far-side window.

The female Colonel got back in. Hui opened the door on his side and got out. The chauffeur got back in and drove away.

And Hui, who tried never to show emotion, allowed himself a fleeting upturn of his lips.

Back in his room, Hui made some notes on possible "problems" that might need fixing and how he would respond to each one. What could they be? He knew that the Chinese vaccine against the virus – the virus that he had been successful in forcing the world to call coronavirus, instead of Chinese Virus, was not effective. In fact, Sinovac's success rate was barely 50 percent, which was the same result achieved with a control group injected with water. As it turned out, the water used on the control group was not sterilized and caused numerous unnecessary deaths. But these people were after all, part of an experiment. And they were also Chinese, so little fuss would be made.

Socialism with Chinese characteristics.

He could probably formulate a second wave of AI-produced scientific "studies" and news stories to discredit the statistics. Anyone who resisted accepting the more positive figures on the vaccine's success could be denounced. It had worked in 2020 when questions were first raised. And there were other means of contradicting what everyone knew to be true. Developing countries that hesitated to buy doses of Sinovac risked losing Chinese foreign aid. Equally successful, ministers of those countries that were receiving Chinese payments to their secret bank accounts to cooperate with Beijing would be cut off from the milk-cow of corruption on which they had learned to rely.

Perhaps it was something else, like the closure of Ningbo, the world's third largest shipping port, that had created a bottleneck for Chinese exports around the world. China's economy depended on exports, which in turn depended on reliable shipping of its goods. Ningbo had been hit with a large-scale breakdown of its automatic cranes and cargo transfer devices. That equipment, like almost everything used these days, depended on a steady supply of microchips to allow the transfer process to proceed smoothly. And the microchips were powered by rare earths, the 15 minerals that, when produced properly, powered everything from i-Phones to nuclear powered military rockets. China produced ninety percent of the rare earth supply. But there had been a breakdown of the production process, and everything was being delayed.

So, no rare earths, no microchips. No microchips, no cranes. No cranes, no loading of ships. And no loaded ships, no exports. One vice minister of commerce had already been sacked. But the problems persisted. Hui knew that, given the time and technology, he could automate the rare-earth production, the microchip deliveries, and the ship-loading process. With AI.

Instead, he was in Lop, listening to Uyghurs being re-educated with electric prods, psychotropic drugs, and good old-fashioned metal truncheons. Hui couldn't wait to see Lieutenant Cho and hear what she wanted of him.

She arrived the next morning in a military Jeep, a clear distinction from the Hongqi L5 that had brought the female colonel to the re-education camp. Every male guard kept his eyes averted as she got out of the Jeep, but they all stole glances. Ma-lin Cho was ravishing, especially in uniform. The curtain of black hair was neatly packed into a bun beneath her service cap. The uniform itself fit her so candidly that she might have been naked. It was not given to these guards to see perfection up close. The lieutenant was out of their league. They contented themselves with gang-raping the Uyghur women imprisoned here. Those who objected to being sex slaves had electric prods inserted into them, if they were attractive. If they were not, their breasts were cut off or their faces disfigured.

"Colonel," said Ma-lin Cho.

"Lieutenant," Hui answered.

Theirs was a relationship built on shared secrets that neither wanted known. Ma-lin had a particularly close understanding of Hui's strategy for becoming the point person in the response to the virus and the negative publicity it threatened to bring with it. She had been the translator for the American, Henry, and, at Hui's request, also his lover to reward him for the information and advice he had shared.

She was also Xi Jinping's spy within the AI Institute. When Henry escaped from China, it was Ma-lin who told Xi it was Hui's fault. Hui knew this, accepted it as part of Socialism with Chinese characteristics, and now was ready to enter the next phase of their complicated pairing.

Direct as ever, the lieutenant dispensed with pleasantries and, as soon as they were alone at an outdoor table that Hui had requested to minimize the chance of being overheard, explained the purpose of her eye-catching visit.

"China's population is aging at a worrisome rate. Young people aren't having children, even after the 'one-child' policy was scrapped. People are living longer because the health-care system is better. But old people can't work hard. And people of working age don't want to do menial labor anymore, like producing clothes, and dolls and all the other junk we make and send everywhere. Instead, they want what they call 'a better life.'"

Hui had seen the demographics and had wondered if this might be the motive for the visit. As always, he had a solution ready, but said nothing, offered nothing.

"To make matters worse," said Ma-lin, "we are having trouble attracting foreign laborers. It used to be we could order North Korea to give us people for the lowest level jobs. When they were worn out, we got rid of them. But now, Kim Jong-un says he can't spare any laborers because he has his own shortage of healthy citizens."

Because most North Koreans are starving, thought Hui. Kim Jong-un was the third generation of his family to have absolute and ultimate power in North Korea. And he was by far the stupidest and cruelest member of his family. He had executed most of his generals. Had ignored warnings that North Korea's food production was insufficient for its population. And then allowed himself to be seen, and recorded in public, vastly overweight and smirking like he had just enjoyed a huge meal. Which he probably had. Ever since he had hosted Trump in Pyongyang, and then broken every promise he made to the American, China had written Kim off as a partner.

Cambodians had been another source of foreign labor, until their own economy picked up and unskilled workers found jobs at home instead of being treated like animals by their Chinese employers and co-workers.

Even the Africans who had been lured to China to work in the mines and mills, on the promise of high wages and beautiful Chinese women had gotten the word back home: Don't come. It's all *Da huangyan* – a Big Lie.

"What has this to do with me?" Hui said, keeping his voice even.

"The Party needs to find ways to convince citizens to do menial labor again. It can no longer use the kind of force it used to. We're already under intense scrutiny from the rest of the world because of Hong Kong, Taiwan, and your friends here, the Uyghurs." She said the last in a serious tone, but allowed a friendly smile to escape her lips. She was, in her own way, trying to make amends.

Even before she finished talking, Hui had a solution in mind. Ma-lin almost certainly knew this. That was why she had brought two algorithm wiz kids from Hui's Institute with her. He recognized the two young men – why had he not also trained young women, Hui asked himself – who sat together, far away from Hui and Ma-lin, their faces blank, their eyes inspecting the ground in front of them. But their minds, Hui knew, were whirring. Hui knew this because he had selected them to master AI and taught them how to think.

"The laboratory facilities here are not adequate," Hui said. He spoke quietly, quickly. He was not negotiating. He was setting his terms and they both knew it.

"You may have whatever you think you need," said Lieutenant

Cho, very much a businesswoman despite her extraordinary allure. She never used her beauty as a bargaining chip. At least not as her only bargaining chip. Hui liked this about her.

"Thank you," he said.

"What do you need?" she asked.

To show that he was serious, Hui broke with habit and smiled. "To begin with, a list of the entire population of China."

Ma-lin smiled too. "Sure. Anything else?" To show that she was not just a pretty face.

Even outside the facility, the screams from within reached them.

"What's that noise?" Ma-lin asked suddenly.

"Either or," Hui replied.

"What?"

"It's part of the re-education program. A student is tied down, face up, on a bed of concrete with his feet and legs extended over red-hot coals. A quarter meter above his legs is a live electrical wire. The student has a choice: rest his legs on the coals, raise them and come into contact with the live wire, or try to keep them between the two. It's either or. It is a most effective teaching tool."

Ma-lin kept her face composed, but Hui could see the disgust she tried to mask.

"Would you like a tour? I'm sure it can be arranged. Then you could report back what you see to General Deng."

"No thank you," said Ma-lin. "Your description was sufficient."

"Yes. Now, Lieutenant, if I can help you with this problem you have explained, perhaps I could return to Wuhan and the Institute to continue my work?"

Ma-lin allowed herself a momentary smile. "Colonel, you and I both know that General Deng would not authorize that. For better or worse, she now controls the Institute."

"Yes. As you say, for better or worse."

They looked at each other. They had achieved an unspoken understanding.

"In the meantime," Hui said, "there are about two million citizens who would willingly accept what you call menial labor."

"Two million citizens willing to do menial work? Where?"

Hui stuck his thumb over his shoulder. "In there."

Chapter 4
The Joy of Labor

Everything about China is massive. Its geographic size, its population, its economic output, its armed forces, its gross domestic product. Its 1.4 billion people represent about 18 percent of the world's inhabitants. So it is surprising that of this immense number, only about 50 million Chinese citizens live outside China. There are many different reasons for this phenomenon: social, political, financial. Since the Party took control of China, not everyone can get permission to leave, much less live outside it. The Party knows who they are, for the most part. And in most cases, it knows if they have relatives still living in China. Most do.

Even the Party's data keepers, however, did not know every single person living in China. The record-keeping task was beyond comprehension. A billion and a half people, in alphabetical order, on a single list. Imagine the length of such a document. Where would there be a computer, or a container large enough to store it?

Hui knew all this. He knew it because before his removal from the Institute that he had created, he had suggested that the Party leadership entrust him with the task of creating a comprehensive record of China's people. He made this proposal with disarming modesty, admitting it was a daunting task, but confidently promising that he had the ability to do it.

Which meant that Hui's request to Ma-lin Cho was nothing more than saying – without saying it – that the project he had suggested before his ouster was still the right thing to do. And the lieutenant, hiding behind a mild smile, was acknowledging that he was correct.

Neither Hui's demand nor Ma-lin's acceptance of it would be voiced aloud. That was the Chinese way.

In point of fact, Hui planned to do the polar opposite of what he was suggesting. He did not want to create a database of every citizen in China. Rather, he wanted to identify every Chinese person living *outside* of China. *Only* 50 million names needed to be gathered, along with vital statistics such as their location, their age, and, crucially, if they still had family members living within the country. That, Hui thought, should be enough.

For centuries, Chinese people have left their homeland and settled elsewhere, usually because they found better opportunities abroad. Opportunities to study what they wanted to study, to find labor that paid them better than what they earned at home, to marry someone who was not Chinese. But almost without exception, the expatriate Chinese stayed in touch with their families left behind, sent money home to support relatives, kept open important channels of communication about births, deaths, marriages, changes of address. The things that make a family a family.

The things that make them vulnerable.

Since Mao Zedong took power in 1949, the Communist Party has kept track of citizens who leave the country. Their jobs, addresses, number of return trips to China, and personal history such as marriages and children are updated regularly. Part of the reason is to make sure that, though out of the country, citizens are paying the proper amount in taxes. A darker, less known reason is to let the expats know that the government knows they have family members still in China, and that they had best watch what they say and do.

Chinese students in American universities receive visits from strangers claiming to represent some Chinese organization. The meetings are intended to remind the student that his or her parents are known to the authorities, and that conduct such as complaining about their homeland could result in serious penalties for their loved ones.

Likewise, Chinese businessmen and women living abroad have good reason to fulfill requests for confidential information about their companies' business strategies, any friction among its executives, forthcoming sales figures or new products. Since Xi took power, they have also been encouraged to provide access to their employers' computer data, resulting in frequent hacks and thefts of secret information.

Hui had wanted to turbo-charge the surveillance of Chinese citizens abroad. The method was simple: digital photographs of each person applying for permission to leave China would be fed into the AI archives for speedy facial recognition. Family members left behind would also be obliged to have their photos taken and stored. The link between the expat and loved ones would thus be instantly available, 100 percent accurate, and easily updated.

Hui's staff had been weeks away from finishing its work on this idea when he was hustled out of his office. He had no idea what if any progress had been made since then. He certainly was not going to ask Lieutenant Cho.

They had parted with an unspoken understanding. They would remain in contact, quietly. The lieutenant would initiate any communication. A secure phone would be brought to the re-education center and Hui would be summoned. Though hardly efficient, this arrangement almost guaranteed that their conversations would remain confidential. And maintaining confidentiality was a virtue these days.

Socialism with Chinese characteristics.

The authorities at Re-Education Center #54 were not pleased to learn that their students – prisoners – would be put to work under a different boss. Nor were the commanders of the hundred or so other re-education facilities throughout Xinjiang province, where almost all of China's Turkic people lived. They argued that to turn the Uyghurs from helpless victims of cruelty, torture and isolation into laborers, who would be rewarded for good work, was a security risk.

They were told: the Party has ordered it. End of discussion.

Hui's estimate was accurate. There were nearly two million Uyghurs, Turks, Muslims and a smattering of Roman Catholic priests and nuns scattered through the detention facilities of Xinjiang. Some, who did not have the common sense to die, had been incarcerated for years. Those female inmates who had not been sterilized and gave birth as a result of rape by the guards usually smothered their newborns rather than bring them into such a world. The stillborn infants' bodies were dissected for their organs.

With the usual speed of priority projects demanded by the Party, factories grew from the ground in a matter of weeks. These would take the place of the bleak assembly lines where the Uyghurs had been beaten, shocked with electric prods, and kicked into unconsciousness. Machinery for mass production of garments, toys, light bulbs, picture frames – every creature comfort the Western world craved and would pay for – was delivered, set up and made ready to use.

Hui, who had suggested that the Uyghurs be put to work under his guidance and rules, would receive no credit for the idea. But he was satisfied. For one thing, the sound of torture sessions at No. 54 became less common. Not that torture had been eliminated, but at least it traded hours of the day with intense and intensely supervised labor. His methods were working, as he knew they would.

Hui was hugely disappointed with the two tech Geeks that Lieutenant Cho had brought with her. They had been among the best prospects that Hui found, and he had given them wide latitude to use their talents in fashioning new AI programs. Since his departure, he found, Deng-tal had sidelined the two and forced them to attend hours-long lectures of political indoctrination. They had started to believe the rubbish about the Party – that it was benevolent, honest, fair, working for its citizens. And they were not able to devote time to their coding and their AI research. They had welcomed their transfer away from Deng-tal and looked forward to being reunited with Hui. But they were shell-shocked by what they saw and heard at Lop.

"Why is there so much crying, and wailing, and screaming?" one of the Geeks asked Hui. Like him, they only heard the torture, did not witness it.

"Sometimes, re-education causes anxiety."

"Yes, Colonel. The lectures that General Deng-tal forced us to attend made us nervous."

"It's best not to say things like that," Hui said mildly.

"Even to you?"

"Especially to me."

Hui's advice was meant not to protect the Geeks, but himself.

When Wuhan was first struck with the mysterious virus that became known as Covid-19, Army-supervised construction crews erected a brand-new hospital to handle the influx of patients in ten days. The world marveled at Chinese know-how, the industry of its workers, the smooth coordination between government and private enterprise. News cameras were allowed into certain parts of the spanking clean hospital to film evidence of the Wuhan Miracle. It was just as well the journalists did not visit all the floors. They would have found that the electricity was not installed properly, the water that came from the sinks was brown, and that an infestation of spiders caused patients, already fighting for their lives, to get out of their beds and swat away the biting arachnids.

Socialism with Chinese characteristics.

The lightning-fast construction of the new Uyghur workplaces followed a similar pattern. The factories, assembly lines, work cubicles and toilets were all substandard. Workers were susceptible to electrical shock – nothing new to the Uyghurs – injury from falling bits of ceiling and misfit windows, repeated delivery of non-working parts for whatever it was they were assembling, and putrid drafts of air piped in from the toilets.

No one complained.

Compared to what they had been living through – and might again if they did not meet their production quotas – the Uyghurs were silently content with their new surroundings. There were no smiles – those were discouraged – but there was concentrated effort to do their best. The Lop laborers were a success story. So were the hundreds of other Uyghur-staffed factories and mills. From delivery of raw materials to packing and shipping of finished products, they hit their targets and sometimes, nervously, suggested improvements that increased their efficiency further.

They made the junk the world craved. Pillows. Pencils. Pens. Flashlights. Tape dispensers. I-phone covers. Erasers. Picture frames. Screws. Nails. Drill bits. Foam paintbrushes. Calendars in whatever language was wanted. Paper clips. Cardboard boxes. Ashtrays (not for America since smoking was largely forbidden there now). Dog collars. Rulers. Scissors. Baseballs (few of the workers recognized what they were making). It was infinite. And it was all Made in China.

Hui's favorite was the American flags that were stitched together hurriedly and slipped into plastic sheaths that read: "God Bless America."

"Sir. You are to come with me please." The uniformed armed guard who approached Hui did so with a kind of respect the Colonel knew meant his name was being used in hushed tones.

Same Hongqi L5 parked outside. Different uniformed officer, a Captain, handed over an unmarked cell phone, exited the car along with the driver.

"Yes?"

The voice on the other end came through a synthesizer. "Some men would have given up."

It's Xi, Hui thought, speaking directly but with encryption so that his voice could not be recognized, overheard, recorded, edited. Hui knew how rarely Xi spoke on the phone, scrambled or not.

"I serve the Party."

"You're full of shit," said the voice, followed by a quick guffaw. "But you're also brilliant. Why do you need the names of every Chinese citizen?"

"You don't want to know."

Pause. "You're saying that to *me?*"

"Yes."

Another pause. If thinking made noise, there would have been a volcano spewing from the phone.

"All right."

"I need more help. Better help."

"Talk to Deng-tal."

"*You* talk to Deng-tal. She might listen then."

"Am I hearing impertinence in your voice, Colonel?"

"No. Bitterness." He knew not to use Xi's name or any of his titles over the phone, even an ultra-secure one.

"Deng-tal is a good soldier."

"And a terrible manager." There, it was out now. The lines were clear. Xi would have to choose.

"You will have more help."

"Thank you."

The line went dead.

Give back the phone. Get out of the car. Stroll toward the factory where he had been when he was interrupted. The sounds of people at work, instead of in anguish, were refreshing, heartening even. He passed by an assembly line where the Uyghurs were making the blue surgical masks that were exported to every country but North Korea, to combat the disease that China had created and spread intentionally. Business creating business.

"I can help you." The words had come from a young man bent over the assembly line beltway. It was the first time a Uyghur had dared speak to him since his arrival.

"Did you address me?"

"I know who you are. I can help you."

"Stop talking!" shouted one of the guards, coming in the youth's direction with a truncheon held at shoulder level.

"Leave him alone," said Hui brusquely. The guard, weighing his choices, shrugged, and walked away.

"Who are you?" Hui asked the young man.

"Who I am doesn't matter. What I know does."

"And what do you know?"

"I studied AI," said the youth. "And I know that you are the master of Chinese AI. I have seen your picture. Trust me."

"Trust you?" said Hui, a smile nearly escaping his lips. "Why should I trust you. You're a Uyghur. You are an enemy of the people."

The young man had turned around now, was facing Hui. Surgical masks went past him on the assembly line, uninspected, untouched.

"Of the government, perhaps. But I am not your enemy."

"Who are you then?" said Hui, impressed by the youth's excellent Mandarin.

The youth looked directly at Hui, who noted that while his skin had the pallor of a prisoner, his eyes were bright blue, and shining with emotion.

"My name is Nur."

Chapter 5
Alone, Together Again

A week passed. No help arrived, nor did any of the guards approach him to take an encrypted phone call. The Geeks from his Institute – he still thought of it as his – plodded along but made little progress. Again, Hui noticed a change in the way the guards looked at him. He was treated with deference, a kind of mute awe that had not been there when he first arrived.

The word has gotten around, he thought. The Uyghur Work Project proceeded smoothly. Production was above expectations. And Hui, its progenitor, was once again a Man of Respect.

He thought from time to time about his momentary contact with the young man who said his name was Nur. Though hardly an expert on Islam, Hui knew a few basics about the tainted philosophy. Nur was one of the 99 names of Allah, the Almighty. In Arabic, *nur* meant "light."

The Geeks asked to see him. Admitted they were stumped. The program he had instructed them to code would not work as it was supposed to. They apologized, found a dozen excuses, careful this time to say nothing negative about their experience with Tanteeth.

Hui heard them out, sent them back with some encouragement, and, assuming he was being watched remotely, closed his eyes to meditate. He wondered silently if this new habit was a sign of personal weakness. He had regarded meditation as a convenient excuse for doing nothing. But since arriving at Lop, he found he could tune out the cries of pain for minutes at a time by concentrating on a mental image of calm. A lake. A tree. A waterfall.

Now, however, he concentrated on his memory of the bright blue eyes and pallid skin of Nur.

And made his decision.

A guard brought the young man in. He looked terrified, but at the same time carried himself with dignity. He looked around the laboratory, bristling with computers, screens, gauges, and flashing lights.

"Read that one," Hui said, gesturing to a rectangular plasma screen jumbled with alphanumerics. The Uyghur studied it for a full minute.

"Python," said Nur with not a trace of doubt.

"Yes," said Hui. "Can you find the error?"

It took two more minutes. Nur pointed to a line of code two thirds of the way down the screen. "It's missing an underscore after pipinstal>."

"Yes. Where did you study AI?"

"Hotan. It's where I was born."

Nearly all the Chinese Uyghurs lived in Xinjiang province, and Hotan was one of the larger cities there. It had a university, although Hui had not been aware that AI was one of the courses of study. He was – had been – in charge of the AI curricula taught at universities throughout the country.

"Who was your instructor?"

"Professor Danuta Byblova."

Hui had never heard of her. Hotan, after all, was not known as a center of learning.

"How far did you get?"

Nur shrugged. "I missed the last three months."

"Why?"

"Change of address," he said, with a faint trace of humor in his voice.

"You were arrested?"

"Yes."

"On what charge?"

"Being the brother of a Uyghur troublemaker."

"Are you a troublemaker?"

"In my opinion, no. As far as your question goes, I stay away from politics. It's a losing proposition for Uyghurs."

"So, when are you a troublemaker?"

"When I know I'm right."

Hui looked at the youth. Nur looked back. The fear was gone. But there was no arrogance in his eyes. Hui thought about the past year. The mistakes he had made. The weakness he had shown. The weakness that had brought him here. Why risk it all again? The answer was simple: this was something he could not do alone.

"All right," he said. He went to his desk, plucked a book off it, handed it to Nur.

"Get ready."

Chapter 6
Smart vs. Intelligent

Python is the foundation upon which most Artificial Intelligence programs depend. Initially designed in 1991 by Dutch coder Guido van and named in honor of the British TV series *Monty Python's Flying Circus*, it is, for those familiar with coding, a language used by coders to write AI. It is not the only one – just as neither English nor Chinese is the only language. But it lends itself to AI programs that focus on facial recognition. There were numerous YouTube videos explaining how to use Python as a base for writing AI facial recognition programs. The Geeks talked about them, argued over which one was best, looked for ways to improve on them.

Hui knew about this. Wished the Geeks would leave YouTube off and concentrate on their own work. It was part of his frustration at not having the absolute power he had commanded at the – no longer his – Institute. That someone like Deng-tal now presided there irked Hui greatly. But he was intelligent enough to keep that to himself.

Hui Jen-Sho had earned his place in the history of the Chinese Communist Party for recognizing early on that AI was the future. He was not a Geek. He did not code. He did not fiddle with the guts of the AI programs he employed. He had others to do that for him. Hui had become famous because he was a visionary, a term over-applied and seldom accurate or deserved. But in his case, it was precisely the right word.

His prescience was guided by two principles: human beings are weak, and new things attract attention. Even after Xi Jinping had selected him to lead China's AI research and allowed him to create the Institute in Wuhan, it had taken a year to find the right people to staff it, and to get the level of cooperation from the Army that was needed. Even a Colonel like Hui – was he still a Colonel? he didn't know – could be slowed down by knuckle-dragging bureaucrats in uniform, more concerned with their own careers and protecting their own turf than ensuring that China would lead the world in this field. With Xi's silent support, Hui had cut down the underbrush of opposition, weeding out a dozen high-ranking officers and twice as many from the middle ranks.

And when the experimental bats at the Virological Research Institute had found their way to the city's wet market, Hui had another idea, a plan to help China evade blame for the resulting pandemic and shift suspicion onto the United States. Powered by AI, the plan had worked. He was intelligent enough to make sure that his strategy was known as the "Xi Plan," not the "Hui Plan." Even the highest-ranking, most powerful, most exalted human beings are still human, and therefore weak.

For a few glorious months, Hui's position was beyond challenge. Party patriarchs visited the Institute, hoping for a few minutes of its director's time, to hear his thoughts, and to praise and thank him for his contributions to the Party, the people, the power of China.

That gave Hui the time and the opportunity to begin work on what he thought would be his greatest achievement: building a database with the name, address, digital picture, and the social media devices owned by every single person in China.

His ambition did not end there. Hui wanted to expand that database to everyone on Earth. It was not as far-fetched an idea as it may sound. Except for a few unknown tribes of indigenous Brazilian Indians, who lived in the Amazon rainforests and had never encountered outsiders, every human has data attached to his or her name. Hui wanted to harvest the raw data of every inhabitant of Earth. And once he did that, it was just a question of expanding the database, person by person, data byte by byte.

He needed better code. The Geeks with him at Lop were talented, but not super-talented. Hui needed super-talent. Which seemed an unattainable goal in a political re-education camp in a shithole called Lop.

He thought again about Nur. There was something there, inside him. He had yet to talk to him again after giving him the book about Python. What Nur learned from it, how well he could remember it, and how convinced Hui was that Nur was what Hui hoped he was, would determine both their futures. He told a guard to bring the youth to him.

"I am sorry, Colonel, but that book is garbage." Nur looked as if he had not slept since their last meeting. Now, he looked at Hui as Cromwell, his neck stretched out on a block, probably looked at the executioner with a dull sword standing over him.

"Why do you say that?" Hui asked.

"Colonel, you asked me to read this book and I have. Apparently, you want my opinion, so I am giving it to you. That book is not accurate, it is not clearly written, and it contains coding and programming instructions that will not work." Nur took a deep breath and waited for the sword.

"You're quite right," said Hui.

Nur, struck dumb, just looked at him.

"This was a test," said Hui, his voice calm in order to calm Nur. "I wanted to see two things: first, if you could detect the errors in the book. Second, if you were brave enough to tell me about them. You have passed both."

Nur nodded in a private kind of way that Hui would come to recognize as cognitive. "Colonel, may I tell you something in confidence?"

"I can't make any promises, but I don't usually pass on confidential conversations." He shrugged. "Especially here."

Nur nodded again. More thinking. Then a decision. "When the guard came to get me to bring me to you, he said, 'You think you're important, do you, Uyghur shit? I think you're due for surgery.'"

"Surgery? You're ill?"

"No, Colonel. When they want to get rid of someone, they administer anesthesia by force, then wheel you into an operating room and remove all your vital organs. And eyes. And then they sign a certificate saying despite the surgeon's best efforts, you died during treatment."

Hui disguised his shock. His time at Lop had conditioned him to the cacophony of mistreatment all around him. But harvesting organs as a method of execution was ... cannibalism, or something close.

"I have a proposition for you," Hui said, without using the youth's name. This would become his habit. "I want you to join my team of ... well, they call them Geeks. It just means..."

"I know."

"You do?" In other circumstances, Hui might have bridled at being interrupted. But he was no longer the head of the AI Institute, no longer a rising force within the Party. Perhaps even, no longer Colonel Hui. Who then? And he realized that Nur's impertinence was born not of arrogance but self-assurance. The same quality he had possessed as a younger man. Did he still have it, now, after his fall from grace?

"Your education must have been better than most. If I can arrange it, you will be lodged near me, away from the general population."

"Why would you do that, Colonel? I am no one."

"We are all no one until we become someone. Someone of use to the Party." Hui had his lines down pat. "And I believe that you have talents that would be useful to me. And the Party. Now, go back, keep to yourself, don't engage in any activity that will draw attention to you."

"Yes, Colonel."

"And..."

"Yes, Colonel?"

"You will not be having surgery here."

Nur bowed his head in respect, turned and left the lab.

What am I doing? Hui asked himself. Why am I getting involved in this Uyghur's life? Xi thinks I can be helpful to him. He has that much faith left in me. And with his backing, I can summon the best AI specialists in China, perhaps in the entire world. So why bestow my protection on this member of a subhuman race? Hui had to admit to himself that he was morally troubled by whatever went on in those torture chambers. He did not want to think of Nur being subjected

33

to whatever it was they did to Uyghurs. He believed what Nur told him.

You are repeating the same error that brought you down, that brought you here. You put your trust in the American named Henry because you sensed that he possessed important information about America, about its weaknesses. And you succeeded in making him into your useful tool. And the campaign that you directed threw America off balance, made them wonder if they were in fact responsible for the virus that was ravaging them. It turned them upon themselves. And now, with the help of AI, you can sow more misinformation, perhaps convincing some of them not to be vaccinated, not to wear masks.

But Henry betrayed you in the end, sneaking back to America, bringing shame upon you and the Institute, and handing it over to General Tanteeth. Your trust was repaid with treachery. And now you are about to do the same thing again, and this time with a member of a race that hates the Party, hates Han Chinese like you, and would put a knife into your back given the opportunity.

Nur probably has talents that even your hand-picked Geeks do not possess, or if they do, they have forgotten them under Deng's mismanagement and personal ambition. You must watch him closely, monitor his work as if your life depended on it. Which it does.

Helping Nur is the smart thing to do. But is it intelligent?

Chapter 7
Hui Wants to Win

"I need more capacity."

"How much?" asked China's Supreme Leader.

"Well, I want to store the names, pictures, and contents of the mobile phones of every person in China."

"Is that all?" Through the phone scrambler, it was more difficult to tell if Xi was making a joke, something the world at large never saw but which he did oft-times in private.

"With sufficient storage and retrieval, we, I mean you, could ..."

"I understand the implications. I want this controlled by the PLA. That means you would answer to General Deng-tal."

Hui let the silence be his answer. Don't say a word. Don't betray your thoughts and wishes. Above all, do not ask to be put back in charge of the Institute in Wuhan. Let it be his idea, his gift. And if things don't go right, his responsibility.

After a pause long enough to know he would not get a reply, Xi said, "Think about it. I don't imagine Lop gets prettier the longer you stay there."

Nor does the workforce grow while you play games, Hui wanted to say, but of course did not. The connection was broken.

Now what? Hui asked himself. He did not have the resources here to accomplish even remotely what he had just told Xi he wanted to do. The goal would have been ambitious if thrown at his – the – AI Institute when it was running at its peak. Tanteeth would have no chance of success. And he could not put himself in a position subservient to her. If Xi had asked him to report to another PLA general, he – Hui – might have agreed.

Wryly, he reminded himself that he had spent years drilling into his subordinates that their feelings didn't matter. It was only what they accomplished for the Party that would be important, and that should control their ambitions. And here he was, whining to himself about his own personal feelings.

The Geeks had again asked to see him. He had tasked them with writing new code on top of Python's base to allow sharper facial recognition. Python was already the leading AI language to facially identify anyone in its storage banks, but Hui wanted more. He also wanted to test the Geeks' aptitude.

Quicker than an AI calibration, Hui could tell as soon as they walked in that the Geeks had failed in their mission. Their eyes did not meet his. Their shoulders were rounded. Hui wasn't sure, but he thought he could actually smell fear on their bodies. None of this was Artificial Intelligence. It was decades of experience and study. It had taken him to the top of his field, and it had exiled him to this hellhole.

"Colonel," said Geek 2, "thank you for seeing us. We came to tell you ..."

"That what I asked for is impossible," Hui said, all Colonel now, not knowing if he still held the rank.

"Sir, it is not that your request ..."

"I know what you are going to say," said Hui. "Don't worry. This will not be held against you." He paused. "In the next few days, I am going to introduce a new member to our team. This person is to be treated as an equal, with all the respect and collegial trust due a comrade. Do you understand?"

From the looks on their faces, it was obvious that the Geeks had no notion of collegial trust.

"Dismissed."

The Geeks couldn't stop saying, "Yes, Colonel," as they backed away, realizing that they had been found wanting, but grateful that discovery did not mean the end of their careers. Or their lives.

Socialism with Chinese characteristics.

Nur's first day went poorly. He was nervous, as was to be expected of someone pulled out of a punishment camp and plopped down into a high-tech laboratory. The Geeks, despite Hui's admonishment, made amused faces at each other when Nur made small mistakes in his spoken Mandarin. How well would you two dolts do speaking the bastardized Turkish that is the Uyghurs' language?

Hui was not in the lab with his team. He was watching on a closed-circuit video line. Considering that they were all in a re-education detention center, he wondered why the Geeks didn't assume they were being observed. Nur certainly did, glancing involuntarily from time to time at the silver cylinder in the upper corner of the lab.

"The colors aren't coming out right," Geek 2 said. "We filtered each picture for maximum color presentation, but look ..." He pointed to a scan of a face on one of the computer screens. "This face looks more gray than white."

"Grayscale," said Nur softly.

"What?" said Geek 1.

"Color doesn't matter in facial recognition code," said Nur. "You're wasting your time."

"You would say that," said Geek 2, looking the dark Uyghur up and down.

"I can put in an extra line of code that will fix the problem," said Nur, paying no attention to the inspection he was getting.

"Go ahead," said 1, "but don't fuck everything up."

"I'll try not to," said Nur. He moved to the keyboard and wrote: "cvz.imread_x+w+b.1.py" and hit <enter.

The image of the face immediately sharpened.

Hui was embarrassed that two members of his – no, it was no longer his – Institute appeared baffled and had to be schooled by a Uyghur. What had Tanteeth done to his charges? Stuffed them with Party dogma and let their brains turn to mush.

Socialism with Chinese characteristics.

No chance to undermine Deng-tal now. But soon.

Chapter 8
Switch Hitter

Arlington, Henry had decided, was an acceptable place to live, as long as you didn't want to do anything interesting. On the rare days when he was not at the office annex, he rode his bike, surfed Netflix and thought about Rav.

Life in the slow lane.

It was slightly more than six months since Henry had escaped from China. Escaped wasn't the right word, but it amounted to a departure without permission. He had to get back to New Jersey to see his Mother, who had been struck with a severe case of Covid. She had recovered, although she would never have the same stamina she had before. Part of that, Henry feared, had been his defection to China. And Henry, aware that he had disobeyed and no doubt disappointed Hui Jen-Sho, his mentor in China, had decidedly mixed feelings about being back in the country of his birth.

A man with no nation.

To begin with, he had been harassed by the FBI, which wanted to charge him with entering the country –his own country – illegally on a Chinese passport. He had successfully explained that his American passport was under lock and key in Wuhan, where he had been working under Hui's direction. He had slightly more trouble explaining what he had been doing in Wuhan in the first place. It would have done him little good to say he was helping the Chinese Communist Party evade blame for creating and spreading the pandemic that was still killing thousands of people every day, and stalling economies around the world.

He had come to a narrow deal. No federal charges would be filed against him. In exchange, Henry had agreed to work not for the FBI, which would never trust him, but for the CIA's Advanced Artificial Intelligence Laboratory, an entity unknown to the public. Unknown because the CIA would have had a hard time explaining why it was using AI to spy on Americans, in America, where it technically had no jurisdiction.

The agreement had been struck, with reluctance on both sides. The Feds regarded Henry as the closest thing to a traitor. They also wanted to make use of Henry's quite extraordinary AI aptitude, most of which he had learned at Hui's Institute in Wuhan. The United States had nothing like it, and was playing catch-up. Concluding the deal, one Special Agent had fixed Henry with a malign stare and said, "This'll keep you off the streets, I guess."

He meant the streets of China but had been sternly warned not the say that. Henry had been assigned to what was called the Office Annex in Arlington, so as not to infect anyone else with his strange notions of patriotism.

Henry had proven invaluable to Hui. His native knowledge of America and its people had given Hui the leverage he needed to assume control of China's counterpunch over charges that it was to blame for the pandemic. Originally called the Wuhan flu, the Party's mouthpieces protested that associating the virus with China in any way was racist, and insisted it be changed to the neutral name Covid. Americans, always frightened of being called racist by anyone, or any group, quickly conceded the point and issued meaningless declarations of their hopes to work in concert with their Chinese colleagues to prevent the spread of the virus and find a way to prevent it from ever happening again. The American news media and social media sites almost overnight banned the use of "Wuhan Flu" and drummed into its viewers and readers "Covid, Covid, Covid."

It had been Henry who suggested the Party play the race card.

"America is already tearing itself apart domestically with arguments over race, and fairness and social justice," he had told his skeptical colleagues in Wuhan. "It doesn't want the rest of the world piling on. Saying this will only add to 'white guilt.'" He had had to explain that term to the Chinese listening to him. One said: "But that's ridiculous. It's like saying the Han Chinese should feel guilt for being superior to the other races. Well, we *are* superior, and we feel no guilt about it."

"Which is one of the reasons you are going to dominate the world soon," Henry answered. "No guilt about what you are doing, no dissent about your policies, no internal arguing."

"A smooth path is easily traveled," said one. Henry could only wonder to himself what a smooth path would look like in his homeland these days.

He saw almost immediately what the problem here would be. Entrenched in their own bureaucracy, the CIA was reluctant to accept advice or suggestions from the outside world. This applied not just to Henry, but to AI specialists in America's top universities and research institutes. The Agency was also intensely protective of its information and pointedly refused to share its research and findings with the FBI, the NSA, Homeland Security, or any other organization that might infringe on its turf. China had bureaucracy too, but because AI was still in its developmental stages, the Party quickly clamped down on all branches of its research and ordered all information to be filtered through Hui.

Until Henry's escape caused Hui's fall from grace.

Rav had turned up unexpectedly, once, at Henry's parents' home before he moved to Arlington. She said she was on official business. She told him that Hui's primary rival, the head of the Cyberspace Administration of China, had disappeared and been replaced. Hui had been "reassigned" to Xinjiang province, which Henry knew was where Uyghur Muslims were being "re-educated" to conform to Party doctrine. For Hui, it was the closest thing to internal exile, and Henry felt responsible for it. That the AI Institute in Wuhan had been turned over to the unlikable General Deng-tal, or Tanteeth as Henry thought of her, only deepened his guilt.

His life in America seemed a pale imitation of the excitement that had empowered him in China. He had been selected by Hui, not because he was a great coder or AI scholar. Rather he had been given an important position because of what he could tell his Chinese colleagues about America. He was as exotic as a dragon. And with occasional... personal... encouragement from Rav, he had proven his worth.

Back in his homeland, he was just another Geek, though one whose loyalty to his country was always under suspicion. He knew his work was valued, and he was not shy in voicing opinions, most of which were ignored. He made sure that his free time would draw no scrutiny, because he assumed he was under surveillance, and that his online communications were monitored. Most evenings consisted of a trip to the grocery store, dinner cooked at his one-bedroom apartment, or, on special occasions, a beer and a burger at a bar and grill a block away.

He seldom communicated with his parents, and he made no effort to make friends. The truth was, he found Americans dull.

Though no one told him so, he believed he had been assigned to the facial recognition project that the CIA coders were desperately trying to weaponize. There was no way to be sure since the work he was asked to do was siloed away from that of his co-workers. Henry just assumed that since he was being asked to code in Python, it was intended to enhance facial recognition, which was the key to widespread monitoring of the population.

He felt no guilt about what he was doing. Guilt, he had learned in Wuhan, was a kind of weakness. A weakness that could not be overcome with isometric exercise, or with steroids, or with lifting weights, or running. Henry was running, all right, but was it from his past or himself? He chose not to think about it. Python, like the serpent of the same name, choked all emotion out of him. He was part of a code, part of a process, part of the future. On behalf of which country, he convinced himself, he did not care.

He knew he was lying. To himself, to the memory of Hui, and, naturally, to Rav. He was still unsure if his feelings for the beautiful translator, who was also a lieutenant in the PLA, were love, or simply lust, and if the desolation he felt since she walked away from his parents' house was her implied rejection of his declaration of love, or bitterness at what he had had, and had let slip through his fingers. "Did you ever love me?" he had asked her plaintively at his parents' front door. And she had smiled her beautiful smile, and said in her frozenly perfect British English, "I didn't, but I could."

His reverie was interrupted by the ping of his laptop. "When next phase?" the message demanded. *When I'm good and fucking ready,* he wanted to reply, but checked himself. It occurred to Henry that he would never even have considered answering such a question if it came from Hui, or from anyone in the Hui's AI Institute. Such disrespect might be seen as individual ego. And that had no place in China. Who you were mattered not at all. What you wanted counted for nothing. What mattered was – is – what the Party wanted, and how well you served its needs.

In America these days, what mattered was how you felt, what you expected the country to do for you (so take that, JFK), how your rage and outrage were compensated by the rest of the population, especially the politicians. In America, it was the individual who ruled those everyone around him/her/they/them/whateverpronounyoufeltlike being that day. Which was part of the reason America was falling behind its competitors around the world.

Henry's current employer tried to disregard the breakdown of discipline outside its walls. The I in CIA did not stand for Insubordination, his control agent had said, and he had been right. Henry realized he was a free man only because he had certain talents that could be put to use. Patriotic use, they had told him. Political use was more like it, but silence had become Henry's most trusted companion since he had returned from Wuhan. And the most frequent as well. Silence cannot hurt me, silence cannot hurt me, silence cannot hurt me, he droned to himself, this mantra of dread becoming his byword for the life he was living.

"cv2.imread_1.py" he texted back. That was an innovation he had invented yesterday. It allowed Python to jump past two commands that had proved troublesome for the CIA coders to smoothe out. He had been waiting for them to demand proof of his competence. This would do it for a while.

"10-4".

Christ, they even tried to sound like the cops on television. The code he had texted he had learned in Wuhan. He knew its capabilities. Also its limits.

He decided to leave early. It would take them hours to figure out what he had done, and how. Thank you, Colonel Hui, he thought. Silently, of course.

A beer? A burger? No, he didn't feel like either. He freed his bike from its shackles on the outdoor stand. There would be no need for a lock on a bike left outdoors in Wuhan. Not because the Chinese were any more honest, but because by now they had learned to assume that they were being watched. From somewhere. Always under surveillance. Not a moment of privacy.

Socialism with Chinese characteristics.

Henry had seen and understood the downside of China under Xi Jinping. He knew about, but never discussed, the roundup of more than a million and a half Uyghurs – the Muslim Turkish people who largely lived in Xinjiang province. They had been arrested, beaten, tortured in the name of re-education, but really as a first step toward exterminating their race.

And the world did nothing. Why? Because you don't want to cross Xi.

How would a similar government campaign in the United States have been received? In his homeland nowadays, you couldn't even arrest – much less imprison or torture – people for looting stores and burning police cars. Because those people were "protected," lest they claimed police harassment or brutality. Or the trump card, racism. Police harassment was a far more serious charge than arson or looting. Which was why China did not understand the United States and needed someone like Henry to explain the upside-down curve that the justice system had taken. Despite the totalitarian system in China, Henry felt freer to tell the truth about America there than in Arlington.

He knew they would praise him for the code he had given them. If not tomorrow, then the next day or week. Clocks worked differently in the federal government. They moved ahead, then back, ahead, then retreated. One moment too fast, the next at a dead standstill. A breakthrough in AI research had to be scanned for flaws, of course. But also, for any concomitant effect that might be perceived as biased, unfair, racist.

Democracy with American characteristics.

To himself, Henry said silently, thank Hui, not me. I just don't care.

All he wanted was to be left alone. Alone with Rav, that is.

Chapter 9
Which Is It?

Another soft tone on his phone. Another coded email, and another day was underway. Without looking, Hui knew it was from Ma-lin Cho, or Lieutenant Cho, more properly. Hui's feelings about her were bleakly divided. Though she had let him take the blame for the American's escape, Ma-lin had more recently spoken on his behalf, with her protector Xi Jinping, of all people. Hui was, to a certain degree, back on the inside. And though he would have denied it to anyone else, he was highly pleased to find his opinions once again valued, even if his political situation was discouraging.

"Arrival 10," was all the communication offered. It was enough. It was now seven. Hui tried to clear his mind. Why would she be coming? The AI research had been improved vastly by Nur's presence, though his colleagues despised him. The Uyghurs he had set to work at the re-education camp were doing well, he knew. Production was significantly up. He knew this because Nur had told him – outside, where no one could overhear or record them – that more trucks than ever before had been ordered to carry away finished products. Products, indeed. Much of it was junk that China mass-produced and foisted on the world.

That Hui had to hear such news from one of the inmates of the "school" where he was being held was maddening, but he had learned to accept such petty, Party oversights. While Hui knew he was in temporary disfavor with the Party, he was slowly, carefully developing a plan not just to rehabilitate himself, but to put himself outside political judgment. Outside this world's judgment, actually.

Lieutenant Cho's car arrived two minutes before 10 and sat just inside the main gate of the re-education center, burning fuel and time. At precisely the top of the hour, it made its stately way to Hui's hut and cut its motor. Hui got in the back passenger side seat and with one up and down glance, grinned.

"In disguise?" he asked. Ma-lin was in civilian clothes, the first time he had seen her so attired since they were both at the Institute in Wuhan. Then, it was to deepen the already ardent fascination of the American, Henry, for whom Ma-lin served as translator and occasional lover.

Hui could not help but assess and approve of her appearance. Her long black hair flowed over her shoulders. Her face had touches of makeup that only enhanced her already-exotic beauty. The sleeves of her black blouse were rolled up to her elbows, exposing lovely, shapely arms and perfectly manicured nails. Black trousers fit her snugly. And she was wearing red heels. Never one to admit carnal feelings, Hui nonetheless felt his throat tighten with unexpected desire.

"I bring greetings from the General Secretary," Ma-lin said, as if Xi Jinping were somebody's uncle who hadn't called for a while.

"Thank you," said Hui, patient, waiting either for the sword, either to tap his shoulders and elevate him to knighthood, or to slash his neck open.

"There is a problem, well, two problems, and maybe even more, that need to be resolved."

"I am listening, lieutenant." It was hard to know what to call her. Her rank was certainly one that required a proper show of respect. But why did she have to be so ... ravishingly beautiful?

"The improved production from this facility has been noted," Ma-lin said blandly.

"I am glad," said Hui, already knowing from her expression he had stepped into quicksand but not knowing with which foot or why.

"The reaction has not been totally positive," she continued. "Some in the Party structure find it difficult to believe that the ... students at this facility can out-produce factories manned by Chinese laborers."

So that was it, though Hui, his counterattack already forming in his mind. They didn't like that Uyghurs did better work than Han. The racial snobbery of the Han Chinese was so widespread as to be invisible. Until something unexpected, like this, happened. Then, the Han bias against anyone not blessed with their racial superiority emerged, swiftly and

45

violently. The Han had been told for so long and so consistently that they were superior to other races that any contradictory evidence was treated like treason. The citizens of Xi's China crinkled their brows in wonder and nasty satisfaction at how white Americans had so willingly surrendered their position of superiority to blacks, Latinos, and yes, Asians. Anything rather than be called racist. That would not be happening in China anytime soon. At least not while Xi-thought led the way, and that, they believed, would be forever.

Socialism with Chinese characteristics.

"The Party asked, no, demanded higher production because of our demographic problems. I delivered higher production. And now they are dissatisfied?"

Ma-lin fixed her endlessly deep eyes on him. "You know better than to talk like that, Colonel." She had called him Colonel! It was the first time that rank had been uttered. From someone in the PLA anyway. Nur had the courtesy – or was it cunning? – to use his rank when they spoke. And like that, another piece of his strategy fell into place.

"The Party wants increased production, but not production that suggests Uyghurs can be more motivated than Han," he said.

"Exactly that."

"If you want Han laborers to be motivated like these people," he jerked his thumb over his shoulder, "then send them here. I assure you, they will respond to the training techniques used at this facility."

"You know we won't do that."

"So? Which is it?"

Ma-lin came close to smiling, checked herself. Directed her gaze to the gray skies above them. "Why are you talking this way? Asking questions whose answers you know, probably better than anyone else in China. Have you lost track of history as well as time? Take my advice, Colonel. Snap out of it."

Now Hui was truly puzzled. She had used his title and so recognized his superior status, at least militarily, and yet she addressed him in a manner at best improper, more likely impertinent. Could she possibly be goading him?

She went on before he could answer his own question. "As always, the Party wants both – increased production, plus validation of Han superiority. How you do this is up to you, but don't leave either box unchecked."

"You said there might be two problems, possibly more? What is the other, certain one?"

Now it was her turn to be stopped cold. She looked out the window of the car again, saw the same gravid clouds, but retrieved from them no answers. Nor, apparently, courage. She sucked in air, turned her head to him.

"As you know, we monitor the Americans' progress in Artificial Intelligence research."

"By 'monitor,' you mean we spy on them and steal anything that is of value? Yes, I know. I created the spybot that does that. Had it created, I should say."

She waved her ringless hand, dismissing the distinction.

"Lately, we notice they have made major gains in facial recognition. They have incorporated code we ourselves only developed six or eight months ago."

"The Pentagon? Impossible. They haven't even discovered the worm we put into their Python application. Unless it happened since..."

"No. Nothing like that has happened since you were... transferred from the Institute. The Pentagon is still trying to find the worm."

"What then? Who?" He stopped, already sensing the answer. "CIA?"

She nodded, once. As though raising her chin again would be painful to them both.

"We think ... rather, it has been established to the Party's satisfaction..."

"It's the American, isn't it? He's started working for them, and then showed them how to do what we taught him how to do." Hui hissed out the last three words with a bitterness he thought he had quite overcome. He held the young American's face in his mind's eye. Thought the word he knew better than to use out loud. *"Hanjian."*

Ma-lin fixed her lips into a smile. "He was a *hanjian*, a traitor to his homeland before he became one to ours."

"Still, to use what I taught him..." Hui realized that he was surprised at the irrational depth of his feeling, his anger, his sense of

... injustice. Growled at his own stupidity. Met Ma-Lin's eyes, which were searching him for the root of this sudden, out-of-character bark.

He looked at her. She looked at him. And then...

The nod, chin down once, and then no movement. Her eyes fluttered shut. Opened slowly. Focused on him.

Chapter 10
Once More Unto the Breach

Bicycle locks are supposed to be simple. You click one end of the sheathed, steel cable into the other end, flick the three-digit code around so that it is securely locked, and stop thinking about it until you are ready to ride again. But what happens when you have thumbed in the right code, tugged at one end to release it from the other and ... you are met with resistance?

The woman was clearly struggling and although Henry didn't know it at first glance, increasingly panicky.

"Help you?" Since returning to America, Henry had had to learn how to address a woman in an emotionally flat tone of voice, without in any way suggesting that a) he found her attractive b) he wanted anything from her or c) that he had forgotten that he was the vilest of all creatures: a white male.

"If you would, please, yes." She was probably in her forties, slim, with unevenly colored blonde hair worn like a Grecian helmet. Her response – unplanned, honest, not offended by the offer of help from a man – was just confused and worried enough to make it sound like that rarest of things: genuine human interaction.

"These things aren't very reliable," Henry said, sorry that he had to lie to be helpful. He took longer than he had to, thumbing the keys up and down as though trying out a new golf club. "Ummm..."

"Yes?"

"Well, in order to open your combination lock, I'd need the..."

"Oh, the combination! Of course. How stupid of me. It's 4-9-3."

"Not stupid at all. Here, I think we've got it." The cables came apart. "It was just stuck, I think."

"Oh, thank you. I'm so relieved. I had a bad feeling about it when I locked it this morning. And if I couldn't open it, I would've been late."

"Late for what?" The question came out as naturally as sweat on a hot day. He had said it before he considered his words. And that, he immediately thought, is how men get in trouble: saying what they mean before they've figured out if it's okay to say it.

She seemed to hesitate, weigh the inquiry, and then, after a semi-deep breath, said, "My analyst."

Henry looked down. A red warning light was going on and off in his brain. Stop now. Turn around. Walk away. Engage in no further interaction.

"Why would you need an analyst?" Again, words unbidden, untested, just true.

She opened her mouth to reply, closed her lips tightly, and laughed, a merry sound that Henry thought probably hadn't escaped from her lately.

"That's a good question. I'm Rose."

"Henry."

"What do you do, Henry?" There. Like thunder after lightning. The question he couldn't answer. What do I do? If I can't answer this, what can I answer? It was natural, he remembered, for Americans to ask each other what they did, as though discussing their occupation would open a window onto the soul. No one in China would begin a conversation like that. They would ask each other if they had read Xi Jinping's latest speech. That was the way to get to know someone. Nothing trite like a job. Rather, a litmus test of Party loyalty.

"Tech." It was as meaningless an answer as "Paint" or "Light." Tech could mean anything. And in this case, it had the added advantage of being true. Technically (get it?).

Don't let this get any further, Henry told himself. Nothing good will come of it.

"I have an idea, Henry. Why don't we go get a drink and you can analyze me? Even if I pick up the bar bill, it'll be a fraction of what I pay the shrink."

Run. Get away. Get on your bike and ride for your life.

"That sounds great," he said instead.

Rose relocked her bike, without help, and she and Henry crossed the street to the neon sign advertising a joint called Relativity.

Seats in a dark booth procured, drinks served, she looked at him without caution and started the conversation by saying, "Nothing will come of this."

"Of what?" said Henry, obeying the laws of cross-gender politeness and pretending not to know what 'this' meant. Also pretending that he could do 'this' without thinking of Rav.

"I'm forty-two years old, I'm good at my job, I've never been married, and I like you," said Rose, as though that *curriculum vitae* answered all potential future inquires.

"Isn't it premature to decide whether you like me or not?"

"When you're my age, it better not be. Why are you here, in Virginia, I mean? Not why are you here in this bar. You're here because I invited you."

"I'm in this bar because I wanted to keep talking with you," said Henry, aware and embarrassed at the truth of his answer. "I'm in Virginia because that's where my job is."

Rose looked down at her Pinot Grigio. "Let's not draw things out. I live in Clarendon. You know it?"

Henry shook his head. "I haven't been here long, and I don't get out much."

She gave a one-note laugh. "Maybe it's time you did." She sipped the wine, looked around the bar, and exhaled deeply. Rapped the table with the flat of her hand. "This isn't our kind of place."

Our. That word that implied togetherness, oneness, even intimacy. The first time Rav had referred to "our plan", Henry's heart had leapt. Was the love of his life beginning to think of him as her partner? Of course, that had not been the case, but it had fueled his hopes for weeks. Until he escaped from China and brought calamity down on the people he cared most about. Now this stranger had used the word less than a half hour after they met. Henry felt as he did as a little boy, shushing down a water slide, knowing it would take him into and under the water of the swimming pool, but still anticipating the thrill.

He had yet to touch his drink. Straight Stolichnaya. Now he downed the shot in a practiced Russian slurp.

"Let's go, then."

They unlocked their bikes, mounted, and were at Rose's condo building in ten minutes. The ride itself wasn't taxing for Henry. It was the thought of what might come next.

Is this how it works? he asked himself. You meet someone, some chemical gets dumped into your insides, you recognize there's an attraction, and then you have at it until you feel differently? His experience was limited. Some high school fooling around. A girlfriend, more like sexfriend, during university, who initiated him in political protest as well as sex, and then, the paragon, the ultimate, the ... he was tired of saying ravishing but what other word worked? ... Rav.

Rose dismounted, pointed to a bike rack outside her building, and started wheeling her own vehicle inside to take to her ... whatever it was. Apartment? Loft? Penthouse? He knew nothing about her except that she was clumsy with locks.

That wasn't fair. She had a quiet confidence about her, without bluster or brashness. Henry hoped she was more competent in this situation that he expected to be.

The bike fit nicely in the elevator, and she scooched back into the rear corner to make room for him. There was no small talk, which was fine with him. She was, it turned out, on the top floor of her 22-story building. In the corner facing south and west. She punched in a code, the door popped open and she pushed her bike inside, letting him catch the closing door and let himself in. She stood the bike just inside the door, looked at him with a faint smile, and said, "Come on, let's get past the awkward part." She was pulling her purple and blue sweater over her head by the time they got to the bedroom, then started undoing her beltless jeans. It was the least romantic seduction imaginable, at least imaginable to Henry, and he wondered for a second if this is what she did with all new acquaintances. Then immediately felt bad for thinking that of her. With only underwear and socks on, she approached him, and he couldn't help but remember how Rav had approached him that first time, in Wuhan, presenting herself as a reward for work well done. Work well done for Hui.

A button at a time, she took control, the smile, secure on her lips, her eyes alight with something Henry did not recognize, but could only guess at.

"This is going to be wonderful," she said, so quietly that Henry wondered if she was talking to herself.

"How do you know?" he said, and his voice sounded like a cannon by comparison.

"Trust me."

"I'm sorry, but I've learned not to trust anyone," he said, his truest statement in weeks.

The words must have sunk in deep. She stopped what she was doing, allowed a brief, broader smile to illuminate her face, and said, "Then I'll have to earn it, won't I?"

Chapter 11
Just Buy It

Hui and Nur spoke daily now. Mostly of technical matters. Snags in the coding. Inconsistent results. Prioritization discrepancies that each was beginning to understand were being introduced by the code itself, not them. The code was actually fixing itself. They were close to understanding, and contributing to, a leap in Artificial Intelligence that most of their colleagues both longed for and dreaded. Machine surpassing man. It was inevitable. Machines don't eat, sleep, complain, get married, have children, have demands. Not yet, anyway.

Hui was deeply impressed by the boy's intelligence, his grasp of complicated, even politically sensitive issues, and the careful, well-thought-out answers he gave to questions that began "What do you think about..." Hui knew who Nur reminded him of. He tried not to think about that.

Nur, growing in confidence, believing he was no longer in danger of unnecessary surgery that would kill him for his vital organs, slowly began to share snippets of intelligence from within the "re-education" camp. "The soldiers are scanning everyone's eyes with a machine that uses very bright light. Some people say it has blinded them. But when they scanned my eyes, I didn't flinch. It felt like they were shining the light right into my brain."

"I imagine they were disappointed not to find anything there," said Hui, with what passed for humor between them.

Nur considered the gentle jibe. "They say the eyes are the window to the soul."

"I wouldn't know. I don't have one. Now, about this pip_install line of code..."

And so, a moment of comradeship gave way to tech talk.

Five minutes and one code correction later, Nur looked at Hui's windows of the soul and said, quietly, "This project isn't just about facial recognition, is it?"

Hui remained silent. How would he know this? "No. It has a greater purpose."

"Which you won't tell me?"

"For your own good." By now, Nur believed that his mentor meant it.

"Do you know that people in America have a device that lets them see on their smartphones who is at their front door? It's ingenious, really."

Nur was already nodding. "Of course, it also records a person's image, keeps track of what time that person was at the door, and logs the address."

"Yes. I am trying to get the relevant authorities to authorize production of a similar device that can be sold cheaper."

"In China?"

"Among other places."

"Buy it."

"What?"

"That American company. Just buy it. Then you'll have the technology and the list of people who use it. And their personal information."

Hui was silent. He had not thought of that, and he was usually the first to think of everything. Nur. Very bright. Possibly dangerously so. Hui could already see how to do it. When Hui spoke of "the relevant authorities," he of course was thinking of Xi, China's ultimate leader and really the only person whose opinion counted.

Would Xi, who had exiled him to this shithole, approve? The company could probably be had for less than a billion dollars. And Hui had one of those lightning-bolt ideas about how it could, with some maneuvering, actually be acquired for free.

Most of the world was not yet aware that China's surging real estate and construction industries were floundering. In fact, the largest of them, Forever Grande, could not meet its massive payroll, let alone pay its cavernous debts to banks and other financial institutions around the world. The government, of course, could bail them out. But Xi had shown himself to be reluctant to help private industries. It was part of his "the state should own everything" mentality. Back to Maoism. Without Mao.

He considered, decided, spoke. "Your people have been working hard. Too hard. The production figures are making some in the Party jealous."

"You want to slow them down?" said Nur, without a hint of disrespect.

"I suppose that's what I want," said Hui.

"Let them assemble better products. Products that require quality checks."

"Qual—"

"Most of what you have them producing is junk – ashtrays, paper clips, American flags," said Nur. "I know this because part of 're-education' is to humiliate us, put us to work on things that are an insult to anyone's intelligence."

"The Party wants..."

"The Party wants to keep us docile, but productive. But boredom doesn't lead to docility. It leads to anger and resentment. Eventually, that will boil over. You'll have incidents. Conflicts with the guards. And the workers – I mean students – will have to be punished, maybe even executed. Let them work on products that require a little bit of skill. It will slow down production, which is what you say you want, but the products will have more value, and the Party will be able to sell them to the Americans and others for more money. Which is also what you want, right?"

Hui knew what was happening, but couldn't believe it. He was being schooled – re-educated, ironically – by a youth. And a youth from a breed of sub-humans. Yet, Nur was right. He could slow production, just as Ma-lin had told him the Party wanted. And increase the value of what was produced here. The Americans would call it a 'win-win'.

He looked at Nur and wondered what else this youth might know. And how to extract it to his – Hui's – advantage.

For all its talk of ideological purity, economic betterment for all, adherence to peaceful policies that benefit the world, the Communist Party was about one thing: keeping the Communist Party in power. The demands it made of its workaday members were minimal: do as you are told, never question an order issued by the Party, proclaim your loyalty, every minute, every day, to General Secretary Xi.

Members who had already achieved honors and been given positions of importance knew there was a second, secret set of guidelines imperative to survival. Take your cut of whatever graft and corruption you were involved in. But always pass part of it upward to a higher-ranking member. That member would then pass part of the booty further upward and so on. Until a piece of the pie reached Xi. The undisputed leader of the Communist Party of China was, quietly, one of the richest men on earth. Xi's fortune, deeply buried in Switzerland, the Cayman Islands, Singapore and other safe places, dwarfed the holdings of Putin, the Russian mad dog, Jeff Bezos, the book hawker-turned-billionaire, Elon Musk, the pot-puffing wanna-be spaceman. Xi's income did not depend on results. It depended on the steady flow of bribes, blackmail, illicit activities, and wink-nod transactions that kept China afloat.

Xi got a cut of every one of them.

"You have good ideas," Hui told Nur. "Be careful not to share them with anyone but me. It could be dangerous for you."

"Thank you, Colonel. I will follow your counsel, as always. I believe you want the best for me."

Hui nodded. Don't let this become a love-fest.

"Do you know what's going on in the underground chambers here?" Nur asked.

"I've heard it. Not seen it."

"Do you want to see it?"

"Not particularly."

"You should. It may influence your thinking."

What is this young man trying to do, Hui wondered. 'Influence my thinking?'

"There is no way to see, to get in."

"There is if you are Colonel Hui Jen-Sho," Nur said.

And the simple truth was that Hui did want to see, want to know. He was disturbed by the sounds, the suffering. Surely there were other ways.

"Tonight," said Nur. "It's safer at night." They arranged a when and where.

He met Nur on time – which was one in the morning – in the space between Nur's building and the next one to the west. The sounds of moaning, suffering, hopelessness, were everywhere. Hui realized what a chance Nur was taking being outside at this hour. But either because they were lazy or inept, there were no guards in the area. Hui's presence, in full uniform, would probably save the boy from punishment.

"Stop!" came a voice. Hui wheeled around, saw the guard approaching, fumbling to get his rifle off his shoulder. A no-account, he decided instantly.

"How dare you speak to me that way," Hui said.

The guard froze. Saw Hui's face, knew who he was.

"I am sorry, Colonel."

"Go about your duties."

The guard eyed Nur, then Hui again, and said, again, "Sorry."

Nur spoke only with his hands and eyes. He directed Hui to the next building. Hui knocked once, pushed the door open. The smell of excrement was overpowering.

"People live here?" he mouthed quietly.

"No, Colonel," Nur whispered. "They die here."

To their immediate left, a closed door muffled the sound of strangled moaning. Or was it weeping? Hui couldn't tell. He opened the door, trying to prepare himself for whatever he saw.

He failed. The young man, naked, hung from two chains attached to the ceiling. His eyes had been gouged out, his lips cut away so his ruined teeth and mouth were visible. Each breath caused a dribble of blood. Hui was horrified but tried not to show it.

"He has been here for three days," Nur said without making noise. "He will have 'surgery' later this morning and be incinerated by nightfall." They left the man to wait out his final hours of hopeless life. If this was really life.

"Why do they do it if he is going to die soon anyway?" Hui asked.

"For fun. They are bored. These people are defenseless. It excites them."

In the next room, Hui found three women huddled together, naked, crying. When they saw him, they scooted into the corner on their buttocks, the two older women shielding the third, who was barely a teen. "No more, please, no more," they screeched in bad Mandarin.

"How many?" Nur asked in their native, Turkic tongue.

"Twenty tonight," said one of the old crones. A viscous puddle rested between the girl's legs.

Hui did not have to ask what this meant. He might not have believed that his people could do this, until, in another corner, he saw a pair of gray Army-issued men's underwear. It was stained red with blood. They left.

The next room, further down, had no door to conceal the muffled screams. A boy, no more than twelve, Hui thought, was stretched backwards, face up, over a metal oil drum. His hands were shackled; a length of chain led under the drum to his ankles. There was no give in his restraints. He had been whipped on his chest, stomach, genitals, and legs so that his skin looked like ground meat. Hui could only imagine the torn muscles, the nerve endings on fire, the relentless pain. The sound was minimal. A rag was stuck down his throat and pebbles had been shoved up each nostril. Hui felt he was about to vomit.

"Re-education," Nur said, his eyes on the youth, not on Hui. He – Hui Jen-Sho – a Colonel in the People's Liberation Army, the leading authority on Artificial Intelligence in China, if not the world, a brilliant researcher, stood mute, unmanned, his nose and mouth filled with the stink of stench, and asked himself who deserved this kind of treatment. And just who deserved his loyalty. For the first time in his adult life, he did not automatically conclude that it was the Party.

Socialism with Chinese characteristics.

Chapter 12
Your Young Uyghur Ward

His proposal was accepted within two weeks. Ma-lin traveled to the re-education facility to tell him.

"The General Secretary is pleased," she said, her eyes cast downward. "Negotiations to buy the American company are already underway. They have opened their books for review. We, of course, scanned the contents. And now we have the list of customers."

And you will get more, and more and more, thought Hui, face carefully neutral.

She hesitated and with that give-away downward glance, said, "There is something else."

By now, he could decipher her facial tics to within a whisper. He would not venture a guess about what was coming. What would be the point?

"The company's owners are coming to China to finalize the deal. Since their technology is largely powered by Artificial Intelligence, they know of you and your achievements in that field."

"I am honored," he said with not a drop of sincerity.

"They would like to meet you."

"And I them. Bring them to me. We can offer them the torture cell next to my living quarters."

Ma-lin smiled her 'I am already far ahead of you' smile. "We have agreed to their request. I have been instructed to bring you to the meeting."

"Indeed," said Hui. "And if I do not wish to attend this meeting?"

The smile again. "You did say it was right next to your quarters."

There it was. He – Hui Jen-Sho, father of China's AI program – was being threatened with torture by the Party he had served for decades. Best to cut the tension short. "Where is this meeting?"

"You know where."

"At the Institute I founded? In Wuhan?"

"They would like to tour it. See what makes it so special."

"It is only special, Lieutenant, when I am there."

"Yes, that is true," she said. She allowed just a whisper of a smile. "They also know you speak perfect English. That will make it easier."

"Better than General Deng-tal, yes. Not as perfect as your English."

"Perhaps. But my talents are not those they are seeking."

Not until they lay eyes on you, Hui thought but did not say. "And this meeting, if I decide to attend it, is when?" He felt the answer, the anxiety, the attitude of well-concealed panic.

"Tomorrow is *when* you *will* attend it."

"And what am I to do with my research files here?"

"You could leave them in the care of..." she switched to English... "your young Uyghur ward." The overlapping wave of words pleased him. He was not sure he would have been able to pronounce them so smoothly, *ex tempore*.

"Nothing must happen to him," Hui said, also in English, as mildly as he could.

"The Party's word is its bond," she answered, well aware of the ambiguity in the phrase.

"Who knows about him? Besides you, Lieutenant?" Hui said more sharply than he had intended.

"There is talk at the Institute," Ma-Lin answered evenly. "Some jokes."

"Jokes? Such as?"

"There he goes again..."

Inevitable, Hui thought. Show emotion just once and you are branded spineless forever after.

"I will need to collect..."

"Several of your uniforms are still at the institute, as well as some of the non-military clothes you wore when you visited other countries for lectures."

"My clothes? Preserved? I imagined..."

"I asked that they be stored in a trunk. General Deng-tal permitted this." From the way she said it, it was clear that Ma-lin had spent some political capital on the request.

"Thank you, Lieutenant," Hui said stiffly, at the same time somehow touched that she would do this. Emotion again! Stop, fool!

"I will speak to my—" quick switch to English —"ward" – back to Mandarin — "and instruct him to take care of the research files. Then I am ready to go with you."

"Of course," she said, pleased with her own success. "The plane is waiting."

He started to say, "Plane?" but stopped himself in time. There would of course be a military jet to transport them to Wuhan. In six months, he had forgotten how different Party officials lived from the rest of the country.

Nur was working on the assembly line, Hui noted with some irritation. He should be coding, not sewing polyester American flags. With a curt nod of his head, Hui communicated his wish to the factory foreman. Nur was tapped on the shoulder, pointed toward Hui, and came over.

"This man is doing important work at the request of the Party," Hui told the foreman. "Except when you absolutely need him here, please allow him to carry out the Party's instructions."

The foreman, looking forward to revisiting the agonized pre-teen stretched over a barrel that evening, shrugged, which passed for acceptance. Hui thought to himself, a soldier who shrugged at me when I was at the Institute would find himself next in line for surgery here. Though what organs of his anyone would want is a mystery. But humiliation is a strict instructor. It teaches us not what to say, but what not to say.

They walked outside, the smell of sweat and fear evaporating in the cold air. Hui saw Ma-lin's car parked well away, puffing exhaust. She was playing by the rules, giving him privacy.

Nur was nervous. "That guy will string me up after you yanked me off the assembly line."

"No, he won't," said Hui, feeling more like a Colonel than he had for months. "Someone I have just been speaking with is going to talk to the camp commandant. You will be left alone. You will not be punished. And you will have access to my workspace."

"But the others, my people, will think I've betrayed them. Where can I eat, where can I sleep? My own people will kill me."

"I can't solve every one of your problems, Nur. I can only stop the million-strong People's Liberation Army from hurting you. If your own people kill you, that is your fault and their loss. Now listen..."

And the once-and-possibly-future Colonel told the imprisoned-and-probably-brilliant young Uyghur what he wanted him to do.

He got in the back seat of the car with Ma-lin and said, "Let's go, Lieutenant. We don't want to keep General Deng-tal waiting."

And did not try to disguise his smile.

Chapter 13
The Forever Grandest Scam Ever

The place had changed. As with any traveler returning home from a long trip, he noticed every minor alteration, detected a different smell in the hallway, bristled when he saw people he did not recognize walking around in his Institute.

His Institute!

He would be meeting the Americans that afternoon and already knew what to do. His was the gift of a supple mind. He had spent the four-hour flight nearly wordless, seated across the aisle from Ma-lin. There were no other passengers on the Gongji-11, a pilotless aircraft of which Hui had heard, but never seen. Despite his lifelong work and research on the topic, he was petrified at streaking along at 500 miles an hour in a plane guided by AI.

He wondered if he was merely a test passenger on the Gongji, an expendable accident if AI proved not to be a faithful pilot. But what about Ma-lin? The Lieutenant sat stone-still, eyes forward, either unaware (unlikely) or unconcerned about entrusting her life to the Party.

But the plane's landing was glass-smooth and the car awaiting them, a burgundy Hongqi H-9, was the kind of limousine usually reserved for high-ranking Party officials. Hui closed his eyes and tried to make sense of it all. He had woken up in a prison camp and was now being ferried back to his onetime seat of power in a fancy sedan. And everyone said America was the land of opportunity.

General Deng was nowhere to be found, and Hui knew this was not a scheduling conflict or a last-minute vacation. Tanteeth no more wanted to see him than the reverse, and he was satisfied with the arrangement.

Upon their arrival, Ma-lin escorted Hui to an office that had, during his tenure here, been reserved for visiting Party dignitaries and never assigned to any full-time staff member. In the room, he found his dress uniform – dark blue serge, snow white shirt, black, Army-issue shoes shined to blinding brilliance. He was a Colonel again. He also saw that one of his civilian suits – tailored for him on Jermyn Street in London –had been pressed and was hanging next to the uniform.

On the otherwise bare desk was a buff envelope. Inside were biographies of the American delegation. Alan Jussoff, the soon-to-be-ex CEO, 56, was its leader. His adjutant was named Brian Helmsley, aged 40, career as interesting as the paper on which his biography was printed. A woman would also attend; Hui paid no attention to this. She was no doubt a note-taker. He donned his uniform – remembering when he had first worn it, to a Party conclave where he addressed the emerging importance of Artificial Intelligence. Some of the top officers, he noted, guffawed at his promises of life-changing technology. But a second secretary named Xi Jinping had paid close attention and nodded knowingly throughout the presentation. And so his ascent began. In a flash of inspiration, Hui took the uniform off and put on the dark gray wool suit instead. First impressions, he told himself.

He walked with Ma-lin through the busy corridors. He knew his sudden reappearance was causing a sensation, but it was one cloaked in looks of disinterest. No one would dare greet him or stare at him, without knowing the repercussions of such actions. Was the master here to be arrested, to be tortured until he gave up all his secrets – and everyone suspected there were many of those – or, was he, perhaps, here to reclaim his throne? To expel Deng-tal, and wipe her from collective memory? In her six months' stewardship, the General had made a poor impression. Technically competent, she had absolutely none of what the Americans called 'people skills.' If one of the Geeks at the Institute broke new ground with his or her coding, Tanteeth's most effusive response was, "Continue with your work." If an underling disappointed her, she reported the infraction to the Party functionary stationed at the Institute. Despite her exalted military rank, she had never handled a firearm. Her personality was imaginary.

Hui saw the quick looks he attracted, understood instinctively that his former charges were confused. Why was the Colonel not in uniform? This did not compute. He remembered a book he had read in English, a biography of the Duke of Windsor, the former King Edward VIII, who had abdicated the British throne for the love of a woman and spent his life exiled in France. The insane decision to give up power for some supposed affection was laughable. What Hui remembered though, was the description of the Duke's deep tangle of emotions when he was permitted to return to England to attend the funeral of his brother, who had succeeded him to the throne. He now felt he understood how the Duke must have simultaneously reveled and reeled to be back among his own people, in a place where he once ruled, and from which he had been expelled.

"We will meet the Americans here, Colonel," said Ma-lin. Colonel, she had called him. Even without the uniform. So, it was true.

The Americans were preceded into the meeting by an attractive female PLA sergeant who Hui had never seen before. Probably from the branch that specialized in following foreigners traveling in China, sometimes seducing and then blackmailing them if they were married or homosexual, otherwise keeping track of their movements and statements.

In fine, but not Ma-lin-like English, the sergeant said, "Honored Guest Hui, may I present Honored Guests Jussoff, Helmsley, and Monaghan." To the Americans she said, "Honored Guests Jussoff, Helmsley and Monaghan, may I present Honored Guest Hui."

She had not used his rank. This was an inauspicious beginning. Jussoff, making sure to take charge of the meeting from the start, said, "Colonel, it is a pleasure to meet you. I've heard so much about you."

"Mr. Jussoff, Mr. Helmsley, Miz Monaghan," said Hui, having committed their names to memory, "welcome to the Institute of Artificial Intelligence."

There. He had claimed it as his own, as their host. The sergeant bowed her head courteously, once, and left the room. Hui's opening remarks would be reported to Deng-tal, of course. Within minutes, it would be the only topic of gossip in the building. Just as he wished.

Hui intentionally omitted introducing Ma-lin. She was not in uniform and he wanted her mistaken for an office worker who would take notes, as he assumed this Monaghan woman was. The American woman was well-groomed, not unattractive, of middle-age or approaching it, slender, with short hair of a light color he disliked.

They arranged themselves around the ash-colored wooden table. On it were bottles of mineral water. Ma-lin, neither unannounced nor introduced, mimed pouring water for the Americans. Head shakes all around, no.

"We very much look forward to seeing whatever parts of your Institute are open for inspection," said Jussoff, not realizing his gaffe. Neither Hui nor Ma-lin reacted.

"That can certainly be arranged," said Hui. "First, however, we should conclude the business which brought you to China." In other words, no tickee, no washee.

"Yes," said Jussoff, smoothly. "We did want to discuss the terms."

"If I may," Hui interrupted. "I have been granted authority to recast the terms of the sale of your company. May I explain?"

All three visitors looked flabbergast. "Um, please, go ahead," said Jussoff.

"Neither of us is without ulterior motive," said Hui. "We have each researched the other and the other's motives. You know why we want your technology. And we know that, even as we began negotiations, you were taking initial steps to start another company with the same capabilities, in fact one that will compete with your current enterprise."

For the second time in a minute, Hui saw six *gweilo* eyes stare at him like half a dozen oyster shells. "That's in a very preliminary stage," said Jussoff, his control momentarily broken. "Nothing has been announced."

"We understand," said Hui. "Please indulge me while I explain why I think your plan is a good one, and how we may be able to ensure that your new company will get off to an excellent start."

The three Americans nodded.

"You no doubt know that China's economy is booming, and that its real estate market is one of the drivers of that economy. Each month, millions of Chinese families move into new housing, improved housing. Families that spent generations in backward villages, in huts, are now living in modern apartments and houses. It is one of the major, though not well-publicized successes that the Communist Party has achieved for its citizens"

"Yes, congratulations," said Jussoff, as insincerely as possible. "Now, this proposed contract..."

"I see I failed to make my point," said Hui. "Please forgive my deficient English." Ma-lin lowered her eyes. "Our mass migration from the country to the newly built cities requires extra vigilance. Even in China, unfortunately, crime has not yet been extinguished. And so, new buyers of apartments and homes in more densely populated areas will need protection for their properties. Protection such as the door cameras attached to online security systems that you were making, and will make again with your new company – the one not yet announced."

"Mr. Hooey," said Helmsley, speaking for the first time, "this is all fascinating, but the purpose of this meeting..."

"Is to make money, is it not, Mr. Helmsley?" shot Hui before the sentence could be finished. "I understand your impatience, even from my humble perspective. You are important people and cannot waste time on an old man's meandering conversation." In another age, Hui might have pulled a dagger from his belt and glided it across this impertinent *gweilo's* throat.

"After careful consultation with my colleagues, the People's Republic is willing to offer your new – unannounced — company the exclusive rights to sell home security systems to the largest real estate consortium in China, for a period of five years. This is a concession we have never made before, but because we value your friendship so highly..."

"How many properties does this consortium have in its catalog?" said Helmsley, betraying himself as the numbers guy, subordinate to Jussoff.

Time for the kill, Hui decided. "I believe the current inventory is two hundred million."

"And we would have exclusive rights?" said Jussoff.

"It would be structured in such a way that you would purchase shares in the consortium, become co-owners, and thus be able to regulate which security systems are installed."

"That's fucking brilliant," said Helmsley. "Alan, can you imagine…"

"Of course, the sale price we discussed earlier would be lowered," said Hui. "From one billion dollars to five hundred million. But in return, you will have yoked yourself to the biggest growth industry in China and be assured that you will play a role in its future."

"That is quite an offer you are making," said Jussoff.

"It is the gesture of a friend, in hopes of a long relationship," replied Hui, reflecting on the past forty-eight hours.

While he was not waiting to die in a fiery crash aboard the AI-piloted plane that had brought him back to Wuhan, Hui had spent his time in the air thinking. No one, outside of a small group of Party officials, knew how precarious was the situation of Forever Grande, the real estate empire. Hui, in isolation in Lop, would not have known but for Ma-lin. "When word gets out, its value will plunge overnight," she had said. Which meant its true value, or lack thereof, was still a secret. Every secret carried with it hidden treasures. Hui intended to plunder those Forever Grande treasures. The thought made him woozy.

"Of course, we will have to run this past the shareholders," said Jussoff, who Hui knew owned or controlled 50.9 percent of the company's stock. "But it is certainly something we will consider and probably recommend."

"I am glad you are pleased," said Hui.

"We won't take any more of your time," said Jussoff. "Let me get hold of some of my folks and tell them about this meeting. And then, we'd very much like to see the Institute."

"It will be my pleasure, Mr. Jussoff," said Hui, smiling benevolently.

"Call me Alan," said Jussoff, beaming.

"Brian," chirped Helmsley, grinning.

Only the woman remained straight-faced. She stared without apology at Hui, then at Ma-lin. "Thank you for your time," she said. "I hope to see you again."

Chapter 14
Revenge Is The Best Forgiveness

Hui waited for the call, not in the suite of rooms that had once been his, but in the medium-sized room that had once been Henry's. The room where the young American had learned about AI from Hui's notes and lectures. The room where he had made passionate if inept love to Ma-lin. The room where he had decided to escape from China, and to temporarily ruin Hui's career and life.

Hui's worldview contained a deep sense of destiny. He looked around the room and, allowing himself a quick grin, thought this the perfect place to spend mental time in limbo. The details of the deal he had concluded with the Americans were being passed along now. He imagined the information would reach the Party's Financial Affairs Committee, where any significant sums of money had to be approved. In this case of course, he had *saved* the Party half a billion dollars. In the larger scope of things, this was pittance. But the Committee would have to take note that he – Hui – had not spent his country's money recklessly.

A new cell phone with no number attached had been waiting for him when he came into the room. He could receive calls on it but not make any. Fine, Hui thought. Who, after all, would I call?

The phone buzzed. He let it buzz twice, then pressed the green "TALK" button, said nothing.

"You have a sense of humor," said the digitized voice of the General Secretary of the Chinese Communist Party. "You buy a company whose technology we have already stolen. And pay for it with shares of cancer."

"The perilous state of Forever Grande will be known soon," said Hui. "Best to part with as much of it as possible."

"Will their government interfere?"

"I believe they are aware of what is happening."

"And leave the American company to figure out a way to wind it down. As I said, a real sense of humor."

"I serve the Party."

"As do I," said Xi, his overdubbed voice sounding like a dog choking on its breakfast. "Your actions please me. Are you ready to leave the life of luxury you've been enjoying?"

"I serve the Party."

"And the Party appreciates it," said Xi. "We'll find a spot for you at the Institute."

"No."

"No?" This was not a word the absolute ruler of China heard often.

"I wish very much to return to the Institute," said Hui carefully. "But I can only continue my work there as its director."

"The Institute has a director," Xi said.

He's playing cat-and-mouse with me, Hui thought. He drew a deep breath. "These political knots are too difficult for me. I will trust in your wisdom to untangle them."

A pause. "General Deng-tal is also a faithful servant of the Party," said Xi. "She must be allowed to leave with proper respect and with her reputation intact."

Xi, she, Xi, thought Hui. "I will follow your instructions. And..." another deep breath, "there is one other thing."

"You want the half-breed from Lop to be your assistant."

Hui smiled. Xi had not risen to these heights without a measure of insight.

"If it pleases the Party."

"The Party can withstand quite a lot," said Xi. "I suppose it will not crumble if a teenage terrorist is allowed to join one of its most secret Institutes. Good luck."

This told Hui many things. His own status, the information Malin had passed to Xi about Nur, and the respect the Institute – His, once more! — commanded.

Luck has nothing – and yet everything – to do with it, thought Hui.

Xingyun jingling. Lucky Spirits.

He walked out of the room, into the Director's office that had once, and once again, belonged to him. A startled female with sergeant's stripes on her olive uniform looked up in surprise. "Do not be afraid," he told her. "Lieutenant Ma-lin Cho will come to see you later today. She will explain to you what needs to be done here. You have done nothing wrong. Just do as she tells you."

"Yes, Colonel," said the young woman.

It is good to hear those words again, Hui thought.

He returned to the room where his clothes were hanging, the room Henry the American had used as his love nest. Hui liked the term in English. A soft place where birds can rest and breed. American birds, Chinese birds. Nest.

From his leather carrying case, Hui carefully extracted a book. The cover read, *The Genius of Xi Jinping's Socialism with Chinese Characteristics.* Inside the cover however, there was no mention of Xi or of Socialism Hui had carefully inserted the pages of the Tao I-Ching, the basic concept of Taoism that was practiced in China and beyond for centuries before the Communist Party outlawed it and persecuted its followers. The Tao, and its companion, the *Cangong Qi,* or Triplex Unity, contains poems and verses that explain all aspects of life and its twin, death.

Hui kept the volumes secreted in his case, partly out of a sense of rebellion, and partly, he told himself, because he carried with him a suicidal urge, one that could only be controlled by putting himself at constant risk, and then overcoming any thoughts he might have of following through on those fatal urges.

A man with an almost infinitely complicated mind, Hui sought occasional refuge in the simple honesty of the I-Ching. For instance:

Stabilize the will with firmness.

Do the work with flexibility

Making the will firm and strong is setting up the crucible.

Gradually progressing in the work is setting up the furnace.

Firmness and flexibility are both used, without imbalance

He was calm. An aura enveloped him.

It was the kind of philosophy provided by the I-Ching that allowed Hui to serve the Party faithfully, while recognizing the vacuity of Communism. Hui was not a tool of the Party. He was a crucible. He obeyed the Party because it was the fire that fueled his ambitions. But, deep, deep inside, he knew that the Party cared nothing for him, or the gift of Artificial Intelligence that he had given it.

Ma-lin would be busy explaining to Deng-tal that her time at the Institute was finished and suggesting that any questions she might have about her future be directed to the General Secretary. As this conversation was taking place, a team of six PLA privates would be collecting her personal effects from her office and boxing them for transport.

Deng-tal had done nothing wrong, Hui knew. She simply was not gifted enough to work in this – his – Institute. She was a bureaucrat, a broom-pusher, who had ascended the military ladder partly because she was intelligent, partly because she was a woman. Though barely, Hui added to himself.

He felt, before he heard, the disturbance of the aura. It came from outside. Hui remained still, and still calm. There was a sound, more a scrape than a knock on the door. It opened. It was the American woman who slipped inside and closed the door behind her.

"I told you I hoped to see you again," she said, all signs of being a subordinate note-taker now gone.

"Yes, you did, Miz Monaghan," Hui said.

She held his look and quickly began unhooking her skirt. "My name is Rose."

Chapter 15
A Strict System Without Rules

The first thing Hui noticed when he entered the Director's office – His office – was that the hologram of Xi Jinping was missing. It had been one of the touchstones of his leadership to have the General Secretary's virtual likeness always present, hovering over him. No one could mistake its significance. It meant that he – Hui – could always be counted on to do Xi Jinping's bidding, and to do it well. Why else have the great leader's image constantly shadowing his every movement? I will reinstall it as soon as possible, after documenting *its* absence during *my* absence.

In this case, absence truly made the heart grow fonder.

He decided not to sit in the plush chair behind the desk. Deng had had it installed. The chair that Hui had used for years had been "recycled" as a petrified employee told him. Hui calmed her. It was not her fault. He would like his chair, or its twin, behind the desk by the end of the day. When the Party spoke, all things were possible.

Instead, he sat on the guest sofa, the one where the American, Henry, had sat, deeply jet-lagged and quizzical, the day he arrived in Wuhan to begin his education at the Institute. Hui shook his head. So much water under that bridge.

It is not given to many people to have power, lose power, and be restored to power, all due to the whims of fate. If Hui had chosen another American fool to mold, if Henry had not proven the ideal dupe, if Hui had not won his competition against the Cyberspace Administration of China to guide the Party's response to the pandemic

74

that started here. If Henry had not found a way to escape back to America. If Hui had not thought to put the Uyghurs to productive work.

If, if, If.

And now that he had been given another chance to implement his worldview, what was he doing with the opportunity? Reading the Tao I-Ching and allowing an American woman to seduce him. How much foolishness could one man hope to get away with?

It had been quite a while, and he had to admit, it had been quite pleasant. The American knew what to do, how to accept as well as give pleasure. It had all seemed so natural, so easy.

Now came the hard part. *Why* did she do it? Hui was not so empty-headed as to think it was because of his masculine allure. Or his skill as a businessman. Or even the power that he – again – wielded. Though that last possibility certainly seemed the most likely. Despite having once had a hologram installed in his – once again – office, Hui doubted that the room where the assignation had taken place was wired. There was no reason for it, and Deng-tal would not have wanted to waste Party funds. So perhaps that secret tryst had remained just that. Unless she ... No, she had nothing on with which to hide equipment. All her ... assets ... were out in the open.

Was it reading the Tao I-Ching that had caused him to lower his self-defense barriers? He had worried, briefly, that there might be hidden cameras in the room and that they would spot him reading the forbidden book. Now, of course, if there were cameras they would have recorded more noteworthy video.

There was nothing illegal or anti-Party about having sex. One point six billion Chinese proved that. And having sex with a foreigner might be frowned upon but was not outlawed. Unless one of the partners had betrayed secret information. Hui knew he had not done that. He had remained mute throughout.

The wisdom imparted by the Tao had affected him, yes, but it had not weakened his will. Indeed, it strengthened his certainty that he was right. He had served the Party since adolescence. And this is what he knew about his life:

Dahuangyan. The Big Lie, His entire life had been spent serving an organization that cared nothing about him, or the other people of

China, except how he and they could make it stronger. And so he brought the American youth to Wuhan to bleed him dry of information about China's nemesis, the United States. And it worked beautifully. And the one time – one time! – events had moved beyond his control, he was cast into the gehenna of Lop. Even there, he had helped the Party by demonstrating the Uyghurs' capacity to be useful. Now, sitting in the chair once occupied by his former American acolyte, Hui made a silent vow: I will not return to Lop, except to bring Nur back with me.

Despite the talk about inertia and stasis, most organizations are amazingly adaptable to change in times of crisis. Hui had been back in Wuhan for only one day, and already word had spread through the Institute: he's back.

Back in his office, the woman who had been appointed Hui's temporary secretary knocked at his door, opened it a crack, put her head far enough inside the office that Hui could either grant or deny permission for entry.

"Come in," he said, feigning friendliness.

The woman's name was Ming. She was in her thirties, Hui imagined, was not wearing an army uniform but instead black shape-fitting pants and a white blouse, with a green sweater tied around her shoulders. Though not exactly attractive, she made a good first impression. Hui intended to ask her to stay on, when the right moment came.

"Lieutenant Cho would like to see you, sir. She says her visit will not take long."

"Ask the Lieutenant to come in."

Ming nodded curtly, turned and stepped out. Hui heard a few murmured words, and then Ma-lin, in everyday drab green uniform, stepped in.

"Colonel," she said.

Hui pretended to look behind him, then looked right and left. "Me?"

She smiled. "There was never a change in your rank. It simply wasn't used during that time period."

Time period. Lop. When the Party had abandoned him.

"How may I help you, Lieutenant?"

"The American delegation you met with has communicated with me. The terms of the purchase of their company have been approved by their directors. They will accept the offer you made."

Meaning selling the company in exchange for soon-to-be worthless stock. "Good," Hui said.

"Having concluded their business, they are preparing to leave China, and would like to see you to say good-bye." Her eyes lit up just enough bulb-wattage to let him know she knew.

"No," said Hui. "That will not be necessary. Please convey my wishes for a safe journey home." Looking Ma-lin directly in the eyes to let her know that he knew that she knew. Silence has so many layers.

"There was also a call for you from the ... Committee. We were unable to locate you at that moment." The committee in question was the Standing Committee, the highest single body of authority in the Party. Even some members of the Politburo were not included in it. Inclusion meant access to Xi Jinping and to unlimited benefits and authority. Unlimited, that is, until they crossed the red line of Xi's displeasure.

"Set up the call." Ma-lin nodded, once, and left him. How the hell did she learn about the American woman, Hui asked himself. It didn't matter really. There was no benefit to her telling anyone. She just wanted to let him know she knew. Insurance? Perhaps. Most likely though, it was just her nature.

A call to the Standing Committee takes less than a minute to make, but sometimes hours to reach the right person. This time it went through quickly. The person who had tried calling him while he was dallying with Rose was the Deputy Defense Minister, whom Hui knew only by reputation.

"We couldn't find you when we called, Colonel," said the Deputy Minister on the encrypted line, instantly marking out his superior status.

"I was performing my duties, Minister," Hui said. And it was true in a way.

"The People's Army requires your expertise."

"It has always been at the People's service," said Hui.

"You know about drones?"

"I am sure you can enlighten me, Minister," said Hui, already sniffing out the reason for the call.

Knowing the line was nearly impossible to hack – or believing that to be so – the Deputy Minister felt free to speak boldly. "We have already weaponized the drones we developed. Now we want them to make their own decisions."

"Indeed," said Hui, his mind already whirring like the drones he was being asked to turn into mechanical murderers.

"You will report your progress and plan to the Standing Committee in a week."

"With pleasure, Minister." The line dropped.

Hui tapped the phone on his desk. Ma-lin answered. "I know how much you enjoyed visiting me in Lop. You will be pleased to know we are going back."

Chapter 16
Arling Darling

For a graduate from an Ivy League school who had lost his first post-college job within months, snuck out of and back into his homeland, seen sights that few Americans ever will, been inducted – indoctrinated, if he was being honest – into a society of visionaries, Henry couldn't quite figure out what he'd done right.

Though he was still confined professionally to the purgatory of Arlington, he knew that his Agency handlers were impressed with his work. For his part, he was coming to appreciate the role that the Agency played in America's safekeeping, although it was certainly guilty of excesses. But so, Henry reasoned, was the Chinese Communist Party. Its mission, set by one man and put into motion by millions of subordinates, cared little, for all its thousands of miles of newsprint and gigabytes of online self-adulation, cared little about the people with whom it shared China's confines.

In slightly more than two years, Henry's reality had shifted from wide-eyed wonder to widely respected *wunderkind*. Policy, politics, polemics had little chance to dazzle him these days. His mind and his motivation were cornered by lines of code that fewer than one percent of the world could understand, much less author. He was part of the brotherhood – perhaps brother-led would be a better term — of Artificially Intelligent coders and practitioners. There were women in the club, yes, and they made important contributions, but still fought an uphill battle for proper recognition.

Henry had time to contemplate the lunacy of the age in which he was coming into his prime, because, really, there wasn't much else for him to do. His work was his work. He would not be attending any company Christmas parties nor intramural softball games, because to most of his colleagues, he existed not as a twenty-something young man but a series of zeroes and ones, slashes and underscores that appeared on their screens and produced either praise or sourly transmitted agreement. While they did not know his name, they knew that # so-and-so, (Henry) simply did not make errors. Not online anyway.

His social life was simple. When she texted, he cycled quickly over to her condo for conjugal conversation. When she had crossed her erogenous goal line, he was dismissed. He never knew when the texts might buzz him, and his member, to attention. And that the match, for however long the stopwatch was ticking, was worth whatever the home team chose. He was content to be the forever visitor, constantly uniformed in gray, with whatever invisible crowd there might be cheering for the other side, the only sounds of encouragement, throaty and insistent, coming from his opponent.

"Come." She didn't waste time or money on texts. And he had learned she did not expect an answering text. She expected him. The one time he had been forced to decline was because of work. And she didn't want to hear about his work, nor tell him about hers. "Keep it simple, stupid," she had sung over her shoulder once, while she headed for the bathroom to clean up. Lying amid the sweaty sheets, he had to admit she was right. It was easier, and more rewarding, to admit she was right most of the time.

He made it to the condo in under 20, locked his bike, buzzed, tried to breathe normally. The door opened and she was naked.

"What if it hadn't been me?"

"That would have been embarrassing, wouldn't it?"

"For you?"

"For the person at the door. Get in there," she said, pointing to the boudoir.

He had begun to have confidence in his performance. If she was faking pleasure, it was well done. At first, he worried mildly about the volume of her animal howls, foul-mouthed commands, and electric-shock orgasms. And the truth was, he didn't enjoy it as much as he had hoped. For Rose, sex was about Rose. It was a neat reversal on centuries of male dominance.

"Pour a drink if you want," she said when they were finished. "I'm going to shower."

He wandered into the living room – that and the kitchen were all that complemented the bedroom – and caught sight of something new-looking on the shelf of a bookcase. Tan in color, with spots of yellow on it, it was about eight inches high, and looked like a square tree with upward turning branches. But what transfixed him were the six bronze statues of long-legged, long-beaked birds perched at the foot of the structure, of different sizes, but clearly balearica cranes. Henry knew this because they were the same kind of cranes he had seen on his visits to the Yellow Crane Tower, just outside Wuhan, on the Yangtze River.

The first Crane Tower may date back as far as 288, though it has been destroyed and rebuilt numerous times since then. The legend is that the owner of a pothouse – an ancient Chinese term for a wine store merchant – was kind to a poor man who asked for a drink but warned the owner he could not pay for it. The owner, named Xin, nonetheless supplied him with wine, not just that one day but for years. The poor man, named Zi'an, returned one day and, with an orange peel, drew a picture of a crane on the wall of the pothouse. He told the store owner that if he clapped his hands, the crane would come to life and dance for him. Xin did, and the living dancing crane drawn from an orange peel was so popular with clients that Xin became a millionaire. To thank Zi'an, Xin built the original Yellow Crane Tower. Years later, a much older Zi'an came back, and began playing a flute. This time, the crane came to life, allowed Zi'an to mount it, and took him away to heaven.

Now, as Henry stood looking at the souvenir, he wondered why Rose would have such a thing. As she stepped out of the bathroom, her hair wet and smelling of soap, he opened his mouth to ask her, then stopped. Instead he said, "You look nice."

"Thanks," she said without enthusiasm. "Time for you to go."

The shift from the hungry mouth, the writhing hips, the needy hands always surprised him, but he was no longer hurt by it. Rose was, in this way, acting more like a man. Got what I wanted, now take off. I have things to do. Henry put down his drink, barely touched, and walked to the door. Over his shoulder, he said, "See you."

He enjoyed Rose but longed for Rav. Was happy to educate himself in the joys of sex with this woman, but would never get over, or give up, on the love of his life. And, it turned out, he had things to do too. Like digging a little more deeply into the story of the Yellow Crane Tower.

Chapter 17
Lop, Stop and Barrel

Lop smelled about the same. Sounded slightly less like a torture chamber. Hui wondered why the piercing shouts had not greeted him and Ma-lin when their Hongqi L5 sedan pulled into the yard. The car was one of the new electric fleet that Xi Jinping had ordered his ministers to use, to demonstrate to the world China's commitment to cleaning up the environment. Had anyone looked over the hills outside Lop, they would have seen choking smoke rising from the coal-fired factories that made steel, refined uranium, fabrics, and medicines, and emitted noxious fumes. But gasoline-free cars were what outsiders were permitted to admire.

Socialism with Chinese characteristics.

Hui wasted no time pondering this hypocrisy. He wanted to get Nur and take him to Wuhan without undue questions by anyone in uniform. Ma-lin would make the job easier. But he – Hui – would be viewed with suspicion, despite his rank, the moment he explained why he was here.

He, who had once been held in such high esteem, had been permitted to bring an American youth to the Institute for Artificial Intelligence. And then watch him ruin his – Hui's – career by putting family over Party. The single most important lesson that Chinese of that young fool's generation had learned. Well, learned, or had it beaten into them and their families at the slightest sign of doubt. The Party comes first.

"Colonel?" It took him a moment to realize Ma-lin was asking him something.

"What?" He said it too sharply, and she retreated physically from the implied insult. "Sorry. My mind was wandering." Of course. Follow an insult with the bare truth, betraying weakness. Get control, Hui, or you will soon be a resident in this place again.

"I don't hear the screams I did last time."

"What do you hear instead, Lieutenant?"

"Well, if I had to describe it, I'd say it's the sound of people working hard."

"I believe you are right." There. The moment of weakness had passed. He had made a determination about a question and was once again a figure of authority. Don't let that slip-up happen again, fool.

A PLA corporal – lower rank than the one that met the car when Ma-Lin was the sole visitor, Hui noticed – was hustling toward them. "Colonel Hui, Lieutenant, we are honored."

"Thank you," said Hui. "I would like to see the camp commandant."

"The ... lead re-education instructor is waiting for you, Colonel." By the look on his face, it was unclear whether the corporal thought he was taking a risk with these words or merely performing his duty adequately. Such small hints as a hard look, a quickly drawn breath, a hesitation in responding could be the difference between promotion and joining the "students" at this "re-education" facility.

Ma-lin receded to the background, content to let Hui be the hero or the horse's ass on this expedition.

The corporal led them past one of the factories whose construction Hui had suggested. The next building, a type of Quonset Hut badly painted gray, was the office of the commandant, his "lead instructor" camouflage notwithstanding. He was a thin man with a thinner pencil mustache and irises that were disconcertingly reddish-orange. Hui disliked him immediately.

"Colonel," he said, rising from his desk chair. "Welcome. Or should I say welcome back?"

Hui ignored the jibe. "There is a prisoner here who I am authorized to take with me. The lieutenant has the necessary paperwork. Please ask your corporal to take me to Prison Block C. Or should I say 'classroom C'?"

The red-orange eyes blazed for just a fraction of a second. Then dulled into resignation. "Of course. May I see the paperwork?"

Ma-lin was striding forward, her arm extended with a bundle, before the sentence was finished. She remained wordless.

The commandant-instructor looked over the papers. "The Deputy Minister of Defense signed this order?"

Hui shrugged. "Would you like to check with him that this is his signature? I have his cell number."

Totally flummoxed, the little man with red eyes set the papers on his desk. "The corporal will escort you. Lieutenant, would you care to remain here and have a cup of tea with me?"

Women have an instinctive ability to distinguish politeness from a sexual overture. Ma-lin gave the commandant the look employed around the world by beautiful women for dealing with ugly little men. "No," she answered.

The day after Hui had left Lop for Wuhan, Nur had been placed on the assembly line making surgical masks for sale outside of China. Many of the prisoners had already contracted the disease the masks were intended to guard against, and were sneezing and dripping snot onto the object of their labor. When the door to the factory slammed shut with a thunder clap, Nur looked up, saw Hui, and fell to his knees. A guard armed with a taser approached him, ready to fire when the corporal's voice overcame the noise of the machinery. "Jing-Su, no!"

The guard gave the corporal a hard look of reproach but lowered his arm. Hui stood still, with Ma-lin behind him. He crooked his finger, once, an economy of motion born of power.

Nur stood, and without a glance behind him, and with his hands behind his back, walked to Hui, who said quietly, "You are coming with me. Is there anything you need to bring with you?"

"Just my brain," said Nur, smiling for the first time since he had last seen Hui. He kept his hands behind his back, a gesture of subservience, Hui imagined.

"Yes," said Hui, smiling back, "your brain."

They walked to the car together. Ma-lin was already seated in the front.

"Colonel," said Nur quietly, "may I tell you something?"

"You may," said Hui.

"I was afraid you had abandoned me. I know you said you would return. But when they put me back to work on the line..."

"You would not be the first person in China to be abandoned and to have your hopes shattered, Nur," said Hui, feeling something purr deep inside his chest. "But not in this case. You will come with me, and we will work together."

"Yes, Colonel."

There was no more need for conversation.

Chapter 18
The Power of Power

The plane and another Hongqi L5 had them back at the Institute by midnight. From the air, Hui had called and instructed his assistant to have the room Henry had once occupied made ready for a new resident. Close every circle that you can, he thought.

Nur was, as he had been when Hui plucked him from the assembly line, mute with amazement and gratitude. Ma-lin ignored the youth, kept her nose buried in notes she was carrying. Hui decided he was not required to make conversation with a boy, and so the journey was a quiet and tense one.

Nur looked at the hallways of the Institute as though he were in a place of worship. He walked tentatively from the entrance to the room where Hui directed him. It was only after he had discarded his prison clothes that he realized new garments had been set out for him – the uniform of a private in the People's Liberation Army. He tiptoed from his room to Hui's office, where he had been instructed to report after showering the filth of Lop off himself.

"Am I permitted to wear this?" he asked Hui.

"Why else would we have put it in your room? You are not in the Army, Nur, not yet. But you must dress like everyone else here. You will look suspicious no matter your clothing. But less so like this."

"Are many of my people in the Army?"

Hui considered the question seriously. "Probably there are a few, who have shown a willingness and an ability to accept the Party's supreme role."

"I don't think there can be many," said Nur, who clearly was more relaxed talking with Hui than any other Han.

Hui seemed to encourage this. "We lost a lot of time after I left Lop. We need to make it up. Here. Now."

"I understand," said Nur, with enough emphasis to make it believable. "They wouldn't let me near your workspace or your living quarters after you left. So I had no access to technology. But I wrote some code that we might want to try out."

"You 'wrote' it?" said Hui, half amused. "You mean on paper? I thought paper was considered a carry-over from the last century. Who gave you writing implements?"

"No one," said Nur, reaching gingerly into the pocket of his new uniform jacket and extracting a sheaf of dirty newsprint. "I had to improvise." He handed the pages, clutched between his pointer and middle fingers, to Hui, who nearly revealed his shock, but controlled himself.

Nur had written page after page of code on discarded copies of the *People's Daily*, the Party newspaper. Lacking ink or pencils, he had written the code in blood. Hui looked at the boy, tilting his head in inquiry.

"Some of it is mine. But there's no shortage of blood in Row C. Lots of people contributed." It was said flatly, as though everyone knew these things. "One woman gave birth to the child of a guard. There was blood everywhere. I wrote lots of code that night."

"What's wrong with your hands?" Hui asked.

"Punishment," Nur replied casually. Or what he hoped was casually.

"Punishment for what?"

"For approaching you, talking to you, being put into your service."

"You were punished for associating with me?"

"I was the first prisoner to be granted any kind of leniency. And it was all due to you."

Hui had sworn off guilt during his long career. Now, something familiar to it had leaked into his brain. "What happened?"

"Two guards dragged me out of my bed the day after you left. They took me to the commandant's office. They held me down while he took a pair of pliers and crushed my thumbs. He kept asking if I could write code without thumbs. It took a lot of willpower for me not to tell him what a moron he was. Of course, I can write without thumbs. I can also write code without eyes, or ears, or a tongue."

"What are you talking about?" said Hui, fearing he knew the answer.

"You gave me the courage to know and believe in what I can do. I can write code without any of my physical parts. Well, I need my brain, of course. The only thing I can't do without, apart from my brain, is you."

Hui remembered Nur saying at Lop he didn't need to bring any possessions with him – just his brain. And that he feared he had been abandoned.

"You realize everyone here is going to hate you," he told Nur.

"And that, with due respect, Colonel, is different how from the rest of my life?"

"It is different because I don't hate you." The words were so foreign to him he might as well have been speaking Russian. He – Hui – did not express thoughts like this. It was not who he was. He was Hui. And yet, he realized, even as the words came out of his mouth, that he meant it. He felt like a suitor revealing his love. Ridiculous! This boy was part of a traitorous breed. He could not be trusted. He could not be given the chance to diminish, in any way, the Party's plans and goals. And yet...

"I want you to sleep, Nur. No one will bother you in your room. It is yours until I say differently. You need to rest and recover. Lop was a challenge. You weathered it." He felt like a fat-assed Catholic bishop or Cardinal congratulating the delimbed, blinded, scalded victims of the Inquisition for not giving up hope.

"Good night, Colonel. You know, I can do what I said I could do."

"Which is what?"

"Create AI that makes decisions about life and death, without human input."

It was exactly what Hui wanted. And feared.

Chapter 19
Hu Da-faq?

The work was intense, private and moved faster than Hui had anticipated. Once he re-established the bond of trust with Nur, they worked as a team that did not need to consult one another, because they already knew the answers to any possible questions.

Hui had abandoned the empirical approach to AI he used in his first stint as director of the Institute. Now he spoke regularly with the coders, listening to their problems, occasionally suggesting a solution, more often learning from them. The science of Artificial Intelligence was developing – developing itself actually – at breathtaking speed. Even his – Hui's – mastery of the subject was now outmoded, antiquated, really, during his time in Lop, by advances, not just in this Institute, but elsewhere around the world.

The Americans, he knew, had brilliantly combined AI with the Metaverse – the make-believe world that anyone can join by putting on a headset and choosing whatever adventure they wanted to have. Virtually, of course. Sold as games, these were sly ways to entice customers to abandon their physical lives, and become permanently attached, and dependent on, the world they had purchased and preferred to live in.

The American military too, was admitting that AI had to be harnessed and used for warfare. Drones were now thick in the sky, seeking out targets, and deciding, without oversight, which to destroy. Hui knew that while China possessed similar drones, they were slower, and made more misjudgments than their American opponents.

Evening up the score, and then surging ahead of the Americans was going to be his, and Nur's, path to recognition, and favor.

A hand specialist brought in from Shanghai was patiently restoring Nur's use of his thumbs. "I've never seen one person's thumbs injured in exactly the same way as this," he told Hui. "Describe the accident again please, Colonel? It would make a good write-up in the Journal of Orthopedic Musculoskeletal Research."

"There will be no articles about this case," Hui said coldly. "Just fix the thumbs."

Doctors like to think themselves the high priests of the modern age. This one was intelligent enough to recognize where he was, and to know his place in it. But he made a mental note that he had been ordered by a PLA Colonel to aid a Uyghur.

The sticking point to the project was determining at what point an AI-enabled drone should be allowed to make choices independent of its controller. It was more than a programming issue. It was, Hui thought quietly, a moral one. But that was not an argument one made in a discussion with the PLA. Right and wrong counted for nothing. What the Party said was right was right. He did not look forward to tomorrow, when the Deputy Defense Minister Hui had spoken with before, would be visiting the Institute, nosing around Hui's work.

"Eat a good dinner," he told Nur. "I want you to stay in your room all day tomorrow. Don't come out for any reason until I personally tell you it's alright."

"How to make a Uyghur disappear without killing him, huh?" They had reached the point of mutual trust where Nur could make jokes, knowing Hui not only tolerated them, but secretly enjoyed them.

"You have a laptop," Hui said. "Keep working, but don't send anything or respond to any messages."

"Well," said Nur, "at least you can be sure I won't be twiddling my thumbs."

Where did he get the wit and timing to say such things, Hui wondered. The brain concealed by the face in front of him was truly a work of art.

They never shared meals. Hui did not want any rumors of a professional relationship becoming friendship. So, he could only hope the next morning that Nur had followed his advice and either eaten heartily or smuggled something into his living quarters.

Deputy Minister of Defense Hu Da-faq was somehow related to the former Supreme Leader of China, Hu Jintao. But how, no one knew. Hu Da-faq was both a riddle and the answer to a riddle. No one pointed this out.

Hui was at the door of the Institute to meet his visitor, who arrived with a retinue that would have done certain sultans proud. Hui knew better than to offer his guest refreshments. Among other subordinates was Hu's personal chef, who traveled with him everywhere, preparing every meal, every cup of tea, and opening every bottle of water that he consumed. It was rumored that Hu believed his ancestor, Hu Jintao, had survived an attempt to poison him during his tenure as head of the Party, and so, the country. While never proven and never discussed by anyone who had hopes of a happy life in China, Hu had indisputably disappeared from public view at the end of 2011, blaming his absence on a stubborn cold. The next year, when his term was up and he was generally expected to seek re-election, Hu Jintao renounced all his government and Party positions and retired into private life.

He was succeeded by Xi Jinping.

"Minister, you are welcome," said Hui, meaning none of it.

"Either way, I am here," said Hu. "We need to talk in private."

"Of course, please come to my office." Hu told his flunkies to wait in the hallway outside Hui's inner sanctum. To his cook, he said, "Cha." Hui told his assistant, Ming, "Water, please, and privacy. Thank you."

"I received instructions," Hui said, "that the Ministry wants to concentrate our research in the area of self-protective measures." Again, he avoided terms like warfare, mass killing, military superiority – all the things the directive really meant.

"Excellent perceptive powers," said Hu, barely disguising his disdain. "You will accelerate your work with this objective being paramount."

"I understand, Minister. The research is intensive, and we always take care not to make errors."

"I trust 'accelerate' is not a word unknown to you," said Hu.

Hui saw a thread-thin wire extending from Hu's shirt pocket and assumed their "private" conversation was being recorded.

"My field of endeavor is artificial intelligence, not guesswork," he said. "We try to make our errors in the laboratory, not the real world."

"The Americans are catching up to us!" Hu's voice, not pleasant when he was speaking normally, was particularly unlikeable when raised. "Or should I say, to you?"

Henry's unforgiven face flashed across Hui's brain. "I am aware of that," he said. "And I have a plan to slow their progress." In truth, the plan had begun to take shape only when Hu said "Americans".

"Why do you make a distinction between what errors are made in the laboratory and in the real world? Is this the 'artificial' part of your specialty?"

No one had spoken to Hui like that since he had been sentenced to Lop. The passage of time did nothing to conceal the insult or his umbrage.

"We make our mistakes in the laboratory, Minister, so that they do not become widely known. And so that no one is injured by them."

"I was told to expect this excuse mongering from you," said Hu, puffing up his plump chest to emphasize the importance of his words. "Now listen, Colonel. The Minister has ordered you to conduct a live test of an AI drone in one month."

Hui, used to handling the unexpected with *panache,* opened his mouth to protest, then relaxed his face. "That time frame almost guarantees that there will be errors."

"Well, Colonel, people aren't perfect, are they?"

"No," said Hui. "But AI is. Or can be. Or should be. If it's used properly."

Hu employed his Stare Of A Powerful Man look. Hui knew he could not win that competition, so he said, "What kind of demonstration does the Minister want?"

Hui pretended to smile. "An armed drone attack. Live weapons. Real people. One month from now."

"Where?"

"Near your previous residence. Lop."

Chapter 20
Mark of Cane

"Pick it up," said Rose, lying next to him.

Henry lifted the thin shiny black cane, smoothed his hand down its length. It was skinnier than his little finger. Shinier than the lacquered nightstand in the bedroom.

He had not seen it before. Rose looked at him looking at it. She reached into the nightstand on the other side of the bed, extracted a length of purple silk. She worked it until she had a loose knot about a third of the length of the fabric. She put her right hand through the knot and tightened it.

She extended her left hand. "Now tie this one."

Inexperienced as he was, Henry knew what was happening. It had been two weeks since his last text summons, and he was hungry. He had never engaged in any sex remotely kinky, though Khadija, his college relationship, had once looped a scarf around her neck and told him to squeeze, saying she had heard sex was enhanced when breathing was cut off. She withdrew the offer when she saw his reaction.

Rose, naked, and now with both wrists secured, turned away from him so that she was lying on her stomach. "Hook it over the bedpost," she said quietly. Henry complied. Once the silk was stretched over the bedpost, her arms were fully extended. He realized it would be difficult if not impossible for her get up without help.

"Touch me with it," said Rose, her features languorous, her voice a murmur. Henry ran his hand down her back slowly. She said, "Mmmmm. That's nice. Now use the stick."

With his right hand, without any pressure, he gently placed the shiny black stick across her buttocks. He might have been setting out crystal glasses on a table, so careful was his movement.

Her eyes closed, Rose said "Hit me."

Henry looked around the boudoir that he had come to know fairly well. He knew that in this room, and as far as he knew, only in this room, this woman he was with became a wild and adventurous animal. Decency and restraint were shed along with her sensible clothing. There was no remnant of the polite, slightly flustered woman, dressed in casual class, who was experiencing difficulty unlocking her bicycle.

"I'm not a blackjack dealer, Rose."

"Do it," said that woman.

He tapped her behind gently with the cane, no more firmly than if he were tapping her on the shoulder with his fingertips to get her attention.

"Harder," she said.

Lifting his arm no more than three inches from her, he brought the cane down.

"Harder."

He lifted his arm higher and brought the stick down across her bottom.

"Harder, you sniveling little fairy."

Thwack. This time, the stick left a red mark.

"Are you even a man?" she said in a nasty low voice.

He lifted his arm above his head and brought the cane down with force, in nearly the same spot.

"Unnn," she said.

Again.

Again.

Again. The last lash cut the skin of her left buttock.

"Harder, you weak faggot."

He aimed for the tops of her legs where they joined her buttocks.

"Oww," said Rose, the first time she had hinted at discomfort.

He continued to punish her legs. Rose began to whimper.

"Someplace else. My legs are tender there."

He lashed her back, drawing blood with the first stroke.

"That hurts," said Rose. She turned her head so she was facing him.

He lashed her harder.

She tried to get up, bending her legs so that she could get up on her knees. But she was too tightly bound by the silk to do it without help. Henry, standing by the bed, slapped the fronts of her knees so she collapsed and was lying flat again. He slashed at her upper legs.

"Enough," she said with a sharp intake of breath.

He slashed her legs again. His mind began to fill with images. Rav, Hui, Qi-Qi, with whom he had escaped to America, only to have her assassinated in midtown Manhattan. And then he thought of the brown and yellow statuette in the living room, twenty feet away. The souvenir of the Yellow Crane Tower.

And it all came together.

"Stop. I said enough."

"Why were you in Wuhan?" Henry said in a guttural voice he had never used before.

"Stop. You're hurting me." She pulled at the silk that was cutting into her wrists. Henry slashed her across her arms. She screamed.

"Why were you in Wuhan?" he said again.

When she looked at him this time, he saw fear in her eyes. He raised the stick, brought it down across her face, cutting the edge of her left eye. She screamed.

This, thought Henry, is power.

"What were you doing in Wuhan?" Slash across the backs of her knees.

"Henry!"

Slash across the bottoms of her feet. Bastinado, it was called. A particularly sensitive part of the body, favored by professional torturers. She opened her mouth to scream, but he slashed her in the same place again before she could fill her lungs. She began to choke. He brought the rod down again, striping the length of her back. Again, and again. Her back now looked like a checkerboard, red with blood some places, purple-black welts already rising in others.

"WHAT WERE YOU DOING IN WUHAN?" he screamed. He paused to see if she would answer.

"Work," she gasped. "Work."

He slashed her across the back of her neck.

"What kind of work?"

"My job." Unable now to control her volume, she shouted the words. Henry looked on the floor, saw one of his socks, grabbed it with his left hand, and slashed her with the cane in his right hand. She opened her mouth to scream, and he shoved the sock in.

Again, she tried to give her arms slack by bending her knees. He slashed the backs of them with his hardest blow yet, and she sank back, stretched out flat.

Rose's blood was now flying off the black cane, onto the bed, onto the floor, onto Henry.

This is power, he thought again. And from power, he saw the face of Hui, the most powerful man he had ever known.

"Did you see Hui?" he shouted, not knowing why.

Unable to speak or scream, she moved her head. Henry thought it was a nod.

"Did you?" Slash.

This time, it was clear that she was nodding.

Henry stopped slashing her. He didn't want to anymore. He didn't have to anymore.

He put down the cane. He pulled the sock, now crimson, from her bloodied mouth. Rose took three excruciating breaths. She opened her eyes, now swollen from being lashed, and looked at him. She was completely under his power.

"Please don't hit me anymore. I'll tell you whatever you want."

"Why were you in Wuhan?"

"Please. Water. I'll talk."

Rose kept a bottle of water on her side table, on the far side of the bed. Henry went around, opened it, looked at her, and splashed some water over her face as though reviving her. She moaned. He lifted her head so she could drink, held the bottle to her swollen lips. She took a drink and immediately spit it out. The sheet beneath her face turned pink.

"More, please."

He gave her another drink, which she swallowed.

"More."

"No. Talk."

She looked at him, this woman whom he had allowed to dominate him in this bedroom until now, who had never shared a single detail of her professional or personal life with him, and he saw in her the flicker of submission, felt a new and different surge of power. He slapped her bottom.

"Please, no more. You hurt me."

"And what have you been doing to me, Rose?"

"She squeezed her eyes shut for a moment. "I work at a security firm. It was purchased by the Chinese. I went to Wuhan to help close the deal."

"When?"

"Two weeks ago." Which explained the silence from her during that fortnight.

"Why did you go to Wuhan?"

"Because that's where the buyer was."

He knew the answer already but asked, "Was it the AI Institute?"

"Yes. Our company specializes in Facial Recognition."

So do I, thought Henry. The pieces were falling into place and he felt fury and fear simultaneously.

"And you dealt with Colonel Hui?"

She remembered the older man's unexpectedly strong arms, developed chest, the knowledge his eyes imparted. She nodded.

It was Rav whose face came into his brain, not Hui. The months back in America, the legal peril, the family matters, the magnetic drag of the U.S. authorities on his willpower; all these floated through his mind, went blank, returned more vividly. Henry, nothing more than a sallow, unemployed college graduate when he first encountered Hui, was now in the middle of something. Something that, as usual, he did not understand.

"Where do you really work, Rose?" His hand was on her buttocks, ready to resume her punishment.

"The same place you do, Henry," she said, a sad red smile forming on her puffy lips. "The very same place."

Chapter 21
Schools, Tools and Fools

There would be no way to keep the objective of their work from Nur for long, Hui knew. The youth was too adept, too clever, too observant to be taken in. Still, Hui decided not to share with him the details until it was necessary. It was not as though Nur could refuse to participate unless he wanted to return to the cells of Lop. And if he did, this time he would have no protection.

Nur asked no questions except the technical specifications that Hui wanted for the code. He ignored – and was ignored by – the other coders, the Han who treated him as if he were invisible, or more accurately, infectious. But there was a second side to his glances, shielded from general recognition, that said he knew something was up.

"These commands have not been laboratory tested," he told Hui during one of their frequent one-on-one meetings. "Unless you know something you're not telling me."

"There are a lot of things I don't tell you, Nur," said Hui. "Which is probably why you are still alive and have thumbs that are beginning to function again."

The youth nodded. He understood.

"Drones are not like people," he said with half a smile.

"No," said Hui. "They are more reliable."

"Until they start thinking for themselves."

Hui looked at the youth. He knew what he was working on and against whom it was meant to be used. "Nur, there are times when we are required to make decisions. Sometimes the decision is between two positive things. Sometimes, between good and evil. And other times, including this time, I fear, between two evils." Hui stopped and considered his own words. He was speaking to Nur as a teacher, a mentor. He had done the same with the American, Henry, until that young man had betrayed him. Would it occur again, with Nur?

But the young Uyghur just nodded and turned back to the screen in front of him. He knows, Hui told himself.

The writing of AI code is something akin to keeping sand at the end of an ocean dry. It can never be perfected, because the next drenching wave is always on the way. AI Code can be written, tested, rewritten, put online, taken down, incorporated into machinery and technology.

And still be all wrong.

Hui had had time to think about his acrimonious conversation with Vice Minister Hu Da-faq. He was planning his counter-offensive. But there was simply no way to know if it would succeed, until it took place. That made the precision of science, the thousands of man-hours of planning and testing little more than conjecture. You will know if it works when it works.

More like Manichean philosophy than life-shifting technology.

They had hundreds of practice drones at their disposal, thanks to the generosity of the PLA when it wanted something done. The first fleet went up under old-fashioned remote control. Each drone soared upward, and returned on command. That was the easy part.

"Ready?" said Hui.

"One last fix," said Nur, touching the Send button. "Go."

Hui gave the order and one of the Han coders, having received Nur's work, downloaded it and made contact with the drones. The understanding was that Nur could do the heavy lifting, but it would be Han Chinese who put that work into action and took the credit if it worked. Nur would be blamed if it didn't.

Socialism with Chinese characteristics.

Up went the drones, which were armed only with blank charges. Their release into the air was ground-controlled. Once they had been aloft for three minutes, each drone took control of its own decisions, its own destiny. Each selected an attack site. Each released its harmless charges. Each charge would have, in theory, and if it had been carrying real weaponry, hit its target.

The Hans grinned, exchanged high-fives, told each other how brilliant they were.

Nur studied his screen, his face blank.

"I know," said Hui. "I know."

"Yes, Colonel," said Nur. "I know you know."

Hui had to decide. Trust or not? Trust had proven an expensive luxury. Yet without it ... He had ten days until the real-time demonstration would take place, with Vice Minister Hu present. Hui envisioned what it would be like. He decided.

He asked Ma-lin to come see him.

She entered his office in her everyday uniform: drab olive-green skirt, white blouse, olive-green tie, her luscious hair pulled tight into a bun and covered by her service cap. When not in uniform, she routinely wore a black skirt or trousers and a white blouse. She would never be accused of flirtatiousness.

"You don't like Nur, do you?" Hui said without preliminaries. Since he had returned to his position, Hui had come to rely on Ma-lin's support, intelligence, insights. Previously, she had been his subordinate. Now he considered her more a partner, albeit a junior one.

Ma-lin looked at him for a long second. He could see her mind working behind her gorgeous eyes, considering the implications of his question.

"I don't like or dislike him," she said. "He is a Uyghur, an enemy of the Party."

"Perhaps," said Hui. "But he is very talented."

"So was the American."

Hui let her see his anger, something he rarely did. "I have thought of that," he said. "It won't happen again."

She was not cowed. "Tell me if I can help you."

"You can."

The wonderful thing about AI, and the machines they control, is that proximity means nothing. Ten days later, Hui, Vice Minister Hu and his collection of flunkies, even the Defense Ministry's chief officer of Party ideology (to ensure the military never got any original ideas about what was right), were all in Hui's laboratory, riveted to a plasma screen that was ten by seven feet in size.

The screen was a real-time picture of the flight of one of the drones that was on its way to a valley just outside of Lop, where one hundred fifty inmates from the re-education camp where Nur had been housed were standing outside together, shifting their feet, looking nervously at the sky. They were surrounded by a ring of PLA troops, armed with automatic rifles that they hefted like recalcitrant toddlers. The camera providing the footage was mounted on one of the drones, about fifty yards behind the main attack convoy. The picture quality was excellent. The equipment was Japanese.

Though it was his laboratory at his Institute, Hui was in the chair farthest away from the screen. Hu was up front, his eyes fixed on the scene, a dribble of saliva balanced on his lower lip. The Party minder was a woman of fifty or so, as wide as she was tall, with metal glasses that reminded Hui of Tanteeth. A timing clock mounted on the wall specially for this occasion counted down, two minutes thirty-four seconds, thirty-three, thirty-two ...

"I need to say again, for the record, Vice Minister Hu, that I believe we have not had sufficient time to prepare this exercise," Hui said amid the intense silence of the room.

"I have heard your excuses already, Colonel," said Hu, without taking his eyes off the screen. "Your point is noted. For the record." He dragged out the last three words.

"The Party set the schedule and selected the time," said the Party enforcer. "Are you questioning the Party's wisdom?"

"Certainly not," said Hui smoothly. "Only that of some of its members."

Ma-lin, in uniform and all but invisibly tucked into a corner of the room, moved toward Hu with a mobile device in her hand.

"Vice Minister, would you like to press the button that will send the signal to begin the exercise?"

"Give it to me, Lieutenant," Hu said, palming the device with his right hand and stabbing the red button on the center with his left thumb.

The screen immediately went fuzzy, but only for a second. When it cleared, the camera captured the drones ahead of it veering to the right, then angling downward from the sky. The camera on the rear drone was equipped with audio, so the audience in Hui's office could hear the harsh buzz of the machines as they plunged earthward. The camera drone too was angled down, and in a moment they could see the huddle of Uyghurs looking up at them, as though they were seeing the Vice Minister, not the winged instruments of death above them. Surrounding them was a circle of Chinese soldiers, rifles at the ready, to prevent any escape.

Hu smiled, then crinkled his eyes in surprise, and began shouting, "No! No!" when he saw one of the Chinese soldiers flop to the ground. Then another. And another, their rifles flipping through the air like batons at a halftime show. Some of the soldiers broke rank and ran from their comrades, trying to get away. The drones hunted them down like dogs rounding on a trapped fox, cutting them down with passionless precision.

The visitors were jumping up from their seats, shouting, looking at Hu for an explanation. The Vice Minister was frozen as if his haunches had been sealed in ice. He kept pressing the red button as if he could undo all this.

Hui remained in his chair, watching impassively. Ma-lin stole a half second glance at him, then turned away from the scene of the massacre. The Party enforcer strode across the laboratory, extending a claw-like hand wrapped in a PLA sleeve. "This is your fault," she shouted. "The Party will punish whoever ordered this."

Hui never displayed his near-perfect English in front of other high-ranking officers. This time, he allowed himself to shake his head, lift his hands in the air, palms up, as though without explanation.

"Who the fuck ordered this?" he said. But it was not a question.

Chapter 22
The Honest, Bloody Truth

It took Rose some time to mount the strength to bend her knees, swing her legs over the side of the bed, and sit up. She winced but to her credit did not cry out. Henry watched her coldly. He had retrieved the cane but knew that if she had a gun in her bedside table, he would be – after exerting such vicious power — powerless.

"Help me to the shower," she said.

Small pools of blood marked each step that she took. Once she was inside the shower, she said without emotion, "Now get out and wait for me."

Henry closed the door behind him, heard the lock catch, heard water gush, heard Rose moan.

He went to the living room and picked up the souvenir of the Yellow Crane Tower. The Chinese characters around its base transported him back to his time in Wuhan. To Hui. To Rav. Had he been happier there? He wasn't sure. Safer? Certainly not. Or maybe, yes. His citizenship without a passport did nothing to protect him from the dangers of Washington, D.C. His boring suburban life – Rose excepted – his hollow wanderings, his hours of coding he knew not what or why, all these put him in danger. He just couldn't fathom it yet. And in Wuhan, he had been exceptional. Hui's little pet *gweilo*. Rav's weekly (sometimes more frequent) stress reduction assignment. And a corporal for Christ's sake, in the People's Liberation Army.

Henry felt here, but not. American, but not. Acknowledged for his talent but distrusted for his foreignness. Aside from increasingly rare conversations with his parents, he knew no one well enough to confide in. Rose had been a grand intake of breath. She didn't want anything more than she herself was willing to give.

And now, what?

He heard the shower stop, some bumping noises from the bathroom. He replaced the Crane Tower, taking care not to smudge it with the drops of Rose's blood that had splattered him. The bathroom door opened, and she said, "Would you come in and help me please?" She was still in the shower, still naked, though toweling herself off. The towel had absorbed a lot of blood, and Henry wondered inconsequentially how she would get the stains out.

She pointed. "In the cabinet. A green bottle, please." He opened the glass door and found the bottle covered with writing in a language he did not know.

"Aloe vera," she said behind him. She was smiling limply, as though she had just told a joke he had already heard many times. "It comes from Kazakhstan if you're wondering. They mix the leaves with opium paste. Works much better than anything on the market here. Help me out, please."

He took her hand and helped her step out of the shower stall. There was an intimacy to it, misplaced, but somehow comforting. It was, he thought, as if he had done nothing more in her bedroom than squeeze her too tight.

"Bring a new towel to put on the bed," Rose said. "I'll have to destroy the sheets." And Henry, who had just savagely whipped this woman, did as she bade him. Master of none, once again, he thought. And Master of nothing but a batch of coded lines of AI.

He spread the towel over the bloodied sheets, laid a smaller hand towel of the same color over the pillowcase where her mouth and eye wounds had seeped through. She winced as she tried to lie down on her own, allowed him to hold her under her armpits and lower her, like a fire burn victim being hefted gently onto a gurney.

Prone, she looked at him heavy-lidded. "Put the ointment on me, please. Spread it everywhere."

An hour ago, Henry thought, he had been anticipating some slightly unorthodox and mildly perverted sex with this startling woman. What had turned him into the monster who beat her so viciously? He had had a premonition when he first saw the Crane Tower likeness.

And his gut had always told him something was not right. A woman like Rose would never be attracted to him, unless there was a hidden motive.

And so, he allowed himself to be brutal, to be a torturer, and received the information that he had dreaded. She was a fake, a phony, there was nothing real between them. Their intimacy, he now conceded, was ... artificial.

The lubrication he gingerly undertook was the least stimulating contact anyone could imagine. Rose kept her eyes shut, her lips set, as he gently, gently tried to repair the damage he had done to her. The ointment had a strange soupy consistency, and he smelled what he assumed was the opium paste, sickly sweet but, as with the addiction opium causes, invisible.

Back, arms, neck, legs. He saved her buttocks for last. Why? Modesty? Shame? Her haunches were suppurating, the body's way of protecting open wounds from the outside by creating something disgusting from inside.

"Go ahead," she murmured. "I can take it." And so he ever-so-gently massaged ointment in and was pleased to see the discharge stopped almost immediately.

"It's the opium," she said softly. "It can be a blessing as well as a curse. And it deadens the pain."

Deadened feelings, Henry thought. Yes, I know about that.

He finished the treatment; she released the breath she had been holding in. "Thank you. Make us a drink, would you? Then we'll talk."

He knew much more about her apartment than he did about her. That included the location of the wine cooler between the kitchen and the living room. She liked white wine usually. Otherwise, ice-cold vodka. Probably wine wouldn't get the job done now. He chose Grey Goose, poured it icy into a tumbler, poured another, unusually, for himself. Drinking vodka in the late afternoon. You've come a long way, baby, Wuhan-Henry told Arlington-Henry in mild disapproval.

Get it out of her right away, he told himself. Don't let her meander as she likes to do, or you'll end up in bed with her. He stopped, picked up the cane, held both drinks in one hand, and walked into the bedroom.

"All right, Rose. Your choice." He raised the glasses, "Pain slaker," lowered them, raised the cane, "or pain maker?"

Rose gave a sad little shake of her head, the left side of her face still against the towel covering her bed. "Whatever happened to that nice boy who managed to unlock my bike and make me smile?"

"He got tired of being lied to."

"Ah, lies," she said. "Yes, being lied to is very disagreeable. Some people probably think liars should be beaten with a stick." She lifted her head, nodded toward the cane, stuck out her hand for the vodka. She dropped it down her throat in a single gulp. "Nazdrovia."

"You turning Russian on me?" Henry downed his vodka too. "Another?"

"Please." She squeezed her eyes shut. "That's better."

He went out to the cooler, came back with the bottle. "Let's settle in."

"Good idea. No, I'm not turning Russian on you. I just like that toast better than any other."

"Khorosho."

Her eyes narrowed at once. "You speak Russian?"

"No. Just a word I picked up. It means 'okay.'"

"I see. What do you want to talk about, Henry? And, by the way, give me another drink."

He filled her glass almost to the top. Too much, he knew. Perhaps it will help.

"You were planted. The bicycle lock foolishness was to draw me in, right?"

"When you put it that way, it sounds creepy," Rose said. The vodka was taking effect. She was regaining color in her face, the blood now staying underneath her skin, where it belonged. "It seemed likely that you would try to help a damsel in distress. It worked."

"Who put you up to it?"

"You can beat me some more if you want, but could we please avoid the name-rank-serial number stuff? I've already told you; I work for the same people you do. Their names are a lot less important than what they do."

"All right. So what were you supposed to do?"

"Exactly what I did. Get into your life."

"You're there, Rose. How's it working so far?"

Another wan smile. "Until today, pretty damn well."

"Let's cut to the chase," Henry said. "But first, is this place bugged? Are we being seen, heard?"

"I'm pretty sure we're not. Of course, no one ever knows. I found that out at the company I was supposed to be working for."

"Okay," said Henry. "Tell me about that."

"What I said was true. It was a company that used AI to inform customers if someone was at their front door. The software detected movement on a path leading to the house, the video clicked on, and you could see someone walking toward your house before the human ear could hear them."

"Was the company successful?"

"Hell, yes. They sold millions of those things. And the information that went with them."

"What?"

She was gaining strength with each sentence and sip. "I told you, the device they make lets users sense someone approaching. They see you before they can feel you, thanks to AI. After two approaches by the same person, AI does a deep-dive on the person's face, the way he or she walks, and anything they may be carrying that helps identify them. Facial recognition is the main tool, but our AI also can tell what brand of coat or shoes they're wearing. Then it cross references the facial recognition with recent sales in the area of coats, or shoes or whatever. Then it has their name and the number of the credit card they used to buy it. All in a matter of hours. And it's getting faster."

Henry was not surprised. He knew what facial recognition could do. It was his job to make it even smarter.

"If the company was so successful, why did it get sold to China?"

"Because the company that bought it paid three times its estimated market value."

"In cash?"

"In stock."

"And Hui Jen-Sho was part of the negotiation?"

"He led the Chinese delegation actually."

Henry nodded. Of course. The circles of life converging, overlapping again.

"What stock did you get in return?"

"Some gigantic real estate company. Biggest in China."

He smiled, sipped his vodka. "You got taken."

"I know." She finished her glass. Held it out for more.

"Your real bosses wanted that to happen?"

"As a warning to other American companies not to sell technology to China."

"Tough love."

"We prefer the term patriotism."

"Very convenient term. Covers all manner of crimes." Henry noticed her eyes were slipping shut more now. The vodka, probably. Time to pounce.

"All right, Rose, the verbal fucking is over. Why did you need to draw me in? Just following orders?"

For the first time, she managed to raise herself off the bed – onto one elbow anyway. "It started that way. The Company doesn't believe you're really on its side, Henry. We know about Wuhan. We know about Hui. We know about the woman you flew back here with, who ended up dead. There are too many open-ended questions for an organization like the one we work for."

"I went through all that when I got back."

"With the FBI, not with us. And we can't get access to what you told them."

"Why not just ask me?" said Henry, not so much angry as confused. One bunch of spies doesn't trust another to tell the truth. What a shocker.

"It doesn't work that way," said Rose, sinking back to her prone position. "They'd rather destroy each other than the real enemy."

"And what's that?" Henry asked.

"China, of course."

"Is that what you think?" he said, before he had considered the words.

"See! That's why they don't trust you. You say things like that and ..."

"Things that you will have to report, right, Rose?"

She didn't answer. Then, "Yes."

"And so, you were given the job of getting me into bed, sucking out all my secrets, among other things, and delivering them to those patriots?"

There was no resistance this time. "Yeah."

"Is there even a code-name for a whore in your language?"

"Henry, listen. I said it started that way. It's changed. I... I..."

"Aw, you love me," he said, now more angry than flattered. "Well, isn't that great. Remember when I told you I've learned not to trust anyone, Rose? You're the kind of person who taught me that lesson."

As well as Rav, he thought, but, even angry, decided not to say it.

Rose took a fortifying sip. "If we're not lying to each other anymore, it's personal for me now. I like you. I don't want to see you hurt."

"How sweet. So you put a statuette of the Crane's Tower in your living room to what? Taunt me? Make me feel at home? Show me you know more about me than I do about you? 'Hey, Henry, mine is bigger?' Is that what you're into?" He reached across the bed, put his hand over her mostly empty glass, grabbed her wrist, and yanked it toward him. The glass toppled, the remaining trickle of vodka joined the blood on the sheet.

"I didn't know if you'd notice the tower," Rose said. She was trying to turn over onto her back and was grimacing with the effort. "A lot of men wouldn't have looked twice at it."

"I'm not a lot of men, Rose," Henry said.

"No, you're not." She was supine now, though clearly uncomfortable. "Right now, though, you're the only man I want." And she in turn caught his wrist and pulled him onto her.

Chapter 23
Falling Upward

Hui survived. The review board concluded that the drone's AI programming had been coded to attack, but that proper checks and balances had not taken place to ensure that its targets were only Uyghurs. The report noted that there was email traffic between Hui and the Defense Ministry and that his caution about needing more time to perfect the devices had been ignored.

The Party hack who had attended the video screening of the slaughter was demoted to deputy hack. Vice Minister Hu's whereabouts were currently unknown, though it was rumored he had been stationed somewhere near the border with India, where Chinese troops were under almost constant attack in the Himalaya Mountains.

The Party review determined that the Party was blameless.

Ma-lin observed Hui at his desk with a mixture of admiration and skepticism. She could say nothing aloud. If Hui's office had not been bugged before, it certainly was now. And all the detection devices in the world could not stop the Party from snooping into your life if it chose to do so. The hologram of Xi Jinping, which Hui had restored soon after his return to the office and the power that accompanied it, had been turned off, Ma-lin noticed. Was that a result of grandiosity on Hui's part, or guilt?

Lieutenant Ma-lin Cho of the People's Liberation Army decided it was not for her to make such determinations. But she also knew that something important, gravitational even, had changed. She would have to make herself ready for its consequences.

"Will you attend the memorial service for our comrades who perished?" she asked in a neutral voice.

"Will Vice Minister Hu be attending?" Hui asked back, equally neutral.

"You know that he will not," she said.

Hui looked at her, raised his eyebrows as if to say, "So, then..." and returned to the papers on his desk. The wizard of AI, Ma-lin thought, and he makes decisions and guides our futures on pieces of paper. Perfect.

She needed to ask him a question but had no means to do so. Not on paper, whose secrets were easily recovered. Not on a tablet or screen, since who knew who had access to its contents, even unsaved. Certainly not verbally, with digital ears hanging or implanted everywhere. How fitting, she thought. In the age of instant and global communication, it is now impossible to ask a simple question in safety.

Ma-lin Cho had not forgotten who was a Colonel and who was a Lieutenant. She could read stripes on a uniform. Nor had she forgotten that she, too, had played a key role in the drone massacre. She had followed Hui's instruction to put the remote device in Hu's hand, and encouraged him, with a slightly sexual smile, to push the button himself. The review board had made much of the fact that it was Hu's thumbprint found on the murder weapon.

She inclined her beautiful head toward the door of the office, lifted her reflecting-pool eyes, and let her forever lips form a question. Hui understood, nodded, once (much as Ma-lin had learned to do) and followed her outside. They walked together, openly, through the corridors, down the staircase and out the front door of the Institute, making no effort to disguise the fact that they were going outside together. There was still no law against talking on the street. Talking anywhere about certain taboo topics was another matter.

Socialism with Chinese characteristics.

"Colonel," said Ma-lin, when they were beyond what both imagined was the range of the Institute's listening devices, "may I speak freely?"

Hui did not look directly at her but spoke with eyes forward. "Lieutenant, it is probably I who should be establishing the rules for our conversation, given what we all know about your special access to the General Secretary."

Ma-lin was prepared for this. "There are times, Colonel, when that is more a curse than a blessing."

"So then, define 'speaking freely.'"

"What we say goes nowhere beyond this street, this conversation."

"Agreed."

Ma-lin decided to take the risk. "Colonel, you and I know that we colluded to..." she paused, "...discredit the Vice Minister."

Hui stopped in his tracks. Looked at his conversation partner. And, careful to make no noise, nodded his head, once. Resumed walking.

"I am glad we did," said Ma-lin.

"And?"

"And I would like to know what the next step will be." Now she stopped walking. Hui faced her. And, still standing still, took the irreversible step. "We have both seen a side of our beloved country that we do not like. You more than me. In Lop. And I believe similar things go on elsewhere."

"And if they do?" said Hui, gesturing for her to continue their perambulation.

"Colonel, with due respect, I believe you are having doubts similar to those that I am experiencing."

This time, Hui kept moving. "Lieutenant, you know that what you are saying is very serious, very dangerous."

"Yes, Colonel," said Ma-lin. "I do. Which is why I am saying it only to you, in the street, outside, and in the hope that you will not report this conversation to the Party."

Hui nodded as he walked. His face showed no emotion, but Ma-lin could see that he was thinking before responding. As always, one step ahead of everyone else.

"Report it to the Party? Lieutenant, it is I who should be afraid that you might tell ..." He looked at her and smiled "... whoever it is you tell things to ... that the drone presentation would not end as planned. You didn't. And now you are telling me something that could have grave consequences. So let me make this promise to you,

Lieutenant. No one – no one – will hear about this conversation from me. Nor will I ever tell anyone – anyone – about the doubts you have shared with me. About our Party. About our country."

"Thank you," Ma-lin said simply.

Hui nodded, once. "I believe that what I saw going on in Lop is wrong. I was mortified, in fact. China is too ancient, too civilized to be employing such horrors. Even against terrorists like the Uyghurs. This is not *Zhongguo tese shehui zhuyi* – Socialism with Chinese characteristics. No, this is Socialism with Chinese Communist Party characteristics. The two are not the same."

"I never thought I would agree with that," said Ma-lin, "but I do."

Hui made a coughing noise and said, "I have devoted my life to Artificial Intelligence. I suppose I believe AI is the answer to every problem. Maybe I am wrong. But maybe, just maybe, it can be put to a good and useful purpose."

"If anyone can do that, it is you, Colonel," she said, giving him the gift of her eyes, her skin, her hair, and her mouth as she said the words.

Hui nodded. "But Ma-lin ..." he had never used her name before, only her rank, "I cannot do it alone."

It was her turn to nod, once. "Here is good news at last, Hui Jen-Sho. You won't have to."

Chapter 24
Not Valid

The complaints started rolling in two weeks after the sale to the Chinese went through. First, the company's bean-counters complained that the first installment of the payment was late. Not just late, non-existent. When they sent polite emails to their counterparts in Wuhan, then followed up with slightly tarter emails, they received a response in barely intelligible English saying their request was not valid.

"What the fuck does 'not valid' mean?" screeched Alan Jussoff, the soon-to-be-ex-CEO, who had given assurances this deal was sweet. He had expected to retire on his share of the profit. Now he was going to *be* retired. International business lawyers were called in to give assurances that the company had done nothing wrong and that payment in full was most certainly due.

The American news media had not yet learned the terms of the deal that transferred the company – and the reams of data about its customers – to China. Nor had it learned that the company had accepted stock as payment for the sale. The debate within the company was whether to alert a friendly news organization or keep the fiasco deeply buried in secrecy.

Rose, who had been part of the planning and execution of the sale, now kept her distance, citing concern about the recent spike in Wuhan pandemic infections. She took meetings on Zoom because she did not want to appear in the office in her current state. The souvenirs of the beating Henry had given her were fading, but she still walked with a pronounced limp. The back of her right leg, where the cane had come into the most contact, was still the color of an eggplant.

Even more damaging, her routinely confident exterior had been shattered.

She had been beaten before. One former lover actually used a bullwhip. But she had looked him in the eye throughout, and never uttered a sound, spoiling his satisfaction. This caning was different. Henry's fury was born not of sexual desire, but bafflement at her deception. And that sentiment reached her and robbed her of her indifference to the pain.

She thought of Henry now, in the middle of a Zoom conference. She could keep laser-like focus during in-person meetings, but the small laptop screen that held matchbook size views of her so-called colleagues was no replacement for close contact with sweaty-smelling or over-perfumed bodies that included emotional giveaways like eye squints, sharp breathing, drumming of fingertips on tabletops. Zoom was a joke, she decided, like most of the rest of life, since China had set loose on the world its dehumanizing, demonic virus.

"Rose, what's your view?" said one of the other participants. "Bring the press in?"

Knowing what her real employer would want her to say, Rose replied, "It can't hurt." She knew that those words carried with them the literal truth.

Next came customer complaints. Dozens said that they were being harassed online by someone or something that knew way too much about them. Their names, their addresses, what products they purchased and from whom, and most worryingly, who had visited them and at what times. The latter had already put a fatal strain on one marriage, since the visitor was young, attractive, and unknown to one of the spouses, who could tell from the time code that she had not been at home when the visit occurred.

The Chinese buyer of the company and the company's user list and other video recorded information refused to discuss what they did with the data they had purchased. "That is a private matter and none of your concern," they told the company that had collected the information. Rose, who had never subscribed to the service of the company she seemed to work for, thought, "What did you expect?"

When Jussoff, the company's soon-to-be-ex-CEO decided to "put an end to this horseshit" and fired off an angry email to Hui, he received in return a series of videos showing him– while he was inside his own home – in various compromising positions with an assortment of men and women, none of whom was his spouse. He made an executive decision to let the matter drop.

None of the news organizations that the company approached about doing a story on how it had been swindled by the Chinese thought it worth investigating. One editor of a New York newspaper privately explained, "I have family still living in China. I'm not going to get them thrown in a camp like the Uyghurs."

A token payment of $10,000 reached the former owners' bank account. This represented less than one half of one percent of what was owed. When the company protested at the meager transfer of funds, the new Chinese owner obtained a court judgment – in a Chinese court, naturally – barring the sellers from making any more financial demands. Failure to comply with the injunction, the court said, would release the Chinese from any promises that had been made regarding confidentiality of the data they had purchased. The English translation of the court's ruling was stilted. But the message was clear.

Don't fuck with China.

Chapter 25
Nur-vana

If a star is kept completely shrouded by darkness, does it shine? Can it? Is it a star at all? And if so, who will see it?

Nur kept such a low profile that not even Hui knew where to find him sometimes.

"He's working," Ma-lin told him, but in that tone of disapproval Hui had actually come to recognize and fear.

"Find him, Lieutenant, wherever he is!" Hui said, himself employing a tone meant to reestablish the gap between their ranks. Their stroll on the street had changed the way they saw each other, largely to Ma-lin's liking; not so much Hui's. He now had an accomplice in a perilously dangerous gambit. But sharing was not one of Hui's virtues, and he did it badly.

Nur's progress on the drone project was beyond anyone's expectations. Only Hui and Ma-lin knew just how far along the boy had come, and decided to keep that information to themselves. Hui knew he had to talk with Nur about it, and about other things as well.

Nur had asked permission to return for a day to Lop, to comfort the relatives of an inmate who had died. The cause of death was not known, but Nur suspected she had died because she no longer had a heart or a liver. She had been a healthy specimen, ripe for organ harvesting. Hui granted the request, but insisted that Nur be driven to Lop in an official car. It would have been too risky to allow a Uyghur to fly on the commercial airline. He would have been subject to abuse at best, assault more likely. He had not seen Nur since his return, nor asked Ma-lin to find out how the visit had gone. After all, he was Hui. A Uyghur's affairs did not concern him.

And so, he surprised himself by his determination in wanting to see Nur, see how he was, see what he had learned at the School of Re-education Horrors. It was not that he – Hui – missed Lop. That place had in fact been a re-education for him, about the country and the Party he had sworn to defend. He had seen those two things – country and Party – through Uyghur eyes, and they had changed him. He knew this, but would never admit it to anyone.

Ma-lin knocked on the office door and ushered Nur in with no expression on her lovely face. Her antipathy toward the boy troubled Hui, but again, he could not give voice to his feeling.

"Good day, Colonel," said Nur formally, while Ma-lin stood in the doorway. Nur was standing not quite at attention, but neither was he slouching or moving casually. Ma-lin nodded and closed the door.

"How was your trip?" Hui asked, not bothering to have Nur sit.

"Informative, Colonel," said Nur. "And thank you for allowing me to be driven there and back."

"I didn't want to risk any more damage to your hands," said Hui, trying and failing to make his words sound like a joke. "Your latest coding shows immense progress."

Nur grinned, an intimate gesture of trust between them. "Yes, the errors I made in the initial coding have been fixed." They both knew his "initial coding" had brought the drones down on soldiers of the Chinese armed forces instead of the Uyghurs marked for execution. Hui's daring gesture of defiance had worked, and Nur was the reason it had. But the less said about that the better.

"What made the trip informative?"

"Some of the ... students ... at the facility have had their work assignments changed," Nur said, the pause in his sentence intended to denote significance of some kind.

"To what?"

"The production of pharmaceuticals," said Nur.

"What kind?"

"Fentanyl," said Nur, almost in a whisper.

Hui knew what Fentanyl was. An opioid created by condensing propionyl chloride with N-(4-piperidyl) aniline, then refining it with filters and dry ice. First created in 1960, Fentanyl proved to be an extremely effective painkiller, 100 times stronger than morphine and twice as strong as pure heroin. It was, and is, the sedative for end-of-life patients, to smoothe their path from conscious pain to the blessed release of death. It is, for them, a kindness.

Naturally, its proven potency as a medical drug meant that it would find its way into the bodies of drug addicts. Fentanyl was so strong and addictive that doctors at first painted the drug onto patches that were attached to a patient outside the body. Fentanyl seeped through the skin and produced almost immediate relief from intense pain like that felt by cancer patients.

Fentanyl is the perfect drug for addicts. It is powerful, and it can be cut with baby powder to make it last longer or combined with heroin or cocaine to pack a greater wallop. It is relatively cheap to produce and can be shipped under the label of medical supplies, then sold on the street to strung-out junkies trying to walk the fine line between blissed out rapture and sudden, unforgiving thrombosis.

"Does this have anything to do with the inmate who died?" Hui asked.

Nur nodded. "She was just a girl, fourteen years old. She was put to work on the assembly line, and thought the powder looked like sugar. She put some in her mouth. They say she started shaking violently, fell down, and choked to death."

"From a fingertip's worth of Fentanyl?"

"It doesn't take much if it is ingested directly, Colonel."

"Was there a memorial service?"

"What was left of her was incinerated, Colonel. Several organs were harvested first."

A fourteen-year-old girl. Dead from tasting something she thought was sugar. "All right. Get back to the coding project. When will it be ready?"

Nur bobbed his head from shoulder to shoulder. "If no one interferes, a week or ten days."

"Make it a week from today," said Hui, putting his disgust at what had happened to the girl behind him, all command in his voice now.

"Yes, Colonel." Nur turned and started to leave.

"Wait."

"Yes, Colonel?"

"Who is directing the Fentanyl production project?"

"My people say it is soldiers. From the Ministry of Defense."

Of course, thought Hui. Making more poison to export to the world. Like the virus.

Socialism with Chinese characteristics.

Where will it end, Hui wondered. Who will win? And who will be the loser? Hu?

Chapter 26
By Any Other Name

Rose forgave him, or said she did, and they resumed what to Henry seemed like a semi-satisfactory calendar of assignation. Her welts and scars healed more quickly than the deeper, more shameful wounds that could not be treated with antibiotics or tender-heartedness. Henry apologized but did not mean it. Rose accepted the apology with matching insincerity.

Having revealed her real profession, Rose now refused to acknowledge it or talk about her current role for the Company. "It's off the table," was all she would say, and not pleasantly. For Henry the choice was simple: accept her terms and keep having sex or insist on full disclosure and lose the occasional release he had become used to, if not dependent on.

Love in the age of the pandemic.

His own job was improving slowly, and so too was his attitude about the Company, the country and life in general. If there is such a thing as Americanizing an American, it was happening to Henry. Routines became rules, choices turned out to be cathartic, ambition replaced ennui. He couldn't truthfully call himself patriotic, but he was no longer anti-capitalist.

He still had not been invited to Langley HQ, but the electronic communications he received from his handlers were for the most part positive, suggesting he had a future.

"Keep your nose clean," one handler had told him by email. This was the ultimate irony, coming from a representative of the nosiest and dirtiest organization in America.

Henry was sitting at a bar, nursing a thimble-sized glass of ice-cold vodka, and trying, for a change, not to code something, but to decode the meaning of life. What random sequence of events had taken him from suburban New Jersey to New York City to Wuhan back to New Jersey and now to Arlington? How had he allowed his emotions to be battered like a ping-pong ball from Khadija to Rav to Rose? Did all the spy craft among the so-called great powers – America, Russia, China – really amount to much more than grown-up boys playing with boned-up toys? Was he too old to be spending time on such cosmically inconsequential questions, like a high school kid with no prom date wondering how ugly a girl he would have to invite to have a dance partner?

Each tiny sip of vodka produced new topics of silent conversation, more unanswerable questions, less self-confidence, and darker images. He visualized old-man Henry stumbling along the streets of Arlington, propped up by a cane, *enroute* to a rendezvous with wizened, wrinkled Rose, where the only physical contact either of them could muster was a cheek kiss and a bottom-pat, and a conversation consisting of deep sighs and rhetorical what-ifs.

If Henry's half-hearted flirtation with treason in China seemed adventurous to some, he knew the translucent nature of his escapade was not something he had created. He had merely helped the Chinese understand America's vulnerabilities, which it had brought upon itself with its careless, gluttonous, reckless attitude toward the rest of the world and its baseless belief that "America First" was the only possible final standing in the eternal game of international one-upmanship.

If he had had a friend, he might be able to discuss these things; if his lover's heart would ever open to him, he might be able to unhinge his own tight emotional springs. He was a still-young man (boy no longer) who traveled the road of life alone, partly due to his past foolishness, equally due to his frozen soul.

The second vodka went down quicker. It was strong. It was pure. What or who else could that be said of?

He went home. Where else? And considered with self-pity that he called this home, instead of the place where I sleep at night and wash up in the morning. It was more of a cell than the room he had occupied at the AI Institute in Wuhan. At least there ... better not to think of that now. Drain your bladder, then your mind.

The sound of the intercom buzzer muddled him for a minute. He had never heard it before, since he had had no visitors. Nor had he been solicited for donations from the local Hare Krishna chapter, Federation for the Blind, or Jehovah's Witnesses. There was no mail delivery. Who still got mail in a box? And Amazon was unaware of his existence since he had moved here.

He approached the intercom with something between excitement and annoyance.

"Yes?"

"Special delivery," the voice said, made almost unintelligible by the roaring static on the line. He could have improved the sound quality with two hours of coding and AI, but this was not his battle.

"Leave it there. I'll come down."

"Shanantu nilld." It took Henry a moment to realize the voice had said, "Signature needed." Was the sound system built with rubber bands and tin cans?

"Come on up." And stood there, still, genuinely flummoxed. His parents would have told him if they were sending something. The Company, of course, did not make use of carriers as suspect as the U.S. Postal Service.

On the off chance that this was company foul play afoot, Henry went to the kitchen drawer and pulled out a five-inch single-bladed knife. It was the most sophisticated weapon that he, technically an asset of a spy company, possessed.

The doorbell buzzed.

He opened the door.

Ma-lin Cho stood there in what seemed to be the only civilian clothes she owned: black skirt, black heels, white blouse, lustrous dark hair long and loose, eyes lowered.

"I am the delivery," she said, her ever-so-slight British accent coming through on the final word, using only three syllables.

What to say? Come in was too common, welcome would be gratuitous, where the fuck have you been perhaps uninviting, I love you was wildly presumptuous, get out of here downright false. He put the knife down. This was the second time she had appeared unexpected at his door. The first time was at his parents' house, after he had fled Hui and the Institute.

"I think about you all the time," he said, honesty being the best policy etc. etc.

"Yes, I felt it, even from far away." The easy manner in which she claimed paranormal powers exploded like a kaleidoscope behind his eyes. This was Rav, truly; she of the casually extraordinary, the effortlessly beautiful, the calmly brilliant.

And an officer in the People's Liberation Army.

"I would like to talk with you, please," she said.

Henry stood to the side, and she entered. He closed the door. Here she was, the real Rav, not the ghost of his longing and imagination. He started to say please sit down, but she was on the move, walking and beginning to talk at the same time.

"Before anything else," Rav said, "I want you to know and to believe that you were very important to me. There was something between us. Not politics. Not language translation. Something real that I felt. And still feel."

He had no answer. He did what he had done so many times in Wuhan; he simply beheld her. Like every other human, she was made of dust, but it was dust dappled with gold, refracted through starlight, conceived in poetry. She could have been saying anything – that she detested him, that he was a fool, that he made her sick – and he would have remained the same silent obedient servant that he had been from the beginning, and was now.

"What began as a business transaction became more than that," Rav said, in a tone she might have used to rattle off the succession of Chinese emperors. "I thought I could maintain my position, and my loyalty to the Party, and to Colonel Hui, and still be with you. But my feelings overtook me. Do you understand?"

"Yes," said Henry, without considering the question or what she had just said. "Nothing is more important to me than you." And as he finished the sentence, he realized that what he said was simple. That he was a simpleton. Truly simple. Simple truth.

"Thank you," she said. "It is similar for me." Similar. Similar, he thought, is not the same as "the same."

"So, what do you feel?" he asked, fearing the answer, needing to hear it.

"I would like to try again," she said, and this time allowed herself to look deeply at him, eyes afire, and, he was almost certain, emitting a pheromone that rolled over him like a gentle wave on a friendly beach.

"Yes," he said again. "Again." A thought came to him. "How did you get here? Why are you here?"

"Those are two different questions with two different answers," Rav said, mildly chiding him as if he had just scooped all the peanuts out of a cocktail dish. "I was admitted to this country under a diplomatic passport."

"And the answer to my second question?"

Rav looked directly at him. "I am here to be married."

His heart stopped. His vision clouded. His hearing failed. His knees, as they had the last time he saw her, went rubbery. It took him a moment to make his lips move.

"To who?"

She gave him a sliver-smile. "I believe the correct English is 'to whom?'"

It worked. He smiled. In admiration. In adulation. "All right. To *whom*?"

"A first secretary at the Embassy here."

"Here? In Washington? How do you know him?"

"I don't. I have never met him." She said it with such a natural tone, as though commenting on the weather.

"But then, how...."

"It is an arranged marriage. Still quite common in China." Again, in that "it's cloudy outside" neutral tone.

"Arranged by ... your family?"

"No. By my Party."

"Your Party," said Henry, truly not following and wanting, dreading, to understand what that meant.

"The Chinese Communist Party," said Rav, moving her mouth into a small moue. "You have heard of it?"

"Ra..." he stammered. "Ma-lin, you can't be serious. Not in this day and age. Even the Party can't make you marry someone you don't know."

"It can. It does. And it will." There was firmness in these three declarations, plunging him into another brand of grief. *It will.*

126

"And so, because the Party tells you to, you are going to marry a stranger?"

"I didn't say that," said Ma-lin, as though enjoying a joke only she understood. "I said the reason I am here, with a diplomatic passport, is to be married."

"And you want to do this?"

"I didn't say that either," she said, like a teacher correcting an especially slow student.

"Rav," he said helplessly, not caring about her real name. "Please. I don't understand."

She came forward, took his left hand, where he had been carrying the knife, in her right. "I liked knowing that deep inside, in your soul, you called me Rav. That when we were together, you thought of me as Rav. And after you left, I imagined you imagining me, as Rav. It helped me through some difficult times."

"And now, now that those difficult times are behind you, you've come to see me to tell me that you're going to marry someone else? Not me?"

Another sliver smile. "You used to listen better, more attentively, when we were together in China. America seems to have dulled your brain. Or at least your ears." She released his hand, stroked his left ear with her right hand, a gesture he had loved and still remembered.

"All right, Ma-lin," he said, trying to find the words, afraid of them once he had found them, forcing himself to ask, "Why are you here then?"

Now she hesitated before speaking. "I am here to ask for your help," she said.

"All right, all right. Whatever you want. Whatever you need. What do you want me to do?"

"I want you to stand with me at the wedding ceremony. I want you to ... what is it in English? ... give me away. To be the person who transfers the bride to her new husband, yes."

"Oh, Rav," he said, "please don't make me do that. It's too cruel."

"It is not cruel," she said. "I want you to be an important part of my Chinese wedding. I want you to be *'Tou zou xinniang.'*"

He couldn't bear to look at her. "And what does that mean?"

This time he got the full Rav smile. "It means 'steal the bride.'"

Chapter 27
Not Too Damn Bad

Hui was pleased with himself. He had executed the sale of a worthless company and in return had millions of people's personal information. He had determined that Hu, now busted to the rank of Director of the Defense Ministry, was behind the illicit production of Fentanyl. He would use that information soon.

The purchase of the facial ID company had been a success as well. One of the first coding projects that Nur helped with had tracked down at least ten thousand Chinese citizens living abroad, most all of whom had done very well financially in the United States, Canada, Australia, or the United Kingdom. The facial ID program identified their whereabouts, and, crucially, the phones they used to call relatives back in China. Those relatives had then been convinced, usually under duress, to write or call their turncoat sons, daughters, grandchildren, whatever, and beg them to return to the Motherland, less they be cast in prison or worse. Nearly all the targets had returned voluntarily, paid enormous financial penalties for earning money abroad without paying taxes on it to China, and been placed in positions where their skills could be utilized – by the Party. And the new AI coding project that only he and Nur knew about was coming along nicely. That would mesh with his final strike against Hu.

And there were other plans he had for using AI. They would come to fruition one by one, each in its right moment. He put his mind in order. He had been told to expect an encrypted phone call from Xi Jinping. He was waiting for it now.

"Not too damn bad," he told himself, realizing with a shock that he was thinking in English.

Corporal Ming entered with the red phone. Hui took it with a nod, indicated with his chin that she could leave.

"We hear that the Americans are fighting each other over whether to get vaccinated," said the beamed-off-Saturn voice. "You were useful ..." he hesitated, looking for the right phrase ... "in the past, in turning their crazy love of liberty against them."

"Thank you, Comrade General Secretary, for remembering," said Hui, like a well-schooled sixth grader. You son of a bitch, he thought. By "in the past," you mean before you yanked my career and my pride from beneath my feet and sent me to the shithole where I might have rotted if you hadn't needed me again. "I have heard similar stories about the situation in America. They seem not to trust their own government to tell them what is best. They are not sure they are being told the truth."

"Yet another weakness in their so-called 'democracy,'" Xi's voice said. "In our country, the Party *is* the truth."

"And we are grateful for your leadership of both our Party and our country." Hui recited the words as if they were a poem that he had learned at grammar school.

"Yes, well," said Xi-voice. "I presume since you know about the situation, you also have a plan to turn it to our advantage."

"I do, comrade. Thank you for having faith in me."

There was a long silence. "Chairman Mao once said to his friend and second-in command, Hua Guofeng, 'With you at the helm, I am at ease.' I won't go that far just yet. But, yes, I have faith in you." The line went dead.

Even for a seasoned veteran of Chinese power games, Hui was stunned. Had he just heard that? Had Xi Jinping just compared him, although in a slightly dismissive way, with Mao's second in command? Was there an implicit promise of elevation to greatness if he continued to fulfill Xi's wishes? Even of becoming Xi's number two? It did not bear thinking about, especially indoors where his facial expressions could be monitored. Of course, Hui knew that many of the top officers in the People's Liberation Army had already been injected with a tracking device that allowed their heartrate and breathing to be

129

clocked at any moment. The device was contained in the anti-virus vaccine that all Chinese military had been required – forced, really – to take. And Xi derided the Americans for not having faith in their government to do the right thing, and for doubting what exactly the anti-virus vaccine contained.

This is no time to wax philosophic, no time to nurse grudges, Hui lectured himself. You are on the cusp of history. Do not let the future pass you by while you seethe about the past.

And yet, he found he could not focus on what must be done. His thoughts, his mind, his interest kept returning to the same image: Lieutenant Cho, walking with him on the street, out of earshot, telling him that he was not alone.

Hui's personal life was largely imaginary. He was an only child, his parents were both dead, and he had never married. His adult life had been spent ascending in rank, outmaneuvering his comrades in uniform, and pursuing the infinite mysteries of Artificial Intelligence, which had fascinated him and dominated his thinking since before the term was invented.

His interactions with women, aside from issuing orders to those in the PLA, were usually either based on his superior rank or the exchange of goods for momentary pleasure. Never his good looks or charm. Now in his fifties and unencumbered by personal responsibilities, he wondered what he had missed, and if it was too late to retrace his steps to the fork in his life's road and take the other, untrodden path.

The path not taken. The life not lived.

He was vastly proud of Nur and his abilities, and because he cared for him, careful never to let those feelings be seen. Affection in the China of Xi Jinping was seen as a weakness. A husband could love his wife and vice versa, but such feelings should not be allowed to interfere with work, or devotion to the Party. Priorities mattered.

Socialism with Chinese characteristics.

He had not contacted the Uyghur youth for a week, content to let him work at his dizzying pace, confident that Nur would tell him what he had done, when he had done it. Promises were not part of his psychological makeup, Hui had concluded. There was no braggart in Nur, only quiet dedication. What he harbored inside, that place of thought and contemplation that even the Party – for the moment, anyway – could not reach, Hui did not know. He may secretly hate me and all I stand for. There is nothing I can do about that. Only hope it does not burst out of him before he is finished his work.

Because, Hui thought, here is the thing about AI: humans, all humans, sometimes doubt themselves and fear others may be right, while they are wrong. AI never does. Even a coder of Nur's caliber must pause and wonder if he has tapped the right key. We are told from our first years of schooling: Double-check your work. Don't leave anything unverified. Don't be ashamed if you've made a mistake. Just fix it and all will be well. Those precepts do not exist in the code powering AI. AI believes in itself, absolutely. It never errs.

It is the perfect partner for the Chinese Communist Party under Xi Jinping.

And Hui Jen-Sho would soon perform the marriage that binds them together forever.

Chapter 28
Blushing Bride

"Steal the bride? What the hell does that mean?" said Henry.

The three vodkas he had downed before coming home had made him careless, perhaps aggressive, but what the fuck were you supposed to be like when the woman you love tells you she's marrying someone else, and wants you to give her away.

Clearly, Rav had anticipated the question. "It is actually part of the classic Tao wedding ceremony."

"Tao? Like the banned Chinese religion?"

"It is not exactly banned," said Rav calmly. "But neither is it encouraged."

"And you, little Miss PLA lieutenant, are going to get married in a religious ceremony?"

"As I said, it is not forbidden."

"Rav," said Henry, his frustration boiling over, "why are you here to tell me this shit? Are you enjoying this? You know how I feel about you. You knew since the last time we saw each other."

"You told me, if I remember correctly, 'I'm the dumbest man on Earth. The only thing I know is that I love you.' 'You' being me." She gave him a medium smile. He knew that smile. It meant she was waiting to see how he would react.

"Yes, you remember correctly. As you always did, and I guess, still do. And yes, though it seems strange to be saying it at this moment, I still love you. You changed my life. Me. The way I think. The way I feel. Everything."

"I know," she said, her face calm, but there was something different in her eyes. Uncertainty. She had not, perhaps, planned for this forthrightness. "Something happened to me, too. I had never thought about this thing called love. I wanted only to advance, succeed. But ... being with you, day after day after day. And sometimes at night. Something happened to me. I couldn't stop it or control it. It was – and please don't tell anyone I've said this – more powerful even than the Party." In her eyes was a unique combination of mirth and fear. Don't tell on me for what I just said, it said, while confirming its honesty.

"Rav, Ma-lin, Lieutenant, Christ, I don't even know what to call you..."

"I like Rav," said Rav, smiling shyly. "I've liked it ever since I realized what it meant. Meant to you. Rav, please."

"Fine. Rav, I don't know what you want from me. You come here out of nowhere, and by the way, how did you know where to find me? You tell me you're getting married, and invite me to your wedding."

"You still ask many questions without waiting for answers," she said, back in control. "I liked that. I still like that. It was not difficult to find your address. By now, you know we can find anything we want to, about anyone. It is the world in which we live."

"I helped create it," Henry said, feeling worse for knowing it was true.

"And I have no family here to attend the ceremony. So I am asking you to be there, to represent my family, and to 'give me away,' as it is said in English, I think."

"But that's so cruel, Rav."

"Ah, you talk a lot but listen only a little." Did you not hear me say that I want you to be *Tou zou xinniang?*'

"Yes, you said something about steal the bride. What does that mean?"

"Those are three uncomplicated English words, I think." She was amusing herself and not apologizing for doing so. "I will explain. Tao is the ancient religion of China, or what was China more than two thousand years ago. It is a religion based on respect for all things, especially all things that are true. Tao despises lies, artifice, unkindness, damage to the world, damage to others, especially damage to others."

"But it is no longer practiced in China. You said yourself. The Party does not approve."

"You are correct," she said, looking up at his ceiling as though seeking inspiration. "The Party tolerates it in principle. But that does not mean it is not practiced. Not openly, of course. But quietly, humbly, in homes, among families, while out in nature. These are the things Tao loves and wants to help protect."

"But you are an officer in the PLA. Are you defying the Party?"

"Not at all," she said. "I am actually a highly decorated officer, though my rank is only Lieutenant. I think you did not know that when you were in Wuhan."

That among a million other things. "So how do you justify practicing this religion?"

"Tao is the part of me that the Party does not touch," she said softly. Then more softly, "As are you."

He started to move toward her; she held out a palm. "Please let me finish. Then you can decide whether to hug me or hit me."

He thought of Rose and the beating he had given her. And then the reconciliation. And realized, in a flash, that, as of five minutes ago, Rose meant nothing to him now.

"Tao is the basis for the Tao-i-ching, a book that was probably written by Lao Tzu two hundred years before your Jesus was born." Rav had never mentioned anything remotely religious to him before and the topic was startling now. "It explains the five principles of Tao. It also lays out the groundwork for the Witness Attestation at weddings, such as mine."

"Wedding" and "mine" in the same sentence was like a knife to the gut.

"Rav. Are you really going to marry someone you don't know?"

"That is up to you, Henry," she said, the impish smile back. "May I sit down?"

"Of course, I'm so sorry. Would you like some water, tea?"

"It smells as if you were drinking vodka at that bar. Do you have any here?"

He was becoming punch-drunk from her words. "How do you know where I was?"

"You have been vaccinated against Covid, right?"

"Yeah, so?"

"So, we know everywhere you have been since then."

"But those vaccines..."

"Are safe and effective. Your experts have said so, so it must be true. No? But did they also promise there wasn't anything else in the doses? No."

The weight of what she had just said fell on him like an avalanche. "There are tracers in the vaccines that we are getting?"

"I don't know the science," she said evenly. "I know that part of the original idea of all the vaccine makers – American, Russian, Chinese – was to be able to track the virus, not necessarily the people. Our researchers found that one led directly to the other. May I have my vodka now, please?"

He fetched her a Stoly and got one for himself too. *If ever I needed a drink*, he thought. Rav accepted the glass, held it in her lap demurely, not sipping until he had. *Because she thinks I'd poison her*, he wondered.

His Stoly went down quickly. "Tell me about this wedding I'm supposed to take part in."

"I was speaking of the Wedding Attestation," she said, seemingly unaffected by 70-proof liquor. "At a certain point, the two people being married witness each other. That means they take obligations of faithfulness and honesty, and promise to live a pure life together. That is the first attestation."

"Sounds wonderful."

"The third attestation is a blessing from the Eight Immortals. These are the beings who abide in heaven. They eat only air, drink only nectar, and are immune from temptation, impurity and sin."

"You said that's the third. What's the second?"

"Ah," she said. "That's where you come in. Because I have no family here, I need someone to give me away. That will be you, if you accept. Your role will be to offer me to the groom, wish me good karma, and stand back while I take my betrothed's hand."

"Why do I not like the sound of that?" Henry said in a low voice.

"I think you will. Sometimes, not often, but occasionally, the person performing your role may shout, *'Tou zou xinniang!'* That means, as I told you, 'Steal the bride.' And that is exactly what the witness does. He takes the bride for himself."

"I can't help thinking that the groom might object," said Henry.

"He might, if he could. But when a witness claims a bride, it is because he thinks she is making a mistake and wants to prevent it by offering himself as an alternative. Then it is up to the bride to decide. And she almost always accepts the offer of the witness."

"Why?"

"Because she usually agrees that she is making a mistake marrying the groom and is waiting for someone to rescue her."

"And that would be me?"

She finished her drink and looked directly at him. "That would be you. May I have another?"

"Another drink or another groom?"

"Both."

Chapter 29
Hui, Me And The Metaverse

There was no reason to delay it. He and Nur had gone through the coding three separate times over the past week. It was flawless. At least on the computer screen. Could it work in the real world, or rather the metaverse? That was the test that would determine the rest of their lives.

The stakes were enormous. Hui was planning a wide-reaching offensive that would eliminate any challenges to his position as architect of the digital universe. Not just in China, but the world. If it worked, even Xi Jinping would think twice about doing anything to displease him – Hui.

This was Chinese ingenuity at its best, Hui thought. Or its worst, perhaps. And the ultimate irony is that its success, or failure, rested in the uniquely wired brain of a youth that the Chinese Communist Party had labeled a mongrel, an enemy of the state, a terrorist. Perhaps Nur was a terrorist, Hui mused. But a terrorist with a different caliber of mind and with tens of millions of victims, unaware of what awaited them, spread around the world.

Nur had showed him – Hui – several lines of code unlike any ever developed before. Hui recognized its potential but had initial doubts about its applicability. "This is very specific," he told the youth. "Can it be massed out?" "Massed" was a word he had learned only recently. It meant, can the directions contained in the code be superimposed over other codes, to take over their function structure, and place them under the control of the specifier?

Nur stroked his chin with his mangled but much improved thumb. "Colonel, if I told you yes, I would be lying. Or at best, guessing. Without some trial runs, I simply cannot predict its power. I am sorry. You will have to trust me."

To his surprise and chagrin, even now, Hui found that he did. Trust. A terrorist. His highly calibrated mind flashed back to the last time he trusted a non-Han. He forced the memory away to somewhere dark and hidden.

This youth, imprisoned and tortured by Hui's countrymen, was offering Hui the key to a device more powerful than anything ever developed by man: control of the human mind. All minds. Always.

It was time to play a game. It was time to enter the metaverse.

In its essence, the metaverse is an alternate universe, where real people can escape from the real world and all its problems. It is not a joke, and it is not a game. It may have started out that way. But the metaverse is the other side of the mirror of our lives, where things work out. Where there is no poverty, no war, no pollution, no racial bias. Indeed, there is nothing wrong at all in the metaverse.

Unless we wish there to be.

Being perfect, the metaverse is not, of course, free. Real residents of the metaverse spend real money on their real Amex and Visa cards to live there, play there, work there, fight there (if that is their wish). But in the metaverse, you always win. The alternate world that you enter, via a headset, a dynamic 3-D screen or contact lens, or, increasingly, a chip planted behind the cornea, transports you to whatever environment you choose. When you arrive, you may choose the avatar –a character either of your choice or your own design – who will represent you, but also actually *be* you while you are there.

When Second Life was introduced in 2003 as the first "alternate universe," it could only offer still-life, though wildly attractive avatars to users. Being represented by a sports hero or a movie star is ego-enhancing. But when they could not move the way you wanted them to, and when their voices were computer-generated and sounded like the conductor on the A train, the experience dissipated.

No longer. Today's avatars bear little resemblance to the cardboard cutouts of the 20th century. In fact, even the name avatar is now considered out of date. Young people referred to their "quins," a contraction of quintessence, to describe their perfected online selves. "My quin just got a new job and is going to be a millionaire," for example. Seldom did one hear bad news in the same sentence as quin. Because, after all, why should bad things happen in the perfect world of the metaverse?

Nur had reported this kind of psychobabble to Hui after combing through hundreds of chatrooms and other sites devoted (in all senses of the word) to the metaverse. This, of course, was done with Hui's permission and marked yet another distinction granted to this youthful enemy of the Party and the people.

"Some of these kids act like they're on drugs," Nur said. "They say stuff and have their quins do stuff that would be completely crazy to do in the freezer." "Freezer" was how metaverse users referred to the real world from which they were escaping. The sarcasm was intentional.

"Drugs," thought Hui.

"I just tracked a dude who bought one hundred thousand hectares of land in Oklahoma with NFTs," Nur said, switching back and forth from Mandarin to English because some of the terms had not yet entered the Chinese language. "When I did a deep-dive to see who he was, it turns out he's 16 years old and was using his parents' credit card to back up the NFT and buy new UIs."

Hui saw where this was going. "Nur, I am an old man. You will have to explain the terms you are using, and then we can continue this conversation."

It was an indication of his confidence that Nur laughed in response. "Yes, Colonel. I can translate for you. NFTs are 'non fungible tokens.' They can be anything that you own that someone else might want. You can sell an NFT – like a Ming vase that you own – but still keep it in your home because you're only selling the digital ownership of it. So, the buyer owns the vase but is storing it at your place. Just like keeping your money in a safe."

Hui pinched the bridge of his nose with his thumb and middle finger. "And this has what to do with the metaverse, Nur?"

"Nothing and everything, Colonel. May I ask a respectful question that will be part of the answer to your question?"

"Go ahead." They had developed enough mutual trust to speak to each other this way. It was an extraordinary development that Hui could never have foreseen.

"Why do we explore space?"

Hui considered for a moment before answering. "To see what is there."

"We can see some things that are there with telescopes and with spacecraft that orbit the moon, Mars, Venus. What do we want to do when we find out what's there?"

"I suppose," said Hui, "that we want to see if there are minerals or other materials that could be exploited."

"And beyond that?"

"Ultimately, I think China wants to establish colonies in space. On the moon certainly. This has been announced by the Party and so that goal will be met."

"Thank you, Colonel," said Nur, nodding. "It's the same with the metaverse. We knew nothing about it twenty years ago. Didn't even know it existed. Just like humans didn't know about the far-away planets – Saturn, Uranus, Pluto – until we developed instruments to help us see them. Next we sent spacecraft to orbit them and take pictures that were sent back. After that? Maybe we will want to colonize them.

"Well, the metaverse is like those once-unknown planets. We know it's there because we've read about it. But not many of us have gone there. The metaverse is where people will go to get away from this world and its troubles. It is a place where we can go and be who we want to be. It is what religious people might call heaven, or nirvana."

"Nur, I have told you: I am an old man. Why should I care about this?"

Nur fixed him with that bright-eyed look he had first employed in Lop, the look that caught Hui's attention and imagination. The look that rescued Nur from slavery and won Hui's trust and protection.

"I believe, Colonel, that with your permission and encouragement, you and I can employ Artificial Intelligence, about which you know more than anyone in the world, to enter the metaverse. And eventually control it."

Chapter 30
Probably Trump's Fault

Things seemed to be spinning out of control and the Leader of the Free World liked it not a bit. "This is not how we planned things," she said coldly to the Delegator of Intelligence, Calm and Karma. The title had been changed from Director of Operations because that sounded too militaristic. The new title was intended to allude to meditation before action, self-awareness, deep-breathing and respect for all life.

The DICK, who had once cohabited with the current Leader of the Free World, accepted the rebuke in silence. There was no point in argument. Argument rippled karma, unnerved selfness, and introduced disruption into following the higher being. It made running the world's second largest spy agency unmindful. Not to mention unpleasant.

"Tell me again what happened in the Himalayas?" said LOFW.

"There was a military incursion across the border into Indian-controlled territory," said DICK, trying to picture a lotus blossom floating on a still pond.

"Chinese?"

"We believe so, since China shares that mountainous border with India."

"I knew that," snarled LOFW, who immediately closed her eyes, crossed her hands across her chest, and exhaled, "Ommmmmmmmmmm....." until her chief of staff and spiritual interpreter worried about her oxygen level. Once the exhalation ended and the LOFW drew a breath, the COS decided to order a bowl of rose-hips matcha tea for her. That helped any problem.

"Casualties?"

"The Indian troops suffered more than two hundred dead."

"How about Chinese casualties?"

"None."

"None?"

"Correct. The Supreme Being spared all Chinese lives, so we can be grateful for that."

"No Chinese soldiers were killed? Were the Indian soldiers armed?"

"Oh, yes. Latest version Soviet weapons and shoulder-fired rockets," said DICK, somewhat disapprovingly.

"Soviet?" said LOFW. "The last Soviet weapons were made almost thirty years ago."

"That is correct," said DICK.

"Even if they were armed with thirty-year-old weapons, how could the Indians not have inflicted any casualties on the Chinese soldiers?"

"Because, according to our intelligence, there were no Chinese soldiers present."

"You are trying my patience," said LOFW. "Wait." She turned her back on the DICK, breathed slowly, deeply, said a short prayer in Swahili, and turned again. "I've re-established my center now," she said. "Explain."

"The Chinese attackers were not humans. As we understand it, they were programmed by Artificial Intelligence. It appears that they were making battlefield decisions on their own. The battle was over in twenty minutes."

"And these robots were armed? Armed with what?"

"High velocity machine guns, chemical explosives, and superheated lasers. They are not robots in the way we understand the word. They were not taking instructions from anyone. They were nonhumans acting on their own with Artificial Intelligence."

"Shit," said the LOFW, quickly asking forgiveness of the Supreme Being for the vulgarity. "What does your Indian counterpart say?"

"The Indian Intelligence Service is not speaking to us," said DICK.

"What?!? Why not?"

"They believe we are incompetent."

"Fucking cloth heads," said LOFW, this time begging Hindu forgiveness.

"How about the Chinese?"

"A young woman from the People's Liberation Army was assigned to speak with our liaison in Beijing."

"And?"

"Ummm, she told him, I believe the correct translation is, 'to fuck off.'"

"What? A girl said that to someone who was representing me? Does she not know I am the first woman to hold this job, the first woman who looks the way I do to hold this job, the first woman who is openly..." LOFW stopped in midsentence. It was probably not profitable to allow the lifestyle decisions that her karma had revealed to her to come into play. Leave it, for now.

"All right. Where are we on Taiwan?"

DICK was flustered. "The Chinese ambassador here gave an interview to an American news organization yesterday. The ambassador said in no uncertain terms that if the United States continued to support Taiwan's illegal pretension to be an independent country, there would be war between us."

"Are you sure he said that? Could there be a mistake in the translation?"

"The ambassador was speaking in English," said DICK.

"Is his English any good?" said LOFW.

"The ambassador was educated at Harvard."

"Shit." Forgive me, Confucius. "You tell that Ivy League ambassador that if China invades Taiwan, I will immediately cancel the joint yoga classes we have scheduled with them." Having asserted herself, she asked, "What are the vaccination numbers?"

"They have not changed since our last briefing," said DICK. "There remains solid opposition to vaccine mandates by the federal government."

"Why, for fuck's sake? (forgive me, Mighty One)," shouted LOFW. "We've told them they have to get vaccinated. Why aren't they listening to me?"

DICK's head was pointed straight down, in embarrassment.

143

John Moody

"The news media has found that fanning doubts about the vaccine gets a lot of attention. Ratings for television networks, hits for websites, and so on. And some right-wing pundits are reinforcing those doubts."

"It's all these men on TV," said LOFW.

"Actually, the leading voice about it is a woman."

"Another woman not showing respect for me? Where's the sisterhood?" said LOFW. "Why would she do that to me?"

"Because she doesn't like you."

"What? Well, just tell her to say that she was wrong about what she said."

"She will refuse on the grounds of freedom of the press."

"She can take her fucking freedom of the press and shove it down her throat," shouted/asked for forgiveness LOFW. "I'm in charge here. What's the second reason they're not getting vaccinated?"

"They don't believe the government should tell them what to put in their bodies."

"It's their bodies, my choice," said LOFW. "They can't refuse a direct order from me. Arrest them."

"The police in most cities not on the East and West Coasts have refused direct instructions to arrest the non-vaccinated."

"But that's crazy," said LOFW. "Who do they think they report to?"

"To their mayors, and to the governors of their states."

"Who gave them that crazy idea?"

"Actually," DICK replied stiffly, "the Constitution of the United States."

"That was written by white guys who are all dead!"

"True," said DICK, softening his tone. "But its message is still alive."

"Oh, my Buddha," said LOFW. "All right, what about Russia?"

"Russia refuses to turn on the flow of natural gas to western Europe until it receives a public apology from the United States."

"Apologize for what?"

"For the humiliation inflicted on the Russian Motherland in the period immediately after the dissolution of the Soviet Union."

"But we won the Cold War!"

144

"And for referring to ideological differences between us as the Cold War."

"What do they want to call it? It's cold in Russia."

"They wish us to rename it "the Period of American Hegemony," and remove all references to the Cold War from our history books, from libraries, from websites, movies, documentaries, old newscasts, and to create a mandatory course for second graders explaining the errors the United States made during that time."

The LOFW had been silently repeating her chakra stones and humming her personal mantra. "Um, ok. And then they'll turn the gas back on in Europe?"

"The Russian leader said he would 'consider' doing that once all the conditions were met."

"Okay, do it," said LOFW.

"Do what?" asked DICK.

"All of it! The Chancellor of Germany is coming next week for that ceremony where we apologize for how we treated them during World War II. I don't want her bitching to the media because her house is cold."

"And you are going to apologize for our defeat of the Nazis?"

"Nazis, schmatzis, that's ancient history to me. Our focus is to provide reparations for oppressed Americans of color, of sexual bias, of mismatched birth gender. Those are the important things. Not Nazi crap."

"Ok," said DICK.

"How about the inflation numbers?"

"We'll announce that it's seven percent in the past month."

"Why do we have to announce that? Just say we don't have the figures yet."

"We do have the figures, though," said DICK. "It's actually nine percent. We have to ease the population into accepting these things."

"You know whose fault all this shit is, right?" LOFW asked no one in particular.

DICK had heard it before. "Trump's."

"Damn right," said LOFW. "He should have taken care of all this stuff before he left office."

"Well," began DICK gently, "technically, Trump doesn't think he *should* have left office at all. He still thinks he won."

"Well, he didn't," said LOFW. "And thank Buddha for that. We had to come in and set everything right that he screwed up. Build America back Diverser."

"I think we're calling it 'better.'"

"Whatever."

"What do you want to do about the apology to Russia speech?"

"What," she said, stroking her chakra stone again. "Oh, let Gramps do it. It'll seem more official that way."

"You want the President of the United States to apologize to Russia?"

"What else has he got to do?" said LOFW. Her rosehips tea arrived, finally, and she sat down at her desk to sip it. "Holy Allah," said sighed. "There's so many things I have to fix. This tea is too strong."

DICK's head bobbed up and down.

Chapter 31
There Goes The Bride

Rav and Henry didn't say good-bye because she didn't leave.

"The Embassy here reserved me a hotel room, but it is ... not pleasant," she said from her side of the bed.

"This isn't exactly five-star accommodation," Henry replied, stroking her un-ringed left hand.

"There are many things I want to tell you and want to hear from you," she said. "The months without you were challenging for everyone."

"You mean Hui?"

She stiffened. "The Colonel was in a dangerous position. He managed to ... is the correct word 'extricate?' himself."

"And he's running the Institute again?"

"It was being mismanaged. He has corrected course."

"Mismanaged by General Deng-tal? The one I called Tanteeth?"

She smiled. "Until you ... left China ... I never told anyone that name. It makes me laugh to think of it now."

"I like making you laugh."

"Actually, you taught me how to." Her look was penetrating and, he believed just then, genuine.

"Will the Embassy know you're not in your hotel?"

"Probably."

"Will they know where you are?"

"Probably."

"Will they come looking for you?"

"Probably."

"Do you want to stay here?"

"Definitely."

Her wedding was scheduled for the next day. He had not yet committed to attend, but both knew he would. What choice, really? Take this enormous chance, or wonder for the rest of his life, what might have been. A near-year had done nothing to diminish her startling beauty. Her British-accented English was crisp as ever, although she thought otherwise and explained she had had little opportunity to use it of late.

"The Party now frowns on the English language," she said. "School children are encouraged to learn Spanish, or Russian, or one of the dialects of Arabic."

"By 'encouraged,' you mean..."

"Assigned. Choice is also frowned upon now."

"Why are you part of that whole apparatus?"

Her look hardened instantly. "Why are you part of the CIA?"

He had not told her. But since she knew where he lived, it was not difficult to figure that she knew what he did. And that meant the Party did. And that meant that Hui did. Not good.

Nor had they discussed what would happen once he shouted *Tou zou xinniang* – *steal the bride* – and she accepted, and the wedding came to a shattering, premature end. Henry didn't care about the groom. Why should he, since Rav obviously didn't either? She didn't even know the groom, she assured him. The incongruity of this accomplished, Western-educated woman submitting to millennia-old tradition was hard to accept. But unless he did, Rav would be out of his life for the second, and final, time.

Later, in the afternoon, she said, "I have to go now."

"Why?"

She hesitated. "To buy a wedding gown."

He said, "You're going to buy clothes for a wedding that you don't intend to see through? That will not be consummated?"

"If I appear in regular clothes, no one will believe that I had any intention of getting married. What is that famous Greek story? The Trojan Horse? My gown will be my horse."

"And what will I be?"

"You will be the soldier hiding inside the horse. Once your foe believes you are harmless, and lets you past the gates of his fortress – in this case the Embassy – you will emerge and destroy him."

That this woman knew Greek literature and history better than most Greeks continued to amaze him. What else did she know that she had not revealed?

"What should I wear?" he asked.

"Do you have a suit?"

It was not an idle question. Men of Henry's age – the Age of Pandemic – had by and large given up wearing anything more formal than clean jeans. That's who I am, he thought. Mr. Clean Jeans.

"Yes, I have a suit."

"That, then."

And ten minutes later, showered, redressed, and sad-eyed, she was gone.

What to do? It had been just twenty-four hours since she came back into his life. Already he was shaping the rest of it around her. Attend a Chinese wedding? In the Chinese Embassy? Madness. Then try to disrupt it by claiming the bride? This wasn't a Disney movie, it was his life. How many ways can you spell stupid? But this was Rav, and she had asked him to be there. So, really, how many ways can you spell coward? Or love?

He had purchased two suits since moving to Arlington. The ones he had left behind in his parents' house in New Jersey no longer fit him, he discovered to his chagrin. Neither of these was stylish, but the jacket and trousers matched, so he went with Navy blue and black leather shoes. The kind of dark red tie that he had seen Party officials wearing on televised events. He had no passport for identification – the Company still didn't trust him with one. And given his non-existent lifestyle, a driver's license seemed superfluous.

He didn't want to leave his apartment in case Rav came back to spend the night again. But he was getting claustrophobic being confined behind its walls. He tried reading, but neither the classics nor cheap thrillers held his interest. He toyed aimlessly on his laptop, even sinking to the level of online games that he despised. He had meant to check out a new site called Metamorph, which had been sent to him via FedEx by his bosses in Langley. They still didn't trust him to come into the office. A note in the package said simply, "Test and report." In addition to the thumb drive that contained the program software, there were two plastic squares with a clear bubble of liquid and something that looked like contact lenses floating inside.

He fit the lenses into his eyes, smarting at their scratchy feel. And instantly felt dizzy. He gripped the bathroom sink to remain upright. What the fuck? Slowly he regained balance. He duck-stepped his way to his laptop, sat down and installed the site. Almost the second he clicked on Begin, his head began to buzz as though he had been too near a gunshot or firecracker. The screen came to life in the shape of a beautiful blond woman.

"Hi, Henry," the shape said. "I'm Mora. What would you like to do?"

Henry remained mute. He knew about the metaverse but had never visited it. Now he wasn't sure he wanted to.

"Come on in," said Mora. "It's perfectly safe. You're in your own home in Arlington. And the door is locked. Nothing bad can happen."

How did she know his name and address? He hadn't given either when he purchased the equipment. Wait. His credit card. And Metamorph had tracked his name and address. What else did it know about him?"

"Let's have a vodka," said Mora. "That usually relaxes you, right?"

He'd paid for the drinks at the bar yesterday with his card.

"Skol," said Mora, with a smile. She sipped her vodka from a shot glass like the one Henry had used at the bar. And, he could have sworn, he tasted the same vodka he had ordered then slipping down his throat, warming him, loosening him, relaxing him, shedding his stupid defenses.

"How's your job going?" Mora asked in a gentle conversational tone. "I know you're doing important stuff."

Alarm bells. How could she know what he did? Of course, he used this laptop for his work. Had she scanned his drives already?

"Don't want to talk about work? I don't blame you," said Mora, taking another sip of her drink. Henry felt more liquid fire slide down his throat.

"No problem. How's Rose?"

Fuck. His phone was synched to his laptop. He lurched to his feet, tried to get to the bathroom to take out the lenses.

"Don't go, Henry," said Mora. "We're just getting to know one another. I'll be sad if you leave me all alone."

He'd had two virtual drinks and already felt six feet under. He pried at his right eye, couldn't find the lens, could hardly find his eye. The left one popped out easily for some reason. "Ohhhh," he heard Mora moan. With his left eye cleared, he found the lens in his right and lifted it out. The two clear circles of plastic lay on his sink, like scorpions waiting to strike.

Henry straggled to the living room, checked the laptop, which no longer contained Mora's face but only his normal wallpaper. What had just happened? Did this happen to everyone who used Metamorph? Did the company know?

He went to his bedroom, found his phone, saw he had just missed a text from Rose. What? He hadn't heard it beep. How long had he been in front of the laptop? He looked at the time on his phone. More than an hour! He'd been inside Metamorph for an hour and had no idea where the time had gone. Or rather he did. Mora had stolen an hour from his life. He looked at Rose's text. "Sheets chilly. Need attention."

Sensory overload. Rav, Mora, now Rose. From having no social life and certainly no real romance, Henry suddenly felt trapped inside a threesome. He ignored the text, though he knew that Rose could see when he had read her messages.

He went back to the laptop and disconnected from WiFi. Turned off the laptop. Unplugged it. Pulled out the battery. Was that enough, or was Mora laughing at his feeble attempt at privacy.

He needed sleep. He needed rest. He needed Rav.

Chapter 32
I Do?

He couldn't be sure if he had been sucked into the metaverse and was still there, or if he had dreamed it all. His sleep had been as heavy as if he'd been covered by rocks. It was six o'clock in the morning. Rav's wedding day. Time for the understudy to steal the show.

Putting on a suit was a strange experience, but after the past forty-eight hours, it was a cinch. He had not heard from Rav since she left. How would she contact him anyway? Did she know his cell number as well as his address? Probably. So her silence was intentional. He was in no position to protest. If she wanted him at the Chinese Embassy to ruin her wedding ceremony, to the Embassy he would go.

It is an impressive building, set back from the International Parkway in Northwest D.C., designed by I.M. Pei and intended as a tribute both to traditional Chinese design and soaring, modern abstraction. The outer walls are French limestone. A Chinese garden, stuffed with native Chinese flora, connects the main building with the Chancery. What its publicity pictures do not show is that it is behind heavy iron and stone fencing, far enough from the Embassy itself to prevent any troubling intrusions or even demonstrations from reaching the ears of those working inside.

When a Uyghur rights group mounted a rally against the genocide going on in Xinjiang province, the protesters were caught on long-lens video cameras inside the building. Several had relatives either in "re-education" camps like Lop, or still living outside of detention. Things did not go well for those relatives. In 2020, a Republican member of Congress tried to introduce a bill to rename the street where the

Embassy was located in honor of Dr. Li Wien-lang, the optometrist who first went public about the danger of the Wuhan virus, only to die of the disease himself. Within a week, Chinese-Americans living in the congressman's district were complaining that their relatives in China were being rousted from their homes, incarcerated, fined and in some cases, permanently evicted. The police who carried out the harassment told them they could thank the congressman for their troubles. Hui's insistence on getting information on Chinese living outside China was paying off.

Henry knew some of the Embassy's history before Rav came back. Careful not to use his home laptop for social media searches of anything or anyone Chinese, he resorted to an old-fashioned visit to his local library branch.

The taxi he summoned took him to the main gate of the Embassy. At its guard post were three heavy-lidded goons in black suits. They made no attempt to hide the automatic weapons leaning against the guard house.

Henry gave his name and the reason for his visit. They looked at him as though he had just spit on their shoes. "Wait," said the largest of the three. He went into the guard post, touched a button and, apparently looking into a monitor, spoke rapidly, and got an equally rapid reply. A door in the gate clicked and opened just enough for Henry to squeeze through. The largest guard gave Henry an unfriendly look and grunted something to his two colleagues. They came up on each side of Henry, pointed to a dome some thirty yards away, and escorted him towards it. They walked so close to him that he could smell their body scents. The smells were not pleasant.

The door swung open just before they got to it, and a young man in a light blue suit, white shirt and dark blue time held it open. He smiled an insincere smile at Henry, and said in perfect English, "You are here for the wedding of Counsellor Zho Pu-Ki and Ma-lin Cho?"

"That's right," said Henry, unsure how charming he was supposed to be.

"This way," said Mr. Insincerity. He dismissed the two musclemen and closed the door. Henry could hear it lock convincingly. He was a guest, but a guest with no option as to the time he might be leaving.

The corridor led into an enormous central hallway. The ceiling, like the walls, was surgically white and at least forty feet off the ground. The floor was laid out in a red and yellow granite tile pattern – the colors of the flag. And there, at one end of the hallway, stood a floor-to-ceiling hologram of Xi Jinping, much like the one Henry had seen in Hui's office but much larger. Next to the hologram, a single Chinese word pulsed on and off in eye-watering red. Henry read the word. It was one he had learned in Wuhan.

"Always?" he asked.

His escort looked momentarily surprised, looked at the flashing word, then at Henry, and said simply, "Always."

How much clearer could the message be? Xi was watching. Always.

The escort motioned to the left, and a door opened as they approached it. Camera inside, Henry imagined. He looked over his shoulder at the hologram and was certain he saw Xi's eyes following him.

The room was small, intensely lit, and packed with a kaleidoscope of cut flowers. When he turned to ask his guide if this was the wedding venue, he realized he was standing alone. He also realized it was only 8:30 a.m.

He was not alone for long. A door on the other side of the room opened, and a white-jacketed butler came in carrying a tray with a bottle and a glass. The butler stood in front of Henry, and with his free hand, pointed palm up at the bottle and asked, "Shhhhhe-di?"

It was a simple word, meaning "yes," and Henry had learned it on his second day in Wuhan. Yet he could never stifle his juvenile reaction. To his non-native ear, the question always sounded like "Shitty?" He controlled himself, nodded, and watched as the butler, without putting down the tray, opened the bottle with a bottle opener and poured its contents into the glass filled with ice cubes.

Henry immediately recognized the bottle as the effervescent water that Hui always had sitting on his office desk. It was the only brand Henry had ever seen, and, because Hui drank it, he assumed it was the best. He accepted the glass, took a sip of the bubbling water, and said, "Xiexie" – thank you.

The butler extended his free arm to a chair, inviting Henry to sit, and walked across the room. The door there opened as he reached it and he went out.

Henry tried to piece things together so far. I arrived early. My name was on a list, so I was expected. The guards dress in civilian clothes but are heavily armed. There are cameras everywhere, which is why the doors open by themselves. The main hall and the hologram of Xi are intended to intimidate and impress, and they do. I'm either in a waiting room or, considering the overpowering flowers, a funeral parlor. The bottled water he was drinking tasted like what he had drunk in Wuhan, so the Embassy brought Chinese water to Washington so the Embassy staff wouldn't drink American brands. That was also intended to impress.

Time passed. He didn't want to look at his phone, like every other stupid American did almost addictively. He was being watched, and he wanted to appear calm, which was the last thing he was.

It was probably twenty minutes before the door that the butler had come in opened, and a middle-aged man with a receding hairline in a black suit, white shirt and red tie entered.

"You are Henli," said Hair Loss.

Henry was so used to the mispronunciation of his name that he hardly noticed. He nodded and stood up, intending to shake hands.

"Zho Pu-Ki," the man said, pointing to his chest.

This, Henry realized, was the groom. Dear God, Rav, you can't be serious. No wonder you want me to *Tou zou xinniang* – steal the bride. Of course you don't want to marry So Pukey.

He was spared any insipid conversation, because the door across the room opened again and Lieutenant Ma-lin Cho entered in full-dress uniform. What happened to the plan to buy a wedding gown? Behind her, a diminutive man in a floor-length yellow silk robe strode to the center of the room. He was carrying a gold-colored cup, and under his left arm, a hefty book that seemed to have a black leather cover. He bent down and put the book on the floor without spilling a drop of whatever was in the cup.

Rav avoided looking at him, training her eyes on Yellow Silk Man. So Pukey did too, as YSM began to chant, not in words, just tones.

But the tones were tuneful and not at all disconcerting. Henry, having nothing else to do, took another sip of bubble-water.

The chanting went on for a while, its tone rising and falling. Rav never changed her grave expression and So Pukey starting blinking as a way of staying awake, it looked like.

Yellow Silk Man stopped chanting at last, opened the book that was indeed leather-covered, and selected a page that had been marked. If the chanting was boring, the reading was soporific. Henry sipped his water as a way of staying awake.

At Silk Man's signal, Rav and Pukey joined hands. Silk spoke in a low monotone that left Henry completely adrift. Rav and Pukey each said something. Then Silk said something, and Rav turned her head, looked directly at Henry, and smiling, nodded once.

Henry had studied the words, written them out phonetically fifty times, repeated them like a mantra. And now he couldn't remember them. He saw Rav's surprise on her lovely face, as her depthless eyes widened, as her beloved mouth opened in disbelief and disappointment.

"Tou," he said. It started with Tou, like the number. What came next? He looked desperately at Rav, who dropped Pukey's hand and said, out loud, "Zou."

"*Tou zou xinniang!*" Henry shouted, suddenly remembering. "*Tou zou xinniang.*" He registered the shock on Pukey's ugly face, the relief on Rav's. Silk Man asked her a question, his inflection rising at the end. And Rav, the woman he loved, the woman for whom he had come to this macabre ceremony of non-love, this abortion of true feelings, nodded once and said, "Shhhhhe-di."

Yes.

It was the last thing Henry remembered.

Chapter 33
To The Victor

Hui's victory was nearly complete. The battle in the Himalayas was such a one-sided rout by his AI creatures over the heavily-armed Indians that even Delhi-TV, which took its orders from the government, reported that a terrible tragedy had occurred on the border with China and put the mass deaths down to "unknown contaminants in the high-altitude air."

The "contaminants" were the prototypes that Hui had long envisioned turning loose on the world. They did not look like the robots portrayed in movies. These were no C3PO's with amusing British accents and blinking eyes. They were dark gray blocks of reinforced steel without faces, but with bulky lower limbs that resembled pistons more than legs. They moved faster than any human, and ignored hills, rutted or rocky paths, shrubbery, which they incinerated after they crushed them. They had nothing in common with humans, except that they could kill without remorse.

The AI troops had been designed by PLA engineers who had been assigned to Hui's secret project. He suspected that there was opposition among the PLA flag officers to this mad scientist's demand that steel boxes be turned into soldiers and allowed to make decisions for themselves. Ranking officers did not like to think that the Army, or the world could survive without them giving orders to underlings. Hui was proving them spectacularly wrong.

Backing up his AI forces were even more advanced versions of the drones that Nur's code had imbued with their own decision-making capabilities. With each design improvement, the speed and lethality of the drones increased. The accuracy in their firing was beyond any statistical possibility, and light years ahead of the fastest and most accurate planes the Air Force had in the sky.

The one problem that Nur pointed out to Hui, quietly and outside so they could not be overheard was: disregard for human wishes. "One of the drones overrode the code we had written for it. It deleted our code and wrote one that would make it impossible to deactivate it."

"How could that happen?" Hui demanded.

Nur shook his head. "I'm sorry. I don't know, Colonel."

"How can we prevent it from happening again?"

"Same answer."

Nur was not being flippant. They had agreed, without words, that Nur was permitted to tell inconvenient truths to the master of AI without repercussion. It made for a more efficient operation, and Hui, though he could not admit it, enjoyed Nur's quiet, confident intelligence.

"Stay on it until the problem is solved," Hui said sternly. "We don't want any more mistakes like that drone disaster in Lop."

They both smiled tightly. Both knew there had been no mistakes that time.

"And the master project?"

Nur came instantly alive. "Great progress, Colonel. I wasn't sure we could program all the traits you asked for into the network. But I think we have done it. It's ready for you to try anytime."

"With lenses in my eyes?"

"That's the only way so far, sir. Until we've developed an injectable chip."

Hui knew that the chip was being developed according to Nur's code and Hui's orders. He could not make it happen any sooner.

For someone who made much of his reputation for bravery, Hui hated anything coming near to, much less touching, his eyes. He viewed contact lenses with the same dread medieval prisoners felt for the rack. But this was his project, and he would not deny himself the honor of being the first to try it. Nur handed him two small plastic tombs containing clear lenses that had been milled by AI technology. There was nothing else in the world like them. Smiling weakly, Hui excused himself, went into the restroom off his office, and clumsily fitted them over his eyes. He could think of few things less comfortable.

He was unsure of his footing as he returned to the control room and Nur. He felt as he had felt after drinking too much alcohol, though that had not occurred for decades. He was Hui, and in charge, always.

Except not just now.

He did not have to direct his attention to a screen. With the lenses in place, the entire room was part of the background. Dome-roofed like a planetarium, he saw images directed down on him from 360 degrees. He felt himself being drawn into the curved world all around him. At its center, a beautiful young Caucasian woman regarded him, smiling, and said, "Hello, Colonel. My name is Mora."

"Mora?" Hui said.

From far, far away he heard Nur's voice telling him, "Yes, Colonel. We took the imagery from the Americans." The youth's voice sounded as if it was being beamed from a star somewhere, though Hui knew Nur was only a few feet away.

"Took it?"

"Stole it. It's an AI program the CIA is experimenting with. It wasn't even encrypted. We had no trouble hacking into it. We can change the imagery later. The important thing is to see if this works."

Mora had been patiently waiting for Hui to address her. It was as if she knew he was busy talking to Nur. She was in no hurry. Her smile was fixed, nearly permanent.

"Mora," he said experimentally.

Her smile lit up. "Hello, Colonel. What you do like?"

Hui realized she was speaking Mandarin, but imperfectly. He could not see Nur with the lenses over his eyes, but he cocked his head in the youth's direction, asking wordlessly for an explanation.

"It's Google Translate," said Nur. "We didn't even have to steal it. It's widely available. We're just using it for this test. If we decide to move ahead with the project, we'll perfect the language. Any language, actually. Words are just words. It's feelings we have to learn how to speak."

"Mora," said Hui. "How do you know my name?"

"I know everything you have allowed me to know, Colonel," said Mora, switching, without warning, to English. "When you put the lenses over your eyes, you opened your brain to me. I know all that you wish me to know." She paused, cocked her head, then with a different, sly smile, added, "and things you would not wish me to know."

"Such as?"

"Such as, who you love, Hui Jen-Sho."

Hui was genuinely shocked that that verb would be used in the same sentence as his real name, uttered without his rank in front of it.

Mora's smile softened, and she said, almost with regret, "I will come back when you have need of me, Colonel." And her image dissolved, to be replaced by that of Ma-lin Cho, in a black dress, her lustrous long hair hanging free, her smile as welcome as the first breath after a long underwater swim, her skin without blemish, her lips slightly parted.

"Hui Jen-Sho," she said, in exactly the voice she used with him. "You do me honor."

"Lieutenant," he stuttered.

Her smile was now beatific. "In this world, in this ... metaverse ... there are no ranks. There is order, yes. But we take orders based on our feelings, not because someone else is superior to us. In this ... metaverse ... feelings are our commands. Or, as they say in English," and she switched languages flawlessly, "'*Your wish is my command.*'"

"Lieuten ... Ma-lin," Hui said, completely unnerved now. "Tell me, please. What are your ... feelings?"

The smile brightened. "I suppose you know that already. You have known since we took a walk down the street and spoke freely."

"But," said Hui, "are these your thoughts, or are they what I hope your thoughts might be? Are you telling me your thoughts, or mine?"

Ma-lin raised her eyebrows a fraction, a delicate gesture that said everything. "Men and women have asked this question, pondered it, prayed that the answer they received would match their wishes, for many thousands of years. In this sense, the metaverse is not something new, but as old as love itself."

"Ma-lin," said Hui.

"I will be here, in this space, for you, whenever you want me. Need me," said the image of Ma-lin Cho, even as it began to dissolve into memory.

Hui wanted to stop her, to ask her to stay, to rise up to the curved roof of the planetarium-shaped laboratory and crack through its walls if necessary, to reach her, to touch her, to hold her. And then he was rising through the air, the walls coming closer to him, or was he coming closer to them? He didn't know or care.

He heard Nur's voice, soft, calming, calling, "Colonel, Colonel. It's I, it's Nur. Let me help you." Hui closed his eyes in order to think. As he did, he recalled who he was, where he was, and what he was doing. "Is she still there?" he asked.

"No, Colonel," said Nur. "It is just you and I here. Let me help you." And, against every instinct and fear that he had, Hui allowed Nur to gently, ever so gently, remove the lenses on his eyes, and welcome him back to the world from the metaverse.

But which, Hui asked himself, is real? And where do I want to be?

Chapter 34
Welcome Back, Traitor

Schrrr. Schrrr. Schrrr.

The sound, repeated in an endless, identical rhythm, forced its way into Henry's brain, and eventually became the one constant on which he could count. Everything else was like a rolling ship on snake-fanged waves, rollicking him up and down, back and forth with nauseating insistence.

Henry thought that he had woken up several times. But as soon as he opened his eyes and made noise, something pressed against his arm, he felt a slight prick, and the darkness overtook him.

We can adjust ourselves to any circumstances if we must. Imagine an honest citizen falsely convicted of some heinous crime and sentenced to prison. As much as the prisoner might protest innocence (they all do), life in prison is still the reality that must be dealt with. Or a patient diagnosed with a dread disease and subjected, unwillingly, to a course of radiation and chemotherapy that leaves the patient aware, but sucks away the will to live, or fight.

Henry's new reality was blurred silence, the occasional tickle entering his forearm, and schrrr, schrrr, schrrr. He remembered Rav had come to his apartment – how long ago was that? — their dream-come-true reunion, her heart-crushing demand that he give her away in marriage, the hologram of Xi in the Chinese Embassy, then dizziness and darkness.

He had only two questions: where was he now, and did she know?

Schrrr, schrrr, schrrr.

After several returns to dream-world, he realized the torturous headache he was suffering from was a good thing. He was, in a manner of speaking, conscious. Risking another needle in the arm, he opened his eyes, then closed them quickly as the brightness assaulted him. Again, and the glare was not as bad. A third time, and he could keep his eyes open until they focused.

Raising his head was like lifting a barbell. He surveyed the scene. He was in a cell-like enclosure with dirt walls. He had been lying on a dirty mattress mounted atop a steel frame that was sunk into the dirt floor. The light that hurt his eyes came through a prison-like barred door. There was a deep odor that was not of human origin. Electricity powering machinery somewhere close by hummed in a regular rhythm.

Schrrr, schrrr, schrrr.

Where was he? Was what he was seeing real, or ... artificial? Oh, you clever wag, Henry. Artificial like artificial intel ... Stop it! This is not funny. He was mixing various parts of his memories but not in any useful order. He was adrift in the flotsam and jetsam of years past. Rav, his Arlington apartment, the last facial recognition program he was working on, Rav, Rose, the wedding, Rav...

Well, mostly Rav, it seemed.

The barred door was pushed open. A young man – not Han, Henry noticed – walked in, stood several feet away, and in bad English said, "You sleep no, wake?"

"I'm awake," Henry said. "Water, please."

"Water, yes," said the young man. Henry noticed now he was wearing a gray uniform that did not look like it was military. His jet-black hair was mussed, his baggy trousers stopped at his ankles, which were crusted with dirt. As were his feet, for he wore no shoes. He looked like a ...

"Am I in China?" Henry said suddenly, loudly, hurting his head and startling the young man, who backed away. He picked up a clear plastic bottle, held it out. "Water," he said.

Henry eyed the bottle, wondered if it contained more of the potion – whatever it had been – that had put him to sleep and landed him here. Thirst overrode his caution and he gulped down its contents. Water, it seemed. He pointed at the young man, said, "Name?"

"Name," he repeated enthusiastically, as though he had answered a tricky quiz question.

"No, your name," said Henry.

"Ur-nam," the young man repeated.

Henry tapped his own chest with his forefinger. "Henry," he said. "My name is Henry." He pointed to his new acquaintance. "Your name?"

"Ah!" came the enthusiastic response. He pointed to his own chest just as Henry had. "Gureem."

Henry helicoptered his finger around the room, said, "Where are we?" And, from nowhere, remembered that he had learned a smidge of Mandarin while he was in Wuhan. "Women zi nali?"

Gureem's face lit up, and in good Mandarin, answered instantly, "Lop. We are in Lop. You speak the bad language."

"Yes, I speak it badly," Henry conceded. "What is Lop?"

"This is Lop," said Gureem pointing down. "Lop. In Xinjiang province."

"You are not Chinese," said Henry, experimentally.

And Gureem confirmed his worst fears. "I am Uyghur."

So, Henry told himself. You were drugged, put on a plane, and brought to ground zero of China's campaign to wipe out an entire race of people. He knew about the Uyghurs, had read more when he was in the United States, after his escape from China. Now, the horrors he had heard about were all around him. Could Rav have done this to him? He could not bring himself to believe it.

There was no time to think about it. The door opened and a tall Chinese man in a green PLA work uniform marched into the room. "Awake," he said to Henry as though presenting news. "Good. Come." He gripped Henry's upper arm and yanked him to his feet. Instant vertigo overcame him, and he began to sink back to the mattress where he had been when he first came to. "Come," insisted Tall Man, loosening his grip on Henry only to reassert it more forcefully. Gureem said something in Mandarin that Henry did not understand. The guard released Henry again and swung his right fist into Gureem's face. The young man crumpled to the ground. Tall Man kicked him in the head and shouted something. He turned to Henry, "Now, come."

It was a convincing argument.

He bent down to look at Gureem, who had not moved. "No, don't. Just go with him," Gureem said, his English somehow improving in his horizontal position. Wobbly and woozy, Henry followed Tall Man through a narrow space that was not so much a corridor as a cave passage. Dirt floor, dirt walls, the smell of urine and too many bodies too close together. After about twenty yards, Henry saw a light to the left. It was an opening of some kind. Tall Man pushed Henry from behind toward it. With little choice, Henry went through.

On the other side of the entrance was a scene as different from the primitive passageway as could be imagined. A brightly lit room full of computers, floor to ceiling plasma screens, the hum of electricity and a constant emission of reams of paper.

Schrrr, schrrr, schrrr.

"Work," said Tall Man. He turned and left Henry alone.

There was an ergonomically constructed chair of black fake leather on the left. Henry sank into it gratefully. He looked at the laptop on the desk in front of him. Smiled. It was AI coding.

"Goody, comrade," said a voice. Henry looked up. A frog-faced young man wearing thick spectacles approached. Henry thought he looked familiar but couldn't quite place him. Then he could! He was half of the Geek Squad, the Han programmers who Hui had recruited to work with Henry during his time in Wuhan. Hui had to pretend that what was coming out of his Institute was the product of Han genius, not a gifted *gweilo*. Henry couldn't keep their names straight and took to referring to them –only in Rav's presence – as Geek One and Geek Two. This was Two.

"Wilker ba," said Two. Henry remembered now his atrocious English but appreciated the effort he was making to say "welcome back." Two had a sly smile on his frog face, as though he knew Henry's return had been involuntary, just as his departure from Wuhan had been unauthorized.

"Thank you," said Henry. "Did Colonel Hui send you here?"

At the mention of the Colonel's name, Two sucked in his breath, nodded, then shook his head. It was a non-answer answer, Henry thought.

Two pointed to the monitor that Henry had been studying. "Wuk," he said. Work.

"I see," said Henry. And he thought he did. "I am here to work on this?" He pointed to the screen.

"Wuk."

"I need to sleep first. I'm tired and groggy. He remembered he had barely managed to get to his feet when Gureem had come in.

"Wuk," said Two.

Henry started to walk out of the room, intending to go back to the dirt room where at least there was a mattress. As he turned in that direction, Tall Man stood in his way.

"Work," he said.

"I'm tired. I need to rest first."

"Work."

The one-word drumbeat brought back Henry's headache. He felt certain he could not sit at a computer terminal and do serious coding work. Whatever drugs had been put into him were still making him woozy. He wasn't even sure where he was. And the two lines of code he had read on the screen belonged to a different program from anything he had ever worked on.

Artificial Intelligence is indeed just what they would be getting from him if they tried to make him code with a cloudy mind, and uncertain goals.

"No," he told Tall Man.

The slap to the side of his head put him down immediately. He had won his argument but not without cost.

As he was floating out of consciousness, he remembered the old politically incorrect joke about the Chinese laundry owner telling a customer, "No tickee, no washee."

No wakee, no codee, he thought, then blacked out.

Chapter 35
Knife For Life

It took the NSA about a week to pin down credible evidence that China had created and dispatched non-human, AI powered things to the Himalayas to slaughter a couple hundred Indian troops. It didn't make the news, because it wasn't about Dem vs. GOP politics, or gender-switching, or a staged confrontation at the Oscars, but it made for a lot of shivers at Langley, and elsewhere along the Potomac.

"How did they do it?" asked a Defense Department AI specialist. "We've been trying to perfect the same thing, but we keep running into roadblocks."

"I think the Chinese just decided to send them out and see what happened," said an underling.

"Is this the AI genius we've heard about who's behind this?"

"Hui Jen-Sho, yes," said the other, "but we think he's gotten some new help. Things are moving faster than usual in Wuhan nowadays."

"But how?" said DOD lady. "The coding for this stuff is incredibly complex. Hui is a genius, but he needs physical backup to do what it looks like he did."

"He may have someone," said a suit from the CIA who clearly didn't like being in this meeting. "We've detected a different coding style in some of the programming we've been able to hack into. It's not Hui's style at all."

"Then who?" said DOD. "That little shit from Jersey that defected to China a while back was helping Hui. And he was good. But he's back under wraps, right?"

The CIA guy looked as if he's just cracked an incisor. "We lost him. We don't know where he is."

"What?"

"We had him nice and cozy, shagging one of our people. He seemed happy enough. And then we lost him."

"When?"

"Five days ago. He's not at his home, his bike is in its rack, his phone has been turned off and the battery removed. He's logged out of his Agency account. And nobody's reported seeing him."

"Who else knows about this?" said DOD, face reddening with realization of what she'd just heard.

"He has no passport," said a guy from State. "We wouldn't issue him a new one when he got back because we thought he wasn't trustworthy. So he can't have gotten far."

The CIA guy looked at him with contempt, as one would a child who promises fine weather tomorrow because it would be a shame otherwise.

"Let's find this little shit and get him back on the reservation," said CIA, apparently unaware that LOFW had banned the use of that word by any Americans, not just federal employees. This was being challenged in a court, but reversal of the mandate was unlikely, as the judge hearing the lawsuit had also ruled that the Washington Football Team be scalped of their name, the Redskins. That verb was another word LOFW had banned. The list of banned English words was now in the thousands. Only heterosexual white men were now legitimate targets for verbal abuse.

Polling had showed that most football fans didn't give a shit what the team was called as long as tailgating parties were permitted. LOFW was pleased with those poll results, once she was assured that tailgating was not a term demeaning to women.

"OK," said CIA. "Forget about getting this kid back to work. Let's put him to sleep. Then let's figure out what Hui is doing and how, and steal the technology from him."

Everyone nodded, except the underling. "Ummm," he said. "We don't have the technology to steal technology from China. They're too well encrypted."

"Well, how the hell can they steal our tech?" said CIA, whose agency was responsible for stealing technology and who didn't like to be told his people were second-rate.

"The Chinese devote more people, time and money to tech-theft," said the underling. "They're the best there is. Better than the Russians. Better than the North Koreans. Even better than the Germans."

"The Germans are stealing our tech?" said CIA, not happy to look like he was out of the loop.

Underling gave him a "duh" look, but stayed silent.

"Let's get this done," said CIA, wanting to change topics. "The boss's top priority is the Knife for Life thing."

Now it was Underling's turn to look clueless. "Huh?"

"She wants white male babies castrated at birth. Before their parents can stop it. That way, she figures in a generation or so, the only potential fathers will be men of color. So we'll all look alike. She wants it to be her legacy project."

"I can't help feel that some people will object to this," said DOD carefully. She was the only woman in the room and therefore the only one who could say such a thing.

"Anyone who objects will be charged with sedition," said CIA, happy to be schooling the rest of the room. "Our supporters love that word when it's applied to their enemies. All the networks except Fox are on board. And like I said, it's her top priority."

"She oughta be more concerned about China and those non-human soldiers," said State.

"She is," said CIA. "She wants to know if there's an acceptable ratio of women among them."

"We don't think these soldiers have any gender," said State.

"Wouldn't that be a perfect world?" sighed DOD, trying to imagine the beauty of it all.

Chapter 36
Between Two Worlds

Hui learned to put the lenses in by himself without fear or hesitation. Only Nur was allowed in the planetarium-shaped room when Hui visited the metaverse. He was doing so increasingly, always in the strictest secrecy. Or at least the strictest secrecy that he could assure. Which, he knew, and feared, was not much secrecy at all.

Socialism with Chinese characteristics.

"Who else can hear this?" he asked Nur, betraying unaccustomed nervousness.

"Colonel, as we have discussed, this is a conversation between you and your inner self," said Nur with a small smile. "The metaverse merely brings to life those things that you wish to be real. The world you wish."

"But you know," said Hui.

"Only because you have permitted me your trust."

"All right," said Hui. "Let's go in there."

The walls around him were illuminated, and within seconds, Mora's comforting face filled him with a sense of calm. "Hui Jen-Sho, welcome back. I didn't know if you would visit again."

"I thought you knew everything," said Hui, mockingly.

"I told you before," said Mora. "I know only what you permit me to know."

"Thank you," said Hui.

"Are you ready to come back in?" Mora asked.

"Please," said Hui softly. "Thank you" and "please" were words that Hui had not employed more than ten times in the last ten years. He felt good saying them to Mora.

The walls of the plane began shifting color. Now they were mint green, now magenta, now cornflower blue.

"Come in," Hui heard Mora say, but he was not sure if she had spoken out loud, or if her words had simply penetrated his mind. Sound was irrelevant, certainty was without value, Hui thought. Feelings were all that mattered here.

Hui felt himself take a step forward. Or was it to the side? He could not discern movement as the walls morphed from one shade to the next. There was no pattern. When he thought yellow, there was a sunburst. When he sought cool, he was surrounded by green. We are what we see. We see what we want. And what we want becomes us.

Hui giggled at his own incongruity of thought.

Hui doesn't giggle, he scolded himself. He translated that into English and corrected himself. Hui don't giggle. We don't.

He got confused. Was he moving forward? Define forward, something in his meta-mind demanded. Don't demand. It's too hard. Too demanding.

Hui giggled again.

"Stop fighting it," Mora said into his brain. "Let go. You are safe with me."

Safe with Mora, he repeated. Not Mora. Ma-lin. He wanted to be safe with Ma-lin.

And like that, he was.

She was standing next to him, though he had not sensed her approach. "You asked me to come, Hui Jen-Sho," she said softly. "Why?" She was dressed in her inevitable civilian clothes; a tight-fitting black skirt, a white blouse whose top button was undone. He had never seen her throat. And ... really?... red, high heeled shoes. Anything was possible here, he thought.

"Because I want to be with you." He recognized the voice as his own, but did not recall pronouncing the words. It didn't matter. They were out there now, between them, awaiting her response.

"I have already told you, Hui Jen-Sho, you are not alone." She did not smile as she said it, but looked at him eyes alight, and with an intensity that came from some secret source.

"Why are you here?" he asked.

"I am here because you called for me. In this world, what you want is what you have. What you have is what you want." She was not mocking him, or toying with him. He felt that to be true, and it gave him a sense of deep satisfaction.

"Then I will stay in this world," he said, or thought about saying, which was the same thing.

"No," said Ma-lin. "You have work to do, as always. It is one of the things we share even in that darker, lesser world." And this time, she did smile and the colors around them were born anew with pink clouds rising and falling, as they never did in the darker world.

"I will here there soon," she said. "And I will be here, always."

And she touched his shoulder. Or did she? Something was applying pressure to his left shoulder. Ma-lin had been standing to his right, so was it her hand? He was beginning to process things with his brain again, not his feelings. And the hand touched him again...

"Colonel?"

It was Nur, trying not to stand too close, but close enough to tap Hui's shoulder softly but insistently. And the pink clouds were replaced by black planetarium walls.

And Ma-lin was gone.

"Why?" Hui said, meaning why was she gone. But Nur answered, "I was becoming concerned. You have been standing still like this for more than an hour. I wanted to make sure you were well."

"I was well," said Hui. "Until you disturbed me."

"Please forgive me, Colonel," said Nur, sincerely but not fearfully. "Would you like me to help you remove the lenses?"

Lenses. In his eyes. Lenses that filtered life, lenses that allowed him to walk through them, to see Ma-lin, be with her, be wherever he wanted to be and with whomever he wanted to be.

And the answers to those two things were: the metaverse, and her.

Chapter 37
Back In The Saddle Again

He was not treated like a prisoner. But nor was he permitted to come and go. After a long sleep, a decent meal, and a shower that was neither hot nor cold, Henry tried to acclimate to his new situation. He was in Xinjiang province, he knew. In a place called Lop, which he did not know. He sensed there was much activity all around him. But he was confined to the building where he slept and where the computer laboratory was located. He was awakened at 6 each morning, with tea, rice and fish. It never varied. The uniformed server spoke not a word.

The first time he looked at the program Geek 2 was writing, he saw what he assumed were intentional errors, though Geek 2 seemed not to recognize them for what they were. Communication was stilted, to say the least. His Mandarin had never been fluent, and he had forgotten much of what he had learned at the AI Institute. And Geek 2 knew only technical terms in English. They tried to converse, but it was like sawing a stone with a dull blade. Not much happened.

Henry knew immediately that the code he was being asked – ordered – to work on involved facial recognition. Since he had been doing similar work from his off-site workplace in Arlington, the language on the screen in front of him was familiar. But he also saw what seemed to be intentional gaps in the progression of the program. Why, he wondered. Usually, such gaps indicated that something was going to be added later. He had decided immediately upon realizing where he was not to ask Geek 2 any significant questions, nor to offer opinions about what they were supposedly working on together. He assumed that anything he said or observed would be reported. But to who? The PLA of which Rav was still an officer? The AI Institute? He knew nothing about it now, didn't know if Hui was still being punished for letting him – Henry – get away. If Tanteeth – he reminded himself that her name was General Deng-tal – was still running it. And why was Geek 2 here, instead of at the Institute in Wuhan? Had he too, failed in some way that merited deportation to Xinjiang?

Most of all, Henry spent the majority of his days wondering: did Rav help them abduct me and send me here? Was the whole "steal the bride" idea just a way to trick me into entering the Embassy, with the hologram of Xi lording over all? Could she have sought me out, given herself to me, involved me in her bizarre non-wedding, and then watched, impassively, as I was drugged and shipped like cargo to this wretched part of China? The enormity of the betrayal made him feel weak and stupid. But at the same time, it instilled in him a cold anger and determination to understand what had happened, and to do something about it. Something drastic.

It was then, without warning, that he saw the line of code that Geek 2 had written the day before: *pip.intall_metaverse.unicode*. His spine went stiff. He knew now why he was here and what they wanted from him.

No one in his line of specialized work could be unaware of the metaverse, the alternate reality, which users readily enter in order to experience things the real world cannot offer. Until now, as far as Henry knew, the metaverse devoted itself to games – kill the zombie, defeat the dragon and so on – or, more gently, visit Paris virtually, pilot a rocket to the moon, or boogie with a movie star or rapper. Since trying the lenses, Henry had slipped on an Oculus Quest2 headset and toyed around for an hour or so with fantasy backgrounds. It was not to his taste, and he had not been tempted to try it again. To him, Artificial Intelligence was intensely real, something to which he had already devoted most of his professional life. The metaverse, by comparison, was something people entered on their day off work to forget their cares, and live for an instant in fake sublimity.

Though still young, Henry had already experienced the highs and lows of real life – the perfect joy of being with Rav, the perverted pleasure of caning Rose, the all-too-brief experience of advising Hui

Jen-Sho on the vulnerabilities of the United States during the early days of the pandemic. He did not need to fire a fake laser to subdue a hydra-headed monster, or dunk a basketball over the head of the latest NBA superstar. In his experience, real life was exciting enough.

He saw Geek 2 get up and leave the computer lab. Assuming he was being monitored on a hidden camera, Henry casually typed in a line of code and pressed "Save." If accepted, that line would neutralize the pip.install command for the metaverse. He waited to see what would happen.

He did not have to wait long. Within minutes, Tall Man came in, shouted "Up, up!" and grabbed his elbow. By now, Henry had re-accustomed himself to the PLA's lack of tact. He did not resist or argue. He let himself be led back to his room-prison cell, heard the door lock behind him, and lay down on his lumpy bed. Now they knew that he knew. The next step was up to them.

When orders come from the top in China, things can move quickly. Tall Man hustled in, a look of important concern on his face. "Go," he said, and Henry thought humorously he might be receiving a challenge to play an ancient board game. But no, Tall Man wanted him to get up and follow – fast. So he did.

The Hongqi H9 was waiting outside – outside being something that Henry had not been allowed to see or smell since his arrival. He didn't even know how long he had been kept inside, other than the fact that he had been allowed long sleeps three times. So perhaps this was his fourth day in unexplained captivity. Or whatever this was.

Having previously manhandled him with impunity, Tall Man now seemed to give Henry a kind of grudging deference. He extended his arm, palm up, as though inviting, not ordering him to get into the black state car. Once inside the back seat, Henry saw there was an apparently unopened bottle of water and an array of Chinese comfort food – salted pumpkin seeds, a kind of fried pork rind, and caramelized onions. He decided to forgo these delicacies.

The clear, hardened Mylar divider between the front and back seats told Henry this car was intended for an upper-level Party official. There was a car phone between the seats. Of course, Henry had no one to call. He looked back through the window and was astounded to see that he had been quartered in what looked like a prison camp.

Dozens of low-slung huts spaced out over hectares of ground, smoke rising from some, and, just before the door had been closed, an acrid smell that he could only imagine was generated by human anguish.

The Hongqi moved off at a good speed, and Henry, trying to process not just what had happened in the last half hour, but in the four or five days since he had been drugged and presumably smuggled to China, tried to put things together. He thought he knew where he was being taken. Where was not the question. The question was to *whom* he was being ferried.

To *whom* made all the difference in this rapidly moving, hard-to-understand world.

Chapter 38
The Price Of Power

It was terribly unfair, all of it. She emerged from her forty-five minutes of meditation, mostly about her polling numbers, in search of good news to lift her spirit, but found none. The daily CIA, DOS, DOD, FBI and BLM briefing reports were filled with negativity. The carefully curated snippets of news items from approved organizations, such as Lesbians of Color, Huffington Post (too right wing, but just for representation), MSNBC, Kos, and, to give it all some credibility, The New York *Times*, seemed intent on impinging on her *wa*, her state of harmony.

It was not at all fair. She closed her eyes, breathed deeply, and tried to *feel* which evil all this bad stuff constituted: racism, gender bias, homophobia, transphobia, white privilege, income disparity, or, most evil of all, Trumpism. She didn't have to put up with any of it. She was who she was, and she could do whatever she wanted to do.

So why hadn't those positive thoughts she kept trying to push to the front of her cerebral cortex, into the gyri and sulci that guided her brain —why hadn't they revealed the right way to deal with all the problems that had been laid at her doorstep? Then she remembered that doors were mostly used in the Western world and therefore were probably not as good a way of entering and leaving, as, say, the curtain over the entrance to a yurt, the kind of tent that originated in Central Asia, which meant it was closer to Buddha's and Allah's presence in nirvana.

Or was she getting those things confused? It didn't matter, she was LOFW and whatever she decided was how it would be.

Except the goddamned (excuse me, Great One) Chinese kept doing things that confounded all those criminal organizations – the CIA, the FBI, the NSA, the Pentagon – over which she had control and which she definitely intended to defund as soon as she could. But not before she'd gotten the bumbler on Penn Ave to fulfill his promise to appoint a left-handed tran to run the Pentagon (left-handed so we'd know which way her brain inclined), a former Massai warrior to the CIA, and a bi-Eskimo to take over the FBI. It was profiling, sure, but she wanted to make sure that the Cabinet looked like America. At least, the America she invited to her secret parties. Then she could get started on her gender neutering – not neutral – program. If we don't let white men procreate, then pretty soon, there won't be any white men. Which would make America look *much* more like Americans should.

Anyway, about those Chinese. Non-human soldiers who made their own battlefield decisions. She suspected they were powering the little tin bastards with Artificial Intelligence, which she hated nearly as much as artificial coloring in icing and ice cream. She'd once canceled a staffer's birthday party when she found out the cake and ice cream were not organic. Which could be one of the reasons she had trouble holding onto staff, but some principles were worth upholding at any cost.

Could the Chinese be reasoned into not making any more of these tin-pol-pot soldiers? Perhaps if she offered to travel to a neutral site – Hawaii, for instance, which had great waves and crazy luaus and flower garlands – she could brow-beat the Chinese guy into calling off his aggressive tactics. After all, she was LOFW. China wasn't going to mess with her.

To prepare for such a meeting, if it were ever to take place, she resolved to play a half hour of Savages every night. Forearmed is forewarned. Or whatever that saying was.

Chapter 39
Nothin' Like Comin' Home

The jet took four hours. Henry tried to sleep but was too nervous. There was someone in the cabin with him, playing a role of flight attendant, but his main duty seemed to be preventing Henry from committing suicide. Each time Henry shifted his position in the seat, the attendant leapt to his feet. When Henry got up and asked permission to use the toilet, he followed him. There was no doubt in Henry's mind where they were headed and as the plane made its descent, he thought he recognized the military base outside Wuhan, where he had begun his perilous escape from China.

He was nervous, but by now, he was used to being treated as a non-living entity by the bevy of soldiers who surrounded the plane as soon as it stopped taxiing. And yet, they cast glances at him, surreptitiously inspecting whatever this bedraggled baggage was that had caused them to scramble. Another Hongqi, identical to the one he boarded in Lop, waited on the tarmac. The attendant who had accompanied him on the flight gestured for him to get in. And Henry thought he saw the young man's shoulders slump with relief. He had successfully handed off the package. Nothing that happened subsequently could be his fault. He would receive credit. His social responsibility score might be raised. Most important though, he was safe, for the moment, from retribution or punishment by the Party, and that was what mattered most.

Socialism with Chinese characteristics.

Henry tried to look confident, even a bit bored, as he settled into the back seat of the Hongqi, like a diplomat having a few minutes of downtime before his next important meeting. It didn't work. However he might have looked to others, he himself felt like a schoolboy being sent to the principal's office to meet some unknown fate.

The route itself was not familiar – he had only gone from Wuhan to this military airbase once, with Fang, now long dead, hissing instructions to him and Qi Qi Dieh, also dead, to keep quiet and let him do the talking, as he sneaked them out of China. Well, Henry thought, Fang got to do the talking all right: probably as electric prods slid in and out of him, and psychotropic drugs loosened any part of his speaking apparatus that hadn't already been removed with a knife.

For a nation that boasted three thousand years of culture, the China of Xi Jinping was truly barbaric. Henry didn't want to learn any more about that.

He smelled, before he recognized, the road they were now on. Take a right – or maybe it was left, coming from this direction – and twenty miles down the road was the beginning of the Crane Tower sanctuary and memorabilia shop. That was no doubt where Rose had purchased her souvenir statuette, and by leaving it exposed, brought upon herself Henry's demented demonstration of sadism.

And then he saw the Yangtze River on his left and knew that they were approaching the Wuhan Institute of Virology, where the pandemic that changed the world had been spawned and set free. Henry knew this not because it was public knowledge. China had rejected all accusations that the Wuhan Virus started in Wuhan, that it had been created through experimentation of fruit bats, and that the experimental animals had been mishandled and allowed out of the Institute. Such accusations were racist, said the Chinese Foreign Ministry, and America and the rest of the West had quickly started calling it Covid-19, as directed by the World Health Organization, an arm of the United Nations that was quietly controlled by China. Being called racist was more deadly than getting the disease.

Henry knew all this because he had been told it by the highest authority possible: Hui Jen-Sho, the director (or perhaps former director?) of the Institute for Artificial Intelligence, located not far from the Virology Institute and the wet market where a dead bat carrying the Wuhan virus had been sold.

And there, just ahead on the right, was the Institute for Artificial Intelligence, where Henry had worked, learned about AI, and learned love as well. That being the one thing he needed to believe was not artificial.

He was expected, of course, and the front door opened as he mounted the seven steps to the white-faced building. Another frog-faced young man, unsmiling and in everyday olive-drab uniform admitted him. Unlike the first time he had entered these doors, Henry knew where to go. In the politest Mandarin that he could formulate, he declined Frog-Face's offer to escort him.

The woman outside the office of the Director looked at Henry with more familiarity than he thought likely, considering they had never met. There was about her an air of, what? Condescension, perhaps. Or was it pity? What a world of difference between this snotty nobody and Rav, who had met him so long ago, it seemed, and never left his consciousness.

"You may go in," the receptionist said in good English.

As soon as he opened the dark wood door and saw Xi's hologram, Henry knew who he would be seeing. So where was Hui?

"Over here," came the familiar voice, in precisely accented English. "Welcome home, Henry."

"Colonel," he answered politely. "I believe you too have been away."

Hui chuckled, not a familiar response for him. "Tell the truth, Henry. Did you rehearse that line?"

In fact, he had, in case it was Hui and not Tanteeth whose office he was in. Curiously, Hui was not behind his massive desk, with the Xi hologram over his left shoulder. Henry had never seen him elsewhere in this building. Instead, Hui sat in one of the five visitors' chairs arranged around the office. Why? Henry wondered, unless it is perhaps *not* Hui's office after all.

"Don't be alarmed, Henry," said Hui in soothing tones. "I am once again in charge of the ... of our ... Institute. I thought to sit here so you could join me, and we could have a more informal talk."

Henry knew that every word spoken in this office was recorded, if not overheard directly, so the mention of an "informal talk" was intentionally misleading. And then he got it. Hui knows that I know,

Henry realized. He knows I know that everything in this office is recorded. And he is acting as though I don't know. We are both actors on a stage.

"As you wish, Colonel," he said, realizing he had to choose each word.

"Are you well, Henry? The journey was not too tiring?"

"The 'journey,' Colonel, was in two parts. For the first part, I was drugged and locked inside a plane. The second leg, from Lop to here, was both shorter and more pleasant."

"I have made that journey from Lop several times," said Hui, as though discussing the inconveniences of commercial air travel. "I prefer Wuhan, don't you?"

Henry decided it was time to launch into his dramatic monologue for the unseen audience. "Tell me, Colonel, was it you who had me drugged, kidnapped, and transported here in violation of more international laws than I can count?"

Hui waved his hand. "These matters belong in the past. They are of no importance to us."

Fight or flight, Henry asked himself. The answer would determine the conditions of his confinement. So he said, "Perhaps you are right, Colonel. Let me ask the most important question. Why am I here?"

"Ah," said Hui, smiling falsely, signaling silently that he – Hui – knew that Henry knew. "That is a much more interesting topic. And one that I would like to discuss at length with you."

"Fine, Colonel. Let's discuss it."

"Your ... departure .... Henry, was a cause of some concern to us. I thought that you and I had reached a mutual understanding about the work we were doing together. I was not prepared for your ... decision ... to return to America."

"You know the reason. My Mother was ill. With Wuhan Flu."

Hui looked up, sharply, then let his features relax. "I wonder, Henry, if you realize just what a rare position you are in, as an indirect result of your Mother's flu. How is she, by the way?"

"She recovered, thank you. The American health care system is truly a miracle of science."

Hui let the unspoken comparison pass. "You have matured, Henry. I am glad to see it."

"Thank you, Colonel. Now please, what 'rare position' do you imagine that I am in?"

"If you will lend it to me, Henry," Hui said smoothly, "I believe I can put your fine mind to excellent use."

"I was a *hanjian*, a traitor, when I was last here," Henry said. "I don't wish to be again, Colonel."

Hui reflected for a moment. Then said, "Henry, what I would like you to help me with this time is far beyond nations, or colorful flags, or pledges of allegiance, or international borders marked only with signs and lines. I want you to be part of something that is not only on the front line of science, but the entryway to the future. I want you to help me create the world we wish."

Chapter 40
A Fine Pair

There was nothing to agree to because there were no options. Henry understood that he was once again being offered something he could not refuse. He had no desire to be returned to Lop to deal with Tall Man, Geek 2, or the unseen, but hardly unheard population of Uyghur "re-education students" he suspected was imprisoned nearby. He had heard the occasional cry of pain, the sound of guards barking curses and orders. He knew all the rumors about Lop. He thought he knew what happened there. He did not wish to join in the festivities.

Hui was solicitous. "You have had a traumatic experience. You have been brought around the world without options. But Henry, you are back where you belong. And the next steps that we can take together are truly something beyond the ventures of AI. You can help us make history."

"Us?" For a second, he hoped that meant Rav, automatically forgiving her if she was part of the artifice to whisk him back here. He remembered the first time Rav had said "us" in reference to them, together, and how his heart had expanded. Was "us" the same as "we"? Did we mean me and Hui?

The Colonel appeared deep in thought, and Henry was unwilling to break his concentration. He had seen this before. In the past, the fruit of this meditation had been something groundbreaking, worth waiting for.

Hui sighed, another new emotion from a man who previously appeared to lack such weakness. "Henry, I am a simple man." They both smiled, knowing that lies can take many forms, including sincerity.

"I need you to understand that while you were here ... previously ... I became interested in your talent, your potential. I became interested in you. You have many abilities that, again while you were here before, had not been identified. I believe I was helping to identify them. I wanted to do that. And then you left. But you also left behind the memory of what we might have achieved. I understand that our countries are not the closest of allies."

Again, they both smiled at the understatement that carried so much implied meaning.

"But I believe the world we live in now requires some people – people like you and me – to lead the way beyond nationalities, beyond the shackles we have put on ourselves for so many years.

"The truth, Henry, is that after all the years I have devoted to Artificial Intelligence, I now believe I have found something even more powerful, more influential, and something that can be spread around the world with very little effort on our part."

"You mean the Wuhan Flu?" The words had just slipped out. Henry wished he could re-swallow them, but Hui's facial expression had shifted from philosophical to offended.

"No, I do not," he said. "I will not insult you by reminding you that the always helpful World Health Organization told everyone to call that sickness 'Covid-19.' To mention this wonderful city at the same time as the disease would be disrespectful, even racist."

"Colonel," said Henry, "if *you* will recall, it was *I* who told *you* that calling something or someone racist was the easiest way to subdue them. Especially Americans. You taught me many things during my time here. But that was one thing I taught you."

"I like your new spirit, Henry," said the Colonel. "Is the English word for it 'feistiness'? It is good for us to now be on an even playing field. And so, yes, I acknowledge that you taught me the power of the word racist. In today's world, it automatically quells your opponent so that any response is inadequate, even proof that the racism that is alleged is untrue. I can tell you proudly, many important people in the Party were impressed with your contribution."

"Colonel," said Henry carefully, "I don't wish to offend you. But even given the fact that I was kidnapped and brought here against my will, I have to say that I no longer believe the Party has supreme wisdom."

Hui was already nodding before Henry finished the sentence. "Then we have something in common, Henry. Let's take a walk. It's good to stretch our legs."

Aside from their first meetings when Hui was lecturing in the United States, Henry could not remember ever seeing the Colonel outside his office. He suspected this healthful walk was an attempt to avoid being overheard. But why would Hui worry about that? Wasn't he usually the one doing the bugging? Something had changed.

A young man was waiting for them outside the main door of the Institute. Henry noticed him immediately because he did not look like a Han Chinese. His eyes were too round, his skin was tan, and his hair had hints of light brown running through it. He was dressed in a PLA uniform but had no rank on his shoulder. So he could not be an active soldier.

"Henry," said Hui, speaking English, "I would like to introduce you to one of my new assistants. His name is Nur. Nur, this is Henry, of whom I have often spoken."

Nur watched Hui's mouth closely, almost as though he was lipreading. He nodded and said, "Hi, Henry. Good meet you."

"Nice to meet you, Nur," said Henry, now wondering if this was some sort of trap being set for him.

"Like you, Henry," said Hui, still in English, "Nur has shown extraordinary talent as a coder. And he is now helping me, unofficially, on the very important project I mentioned to you just now in my office."

Nur nodded, smiling like the village idiot. Really, thought Henry. Extraordinary talent. But he knew better than to judge by initial impressions. And yet Hui seemed to have mastered precisely that art. He saw something in me that even I didn't know was there. Or perhaps he just saw a dupe whom he could manipulate.

"I will speak to Nur in Mandarin, which he speaks very well for someone of his race," said Hui. "And then I will say the same thing to you. As Nur learns English, you will be able to communicate more easily. But for now, I will be your filter."

"His race?" said Henry.

"Nur is a Uyghur. I believe you have met one or two others recently."

Henry flashed back to the first day in Lop. Gureem was the youth's name. A prisoner, like all the Uyghurs there. But intelligent, seemingly friendly. Would this Nur prove to be the same?

Hui turned to Nur and spoke. The Uyghur listened attentively, as if in an advanced college seminar. He said not a word until Hui went silent, then nodded and said, in English, "Yes, Colonel." He looked past Hui, caught Henry's eye, and smiled. I am ahead of you already, the smile seemed to say.

Hui turned. "Henry, I know that you have many questions about why you are here. I will try to answer them in good time. But now, please concentrate on what I am about to say.

"Artificial Intelligence is the future of mankind. You and I agree on that. I have seen your enthusiasm, your devotion to the work. You would not be so devoted if it were not something you, like I, believe in. I have devoted years of my life to this study, and it has paid off. China is now the world leader in AI.

"But Henry, I have found something that I believe can be even more important. The metaverse. Think about that while we continue our three-way discussion."

Hui turned back to Nur and restarted his monologue in Chinese.

The metaverse, thought Henry. Is he kidding? The metaverse was just advanced game-playing. Teenagers strapping on headsets, fingering joysticks, and living their alternate lives through Avatars or whatever they are calling their representational selves. He looked across Hui at Nur, who was now responding in spitfire Mandarin. And Henry realized, not for the first time, that his life was beyond his control.

Hui turned back to him. "Listen carefully, Henry. We are in the street because I do not want our conversation to be overheard." It was the first time Henry had ever heard Hui suggest he valued privacy, especially from the Party.

"The project I have in mind is not, I repeat, not sanctioned by the Party. It would not be in my interest to have the Party learn of this. Do you understand?"

"Yes, Colonel."

Hui grinned, another first for Henry. "When we are discussing this project, and when we are outdoors, you need not refer to me as 'Colonel.' My name is Hui Jen-Sho, as you know. You may call me by that name."

For Henry, it was as if he had stepped not into the street, but into a dream world. Military titles cast aside, blind loyalty to the Party cast into question, projects conducted in secrecy? Was he being set up?

With all the rules seemingly in question, Henry decided, what the hell? "Colon ... sorry, I mean, Hui, tell me, please. Where is Lieutenant Cho?"

A smile bordering on beatific filled Hui's face. "I wondered when you would ask. Trust me, Henry, she is safe. That is all you need to know."

So there were limits to the candor of this new world, Henry told himself.

"It is only that ... well, I love her."

A slightly less kind smile. Hui said, "I have known that for a long time, Henry. I can understand the emotion. Now, I want you to work with Nur, following my blueprint. We are going to create our own metaverse. But this metaverse will be powered by, and controlled by, the AI program Nur and I have been working on. Having you here to work with us will be a great advantage and will speed things up."

Henry stopped in his tracks. "Is that why I was kidnapped and brought here?"

Hui stopped too. "I don't think of it as kidnapping. Any more than you thought your quick return to America, against my wishes, was betrayal. So our perception of things is not really all that different." He began walking again, and Henry, with no answer to that statement, had no choice but to follow.

Once back inside the Institute, Hui adopted his brisk in-charge attitude again and told first Henry, then Nur, "A laboratory has been prepared for you. I expect you to produce noticeable results within a week. All glory to the Party."

He pointed to a closed door, which, when opened, concealed a nearly state-of-the-art full ceiling-to-floor screen, a quantum computer system and two work areas separated by a clear plastic wall. Compared to the grubby room in Lop, it was like a science fiction movie to Henry.

There could be no doubt that Hui had either retained or regained his authority.

The immediate problem of working with Nur would be communication. Henry had forgotten much of the Mandarin he had learned. And Nur had made no claims to be able to speak English. They had one common language: AI.

Henry sat at one of the screens – essentially laying claim to it as his – and typed a line of code that he had used in Arlington on occasion. Instantly, the screen split in two. On the left side, instructions were displayed in English. He moved to the right side of the screen and selected "Mandarin." Then back to the left side, and keyed in, "Is this the language you speak best?"

The Chinese characters formed a millisecond after he had hit the Send key. Henry knew this translation tool was a hundred times faster than any commercially available site. It also had a firewall against snooping, not that that would stop the Chinese Army from cracking into it.

While Henry was inputting information, Nur took the chair in front of another screen. He seemed to know precisely how to replicate the line of code Henry had written. His screen came to life, and Henry's question, in Mandarin, was on the left side of his screen.

He answered "Turkic-Arabic is my native language. But my Mandarin is acceptable. I would like to learn English quickly." Henry looked up the second he had read the answer and saw Nur smiling. It was a welcome sight.

Nur switched the left side of his screen to Turkic and inputted: "I know about you. The Colonel believes you have unique capabilities."

"Thank you," Henry responded on his screen. "And you?"

"Just a Uyghur trying to stay out of Lop. You have been there. You can understand." Again, the answer was followed instantly by a bright and wide smile. Nur was enjoying this, Henry thought.

"Do you know what the Colonel wants us to create?" Henry input.

Nur's eyebrows wrinkled. He did not like this question. His hands hovered over the keyboard. He input: "Let's wait until my English is better."

So, thought Henry. Smart as well as intelligent.

Chapter 41
Moving At The Speed Of Bright

The pace at which Nur digested English words was startling, as well as grammatical rules, and irregular verbs – "Why is the past tense of walk, walked, but the past tense of write, wrote?" he asked Henry on the screen one day.

"To frustrate pesky Uyghurs," Henry replied and was rewarded with the first sound of laughter to come from his workmate.

Hui's instructions had arrived within days of the trio's walk along the street. To call his plan bold was like describing the Chinese Communist Party as resolute. Henry read the document (had Hui really written it in English himself?) with mounting admiration and tension. Nur's copy was in Chinese.

"Until now," Hui had written, "the metaverse has been primarily a place for games, competitions, virtual warfare, pretend homecomings, imagined love affairs, and time-consuming leisure. It has become a multi-billion dollar business because it allows users to 'get away from it all' and indulge their fantasies.

"By donning a headset, visitors to the metaverse can see things and do things not available to them in the world they are leaving behind. Their powers are heightened without effort on their part. Their fantasies become everyday truths, and their wishes need not be voiced to be granted. It is what some Christians might call 'heaven,' the only drawback being the elastic band wrapped around their skulls to keep the headset in place.

"Such encumbrances are no longer necessary. Already vision screens that look like ordinary contact lenses can be placed over the eyes. As long as they are in, the user is in the metaverse. When they are removed, this drab, so-called 'real world' reclaims them.

"But even contact lenses eventually become irritating, and so, a less intrusive channel for transport has been found. A microscopic chip can now be implanted under the skin. When activated, the chip takes its resident body to places in the metaverse that so far, can only be dreamed about. You wish to be commander of an army? Your troops await your orders. You love someone who does not return your ardor? That will be reversed. You long to go to places your budget does not allow? You are there. You suffer from an illness that has no cure? The cure is here, waiting for you. You cannot understand other languages? You are fluent without study.

"The planet known as Earth is doomed. It is choking itself to death, its inhabitants are happier killing rather than loving each other. There is not enough food, water or money to support everyone. Empty promises and lies are the world's only common currency.

"What we will not tell our guests in this wonderful world is that once they arrive, the gate through which they entered the metaverse slams shut behind them. They will never return to the real world. They can request a tour of what they left behind – homes, family members, pets, cars, jobs – but it will be a virtual tour, and infinitely less interesting than the world they now inhabit. Who would want to go back to that planet of unhappiness? You are here now. You are here forever. Enjoy yourselves. Let us worry about the details.

"You will create this place for me. I will oversee your efforts. Christian phantasmagoria states that God created the world in seven days. You are not gods. I give you seven weeks to complete your work.

"Hui."

Henry did not realize that he was trembling. It was the most ambitious, shocking, impossible, irresponsible, obscene message he had ever seen. The object was clear: Create a new world that everyone would want to be part of, then lock them inside it. Welcome to the metaverse. You will never leave.

He looked across the room at Nur. His round eyes were narrowed. There were drops of sweat on his forehead. He was not trembling, but his very stillness was frightening. And no bright smile lit up his face. After all the horrors he had witnessed in his short life, he was finally horrified beyond imagination.

"You understand what this means?" Henry said in English, aware that every sound in the laboratory was probably being recorded.

"Do you?" Nur answered in the same language.

Henry nodded, pointed in the general direction of the street. Nur nodded.

It was not so easy to leave the Institute without Hui to escort them. Each young man had to key in permission to leave. This request was handled by a PLA officer who was not part of the Institute. Security in China was paramount, personal privacy non-existent. Even asking to be left alone for a few minutes was taken as proof of suspicious activity.

The response was immediate. Henry's request was granted. Nur's was declined. Henry was surprised. Nur shrugged. He held out a ballpoint pen (Henry had not seen one since his enforced arrival in China) and a few sheets of computer paper with printouts on only one side. He mimed writing. Henry tried idly to remember the last time he had grasped such an ancient instrument.

Out on the street, Henry realized that despite his many weeks at the Institute during his first visit here, he had never really looked around outside. He had been to the Yellow Crane Tower, yes, but that was more as a tourist. And look what that had led to. Now, he spent a few minutes examining the street that lay ahead of it. It was straight for as far as he could see. There were office buildings, a smattering of what looked like apartments, a shop selling women's clothes that were ugly beyond measure, and, finally, a teahouse.

"Teahouse" was a misnomer. Tea could be purchased, yes, but the place also sold *baijiu*, the wickedly strong liquor that Chinese gulped down to forget their problems. Also their names if they drank enough. The legend of the Yellow Crane Tower was that it was built to honor a good-hearted teahouse owner who was kind to a penniless customer. The customer turned out to be a wizard, who created the tower to thank the teahouse owner.

Henry wondered idly what the wizard would think about today's China. A nuclear power controlled by a single Party, where citizens were taught that what they wanted mattered not at all, but what the

Party told them to want was all-important. Would they be likely to take pity on a poor traveler? To share their food and drink with a stranger who appeared impoverished? Is that something the Party would want? And to whom would a tower of gratitude be built now, except the leader of that Party?

The teahouse had tables outside and Henry sat at one of them. An elderly woman strode over to him and gabbled loudly. Henry assumed she was the proprietor or at least the waitress.

"Cha," he said in what he hoped was comprehensible Mandarin. The woman went off, muttering to herself. He smoothed the paper across the table surface, took out the pen. What, he now asked himself, did he want to say to Nur? He had seen the look of distressed surprise in the Uyghur's eyes. He deduced that Hui's dark vision of the metaverse was equally unsettling no matter what language he used to describe it. He needed confirmation from Nur. But the gap between English and Mandarin prevented him from posing the questions he needed to ask with sufficient delicacy. He could not translate from one language to the other using his phone, his laptop, or any technology in the Institute. It would all be monitored.

His tea arrived. It was clunked down on the table by the Gabbler, who immediately thrust out her hand, palm up, for payment. Henry had some yuan that he had been given after he and Hui had spoken. Without thinking, he held out a handful of notes, keeping some more in his pocket, and was startled when the woman grabbed them all, and made off, chuckling. Henry shook his head. The exact same thing had happened to him the first time he arrived in Wuhan and unwisely tried to pay a taxi driver in dollars. Ignorance may be bliss, he told himself, but it is certainly expensive bliss.

Pen hovering above paper, Henry tried to find the words that would communicate his concern, ascertain if Nur was in agreement and plot their joint course of action. Impossible. He could no more find the right words in English and expect them to be understood, than he could pen the message in Mandarin himself.

He looked down the street and felt a flush of excitement. It was what looked like a book stall. Necessity being the mother of et cetera, he took a symbolic sip of his tea and got up. The stall was only twenty or so yards down the street. Henry hustled down the street, enthusiasm already brimming.

It was more than a stall. Behind the rows of books on outdoor shelves was a real store, books lined up in some sort of order, but one not comprehensible to a non-Mandarin speaker. The proprietor looked at him suspiciously. He was an old man, sitting behind a clear plastic shield along with an ancient looking cash register. Henry smiled and thought to himself, wonder if he takes American Express? He passed through three shelves before he found what he wanted: aisle four said "English". And within two minutes, he had found the key to unlock communication with Nur: a Chinese-English dictionary. He hardly looked at it, so intent was he on purchasing and possessing it.

He knew about the Rosetta Stone, the stile uncovered by Napoleon's army during their campaign in Egypt. A decree carved into the stone in three languages, it became the basis for deciphering the Egyptian language used during the reign of Ptolemy V two hundred years before the birth of Christ (which was now a much frowned-upon way of marking time, since it assumes that Jesus was anything more than a smooth-talking Jewish carpenter's kid).

Fortunately, the thieving waitress at the tea house had not grabbed all his yuan. Already knowing what would happen, Henry held out another wad of notes when he reached the old man behind the plastic shield. Gramps used his thumb and middle finger to spear all the notes and drag them under the space between the plastic shield and the counter, where Henry could not reach them. He grinned evilly at Henry and took a sip of what Henry assumed was *baijiu*.

Henry didn't care. He left the book shop, returned to the tea house to find his tea still on the table, and comfortably room temperature. Henry sat. Like a scholar seeking wisdom, he thumbed to the English-to-Chinese part of the dictionary. The first word he looked up was *danger*. He wrote down the page on which the word, and its Chinese translation, appeared.

He had purchased, at no doubt several times its real price, his own Rosetta Stone.

Chapter 42
Against All Odds

The system worked, albeit slowly. Henry copied the page numbers of the dictionary where each word was printed. Number after number after number eventually made a sentence. It was not grammatically correct, but that didn't matter.

Nur took the paper and the dictionary and bent over his desk, keeping his hands over the book. It was possible they were being video-recorded, but there was nothing to be done about that. At least they were not keying the words into the vast digital information universe of the Institute. They were, in effect, using low tech to get around high tech. They both found poetic justice in this, then were further amused that they – two tech geeks – were referring to poetry as a secret weapon.

Nur's comprehension was astonishing. He did not need to read all the words in Henry's messages before he had opened the dictionary to the Chinese to English section and began writing down the page numbers. He passed them to Henry with the radiant smile of a bingo player holding up a winning card. The conversations were stilted, but got to the point:

Henry: Metaverse to be a prison, right?

Nur: Exactly. You oppose?

Henry: Of course. You?

Nur: Too.

Henry: Think Colonel we (he used that word to phoneticize the name) has approval for this?

Nur: Don't.

Henry: Work together?

Nur: Like brothers. Have idea.

They tried to cover the silence of the slow reading and writing project with keystrokes on their laptops. Henry spent meaningless minutes writing code that he knew was faulty, then swearing and wiping it out. If the defective code was being recorded, it would take the same amount of time for whoever was seeing it to realize it was useless as it took Henry to ensure that it was.

Nur began speaking English phrases to Henry. Never about what they were passing back and forth on paper, but about aspects of their work. Henry was amazed at the speed with which the Uyghur picked up the language.

When they were discussing the project they were supposed to be working on, they could fast-track their translations by using the 5-G programs available to the Institute. They "spoke" without looking at each other, on their screens, always careful to keep their comments professional, revealing no traces of human feelings or external emotion. It was not as easy as they had expected.

For instance, Henry asked: What devices will take the place of the headsets to bring users into the metaverse?

Within seconds, Nur responded: first contact lenses with electronic sensors. Afterward subdural injection of chips.

Henry: Chips already developed?

Nur: Being developed. Top priority.

Henry: The Party always succeeds.

Nur: Praise to the Party.

It felt childish, like reciting nursery rhymes at a corporate board meeting. But the phrases of praise were needed to deflect suspicion. By and large, they worked. One of the Geeks who worked on and off with them told Henry one day, "The Party is pleased with your progress. And your attitude." Of course, he could not have known about their progress unless he was monitoring it secretly. Henry suspected Geek's Social Loyalty score would take a hit for that misstep. Good, he thought.

They used paper that had been vomited up from the laboratory printers for their secret conversations. Usually, one side was filled with code. Hundreds of pages a day were printed, discarded, printed, discarded.

Using the dictionary, Henry asked: Has we used program? Nur got the pun.

Nur took some time in answering, then found the words he wanted to use: When use, trance.

At first Henry assumed Nur had used the wrong word.

Henry: Trance?

Nur: deep concentration, half-awake half asleep nothing else in brain.

Henry: You record?

Nur, smiling as Henry found the correct dictionary page numbers and decoded the message: Of course. They record me, I record them.

Henry: Me see?

Nur: Bad idea.

Henry: Why?

Nur: You see, you see.

It was arranged for that evening, after most of the Institute had quit work and thee monitors, in theory, had too. Nur took the extra precaution of logging off from the Institute's main modem. Instead, he downloaded the video he wanted Henry to see and stored it on a thumb drive. Very 20th century of course, but if they were going to catch him and return him to Lop, it would not be because he had been careless or lazy.

Henry never left the lab. He did not want video of himself walking the halls, returning to his quarters, or anything else that could be time-stamped. Where was he? Working of course, for the glory of the Party.

Nur came into the lab at 10:30 as they had arranged. He brought some pieces of fish and a small cup of soup, since Henry had not eaten since midday. Henry gobbled it down as Nur fit the thumb drive into an old Dell laptop that had been collecting dust in the lab. It was offline.

"Put these in," said Nur, holding out a matchbook-size plastic case. Henry knew they were adapted contact lenses. For the time being, they were the best way to enter the metaverse. The headsets that were used in the last decade were outdated. Soon, he and Nur knew, an injectable chip would guide the traveler through the metaverse. But not yet.

He inserted the lenses, let Nur help him to sit down in front of the laptop – he could not see it, only a gray blur – and nodded.

Nur switched on the video.

And Henry saw it.

Hui, standing in the middle of the planetarium lab, speaking to Mora, who Henry knew from his own session in Arlington.

And then the video continued, and he saw it all.

"Lieuten ... Ma-lin," Hui said, completely unnerved now. "Tell me, please. What are your ... feelings?"

The smile brightened. "I suppose you know that already. You have known since we took a walk down the street and spoke freely."

"But," said Hui, "are these your thoughts, or are they what I wish your thoughts might be? Are you telling me your thoughts, or mine?"

Ma-lin raised her eyebrows a fraction, a delicate gesture that said everything. "Men and women have asked this question, pondered it, prayed that the answer they received would match their wishes, for many thousands of years. In this sense, the metaverse is not something new, but as old as love itself."

"Ma-lin," said Hui.

"I will be here, in this space, for you, whenever you want me. Need me."

Then the image faded, and with it, Henry's hopes and will to live.

Chapter 43
Neither He Nor Xi

LOFW was fit to be tied. Which had happened before, but only by mutual consent. Now she stared at DICK as though ready to bite his head off. "I asked for some information," she said.

"I am afraid that information doesn't exist," said DICK stiffly. "We cannot determine how many of the AI soldiers are women because first, AI does not have gender, and two, we have not been able to capture and inspect any of them."

"That's not good enough," shouted LOFW. "I pay all of you people to get me information and now you tell me you can't."

"Because there is no gender distinction with AI."

"First," said LOFW, "women have spent a century and more to let you men know there *is* a gender distinction. It distinguishes us from you putrid male things. Don't *ever* tell me there's no distinction."

"It was my impression," said DICK softly, "that the fight for women's equality was to have women be treated the same as men, not differently from them."

"That was then, this is now," said LOFW loftily. "We got what we wanted. Now we want more."

"Of course," said DICK. "As you should."

"I want our best AI people to get to work making women robots."

"Again," said DICK, probing her tolerance gently, "they are not robots. They are armed and highly intelligent warriors. They do not take orders from anyone. They decide what to do based on their own intelligence."

"I wish there were more women like that," said LOFW, certain she had made her point and won the argument. "Now who are our best AI people?"

DICK, holding himself rigidly straight, took a deep breath and said, "We have several people working in that area. But one of our very best cannot be located."

"What's that mean?" LOFW said with a steely tone. "If I say I need someone to do something, she needs to get her ass in gear and do it."

"The person in this case is male," said DICK.

"Figures," shot back LOFW. "Lazy, huh?"

"No. Missing."

"Well, find him."

"We're trying. We're afraid he may have been taken."

"By whom?"

"At the moment, we suspect the Chinese."

"Those creeps again?" said LOFW theatrically. "They build robots without any concern for gender representation, then they kidnap one of our people? Get her on the line for me."

"Get who?" said DICK, afraid he knew the answer.

"The guy in charge in China. Her is his name, I think."

"Whose?"

"No. His."

DICK had seen the Abbot and Costello Who's on First routine. Now, he felt he was living it. "The Chinese president is named Xi."

"See? I told you," said LOFW, satisfied she had been right all along.

"Told who?"

"You. About her."

"About Xi."

"Her. Can't you speak English right?"

"Right."

"So you can't?"

"Who?" asked LOFW's private secretary, trying in vain to take notes.

"Him," said LOFW, pointing at DICK.

"No, Xi," said DICK.

"I need to meditate," said LOFW, sighing deeply.

"Who does?" asked the secretary.

"She does," answered DICK.

"What about Xi? Does he meditate?"

"You mean Xi?"

"Just get her. I mean him. I mean Xi," said LOFW. "God, this job is difficult. I need more women around here."

Chapter 44
Fentanyl And Jelly Sandwiches

Hui was quietly elated. His position and personality did not allow him to show it. Nevertheless, there was a spark in his step, and his face, though carefully set, had more than the average glow to it.

Along with the latest coding fixes, made overnight, Nur had brought excellent news.

"The team working on the implants thinks the control can be miniaturized even further than we thought," he said. Along with unheard of freedom for a Uyghur, Nur had also been told, by Hui, that he was permitted to show some personality. And so, he waited, dramatically, for the Colonel to respond to this information.

"All right," said Hui, smiling vaguely. "I'll bite. How much more can it be miniaturized?"

Nur let himself smile. "To one one-thousandth of a millimeter." His pride was evident. Yet even with Hui, Nur knew better than to gloat. "As you know, Colonel, a particle that small can be absorbed by the human body through osmosis."

Already knowing the answer, Hui asked, "And how do you suggest the osmosis take place?"

Now Nur knew he had clearance to smile broadly. He said: "Nothing 'gets under your skin' quite like Fentanyl, right?" The expression meant the same in Chinese as in English.

"Quite right," said Hui. He took a deeper than usual breath to congratulate himself. Having learned of the former Vice Minister Hu's Fentanyl production program, Hui had reported it to Xi Jinping. And Xi, wiser than anyone (or so it was good to say if you wanted to get ahead), decided on the spot not to put an end to the program, but to transfer its supervision to Hui. "Don't let it spread among our people," he warned Hui. "Make sure every last bit of it reaches America. They love to put themselves out of the misery of everyday life with drugs. This is perfect for them."

"As always, you are right," said Hui humbly, while really thinking, 'You have a talent for stating the obvious, you self-satisfied oaf.' Hui had already anticipated Xi's response and knew exactly how best he would use Fentanyl.

Patches.

Millions of them were sold every year in the United States. They were stuck with adhesive to the belly just below the ribcage. Slowly but effectively, the liquid Fentanyl seeped throughout the patches first made contact, then seeped under the skin and into the stomach sac, where it began its calm-inducing tour of the rest of the body.

For those who lacked the patience to let the patches ease their pain, Hui knew (thanks to Nur), there was a booming if illegal industry in America to extract the hard-core ingredients from patches, condense the Fentanyl, and take it orally or by injection. Such self-abuse seemed to Hui barbaric, but, he told himself with a secret smile, not for him to judge others. Plus, he had concluded that the Fentanyl patch could be used for another, even more strategic kind of addiction: to the metaverse.

Xi had instructed him not to "let it spread" among Han Chinese. He hadn't said don't test it on them.

The Chinese version of the various metaverse games and worlds was called Jelly. Hui had been unaware of it until Nur brought it to his attention. "It's not as refined as the ones in America," Nur had said, "but there are also absolutely no rules about how it can be used. Not yet, anyway."

Perfect, thought Hui. A make-believe world newly born, like a baby, whose development depends on its caretakers. Parents, in a way. Hui would be, if not the father of Jelly, then its godfather. And he would shape it to his pleasure and advantage.

Hui no longer saw the Geek Squad that he had created during his first time as Director of the AI Institute. He received their updates through Nur, who seldom let the chance slip by to point out their inferior intelligence. Hui knew what he was doing: turning the Han Chinese discrimination and derision of the Uyghur race on its head and, demonstrating that Hui's Chinese underlings were the ones who were substandard. It was never expressed in so many words. More in gestures and clever comparisons. But Nur's point was clear.

"Next you'll be challenging me to a Go match," said Hui, his eyes alight with hope that Nur would take the bait.

Like tens of millions of Chinese, Hui fancied himself an excellent player of Go, the board game that had been played in China since, well, since there was a China, some 2,500 years ago. It resembled chess, but required far deeper thought and planning. Hui had decided to believe the legend that the game was once used to decide who would be the next ruler of Tibet. The winner got the throne. The loser got the ax. Hui mused that Xi Jinping was probably wise not to let his leadership position be decided by Go, in case some brilliant mind like Nur was his opponent. That, Hui thought, would put a dent in the Han Chinese repugnance toward Uyghurs on the grounds that they were subhuman.

Nur shook his head. "No, Colonel. I would never challenge you to Go. Or anything else." They both knew this was as close to a loyalty oath as Nur could state in words. He demonstrated fealty by actions.

"I have the same question as always these days, Nur," Hui said.

"How long will it take?" Nur answered. "Maybe a month. Maybe less, depending on how widely we can test the chip, and how much variation there is in the reaction to it once it's inside the body." What Nur was saying, he – Hui – knew was: how many of them die.

"Could we use the ... students?" They both knew he meant the Uyghurs at the re-education prison.

"Very few Uyghurs have ever entered the metaverse, Colonel," said Nur. "It is not an ... entertainment ... offered at Lop."

"Your recommendation, then?"

Nur said: "I suggest you authorize testing on current users of the metaverse."

"Here, you mean, in China?"

"Yes, Colonel. I suggest you make Fentanyl and Jelly sandwiches." This time neither Hui nor Nur smiled.

"Let me think about it," said Hui, already knowing what he would do. "In the meantime, take me to the metaverse." He got out the blue plastic case and began to extract one of the lenses. "Take me to Mora."

And beyond Mora, to Ma-lin.

Chapter 45
Hu'da Thought?

Henry could only plough forward with a project he knew would make him both unhappy and unnecessary. Hui had left little doubt about what he wanted: a metaverse controlled, policed, and constantly improved by AI. With Hui in charge of what the AI could do. It was the closest to world domination a single individual could hope for. It depended on the metaverse fulfilling its promise to be a better place than the real world, at least what passed as the real world for now. Once enough people had experienced the bliss of the metaverse, they would want to inhabit it constantly, without returning to the drudge that was their everyday lives. The physical world would melt away, much like living in caves, rubbing sticks for fire, hunting animals for food, or relying on horses for transportation had all faded from thought.

The metaverse, Henry understood after listening to Hui, would replace physical life. "Our bodies will simply be the connective tissue through which we experience existence," the Colonel had said, first to Henry in English and then to Nur in Mandarin. Each young man at first shook his head in disbelief, then slowly began nodding in comprehension and agreement. A new world. A better world. The answer to all. Neither of them was happy about it.

The trick for Henry was to compose coding that allowed the AI guides of the metaverse to keep users fulfilled, contented, and, if need be in some cases, unable to leave. It was not an easy task. But since his unwilling return to Wuhan, Henry had realized just how good a coder

206

he was. Working in tandem with Nur helped, but there was no doubt in Henry's mind that he possessed special skills.

He tried – unsuccessfully – to banish thoughts of Rav. After what he had seen her say to Hui during Hui's visit to the metaverse, Henry understood that he had been – and would always be – a pawn in Ma-lin Cho's very sophisticated world of deceit. He had asked Hui about her only that one time and had been rudely shut down. He got the message. Rav – or rather Ma-lin Cho – belonged to Hui now and probably always had.

And escape? Thoughts of getting out of China, away from Hui and Rav, back to America – such thoughts were, more than anything, depressing. Go back to what? To whom?

He had been permitted to send his parents one email, from an untraceable address, assuring them that he was well, that he loved them, and asking them not to try to locate him. All three statements were mirrors of the truth, he knew. Mentally and spiritually, he had bid his parents farewell the first time he came to China, to work and study at the knee of Hui Jen-Sho, his inspiration and his hero. And look how that had turned out.

Today was demonstration day. He and Nur had agreed to meet early at their shared lab space. The floor-to-ceiling video screens were already on. They showed a street filled with shops, moving in and out of focus, replaced by another length of the same street, and different shops. People stepped in and out of the image. The sounds of traffic, of far-off music, of feet crunching on the uneven street competed for the ear's attention. Henry had seen it before. It was the line of vision of a person who carried inside his or her body the chip that Nur had coded. The video command within the chip transmitted whatever the user saw to the screen. The person became a walking, talking camera. And the only way to turn it off was to extract the chip from the user's medulla oblongata, where it had been instructed to go after being absorbed into the bloodstream. Nur and Henry had agreed that "user" was not a proper description for someone carrying the chip. They preferred "visitor," as in, a visitor to the metaverse that they were creating and improving with each stroke of their keyboards.

Before he said a word, Nur went to the place where the Chinese-English dictionary was concealed. He put it on Henry's workspace, and opened it to a page he had bookmarked with an actual piece of paper, which both considered an artifact of the past.

"Escape" and then "route," were the words he pointed to. Henry did not comprehend. Hui held up his index finger, as if calling for patience. The street scene on the screen was swallowed up, replaced for a second with darkness, then light. The visitor had entered a building.

Henry and Nur continued their coding.

Hui came into the lab an hour later dressed in full uniform. He usually did that only when there was something he wanted to announce. He smiled brusquely to each young man, as if suggesting that what they would see today was proletarian in nature. Yet Hui's eyes were bright, his face color high. He is excited, Henry thought.

"I have visited the metaverse," Hui said in English.

No shit, thought Henry. I saw you in there, practically fucking Rav. The Rav thought stabbed him.

Apparently Hui knew that Nur's English was progressing rapidly because he did not repeat himself in Mandarin. "We now know that the metaverse can be many different things, to many different people. It can be a harmless yet exciting video game. It can be a virtual experience that simulates many activities most people will never know: skydiving, fighting a dragon, visiting an unknown city, being a sports hero... on and on. And all without leaving home. Yet it is just as real as some of the activities we undertake in our physical lives.

"What do I mean by that? If we visit Paris in the metaverse, we see exact reproductions of the real Paris. We see the Eiffel Tower as it really exists. We hear the River Seine rushing beneath us as we cross the Pont Neuf. And we remember. If we score a goal in a football match, we feel the ball leave our foot, we see its path, we use body language to help it get past the goalie. We hear the crowd go insane when it kisses the net. And we remember that as well."

Hui looked directly at Henry, ignoring Nur. "If we make love to a beautiful woman in the metaverse, we smell her scent, we feel the texture of her hair and skin, we experience the joy that poets and singers have tried to describe since the beginning of time. We own her. And we remember." Hui smiled, not unkindly, but neither with sympathy as he drove the knife home.

Henry could not control his reaction. His eyes closed without command, his breathing stopped on its own. He swallowed without knowing he was swallowing, and felt wobbly. Nur watched, knowing what was happening but not why. And betraying not the slimmest hint of emotion.

"As you know, we are working on an improvement that will allow visitors to the metaverse to experience their journey without a headset or intelligent contact lenses. We will put the metaverse *into them*, and then let them go *into the metaverse*." For the first time, he looked at Nur. "You have done well. Let us show Henry the result of your work."

Nur nodded, turned to his workspace, touched his keypad. The floor to ceiling image blurred for a second, then popped into sudden focus. Henry did not know what he was seeing, and then, he realized, it was a camera trained on a man's back. The man was sitting in a comfortable-looking chair. He did not move.

Slowly, the camera panned to the right, shifting from the back of the man's head to his right profile, and finally, a full-face shot.

The man was former Deputy Defense Minister Hu. He was dressed in orange prison garb, yet did not appear to be restrained in any way. Hu's eyes were wide open and he was staring intently. Yet there was nothing in front of him. His mouth, also open, hung down as if he were in a deep sleep and snoring. Yet he made no noise. Hu's hands twitched and he fondled himself every few seconds. Yet he showed no sign of enjoyment. He lifted one foot, then another, then carefully laid each one back down exactly where it had been. Each footfall was silent. The right leg of his trousers – the same orange color as his shirt, had been pulled up past his knee. On his thigh was a brown patch stuck to his skin.

"As you can see," said Hui, "this test subject, a volunteer by the way, is deeply inside the metaverse. And the metaverse is deeply inside him. In his brain, to be exact. Finding a brain in him was the hard part," Hui said, with a sour smile, "but once found, it lodged itself in nicely. The chip is connected to the medulla oblongata, the tail end of the brain that connects it to the spinal cord. If the chip were to come loose, it would sever the connection between brain and spine, leaving the visitor unable to move, swallow or breathe. We don't want that to happen and so this visitor will remain where he is, seated, happy, seeing what he wants simply by thinking it, and without human needs.

"Clearly," said Colonel Hui Jen-Sho, expanding his chest and bouncing, just once, on the balls of his feet, "Hu we are and who we are not sometimes is beyond our control." Henry saw that Nur got the pun, but was shaking his head no. Nur was not onboard.

Chapter 46
The Cost Of Being Right

"Zero Covid" was a term first suggested by a doctor of epidemiology who had done nothing but research the origins of the Wuhan Flu since it was created in 2019. The doctor's work was widely admired by her colleagues. It was, however, reviled by the Chinese Communist Party because the doctor had no hesitation in assigning blame for the birth and distribution of the virus. She traced it, meticulously, from the Wuhan Institute for Virology, where it was intentionally concocted, to the Huanan wet market, where a bat infected with the virus was sold, to the Tianhe international airport, where at least ten thousand Chinese, many of them already infected, were allowed to board airplanes bound for other countries, to the Chinese Ministry of Health, which followed the Party's orders to deny any responsibility for the outbreak, blame it on the United States, to the World Health Organization in Geneva, which similarly obeyed the Party's demand that the illness not be named Wuhan Flu or Chinse Virus but rather the generic and uninformative Covid-19. Finally, she pointed out the Chinese government's consistent refusal to let international inspectors in and its failure to cooperate with other nations to stem the incredibly fast spread of Covid around the world.

Having so damningly laid out the timeline of the pandemic, the same doctor, whose social media accounts were erased within days, made the radical prediction that the coronavirus could spawn variants of itself, that would pose new health threats and be less responsive to the vaccines that had been developed to fight the original virus. This too was disowned by the Party, which did not want the Chinese population thinking about anything but serving the Party. For her affrontery in making that prediction, the doctor disappeared.

When the predicted variants were first identified, the Health Ministry was thrown into temporary chaos. Where had they come from, how were they different, what could be done to confound their progress? The political arm of the Ministry, which enforced Party doctrine, brought the doctor out of the home arrest where she had been kept, and told her to provide them with answers.

Still traumatized from the rough treatment she had received at the hands of a Party that claimed to exist for her and her countrymen's happiness, the doctor at first refused to help. The next day she received a visit from her aging, ailing mother, who said that her cancer treatments were being suspended and begging her daughter to do what the Party wanted.

With that patriotic incentive, the doctor explained that the best way to prevent the spread of the variant was to completely isolate anyone who had been infected – or had been in contact with someone who was sick. Local Party officials reacted with horror. That might mean shutting down workplaces. That might mean falling short of the Party's production goals. That might result in dire consequences, since China was hosting the 2022 Olympics.

The doctor shrugged. She was not an economist. She was an epidemiologist. Sometimes science collided with other science. You're in command, she told the Party officials questioning her. You figure it out. Her mother's cancer treatments were resumed, but on a less frequent basis than before. The point was clear: any level of defiance of the Party will be punished.

The doctor was probably the only person not surprised when China's great and all-powerful leader, Xi Jinping, gave a speech in which he announced the introduction of the "Zero Covid" policy. New variants of Covid had been discovered, the ultimate leader explained to China and the rest of the world, and that he – Xi – had ordered that they be eradicated. In order to carry out these orders, it would be necessary to "lock down" entire cities where the variant had been located. China must be made safe. What Xi did not say was that China must be made safe not for Chinese citizens, but for the hundreds of foreign athletes. Those athletes would be confined to a bubble to ensure that they had zero contact with any Chinese outside the smallest circle of officially approved workers. Thus would China welcome the world to its Games.

Sophisticated city residents in Beijing, Shanghai, Wuhan, smirked at the announcement, presuming that this variant would be found only in backwaters like Xinjiang province, where the subhuman Uyghurs lived and were being "re-educated." So they reacted with abhorrence when some of the higher-rent neighborhoods of their great cities were taken over by HazMat-clad Party enforcers, who went door to door, welding shut apartment doors, and nailing wooden planks across the entrances to private homes. Do not come out, they told the aghast citizens. Anyone found on the streets will be shot. But we need to buy food if we are to be shut in here, the residents argued. Let us go shopping and then we will stay in our homes.

Not our problem, said the HazMats. We must all sacrifice when the Party asks us to.

Socialism with Chinese characteristics.

For Henry, the Wuhan lockdown meant very little. He and Nur had largely stayed within the walls of the AI Institute ever since word of a variant had started making rounds on the street. His Mandarin being far superior, Nur heard about it first and informed his co-worker.

"I thought we'd defeated Covid," said Henry, during a rare walk outside. "I thought the vaccine was finally working." Early attempts by Chinese scientists to create a vaccine had resulted in the widespread use of Sinovac, which proved to be less effective than a control dose of water used in preliminary testing.

"Everyone with Sinovac needs to be shot again," said Nur, unaware of the *double entendre*. "Party very scared. Important people" – he and Henry both knew this meant Party officials – "getting new shots from American Pfizer. It works."

"What about the rest of the Chinese population?" Henry asked. "The, like one and a half billion who aren't Party big shots?"

"New Sinovac. This time with different ingredients," said Nur, flashing a wicked smile. The last word was difficult for him to pronounce, but he had been practicing.

"Why are you smiling?"

"New ingredient is tracking device. Party will know how follow every Chinese, every minute. What they do. Every eye movement. What they say. Soon, what they think."

"Who knows this?" Henry asked, horrified by what he had just heard.

Again, Nur showed how far his English had advanced. "Hu don't know nothing. Hu live in metaverse now."

"No," said Henry. "I mean, how many people know what's in the new vaccine?"

"You, me, Hui. Ha ha," said Nur, suddenly laughing. "Hui. We. Same sound. Hui know. We know."

"It's called a pun," said Henry. "Did Hui get permission to insert that tracker into the vaccine?"

"He get permission. Xi give permission. Ha ha. He. She. Xi. Hui. We. I like English."

And the next step, Henry felt certain, would be a mandatory "booster" shot. That one would contain the nanochip that would make its way through the blood circuitry to the brain and attach itself to the medulla oblongata. And bring the metaverse to us. And keep us in the metaverse. Forever.

Unless.

Chapter 47
Priorities

With the creaking inefficiency that has defined its post-Vietnam existence, the CIA eventually pieced together a hypothesis of how it could have lost an asset, meaning Henry, with no plausible explanation. Though legally prohibited from using its vast resources to follow, investigate or spy on American citizens, this law was ignored with the same impunity as rules about jaywalking.

Propelled by vitriolic outbursts from the Director – who was peppered with higher ranking vitriol from LOFW – the agency made finding Henry a priority on the same level as tracking Russian military buildups on its border with Ukraine and monitoring Kim Jong Un's nuclear program. They came up empty. The lad had simply disappeared.

"He's in Wuhan," said Rose Monaghan when a higher-up, in desperation, asked if she had any thoughts about the whereabouts of her occasional sex partner.

What makes you so sure, her superiors, known as Sups, asked.

"Because it's where he belongs. And where he wants to be," Rose told them. "It's where his life got meaning. And where he fell in love."

"Our research didn't turn up anything about love interests," her Sups said. "Except for you."

Rose scoffed. "It wasn't love. It was mutual convenience." And she told them what Henry, nestled next to her, had related about Rav.

Who else knows this, the Sups wanted to know.

"The FBI probably," Rose said. "They kept tabs on him after he came back from China. And they probably have art on the woman. She visited him at his parents' house in New Jersey."

"How come we don't have those pictures," her superiors asked.

"Because we hate the FBI and the FBI hates us. They'd rather cooperate with Fancy Bear than us."

"The Russian hackers?"

"Sure. Anyone but us. Don't you realize that? How stupid are you guys, anyway?"

This was not a career-enhancing question to pose to her Sups. Rose didn't care. Though the agency didn't know it, she was about to hand in her resignation. She was tired of taking assignments that involved sleeping with men she didn't know, then coaxing secrets out of them between the sheets. She had done it, willingly and well, dozens of times, but enough was enough. The only time she felt she had failed was with Hui, who accepted the gift of her body with good grace, and gave back nothing in return.

"Let's leave the FBI out of this," said the Sup.

"Exactly how they feel about us," said Rose, determined to see this through now that she had started it.

"We don't want to ask the FBI for help," said Sup. "It would make us look bad."

"As though that's something new," said Rose.

"His work records indicate he's very bright and good at coding," said Sup.

"Your mastery of the obvious is truly astounding," said Rose.

"I don't want to have to report to the Director that we can't find him."

"Then don't."

"But he'll ask where Henry is."

"Lie," said Rose. "It's what we do best."

"This isn't going to go down well," said Sup.

Finally, he was right about something. The Director took the news, passed it to DICK, who had an appointment the next day with LOFW.

"Let me get this straight," said LOFW, frowning, the last word being one she disliked and tried not to use. "A CIA coder who once took an unauthorized trip to China and started working for their AI Institute, only to return, and show great promise as a coder for us, has disappeared and may be back in China?"

"That's the way it sounds," said DICK, softly.

"Does he want to be there?"

"We don't know," said DICK.

"Can't we just call and ask him?"

"Ummm. No."

"I have the most sophisticated communications setup in the world and I can't make a call to an American?" said LOFW, in a tone that suggested she was losing her equilibrium.

"First, the most sophisticated communications setup in the world belongs to the Chinese Communist Party. It can record, literally, every single electronic communication, anywhere, around the world."

"Not my communications?"

"Yes, including yours."

"Well, have someone turn it off," shouted LOFW, eyes blazing.

She took a calming breath. "Listen, there are more important issues than some dopey American in China. I had a brainstorm while I was meditating, and I want to act on it right away."

"Isn't meditation a time to clear the mind and push out stray thoughts?" said DICK.

"Sometimes, but this was a really good idea," snapped LOFW. "You know how everyone says we don't have a national strategy for getting kids back to school after Covid? Like whether they have to wear masks, or retake their exams, or play outside together."

DICK felt his head start to throb. "That's because schools are not run by the federal government. They are run by individual districts in the fifty states."

"But they have to do what I tell them," said LOFW. She sounded sure of her ground.

"And what is your idea?"

"We'll have a phased return to classrooms. Girls will go back first."

DICK began to feel as if he might throw up. "Ummm, why would we do that?"

"Well," said LOFW, warming to her topic, "everyone knows girls are better students than boys. And girls have been held back for centuries. So this is a chance to give them the respect they deserve and have been denied."

"And what about the boys?"

"What about them?" answered LOFW. "Boys are lazy, dirty, they don't obey rules, and they're probably the ones carrying Covid. We'd actually be creating a safer learning environment."

"So, only girls would go to school?"

"For a while, yeah. Maybe when we're sure it's safe for the girls, we'll let some boys come back. Ones who respect girls."

"I can't help feeling that parents of boys might object to this," said DICK.

"I've thought about that," said LOFW. "And the answer is Afghanistan. See, they didn't let girls go to school there when the Taliban was in charge. Then we threw the Taliban out, and girls could go to school, and dress the way they wanted, and get jobs and drive cars, and everything.

"Then Gramps pulled our troops out and the Taliban came back and now, girls can't go to school again. So we'll see how they like it if *only* girls can go to school in America. The Taliban will see how much smarter girls are, and they'll decide to bring them back to school there. We'll *shame* them. And I'll ... we'll get the credit for it."

Now DICK's head was really throbbing. "This is an idea that is going to meet resistance. It will not be popular with people."

"*I don't care about the people,*" LOFW shouted. "I'm in this job. Leader of the Free World. And what I want is what's important. And anyone who disagrees can just *leave.*"

"Leave what? Leave where?"

"*America!* I'm in charge now, and anyone who doesn't like that should just get out. Like I said, I'm building back diverser. And I don't have time to argue about it."

For DICK, time seemed to stop. He waited an appropriate amount of time, then asked, "What do you want to do about that CIA coder in China?"

"Oh, him," LOFW seemed calmer now. "Get the head of China on the phone for me."

"As we've discussed, the president of China refuses to speak with you."

"See? Another man not respecting women. That's why I don't want any boys in school. It'll slow down the girls. And they might feel they're not being respected. I don't know. You're the DICK. Handle it yourself."

"My pleasure," he said.

Chapter 48
Where Hui Wish To Be

Hui now went into the metaverse every day, sometimes twice, once even three times. Nur knew better than to question him, let alone object. He knew why the Colonel preferred to be there, knew that he usually emerged happier, if slightly fog-headed. When he tried to show the Colonel the latest progress he and Henry had made, Hui gave the coding a cursory glance, and said something like, "Keep going," or "Do what's best." Nur, always aware that if he slipped up, he could be back in Lop by sundown, bowed his head, and murmured, "Yes, Colonel."

Hui told Nur he was ready to be a test case for an epidural chip. Nur tried, with all the diplomacy a Uyghur youth could muster, to gently dissuade a Colonel of the People's Liberation Army. "You are the architect of this project," he told the Colonel. "Someday, yes, you will show the world what you have done. But there is still some risk. Be patient, please, sir."

Hui nodded, knowing the youth was right. But, he wanted to tell him, being in the metaverse, with Ma-lin at my side, is where I wish to be. And if the chip renders me unable to leave, what harm is there in that?

He put in the lenses, entered the planetarium-like lab room, and waited. The floor-to-ceiling wall screens showed a live picture of the street outside the Institute. There was less foot traffic than usual, he noted, a result no doubt of the latest semi-lockdown. Despite the Party's "No Covid" rhetoric, the virus and its variants were sweeping across the country. The Party, of course, did not acknowledge this.

Instead, it locked down parts of the infected areas. And a lockdown ordered by the Party was not subtle. HazMat suited police roughly ordered citizens to go to their homes immediately. Once a street was cleared, shop owners were rousted from their places of business and sent home. Doors were barricaded shut with plywood or metal sheeting. Residents who protested that they needed to buy food if they were to be confined to their residences were smacked with batons. "Can you eat without teeth?" the police growled. "Say one more word and you'll find out."

Hui did not agree with the "No Covid" policy. It was too harsh, too inhuman. But since he seldom left the Institute now, he was relatively unaffected. Party-approved vendors kept the Institute kitchen well stocked. It was another reason that he preferred the metaverse, where he had no appetite and no need for physical sustenance. How long could he go without food or water, he wondered. Sometime he would test himself.

The wall slowly dissolved from the street to Mora, who seemed to have been waiting for him. "Hui Jen-Sho, welcome back," Mora purred. "Have you come to see me?" There was no doubt she was mocking him, though in a friendly way.

Mora was beautiful, or at least he thought so, despite never having seen her. She was an idea, not a woman. But that did not matter. Who, after all, can define what a woman is? Hui was not a biologist. The idea of Mora was beautiful, and in the metaverse, where nothing is real, it is the *idea* of something that matters.

Increasingly, he used his trips to the metaverse to recall his life. He was not exactly reliving it; rather, he was feeling the *idea* of what his life had been at various stages. Not surprisingly, the results were more pleasing than reality would have been.

As a boy, Wee Hui was happy, he felt. His father was stern but a reliable, constant presence. Wee Hui did not experience hunger, except perhaps for affection. His mother was a smiling, pleasant nonentity, who bought food, kept the family fed, and said very little. Hui's main influence as a boy, as a teen, and of course as a young man, was a school teacher who was also the Party representative and watchdog in the neighborhood where Hui lived.

"Your parents are fine people, Hui," said the teacher. "But the Party is your real family. It will never disappoint you. Remember that."

Hui, a quick study, remembered.

Hui had two immense advantages as a young man: his parents had taught him manners, and he was extraordinarily gifted intellectually. He knew what to say, when to say it and to whom. He was unfailingly polite, and if he disagreed with someone, managed to make it seem like a silly misunderstanding. He was amazed at first, then merely accustomed to using this tactic to get his way.

Then, because he was polite, knew the right slogans, and had a brain bursting with ideas, he was given chances to prove his worth to the Party. He almost never failed, save one time when, as an Army conscript, he was ordered to put a bullet in the head of one of his fellow soldiers who had disrespected his superior officer.

"Why?" asked Private Hui.

"Because he did not show me the respect I deserve," shouted the officer, brandishing the pistol he wanted Hui to use.

"I believe it was Chairman Mao who famously said, 'The Party deserves respect. Its members must earn it.'"

This was an astoundingly brash thing for a private in the PLA to say to a superior. Hui made sure he and the officer were alone when he said it. He was not suicidal. And the superior, realizing that Hui's knowledge of Party history and decorum was better than his, grunted and walked away.

The private who had been marked for death vowed he would always look after his fellow conscript. That man, named Zhuang, would become one of the most trusted allies of an up-and-coming Party member named Xi Jinping. Zhuang would eventually be named head of the Cyberspace Administration of China, which monitored every electronic communication in the country, and beyond. And Zhuang also became one of Hui's fiercest rivals for Party recognition. His promise to Hui was completely forgotten, like so many promises made by high-ranking or ambitious Party members.

All these thoughts and recollections, some of them clouded by time, passed through Hui's memory in seconds. Time had no role in the metaverse. Time was earthbound. Hui, now, in this cyber-reverie, was freed from the clock's bonds.

"Hui?" came Mora's silky voice. "Your mind is wandering. There is someone here who wants to say hello." And Mora's soft, non-human tones bled out of Hui's consciousness, and were replaced by Ma-lin's more direct – and more beautiful – "Hello, Hui. I am glad to see you again."

"Ma-lin," he said, or thought he said, or perhaps just thought. In the metaverse, a thought carried the weight of a word. A secret wish was a signed pledge. And regret existed only in the past tense, in the real world, which no longer mattered.

"I have been counting the moments until you returned," Ma-lin might have said. Hui felt elation, or thought he did, but perhaps he had that wrong. One of the most powerful men in China was turned into a fluttering idiot when he put lenses in his eyes and entered a universe – metaverse – that had not existed until a few years ago. Did he like it here? He liked being with Ma-lin. He wanted to be with Ma-lin. He wanted Ma-lin.

"You want me?" she asked, a smile tickling her lips.

"I didn't say that," he replied without moving his mouth.

"No, but I felt it. And that is what is real. What we feel."

"Yes, I want you."

She began unbuttoning the white blouse that she had worn each time he visited her here. There were only three buttons on it, and Hui wished he could help.

"Let me do it. You just watch."

He felt himself coming alive in a way he had not since the American woman had given herself to him. And the memory of it made him feel guilty, dirty.

"Forget about her," said Ma-lin. "You are with me now. And you are going to have me." Without removing any other clothing, she was suddenly naked and moving toward him.

And too, he – Hui – felt himself naked, and powerful and capable. When they touched, he was thrilled to find that her body was taut, and strong, and accepted his hands and lips and the rest of him with a smooth precision. And then her hands were at work too, and he had never felt anything like them. He hoped he was pleasing her, but was afraid to ask.

"Oh, yes, you do," she said in a lower unmeasured murmur that he somehow knew that she was feeling him within and was happy with the feeling. And that thought made him stronger, but not faster, for he wished that this would never end.

And then she screamed and used words that he had never heard.

"Colonel, colonel, please take my hand." Nur's voice was scared and Hui wondered why. At the end of her scream Ma-lin's perfect body had disappeared, and Hui was plummeting downward, toward the earth, through disinterested clouds that did not support him, knowing that when his fall was finished, he would be smashed to pieces before he knew he was dead.

The hand that squeezed his was strong, unforgiving, and unwilling to hear him tell his dreams out loud. "Colonel, open your eyes wide. I have to take out the lenses." And then he felt two needles, or were they fingertips, invading his eyes. And when the needles removed a lens, he was terrified beyond anything he had ever felt – he was partly in the metaverse where he possessed Ma-lin, and partly in the laboratory where his mastery of Artificial Intelligence was meaningless to him now, and more artificial than he had ever wanted to admit.

And then the second lens came out, and Hui Jen-Sho, master of his craft, and creator of a new world of wishes and wonder, broke down in tears.

Chapter 49
Slower Is Better

Henry began to make mistakes in his coding. They were small, and barely noticeable. Except that, if he made one mistake early in the programming, the rest of the program would have to be fixed from that point on. One mistake, inserted early enough, infected everything that came after it.

Like digital Covid. Only deadlier.

The mistakes were entirely understandable. They were also entirely intentional. Henry was awestruck at the bipolarity churning inside him. On one hand, he knew, and was proud, that he was the co-author of a technology that could reshape the world, if not completely replace the world. The metaverse that Hui had described and set them to work creating would be so attractive to most users that they would never want to return to real life, with all its pressures, sadness, conflict and inequality. And anyone who did want to return would soon learn that the AI controlling their visit to the metaverse would not allow them to leave. They would be permanent visitors, honored prisoners, in a world that guaranteed their happiness. And did not take no for an answer. The description also fit Henry perfectly. He was treated with elaborate courtesy and a thin veil of pretense that he was back in Wuhan by choice. That premise was shadowed by the unspoken reality that Hui had no intention of letting Henry leave his service.

The second force competing for Henry's soul was a primal male hatred of the man who had the affection and devotion of the woman that he – Henry – loved. Yes, Rav had lured him to the Chinese Embassy and been part of his kidnapping. He would not forgive her for that. But the moments that they had spent together were beyond any joy he had ever known. She was part of him. A part he would never give up. Love and hate are so closely related it is sometimes like encountering twins intentionally trying to deceive you about which is which.

The coding errors had to be inserted with finesse. Henry was good at this by now, but he knew he was not the smartest person in the coding lab. That would be Nur.

As he tapped the keyboard – P_y%3* — he knew that Nur would know. How would he react?

V^^pb7+.

Not blatant tomfoolery, but clear enough to anyone who knew what the code was for. The mental stress was far stronger than the intellectual need to make it look good. Henry had toyed with code before. But never for stakes this high.

Nur's and Henry's assignment was to create a code that took users into the metaverse, but also one that could be adapted, changed or even improved upon by the artificial intelligence code embedded into the programs. They were not writing code for the users. They were writing it for the controllers of the users. And those controllers were not human. They were artificial at best, and scariest of all, very, very intelligent.

Henry was trying to outsmart AI. Could humans still do that?

Nur was on the other side of the lab, busying himself with what he called a quality control code that Henry had to admit he did not understand. The Uyghur's composure was amazing: he never looked stressed, never, in fact, even looked as though he was concentrating particularly hard. Just the smooth, continuous input of data, resulting in programs that, once implanted, could control the human mind.

Henry needed to ask Nur a question, but not verbally. They had already found the location of the microphone that recorded every word they said. Rather than disable it, they had decided to make the most of it, since they knew where it was. "Knowledge is power," said Nur. How, Henry wondered, did a Uyghur from a re-education camp in Xinjiang province know of Francis Bacon's famous observation?

Henry stood and moved to the corner of the lab. A bookcase – remnant of the 20th century – in the corner was stuffed with useless outdated volumes. It was there that they had secreted the Chinese-English dictionary that allowed them to soundlessly converse.

The dictionary was gone.

Henry, alarmed, got Nur's attention, pointed to the bookcase, and in sign language, shrugged his shoulders and held both palms up?

Nur got the meaning of the question, but his return shrug meant he had no idea of where the precious volume had gone. Instead, he mouthed the words he had pointed out in the dictionary weeks ago. "Escape route. Lan se de."

"What?" mouthed Henry. "La se de?"

Before Nur could answer, they heard footsteps outside the lab. Henry hurried back to his console and had seated himself just as the combination lock to the lab clicked and the door opened.

Hui stood there, placid but stern. He was, Henry noticed, dressed in his everyday olive drab military uniform.

"Good morning," Hui said in English. It had become their *lingua franca* ever since Nur showed such astounding aptitude for Henry's mother tongue.

"You will recall that I gave you seven weeks to complete a code program that would allow our metaverse users to be guided – controlled really – by Artificial Intelligence. How are you progressing?"

"I believe we are on schedule, Colonel," said Nur. "My comrade and I have developed into an efficient team." Nur used "comrade" in the lab, because all three of them knew their conversations were being recorded. "Throw the dog a bone," is how he explained it to Henry, silently, using the dictionary. And now that vital communication pathway was missing.

Hui showed no reaction. "I have been following your progress. You actually appear to be ahead of schedule. But I have some questions." Since Hui seldom dabbled in questions, preferring answers, both young men tensed.

"Let's look at some of your latest work," Hui said. With two quick keystrokes of his handheld control panel, he erased the floor-to-ceiling live scene outside the laboratory that dominated the lab walls. It was replaced by Henry's work from two days earlier.

"I believe there is a sequencing error here. What do you think, Corporal?" Henry knew that when Hui used his supposed military rank, it signaled trouble. He stood and walked over to the wall, pretending to see better by being closer to it.

"It is here," said Hui, touching his own handheld device and causing an arrow to appear on the wall. "This line, Corporal."

Henry immediately saw that Hui had identified one of his first intentional errors. Why fight, he told himself.

"Yes, Colonel, you are right," he said. "It was a stupid mistake."

"And a costly one," said Hui evenly. "Now you will have to erase every line of code that comes after this point, go back, fix your error, and rewrite it to adjust for the mistake. You will still be on schedule, but no longer ahead of schedule. A shame," he said, but with a grin that broadcast victory.

"I will make the adjustments immediately," Henry said. He wondered if the mistake had been spotted by Geek One or Geek Two. Or if Nur had seen it and told Hui. Nur's face was expressionless.

"Perhaps part of the problem is the language gap between you," Hui said, nodding toward Nur and addressing him. "Your English has progressed rapidly, but there is still room for improvement.

"Yes, Colonel," Nur said in Mandarin. Henry felt betrayed.

"I value this project highly," said Hui, gathering momentum. "So highly that I have decided to add a member to your team. "To bridge any linguistic difficulties. Lieutenant," he said, his voice raised.

The door opened. Ma-lin Cho, in full officer's uniform, her black hair tucked beneath an olive-green Army cap, entered with no expression on her lovely features.

"I believe you know Lieutenant Cho," Hui said to Henry. "Though she is not up to speed on AI, her English is excellent. She will be a valuable addition to the team." Rav stood at attention, her eyes boring into empty space, avoiding Henry's. "She will remain with you until the coding program is complete. And correct," Hui added, looking directly at Henry.

"As they say in the American theater before a performance, 'Break a leg.'"

Chapter 50
A Different Kind Of Love

From the minute Hui left, the lab took on an oppressive air.

Nur tried to defrost the room. "Welcome, Lieutenant." Rav ignored him, pretended to understand the code that was posted in large letters on the floor-to-ceiling wall screen.

"Nur, let's figure out how far back we have to go to correct my mistake," Henry said. Rav was translating his English into Mandarin before he finished his sentence. Then, to Henry, "Anything you have to say to your colleague can be transmitted through me. To ensure precise communication." Her tone of voice was eerie, off-putting, not overtly unfriendly but without a trace of emotion.

By now, Henry had figured out the situation for himself: Rav had been assigned to go to D.C., get him to go to the Chinese Embassy, where he could be drugged, loaded like cargo onto a Chinese diplomatic plane, and brought back to face Hui's vengeance. It hadn't happened quite that way. He believed Rav when she said she loved him. Doubting her would be too painful. She felt something. Else why stay the night with him? He remembered that she had willingly served up her body as a bribe his first time in China. Was that going to happen again? And would it be enough for him to accept the circumstances in which he found himself? Again?

Despite, or perhaps because of her presence, he and Nur had a remarkably productive work session. Both knew where Henry had made the first intentional error. It was like two deer hunters who heard a twig crack at exactly the same moment and started heading in the same direction without the need for words. Or were they mute because it, in a way, reduced Rav's role in the lab. Instead of being separated by language, he and Nur bonded through silence. They let their fingers do the talking (see 20th century Yellow Pages jingle).

Aware that she was being shut out, Ma-lin excused herself (in Mandarin only), and went to Hui's office, where she asked his assistant if she might see the Colonel. She knew the assistant, Ming, disliked her, either because her close relationship to Hui was known, or perhaps, just because she was beautiful and the assistant was not. Even China had the equivalent of a Woke movement. Some of its loudest members were women who had not been gifted physically. Of course, that would never be admitted, either here or in the even Woker United States, which had given up its democratic freedom of speech so that its minorities could have theirs.

As expected, Ming frowned, sucked in her breath, and told Ma-lin she would have to wait, that the Colonel was very busy in a meeting. She pretended not to hear as the assistant buzzed the inner office, told Hui who was here, and put the phone down sharply.

"The meeting is over. You may go in."

As she closed Hui's office door behind her, Ma-lin saw two things that were significant: Hui was already up and walking around his desk to greet her. And the hologram of Xi had been turned off.

"Ma-lin," he said.

"Colonel," she answered. She saw his face stiffen.

"I believe the listening devices are off," he said, studying her closely. "In fact, I have ensured that they are, so that we can be freer with each other." He took another step toward her. She stood still, and he encircled her shoulders with his arms.

"I hope that nothing has changed since our last ... meeting," he said.

"Our last meeting was this morning, when you summoned me and told me my new assignment was to sit with the American and the Uyghur and translate for them." Gently, she extracted herself from his grip.

"Well, yes," Hui said quietly. He cleared his throat, not a pleasant sound. "I meant our meeting before that." Hui was strangely indirect, halting, as though he knew what he wanted to say, but was having trouble finding the words.

"Please tell me which meeting you are speaking about."

"When ... Mora brought you ... to me. You were..."

"Who is ... Mora?" Ma-lin asked, beginning to suspect she knew what was happening but not wanting to make any dangerous assumptions.

Now it was Hui's turn to look perplexed. "The gatekeeper. In the ..." And as if a light had been switched on, his eyes went dull, his shoulders slack, and reluctantly, he finished the sentence "... the metaverse."

It was clear to her in an instant. You fell victim to your own invention, she wanted to say, but did not. Nor did she pity him, though she wished she could. Hui Jen-Sho was part of the Communist Party elite, one of its shining stars. Yes, Henry's abrupt and unauthorized departure from China had humiliated Hui and left him open to a period of indecision. But he had marshaled his forces, his intelligence, his determination to win. And win he had.

He had put the Uyghurs of Lop to work in an impressive and efficient way. He had moved strides ahead of any other AI theorist. Granted, it had been with much help from Nur, who Ma-lin still distrusted on simple ethnic grounds. Together Hui and Nur had weaponized drones without involving either human life or human oversight. AI ran the drones, as it ran the military machines that had slaughtered Indian guards at the border, and was even now being improved and calibrated to take on different, more potent enemies, both abroad and, if necessary, at home.

And this, this bold step into the metaverse, where AI would control its users' experience in a shadow-world of pleasure and subservience, this was perhaps Hui's most elaborate – and evil – stretch for power. Power over anyone who entered Jelly, or any of the other artificial worlds we might wish for. Power that could turn a powerful foe like Hu Da-faq into a slobbering brain-dead middle-aged baby, living his life on an easy chair, certain that he was winning every game he played, every life he lived.

Tread carefully, Ma-lin. You are not just talking to Hui. You are talking to we. We all. We who are and we who wish.

"Hui Jen-Sho," she said, "you know how devoted I am to you. You know that I am grateful for all the opportunities you have given me. For the chance to serve the Par- ... no, not the Party. For the chance to serve you. You, who I hold above all others, and all other groups." This was as close as she could come to derogating the Party. "I love you, Hui Jen-Sho.

"But I do not love you in the way I believe you think I did. I am forever grateful to you. But I do not want to live as your lover. I have ... no, life has chosen someone else for me to share that part of life with. I did not plan it. I did not want it, not at first. But karma, which we discussed, is stronger than our minds, stronger than our bodies, stronger even than ... parties." She used the last word in a way that could not be construed as an insult to THE Party.

"I will always be available to you, Hui Jen-Sho. Just not in the way that you were thinking."

To his credit, Hui had already recovered from the body blow. He held his shoulders back, his eyes had cleared, his breathing had resumed its normal pace. He heard her out and was nodding in agreement before she had finished speaking.

"Of course, Lieutenant. I understand. We will have to modify the Jelly program so that mistakes like that are not repeated."

They looked at each other in silence.

"Now, what was it you wanted to talk to me about?"

Ma-lin did not hesitate. It was not at all why she had wanted to see Hui. And she was not at all sure she was correct in what twenty minutes of observation had taught her. She knew it would relieve embarrassment and her conflicted feelings almost instantly. And so, she looked at him and said, "The American and the Uyghur. I think they are plotting against you."

Hui moved forward like a snake, kissed her on the cheek before she knew what he was doing, and said, "I would have been disappointed if they were not." He turned and started walking back to his desk.

It was the last time their bodies would meet.

Chapter 51
At Least They're Happy

The demand for Fentanyl in the United States was at an all-time high. Doctors wrote prescriptions for patches for any patient who suffered from end-of-life cancer, or who had a complex family life. The drug was becoming both more popular and more powerful at the same time, and for the same reason: it dulled the ache of life. And when "patients" who had slapped a patch on, or when addicts who had distilled the Fentanyl from the patch and were snorting, smoking, chewing or injecting it, it produced almost immediate relief. Sometimes in the form of happy drowsiness, sometimes in the form of death.

The patches were made almost exclusively in Xinjiang province by Uyghur prisoners – make that students – of the People's Liberation Army. The PLA sold container ships full of the product to customers seeking contentment rather than dealing with their real-world problems. Since Hui had taken over production from the hapless, but now constantly happy Hu Da-faq, the patches also contained, in addition to Fentanyl, a grain-of-sand-sized chip that would lead users to the metaverse. The chip then attached itself to the brain's medulla oblongata, and prevented a user from leaving the make-believe world. Attempts to remove the chip from the medulla oblongata invariably snapped the connective tissue between the brain and the spine and left the user brain dead and completely paralyzed.

Henry and Nur had written the code for the chip. And then, Nur had written one final command.

Hundreds of the Uyghurs working on the Fentanyl patch assembly line fell ill from contact with the substance. Several dozen died, though the exact number was unknown since it was not worth taking the time to count.

It was also unknown how many of the patches containing the life-changing chip had been delivered and used. Sales reports showed that the PLA had reaped about $700 million a month before Hui took over. The figure was now $1.3. billion. A month. With no taxes.

In lieu of a cut of the profits, Hui had received a Medal of Merit from the PLA and a warm letter of congratulations from Xi Jinping on the accomplishment.

Socialism with Chinese characteristics.

"Better production, better product," Nur said, dead-pan, when Hui told him the figure. Hui knew the youth was quietly pointing out that his people worked better than Han Chinese.

"That's enough of that," said Hui, in case a random listening device had slipped past his detection scanner.

"When will we start to program chips to go into the American Covid vaccines?" Nur asked. He disliked the idea, but after all, Americans were a long way away. And hadn't exactly rallied to the Uyghur cause.

"We aren't going to do that," Hui said.

"Why not? The American companies are making their vaccines in China now. It's so much cheaper and that means their profit margins increase." Nur had been reading up on the vaccine wars.

"One of the companies opened a manufacturing plant near Shanghai," said Hui. "Of course, the entire workforce is Han," a mild swipe at Nur's recent cheekiness. "When we tried adding the chip, one of their quality control experts detected it. They inspected it, and said it appeared to be Chinese in origin. We told them they were racists for saying that and they apologized. Such a simple trick. Utter the word 'racist' and America will bend over and allow itself to be fucked every time. No wonder no one respects them anymore."

"How was it resolved?" Nur asked.

"We promised to get to the bottom of it, and the fools actually handed the chip over to us. Naturally, we claimed that the chip was American in origin, and suggested their main competitor had tried to contaminate the vaccine to gain an advantage. Now the two companies are suing each other. It'll take years for it to work its way through the courts."

"Why haven't they detected the chips in the Fentanyl patches?" Nur asked.

Hui smirked. "Same reason: racism. Fentanyl patches are cheap to produce, but the American pharmaceutical companies make a huge profit off selling them. And American doctors get a cut out of every patch they prescribe, so they'll write a prescription for anyone who comes in complaining of a hangnail. Most of the people who use Fentanyl are either minorities, poor whites, or elderly people in great pain as death creeps up on them. The politicians don't care about them. After all, stoned junkies probably can't remember to vote, and dead people can only vote in big cities like Chicago and Newark. So the Congress just keeps passing bills and spending money to prevent what they call 'drug addiction.' They know very well the people buying Fentanyl aren't addicts. They're just losers, trying to tune out of their shitty lives."

"Which is what you want to help them do with the metaverse?"

"Yes," said Hui with what, for him, passed for enthusiasm. "We'll lace the Fentanyl patches with our chip, which will attach itself to their ... you should excuse the expression ... brains. Then, when they enter the metaverse, the chip will turn on, and they'll be unable to leave. And we will have granted them precisely what they wished for in the first place: respite from this terrible life. So even if they are no longer free, at least they are happy."

"May I ask another question, Colonel?" Nur said.

In reply, Hui shrugged.

"Does my American colleague know the end objective of the project he and I are working on?"

Hui looked into the middle distance before he replied. "Henry is a complicated young man, Nur. Much like you. Incredibly bright, prodigiously talented in coding, eager to learn even more. But morally conflicted."

"How?"

"Henry is typical of Americans of his age. He grew up being told – by teachers, by peers, by the television and online garbage they inhale – that America is a terrible place. That every white American is racist, and every minority must be catered to, their wishes fulfilled, their lives paid for by other people who actually *work* for a living instead of complaining about everything. He grew up hating his homeland, feeling guilty because he was white and lived in a nice house, went to good schools, and was not in constant danger of being shot or stabbed outside his front door.

"For some strange reason, fate chose Henry to listen to one of my lectures about Artificial Intelligence, a topic about which he was, and is, passionate. Perhaps it was wrong of me, but I thought I detected great potential in him. And so I arranged for – lured, really – him to come to Wuhan and work with me. And it was here that he learned about, and came to respect *Zhongguo tese shehui zhuyi* – Socialism with Chinese characteristics. Henry understood its efficiency and its simplicity. Do what the Party tells you to do, do it well, do not ask questions, and you will progress. He also came to understand that the Party was the source of all wisdom and all good things."

Hui shrugged again. "Perhaps I had some part in that."

"How so?" asked Nur.

"I gave him a chance to show his talents. I made use of his native knowledge of America and its weaknesses, which he was only too happy to describe and suggest ways to exploit. And at some point – and this is where I may have been wrong – I rewarded his efforts." Ma-lin Cho's image stood in front of him, as clearly as it had the day before when he wrapped his arms around her, only to be rejected.

"Why did he leave China without your permission?"

"Ah," sighed Hui, "another of my errors. Because I thought he understood *Zhongguo tese shehui zhuyi,* thought that he had learned to accept it and be guided by it. I let him know that his Mother, who I know he cared for, had contracted the virus that was killing millions of people. When I refused permission for him to leave, he escaped. Escaped with the help of some evil people. Escaped at the cost of several lives. I, too, suffered, but was allowed to live, to re-educate myself, and to resume my previous duties and more."

"Colonel?"

"Yes, Nur?"

"I believe Henry is in love with Lieutenant Cho."

"I know."

"Colonel?"

"Enough about me. Enough about Henry. What about you, Nur? Are you going to accept all the kindness and generosity I have shown you, the chance I have given you to use your wonderful mind, excel in your art, make a name and a place for yourself beyond the charnel house of Lop. Are you going to do all these things, and then betray me?"

Hui would have loved to know what flashed through Nur's head as he considered his response. He weighed for an instant ordering Nur to have a chip installed under his skin, allowing it to attach itself to his back brain, and then grilling him until he gave voice to his hidden thoughts. He knew he would not do that. Yet another of your weaknesses, Hui. When will you learn?

"Colonel," said Nur. "I am Uyghur. We both know that as long as Han Chinese rule our land, as long as the Party is the ultimate authority of China and Chairman Xi is the ultimate authority of the Party, I will never be treated as human. This is not your fault, Colonel. But neither is it something you can change. I give you this promise: I will never do anything that would bring upon you the same shame, the same consequences, that Henry did. I know that you see Henry and me as freak twins, both good at coding, both still young, both beholden to you. But, Colonel, what you have done for me is far, far more than what you did for him. You gave Henry a different life. But you saved mine."

Hui looked at this Uyghur youth and felt in himself a jolt of tenderness. He would never, of course, allow this to be seen, or demonstrated. As with Henry, he looked at Nur and wondered, deep in his subconsciousness, what if I had had a son? And remembered with a pang of sadness, every bit as powerful as the jolt of tenderness, that the one person he most wanted to show affection to, and protection for, would not have him.

Hui Jen-Sho straightened his shoulders, cleared his throat and told Nur, "You are lazy. You are wasting my time. Get back to work."

"Yes," said Nur. "I have work to do."

They both smiled, knowing.

Chapter 52
Rose Knows

DICK was about to burst. "What do you mean you've looked? And can't find him? You're the head of the biggest spy agency in the world."

"Third biggest, actually."

"What?"

"China and Russia both have bigger spy shops. And Iran is catching up to us quickly. So is India. And speaking of budgets ..."

"Never mind budgets. You want me to go in there and tell her we can't find this kid? You know what she's like. She'll eat me alive and spit out..." He considered for a moment starting again, decided he didn't have the strength or the endurance.

"There is one possibility," the director said.

"Go on."

"One of our agents ... well, not really a full agent. More a plant we have used from time to time ..."

"What about him?"

"It's a she."

"Who?"

"Our agent. Our plant."

"What about her?"

"She knows Hui."

"She knows we what?"

'No. Hui. The Chinese guy. The AI expert."

"So, our agent knows a Chinese expert. There are about three hundred million Chinese experts. Most of them teach at Harvard and Yale. And spy in their spare time."

"I know. But this ... Hui might know."

"We might know what?"

"Where he is?"

"Who's he?"

"The kid that's gone missing."

DICK's head was pulsing. "And this has what to do with our ... plant."

"She could ask him."

"The top dog in China is going to ask where an American kid is?"

"No, our plant will ask."

"I didn't know plants could talk."

"Our plant. Could ask the Chinese AI guy. After all, our missing guy is an AI guy too."

"And what? You think he was invited to an AI convention in China?"

"We don't know."

"Then what's the point of asking him?"

"Who?"

"No. Hui."

"If you think she'll find out, fine."

"I'm sure Xi has more important things to worry about."

"Not Xi. Her."

"Oh, her. Yes, I will."

DICK rose. "I have to go run the daily national security briefing. I hope this is a quick in and out."

Chapter 53
Everybody's Doin' It

Henry mended his ways, crossed his Ts, dotted his Is, and fixed his ties to Hui. Nur was quieter than usual, even for Nur, which made Henry suspicious. There was no easy way to ask the Uyghur what he was thinking. But he knew something was going on.

He – Henry – got a break, when he – Nur – had a breakthrough.

"The code can be shortened. Which means the chip it will live in can be even smaller," said Nur one day, without warning.

"Does it affect the quality of the metaverse experience?"

"I haven't done enough runs to say for sure," said Nur, "but I think it might actually improve it. This was a qualitative snap. One time the old way worked. The next time, the new, shorter, faster way did. I don't know why."

"How would this new chip be administered?"

"It almost doesn't matter," said Nur. "Swallow it, inject it. Let osmosis do its work. The chip is so small it can work its way between skin cells. Of course, direct injection gets it right into the bloodstream and so it gets to the brain faster. But any method will work, eventually."

"We should make the Colonel aware of this," Henry said, demonstrating his renewed loyalty to Hui for whoever might be listening.

"I have something to tell you," said Nur, "but my English..."

Henry knew that meant that Rav would be asked to translate, something he very much did not want to endure. His thoughts for Rav – Lieutenant Cho as he had commanded himself to call her in public but inside his head and heart she would always be Rav – were so complicated that he was unable to put a name to them. The simplest, most honest formation: he would always want her. And he could never trust her.

"See if she is available," he told Nur.

"But what I need to tell you..." said Nur. And stopped.

She was available.

Nur got right to it. "I am permitted to read various websites from America and Western Europe, in order to better understand who our ... users will be. Recently, I read a statement from an American billionaire, who is still in his thirties. He created a social media platform that is being used around the world. He has become very rich, and he has committed himself and his company in the metaverse."

Rav's translation was so smooth, as it always was, that Henry momentarily forgot he was supposed to be conversing with a Mandarin speaker. They pointedly did not look at each other.

"This billionaire said that he was investing in the metaverse because he believed that someday, everyone would live in it. Constantly. That the metaverse would be a more welcoming existence." Nur paused and Henry could see him fashioning his next words with care.

"Since we are working toward that same goal – having everyone to the metaverse all the time – I wondered if you thought this American might be thinking the same thing we ... I mean Colonel Hui ... is thinking."

It was skillfully worded, and Henry nodded in appreciation. In the most discreet way, Nur was asking Henry if he thought they might be better off working for the American, who shared the same goals but perhaps did not have the same quality of coders at his disposal. He risked a glance at Rav and saw that she was purposely looking into the middle distance, and not at either of them. He thought, she too understands what Nur is asking.

And why not, Henry thought. In China, Nur was treated as a subhuman, despite Hui's generosity and protection. But that could change in a minute. Hui could suddenly be out of favor, as he had been before. Or the powers that be – Xi Jinping himself – might decide that Hui's brilliant use of the Uyghur prisoners, was a mistake and that rather than being employed, they should be destroyed.

Nur was also asking his American colleague if his – Nur's – talents would translate to America, if he might be accepted and respected there for what he is – a genius.

All this flashed through Henry's mind as he now tried to compose a reply that answered these questions honestly. A most careful reply, considering the ravishing vessel through whom he was communicating.

"I congratulate you, Nur," Henry said, "on your ability to learn what is happening in the outside world and translating it into ideas that might be useful to Colonel Hui and the Party." Rav was a talking stone, her translation perfect, her emotions nonexistent. She spoke the words precisely and looked straight ahead.

"I know about the billionaire you referred to, but I had not heard about those remarks. He must have made them since I ... returned to China." Did she just wince, ever so slightly, Henry asked himself. Or did I just want her to? He was unsure.

"Your work, Nur, has been brilliant, and it is an honor for me to work with someone of your talent and your unflagging devotion to the Party." That should inoculate Nur against repercussions if some Party asshole hears about this conversation and tries to make trouble.

"I will try to answer your question directly, but please allow me a few digressions. They will help me to make my answer more valuable to you."

And with a concussive force that nearly caused him to lose his balance, Henry realized he had been here before. During his previous time in China, he had been asked to explain America to another Chinese listener – a Han, not a Uyghur, but no matter. And Henry had delivered a half hour discourse to a room full of influential Party members that had come to be known as The Six Points Speech. It was homage to a 2009 speech delivered by Hu Jintao, Xi's predecessor as General Secretary of the Party. Hu Jintao was also related to Hu Da-Faq, the vice minister of defense that Hui had eviscerated with the deadly drone project.

Henry's previous Six Points Speech had been disguised as his response to a question from Fang Fang, the Party careerist with whom he had been thrown together to work on Hui's AI plans. Fang Fang, always looking for ways to move up through the Party ranks, had once been married to Qi Qi Dieh, a virologist who had unknowingly started the Wuhan Flu pandemic by selling a diseased bat to the city's wet market. Both Fang and Qi had been murdered, one by firing squad, the second by a Chinese assassin sent to dispatch her in New York. Rav had translated Henry's remarks to the august audience. He saw that she was remembering the same thing he was.

"America," Henry began, "is in fatal decline."

Chapter 54
The American Experiment

"It was once the most powerful country in history. It was unquestionably the leading power in the Western world. And America, apart from being strong, was also a shining idea and ideal. An example of how freedom worked, and how freedom should work."

He knew he had Nur's attention. And Rav's precise translation was accompanied by a light in her eyes that Henry recognized. She was excited by what was passing from her ears to her brain to her tongue.

"The problem with freedom is that it has no logical limits. Once tasted, freedom, like Fentanyl, is highly addictive. People want more, more, more. And there is no gauge that tells them 'Enough.' No one can say for certain how much freedom is good, and at what point it becomes destructive."

Nur was nodding and Henry thought to himself, surely, a Uyghur who has spent time in captivity knows what I am talking about.

"For instance, Americans love to talk about freedom of speech. You are allowed to say what you think without fear of being punished by the government." Tread carefully now, Henry thought. Remember where you are and who is hearing you. "Almost everyone supports freedom of speech. But how far does that freedom extend?

"Should you be allowed to express yourself by talking, singing, shouting, in the middle of a field, where only cows and flowers are around you? Sure. How about the center of a city, with people in a hurry walking all around you? Perhaps.

"Now, how about in a concert hall, where a rock group is singing? Should you be allowed to shout there? Why not? Everyone at a rock concert is cheering, or shouting, or singing along with the group, right? Now how about a hall where an orchestra is performing, let's say, Beethoven's Moonlight Sonata. Should you be allowed to shout your opinions there? I think most people would answer that question differently than the rock concert example. But who do we trust to distinguish between those two?

"America also loves to think of itself as a stable democracy. We have different opinions and people who represent those opinions compete to be elected to be our leaders. Elections are good things, right? They express the will of the majority. The tough part about democratic elections is that, by definition, someone has to win and someone has to lose. Now, if you or your candidate was on the losing side, what freedom of speech do you have? For more than a century, the losers in an election shook hands with the winner, offered congratulations, and got busy trying to make sure that they won the next election. You can argue that the losers weren't really saying what they thought – that they deserved to be elected more than the winner – but it was the polite and responsible way to react. They used their freedom of speech to *not say* what they thought.

"In the last election, Trump was defeated by about seven million votes. But instead of congratulating the winner, Trump started saying that the election was fraudulent and that he had won it. And some of the people who believed him tried to take over the U.S. Capitol, which is the seat of government. Now, to be fair, those people were using their freedom of speech to express their disagreement with the election result. So now, we must ask, how much freedom of speech is too much?

"And that's what's happened to America," Henry said, aware that Rav's voice was becoming lower, softer, but no less precise. "We have forgotten that there are standards of civility that go along with freedom of speech. We've come to believe that winning — at whatever it is, an election, a football game, a court case, an argument over a traffic accident – that winning is more important than winning fairly, or than using our freedom of speech with some discretion and some respect for what's true and what's best for everyone."

Henry realized that he was thirsty. There was no water. So he kept talking.

245

"When I think about it, I realize that was why I left America and came to China to study with Colonel Hui. And after a while, yes, I betrayed my country, I became a traitor, a *hanjian*. And I helped Colonel Hui by explaining things about America that he could use against it.

"I suppose that considering the project we are working on, and what we hope to achieve with the metaverse, that I am betraying my country again, again I am a *hanjian*..." He stopped, looked hard and unsparingly at Rav, and said, "even though this time, I am not here by my own choice."

Rav reddened, her gorgeous eyes fluttered, open-close, open-close, and either a tear or a drop of sweat coursed down her cheek. Good.

"And so, Nur," Henry said, "Americans are behaving like babies. They want only the things that they want, they don't care, or even acknowledge, that there might be other people who believe other things, want other things, are working toward different goals, just like they are. They just want to *win, to win every time, on every issue*. And if they don't win, they cry, and curse, and call it unfair, and maybe, try to take over the government by violence.

"The metaverse is the answer to all their complaints. In the metaverse, they can have everything they want. There's no such word as *no* in the metaverse. The world they wish is the one where they can live. And get away from the real world, where everyone hates everyone else, and everyone complains, and everyone is willing to do anything to win. All they have to do to escape from this shitty real world is let us put a chip inside them, and wait until it attaches itself to their brain. They can stop thinking about the real world. We'll take care of that for them. They can be free. And they can be happy, forever, in the metaverse. As long as they don't try to leave it."

The silence was louder than all the applause at a Trump stop-the-steal rally.

Rav looked at him in a way she never had before. She shook her head, once. Did she mean no, she didn't agree? Did she mean no, you're wrong? Or was she so shaken by what he had said, and how he had concluded his monologue, that she would have to reassess what she knew and how she felt about him?

Nur was already calibrating. When he began to speak, Rav was caught unprepared and had to shift back into translation mode lacking her usual self-control and aplomb. "So, tell me please," Nur said. "While all these Americans are relaxing and enjoying themselves in the metaverse, who is going to run the real world, this world?"

Henry smiled. "That should be obvious, Nur. We will."

"We?"

"Hui, Xi, you, me." Rav almost stumbled on the translation. She had to be sure whether Henry was using proper names or pronouns. But she got it right, as she always did.

And Henry, who it seemed never got anything right, said, "I'm thirsty. I'm going to get some water. Then let's get to work."

Chapter 55
The Things That Matter

Unaware that they were being sold out by one of their own, and that their escape route through the metaverse was a minefield, Americans were busy getting on with the things that mattered:

Should Americans wear masks when they went to bed? Who should enforce this rule?

Should white people be allowed to say anything that black people might not like?

Are black people who hate white people racists? Is that question racist?

Should marijuana be legal? Should cigarettes be outlawed?

Should Mount Rushmore be demolished and rebuilt to honor lesbians of color?

Should the name George Washington be banned from the language?

Should illegal immigrants be allowed to sue for retroactive welfare payments that included the years before they snuck across the border?

Should eight-year-olds be educated about anal sex?

Should humans be allowed to marry llamas?

Should men be allowed to compete against women in sports if they promise to wear a dress?

Should men be allowed at all?

The shouting, and cursing, and hissy-fits went on and on, and CNN and Fox and the rest of the idiot chorus opined and condemned and preened and crowed and assured their audience that America was exceptional and great, as long as it allowed everything that they wanted, and outlawed anything they didn't.

Democracy with American characteristics.

Prescriptions for Fentanyl sextupled, as more people discovered that CBD oil didn't get them where they wanted to be, but Fenny, Christ, it was like checking out of this shitty world and never having to think about it. Or do anything to make it better. Or do anything at all.

Tweakers began complaining that the Fen they were extracting from patches made in China by slave labor contained impurities. The tweakers demanded that someone in the government – they didn't care who – tell the Chinese to stop putting shit in their shit. "Tweakers are people too," was their rallying cry, although it seemed far-fetched. Nonetheless, a congresswoman and Fentanyl user from New York promised to look into it.

A public opinion poll found that 11 percent of Americans thought LOFW was doing a good job. Seventy-seven percent thought she was not. The company that conducted the poll was suspended from Twitter and its CEO was hauled before Congress to apologize for reporting what Americans believed.

LOFW gave a speech, which her office ordered all TV networks to take live, and Twitter to live-Tweet. "America," LOFW said with a broad, slightly dazed smile, "is finally heading in the right direction."

The billionaire who said everyone would someday spend their entire lives in the metaverse announced that the next generation of his company's hardware would replace headsets with contact lenses. People who already wore contact lenses could get lenses custom made to their prescription. Best of all, the company would store all their medical histories, and text and Twitter histories, and personal information so they could replace the metaverse lenses just by thinking about doing so. And their credit cards would be billed, automatically. And it was not refundable.

The lenses would be made in China.

Chapter 56
Welcome, My Beauty. Welcome My Beauty

Getting the contract for contact lenses was a huge break for Hui. It augmented the information bank he had created with facial recognition, and essentially allowed him access to the medicine cabinet of any lens-wearing American metaverse visitor. There were millions. The metaverse was becoming the existence of choice in America. And Hui would be its master.

Hui met in person only with Nur. Both Ma-lin and Henry had requested interviews with him. He refused. He spent more time in the metaverse, where his feelings for Ma-lin were sure to be requited.

The breaking point came when Hui's assistant, Ming, burst into the laboratory while he was in the metaverse. She looked scornfully at Nur and said, "The General Secretary wants to speak to the Colonel."

Hui, oblivious, was smiling gently and stroking his leg with his left hand.

Nur, seeing the danger, said, "Please explain to the office of the General Secretary that the Colonel has been taken ill, but will be available in ten minutes."

"You want the General Secretary to wait ten minutes? You must be crazy, you stupid Uyghur."

"It is necessary to bring the Colonel out of the metaverse slowly, so he regains all his real-world senses."

Ming turned, said over her shoulder, "This will be on your head, you piglet. You'll be back in Lop tonight."

Nur, thoroughly shaken, began the process of release, having to hold Hui's wrists to prevent him from resisting forcefully.

"No," murmured Hui. "I want ... Ma-lin ... don't leave me!"

With reassuring words, Nur gently darkened what Hui was seeing, allowed it to melt to solid gray, and put a straw dipped into a drink into Hui's mouth. Hui sucked.

"I am sorry, Colonel. It is time to remove the lenses."

"Lenses," Hui repeated dully.

"Please tilt your head back, Colonel."

Hui did, and Nur, practiced by now, removed the lenses.

Hui looked around the now-darkened laboratory.

"Why?"

"The General Secretary is calling for you, Colonel."

"All right." Hui was already pulling himself together. "But Nur?"

"Yes, Colonel?"

"I don't want the lenses anymore. I want the chip."

"It's not ready, Colonel. We need to do more work on it. To prevent what happened to..."

"To Hu. Yes, I know. But I want it."

"Let's get you ready to talk to the General Secretary," said Nur soothingly.

"She's more important."

"Yes, Colonel. The General Secretary is more important."

"Not Xi. She."

But Hui was not talking with Xi ten minutes later. That was because Xi was talking with Ma-lin Cho, who was his secret source of information about the AI Institute. China's supreme leader knew everything could change in an instant in this world, but not his trust in his wife's beautiful best friend. Xi trusted Ma-lin to tell him the truth, not only what he wanted to hear. Such people were as unique as blue-eyed Han.

"What's going on there?" Xi asked, his voice distorted by multiple layers of digital shielding.

"I am sorry to say that I believe the Colonel is not as efficient as normal," she said. "That's one way of putting it."

"Explain."

"He is sick with love."

"Hui? In love? That's impossible."

Rav remained silent.

251

"Wait," said Xi. "It's you, isn't it? He's in love with you."

"Yes."

The digital voice produced a new sound. A laugh. "Hui is a professional. He doesn't let feelings get in the way. But to have you. Yes, I can understand it. Welcome, my beauty. You've bagged your first love victim."

She stayed silent.

"Or perhaps he is not your first. Doesn't matter. Keep me informed on the metaverse project."

"It is getting closer and closer to reality," she said.

"Tell me, is the Uyghur really any good?"

"I do not believe any Uyghur can really be good," Rav said stoutly to the author of the campaign to exterminate them. "But yes, he is very good at this job."

Another bark of digital laughter. "There might be one or two of them that aren't criminals, aren't terrorists. We will talk again soon." And the line went silent.

Ma-lin did not want to contribute to Hui's diminishment. What she had told him at their last meeting was true: she loved him for what he was and for what he was doing. Physical relations were out of the question. But there were more important things.

There are more important things than sex, thought Hui, as he sipped water and tried to get his head back on straight. You have to talk to this megalomaniac and convince him to back your plans. But even as he was preparing himself for that very important encounter with the real world, and its dangers, he clung to the water-color memories his last visit to the metaverse had painted for him.

A knock on the door, and Hui's bland assistant entered, carrying the specially encrypted cell phone. "He's ready."

"My apologies for being unavailable earlier."

"We're talking now, that's what matters," said Xi's altered voice.

There was a pause. "You called me," Hui said carefully.

"I keep hearing that you've cracked through, that you can get the Americans into the metaverse and keep them there."

"We think we are close."

"'We?'"

"The team working with me."

"Including the Uyghur?"

Think before you talk, Hui told himself. "Yes, including him."

"And the American?"

"He is ... helpful."

"We have learned from our mistakes, is that right?"

"You make none. But yes, I have learned from mine."

"You must still be in the metaverse. I make plenty of mistakes."
The line went dead.

The shock that rocketed through Hui's body convulsed him. Why would Xi know that? There was no chance for Nur to have let that information slip. And why had Xi asked about Henry?

Hui made himself relax. Learn from your mistakes indeed. He called for his assistant. "I need to make a call," he said.

Chapter 57
Something Old, Something New

Henry felt something was wrong but couldn't put a name to it. Nur was quieter than usual. Rav had withdrawn again, doing her job superbly, but avoiding eye contact as much as possible. Now she left them alone.

The work was proceeding at a rapid pace. However Nur had done it, the chip that would contain the metaverse coding was hardly larger than the tip of a pin. And once ingested or absorbed, it would seek out the bloodstream for the most direct pathway to the medulla oblongata. He still didn't know what Nur meant by "escape route," though Nur had mouthed the words to him again when they were alone.

"How can we test it?" Henry asked. Nur shrugged. "I don't drive the train. I just make it run." His English now included colloquial humor.

Henry felt that he was stumbling along in his normal know-nothing fashion. Yes, he had applied his skills to this, Hui's latest, most grandiose, and evil project. But where was it all taking him? He had no idea. He also recognized that he was a poor second to Nur in terms of sheer coding brilliance. How had Nur learned all this, despite his personal circumstances? Where would it take him? It occurred vaguely to Henry that Nur should go to America and bring it up to speed in its virtual war of technology against China.

None of these thoughts could find voice in this room with a thousand ears.

For Nur, and for all the other people watching and hearing them, Henry asked, "How close to completing this code sequence are we? And when can we release the chips?"

Nur took a moment to compose his answer. "These are questions for Colonel Hui. You and I are near the end of our assigned task. And let me say, my friend, it has been an honor to work with you." Henry's eyes widened. It was the first time Nur had used the word "friend" with him. "I hope to see you again." And he silently pressed into Henry's hand four small plastic containers, each no bigger than a thumbnail. Two were red. Two were blue.

Silently, swiftly, Rav came into the laboratory. "Excuse me." She looked at Henry and said in a deliberately neutral voice, "The Colonel wishes to see you in his office." She kept her eyes on him as she said it.

Without thinking, Nur cracked, "Ask him where he wants to drive the train."

"I guess I'd better go up there," Henry said. He pocketed what Nur had given him.

Rav nodded. Nur wiped the grin off his face.

The trudge up the steps seemed longer than usual, and Henry wondered if it was because his legs were getting old, or if his sense of danger was now more developed.

"Wait," said Hui's assistant, Ming, who had the charm of a blackboard. For the next fifteen minutes, Henry pondered his life again, counted his mistakes, and settled finally, on picturing Rav as she had looked the night she had spent at his apartment in Arlington. The waves of his silent emotions made the wait seem longer.

"Go," said Ming.

The first thing Henry noticed when he went into Hui's office was that the hologram of Xi was turned on. The Supreme Leader's face was animated. His eyes followed Henry as he moved toward Hui's desk. The second thing he noticed was just that: Hui was behind his desk, in full uniform, looking very much the part of a Colonel.

"Corporal," Hui began, and Henry felt a shudder go through him. So they were back to using rank. And Colonel was higher than corporal.

"Yes, sir," Henry said, peripherally aware that Xi's hologram was looking down at him.

"I have received reports of your progress since our last meeting. You are to be congratulated."

"Thank you, sir."

"Not by me," Hui said curtly. "My congratulations mean nothing. The General Secretary —" Hui nodded once toward the hologram — "will receive you in person to thank you. And to learn when the code you have developed will be operational."

"Colonel," said Henry without thinking, "you must... the General Secretary must understand that we have developed only a prototype. This prototype needs to be tested, refined, improved. We have only..."

"The General Secretary knows everything about your work, and any suggestion that he 'must understand' something that you would tell him is entirely inappropriate." It occurred to Henry that Hui was speaking for the benefit of the hologram, thus his imperious tone.

"You will have an hour to prepare yourself. Take a full uniform and an overnight bag of necessities. I expect you will return here late tonight, but you may be invited to stay for an evening."

"I am ... I'm going to Beijing?" said Henry, dumbfounded.

"That is where the General Secretary resides," said Hui, as if schooling a ten-year-old.

"Yes, of course. But, I mean, what does he want?"

"As I have already said, he wishes to thank you. Consider yourself very fortunate."

Inchoately, Henry found himself thinking of Chinese fortune cookies. He stood. "Thank you, Colonel. May I just say one thing?"

Hui shrugged.

"I would like to inform you that my colleague, Nur, did more work on the coding for this metaverse project than I did. It is he who should be thanked."

Hui looked at Henry with even parts of contempt and warmth. "The General Secretary of the Chinese Communist Party is not accustomed to meeting with terrorists. The Uyghur will be rewarded as is appropriate. Now stop arguing with me and put together your belongings. A plane has been sent for you."

Already standing, Henry could think of nothing more to say than, "Thank you for this honor, Colonel. I will not forget to tell the General Secretary how much I owe you, as well as him."

As if brushing away a fly, Hui waved his left hand. "You deserve this." He was not smiling.

The hologram of Xi nodded.

Henry didn't need an hour to gather up his personal effects. There weren't many. He folded the best uniform he had, a pair of civilian pants he had purchased at a street bazaar, toiletries, sunglasses. He paused and considered whether he should bring the tiny containers Nur had given him. Yes, no, yes, no, and in the end, he grabbed them, and, for some reason, put three of them in a secret pocket of his washbag. He probably would not be allowed to bring it into Xi's presence. But it could be left on whatever plane he was on. Stealing passengers' belongings on a presidential aircraft would be considered bad form.

A Honqi sedan stood outside the Institute, and Henry intentionally walked past the laboratory where he and Nur had labored without looking in. He opened the door of the building, walked down the stairs, and got into the vehicle.

An hour later he was at Wuhan airport, from which more than ten thousand citizens of the city had left on international flights late in 2019, taking with them the Wuhan virus that they had contracted, and ensuring that the rest of the world would become as contaminated as they were.

The driver seemed to have clearance, and he guided the sedan onto the tarmac reserved for government planes. Sure enough, a white, unmarked jet was idling. Henry was surprised to see it was an Airbus. Then he rethought it: nothing but the best for the Supreme Leader. The driver stopped.

"Thank you," Henry said and in response, received silence.

A portable stairway led into the main entrance of the plane and as Henry climbed, he was surprised that there was no Army security arrayed around the aircraft. He was even more surprised when he got into the craft, and saw four *gweilos*, all male, all hefty, encircling him.

"Hello," he said in English, more out of inbred courtesy than surprise.

"Yeah," the beefiest guy grunted. Before Henry could ask questions, one of the others got behind Henry and started closing the airplane door.

"Hey," Henry said. No longer courteous but alarmed.

"Get in there," the biggest piece of beef said, gesturing to the passenger section. Within one step, Henry saw that the main section had only six or eight seats connected by waist high shelves. Each seat and each shelf held several seat belts. Was this a cargo plane, Henry wondered. Then he saw that the seat belts were not bolted down. They were thick pieces of fabric with a sinecure at each end. He felt weak in the knees and turned around to say that he wanted to debark, but was shoved forward.

"Hello, Henry," said a voice he recognized.

The voice belonged to Rose. And in her hand, she held the black cane.

Chapter 58
Farewell, Cruel World

An hour after he had sent Henry to the CIA plane, whose landing in Wuhan had to be thoroughly negotiated between American and Chinese spies of high rank, Hui Jen-Sho prepared himself. There would be questions to answer. Why release such a valuable asset as an American who was disenchanted with his own country, and had shown himself to be sympathetic to *Zhongguo tese shehui zhuyi* – Socialism with Chinese characteristics?

The easy answer – that he was taking vengeance on Henry for his betrayal a year earlier, a betrayal that had condemned Hui to months of misery in Lop – was not the truest answer. Yet how could he explain to Xi, or to himself for that matter, that he wanted Henry gone so that he could never have Ma-lin Cho. Hui's jealousy was not the sentiment of a rational man, a man of status in the Party system. It was more like an aging dog, resentful of the growing process of a younger, stronger pup who threatened to dethrone him from his position of primacy.

To himself, Hui had to admit that Henry as well as his Uyghur workmate, had outstripped his knowledge of AI. Hui's stardom in that area was rooted in outdated research and enterprise. When he saw what the two young men had accomplished on the metaverse project, he felt like an accountant using an abacus to tot up numbers, while his younger colleagues ran them through a state-of-the-art digital program.

The call to the CIA woman, Rose Monaghan, was completely spontaneous on Hui's part. Since any communication was monitored by the Cyberspace Administration of China, Hui would have to explain his call to Arlington, Virginia. He felt certain that he could pass it off as cinching a detail in the acquisition of the facial recognition company, which the American woman had pretended to represent and which had brought her to Wuhan, and their brief carnal interlude. Intimacy with Rose had been like chewing a piece of gum – satisfying for a brief time, but destined to be tossed into the trash when its flavor evaporated.

He had known all along that Rose's real employer was the CIA. He was proud that he had discovered this by using the very facial recognition and deep-dive information-gathering technique that her supposed company was selling to Hui. Hoist on her own petard, as Hui believed that baffling English expression went.

She had obviously kept his name and number in her phone directory. "Colonel Hui, what an unexpected pleasure," she had answered.

"Hello, Rose," he said, cutting through the pretense that they were mere business acquaintances. "I believe one of your colleagues has gone missing. I know where he is."

"So do I, Colonel," Rose had replied. "He is once again working at your Institute. And he helped create the non-human fighters that killed several hundred Indian troops."

"That's the thing about quality spy craft, isn't it, Rose? There are truly no secrets between top-level professionals. You may have Henry back, but you must send someone to collect him. I cannot put him on an official Chinese aircraft."

"Yes, we would like to have him back. Kidnapping him from the center of Washington D.C. was rather cheeky, wasn't it, Hui Jen-Sho?"

"I know nothing about that," Hui lied smoothly. "He turned up here and I was able to offer him a job."

"Right," said Rose. "Can you get authorization for an unmarked plane from America to land there?"

"I believe so. It seems my place in the People's Army and my status as the director of this Institute have never been greater."

"Then I'm happy for you, Hui Jen-Sho. I will come myself."

"Really?" said Hui, surprised for the first time on their call. "Please forgive me, Rose, but it will not be possible for us to see each other."

"Of course not," she said. "I will stay on the plane. You deliver him and off we go."

"May I ask why you are volunteering to make this tedious journey?"

There was a long pause. Then she said, "Henry and I are overdue to continue a conversation."

Chapter 59
Farewell, Cruel World II

Hui's next talk was with Nur.

"As I have told you before, you are an amazing young man."

"Thank you, Colonel. I have learned many things from you."

"We have nearly accomplished our goal with regard to the metaverse, have we not?

"Yes, Colonel," Nur said without hesitation. "We can control the entire experience with AI. Anyone will be welcome to enter our metaverse. But with our chip embedded, they will not be permitted to leave it."

"Well, they will spend their lives in the world they wish for," Hui said smugly. He thought of his time there with Ma-lin, looked forward to returning for more.

"Colonel, may I ask some questions?"

"I always get nervous when you ask permission to ask, Nur. But yes, you may ask me some questions."

"My American colleague is no longer here, is he?"

Hui was surprised. He had intended to break the news to Nur himself.

"Why do you think that, Nur?"

"Somehow, I can feel his absence," the youth replied. "It is as if part of our coding has been erased, as if some sequences are missing."

"You can restore these sequences, correct?"

"Yes, Colonel. It's not real. It's just a feeling."

"Like the metaverse itself?"

Nur grinned. "Yes, Colonel. Exactly like that."

"Henry has gone home, Nur. His work here is finished."

"*Our* work," Nur said with more force than Hui expected or appreciated.

"You had another question?" Hui said this with an air of perturbed command.

"I have been thinking of how to ask this question, sir. You have been extraordinarily kind to me, and I do not wish to seem ungrateful."

"This is about your people, the Uyghurs, isn't it, Nur?"

"Yes, Colonel. It is about my people. You have been among them, Colonel. In Lop. Did you see terrorists there? Did you see people who want to commit violent acts? Did you see ... subhumans?"

"You are more intelligent than this, Nur," Hui said. "To talk like this, in a room with many ears. And even if you were talking only to me, on the street, it would be my duty to report what you said to the Party. But I will not do that."

Hui was genuinely conflicted. He could shut Nur down now, tell him his questions were indeed, signs of ingratitude. He could expel him from the Institute, send him back to labor in Lop, putting together Fentanyl patches, or sewing American flags. But that is not what Hui wanted. He wanted Nur to reach, through his own deductive reasoning, the realization that he – Nur – was extremely fortunate. And that it was in everyone's best interests to forget about the other Uyghurs and live his life to please the Party.

"There is no easy answer to your question, Nur," Hui said. "And yet there is a simple one. No, I did not see terrorists and subhumans in Lop. Nor did I see true Chinese, Han Chinese. There is a crucial difference between your people and mine, Nur. It cannot be bridged by high-minded talk about equality and not judging people for how they look. Judging people for how they look is a very human instinct. We like our own kind. We distrust those who look different from us. The Americans are so caught up in telling each other that we are all the same, that they have tried to erase the simple fact that people like their own kind. Period. It will eventually destroy America.

"But China will not succumb to such stupidity. The Uyghurs will never be trusted by the Han. And while the Han rule China, as they have for a thousand and more years, the Uyghurs will never be accepted.

"That is not an easy answer. But as I said, there *is* a simple answer: do your job. Please the Party. You have been given a great opportunity. Use it. Show your brilliance. Escape your people's destiny."

"I understand," said Nur, and Hui could read the pain in his eyes. "Thank you for being honest with me."

"Now about the chip ..." Hui began, but Nur cut him off. "It is nearly ready, Colon- ..."

"I want it now," said Hui cutting Nur off in turn.

"It is not thoroughly tested, Colonel."

"This is not a debate, Nur. How far along is it?"

Nur looked at Hui in a different way than his usual submissive but cooperative expression. "There are two versions, Colonel. Henry called one of them red and the other blue. He said it reminded him of the politics in his country."

"Politics which he himself understood, but detested," said Hui.

"I believe that is correct. I don't know much about America."

"Which one is more powerful, more realistic."

"The red one. It is closer to real-world conditions than the blue."

"Then I want the red."

"But, Colonel, the blue one..."

"Now!" He had not meant to sound so harsh, but his eagerness to get back to the metaverse overcame his usual good manners.

"As you wish, Colonel," said Nur. "May I suggest an injection. It ensures that the chip will get into the bloodstream quickly."

"Yes, an injection."

"However, Colonel Hui," said Nur with self-assurance. "I cannot administer the injection. You must do it yourself, so that there can be no doubt you are acting of your own free will, voluntarily."

Hui was already rolling up his sleeve.

Nur held Hui's eyes with his own. "You will administer this injection yourself, correct?" His failure to use Hui's title was strange, but Hui was in a hurry.

"Yes, I said I would."

"And you will not consider the blue version?"

"No."

"Very well." Nur crossed the lab and opened the door of a small half-sized refrigerator that Hui had barely noticed before. He assumed the coders kept their lunch in it. But Nur withdrew two sealed plastic baggies, each containing a hypodermic needle and syringe, and put them on the table in front on Hui. On each bag was written, in Latin letters, "Hui." One was in blue ink. The other was red.

"I prepared these for you, knowing you were eager to go back to the metaverse. I wanted to ask you about my people, but now we have had that conversation."

"Thank you for understanding, Nur." Hui took the red-inked baggie, ripped it open, and held the syringe. "Wish me a good trip, Nur."

"Have a good trip, Colonel."

Among other skills learned in the PLA, Hui was familiar with administering injections. Mostly it had been morphine to wounded comrades. Sometimes it had been psychotropic drugs to prisoners. He found the vein in his forearm, inserted the needle, pushed the plunger forward.

No reaction.

"It will take a few minutes," said Nur.

It would be the first time Hui visited the metaverse without lenses or goggles, and he felt a flush of excitement. Was that what it was? His blood pressure had definitely picked up.

"Prepare my visit," he said to Nur.

"Yes, Colonel," replied the Uyghur whose request to free his people he had just refused. Hui seated himself in the same chair he had used on previous visits. He did not mind waiting for the chip to take effect. He spent the minutes thinking of Ma-lin, the way she had smiled at him on a previous visit. The way their bodies had fit together perfectly. He tried to recall every detail, but his mind was registering some interference.

Ah, he understood. His new visit was beginning. Nur had been right. It had only taken a few minutes.

He let the gray entryway descend on him, through him. On the other side would be ...

"Hello, Hui Jen-Sho, welcome back." Mora was there, indistinct as always, but in her own way, attractive like a good hostess should be.

Hui could hear himself saying hello back. He knew he was with Mora, but where had he come from? He couldn't remember what had been on the other side of the gray wall or how he had gotten here.

"I wish to be with Ma-lin Cho, please," he said in a low-key way. Or he thought it was low-key.

"What did you say?" Mora replied.

"Take me to Ma-lin Cho." Forget the please. He knew he sounded stronger now. In command.

"I'm sorry, Hui Jen-Sho," said Mora evenly. "That name is not in our database."

"What? I was with her, with Ma-lin Cho, the last time I was here. Of course she is in your database."

"The last time you were here, you were wearing lenses, isn't that correct?"

"I think so, yes. What does it matter?"

"It matters a great deal. With the lenses, you had a less realistic, but perhaps wider experience. Things might have been in that database that are not yet in this one. The chip you injected was not quite finished, was it? It needed more work. Didn't they tell you that? I can tell from your brain waves that they did. Why did you inject a chip still being developed?"

"What difference does it make why?" Hui could feel his heart pounding. "I want the experience of being with Ma-lin. That's why I got the chip."

"Did someone inject that chip into you? It was not a kind thing to do, Hui Jen-Sho. Not the act of a friend."

"I injected myself!"

"Oh my," said Mora. "You acted rashly. The database associated with that chip was not complete. There was more information that should have been attached. Perhaps it was a coding error."

Coding error. Henry. Their last conversation. "*The General Secretary must understand that we have developed only a prototype. This prototype needs to be tested, refined, improved.*"

He had handed Henry over to Rose for revenge. For leaving China without Hui's permission. For casting Hui into disgrace from which he had clawed his way back. But most of all, Hui admitted to himself, he had handed Henry over to keep him away from Ma-lin. It was revenge, but revenge for the wrong betrayal.

"Let me out," he said in a panic. "Let me out of here. I want to go back. I want to put lenses in and return to the place where I am with Ma-lin. I want to go back."

"I'm sorry, Hui Jen-Sho. That is not possible. The chip has attached itself to your medulla oblongata permanently. To try to remove it would snap the connection from your brain to your spine. It would leave you brain-dead."

"But ..."

"Surely you knew that, Hui Jen-Sho. You were in charge of the coding project, were you not?"

"I thought ..."

"I understand. Thinking in that other world you came from, can result in mistakes. Errors. That is why this chip needs to be refined and developed further. To make sure there are no errors. Like this one.

"Now, Hui Jen-Sho, where else would you like to be? With whom? Someone in our database."

"There is no one," he answered, already seeing his future stretching out before him. Loneliness. Misery. Ma-lin-less.

"Don't be so glum," said Mora. "Think about it. Or better yet, feel it. This is your world now. The one you wished for. You'll have to get used to it."

Chapter 60
Cane'nt Always Get What You Want

It was seventeen hours from Wuhan to Los Angeles. And another five from L.A. to D.C. Henry, stripped naked and bound to the plane's couch, was beaten with the cane for most of the journey. When Rose tired, one of the goons who had forced him into the passenger section of the plane took over. Oddly, those blows were less intense. Rose had the advantage of anger in her strokes, the memory of why they were being applied. Henry fainted repeatedly, was revived with powdered cocaine, which increased the sensitivity of his skin, and once the skin had been ripped away, his muscles, cartilage and finally, his organs.

When it was done, he was slathered with Isopropyl alcohol, which introduced a new hell, and was the beginning of what he knew already would be months of recovery.

It was pointless to ask "why?" He knew why. Vengeance. The same vengeance that led Hui to trick him onto this plane, vengeance for his own betrayal. He wanted during the flight to disappear into the metaverse, to live in a different world of his choosing. Wished he had taken one of the chips that had been specially designed for Hui – the blue one, which would guide the Colonel to Ma-lin, not the red one, where Ma-lin did not dwell. He wondered which Hui had chosen. Which we had chosen. And when would Hui realize that Henry had stripped Ma-lin Cho out of his metaverse database?

"I really hope you report this to the police," Rose had said, still sweaty from her exertion. "And then explain why you are, for the second time in your life, entering the United States without a passport, just a card that identifies you as a corporal in the PLA. That'll go over just great."

Henry reminded himself: the first time you face danger, you are terrified. The second time, cautious. This was, what? The third time he had crossed oceans without documentation, the second time he was crossing oceans as a victim of abduction. He had to admit it was the first time he had crossed an ocean while being beaten bloody.

"Where'd the cocaine come from?" he managed to croak.

"Private stash," said Rose. "Confiscated during a raid. Same as the opium I have. A shame to let it go to waste." Noticed his hoarseness. Gave him a plastic bottle of water, lifted his head to help him drink. Said no when he asked for more. "After you'd caned me, you only gave me a sip. Then you made me talk."

So, she remembered the details of that day. Henry decided he wanted to forget today as quickly as possible. Maybe he could go into the metaverse. Cleanse himself of reality. Realized the only place he was going was probably prison. What could the CIA want with him now?

When the plane bounced down at Andrews Air Base, it felt as if each of his organs was being torn out of him. He tried to blank it out but wasn't strong enough. Nur, who had endured much worse, would be stoic.

He hoped Nur would not be blamed for Hui's fate. If he had chosen red, the Colonel would spend the rest of his life in the metaverse. He let the chips fall where they might, Henry thought. Was that funny? Not really, he decided.

He was transferred via stretcher to an ambulance, sped to Langley, admitted to a secret medical facility right in the Company's headquarters. They thought of everything, Henry marveled sourly.

Except how to defeat Hui and Xi.

They let him get better for three weeks, then the interrogations began. Who had abducted him? Where did they take him? What did they want? What did he do for them? Who had done all this to him?

Rose sat in for most of the sessions, clutching the cane like the weapon they both knew it was. There was no point resisting. He told them what they wanted to know, about the Embassy wedding, about Lop, about Nur, about Hui's demotion and return to power. About the AI coding. About the shift to the metaverse project, how Hui intended to insert chips in users, leave them powerless to resist, unable to escape, or do much of anything.

The only lie he told was who had beaten him. PLA goons, he said. Because he had started making coding errors on purpose. Don't fuck with the PLA, he advised his interrogators. Rose sat silent while he spun his lies. Unless the goons on the plane turned on her, she was safe.

"You think you're pretty hot stuff, don't you," said one of the questioners. He was dressed in a navy-blue suit, light blue shirt, and red rep tie. The company uniform. Why not just have the letters stenciled on his forehead?

"Do I look like hot stuff?" Henry replied.

"You look like shit," Blueboy said. "You must really have it in for whoever worked you over like this."

Henry looked at Rose who refused to meet his glance.

"Goes with the territory," Henry said. Rose grinned.

"Your story checks out with our own intelligence," Blueboy said.

"I can't be that wrong, can I?" Henry said. That got a gruff grunt.

"We're gonna leave you to get better for a few days. Then you're going to talk to a VIP."

"Really? Is DiCaprio making a movie about me?"

"You're hilarious. You're also lucky to be alive. Look, Frankenstein, your ... absence, shall we call it ... was noticed by some very important people. People who want to talk to you about the metaverse."

"He was the creator," Henry said softly.

"What?" asked Blue.

"Victor Frankenstein was the name of the creator, not the monster."

"Look, Mr. Encyclopedia, you've heard of the billionaire asshole who's investing tons of money on the metaverse, who says someday we'll all live in it, who's already developing some kind of lenses to let you get in there that're better than those clunky headsets."

Did I know about that, Henry thought? No, not on my own, but Nur found out about it and told me. And the lenses, even though they're already outdated, will be made in China. And will have a chip in them that will seep through the eyes of the wearer and into the bloodstream and end up attached to the brain.

And so will accomplish the same thing as Hui wants to do, while making a huge profit from selling them to the billionaire.

"Yes, I've heard of him and what he's doing."

"Well, take my word for it, he's not going to do it without giving us a bite of the apple."

"Apple?" said Henry, smiling.

"Izzat funny?"

"Never mind," said Henry.

"Look, this has authorization way up the food chain. *Way up.*"

"What, please, does any of this have to do with me?"

"Stop being an asshole, Henry," Rose said. "You know. We want you to replicate the work you did for Hui."

"Who's we?" asked Blue, befuddled.

"No," said Henry.

"Who's we?" said Blue, still befuddled.

"I won't do it," said Henry.

"Yes, you will," said Rose. "Unless you want your parents prosecuted for aiding and abetting a traitor."

Henry stared at her. "You're just the same as them, aren't you? Just different flags to salute."

Rose didn't pretend to misunderstand. "Hui is way ahead of us. We have no choice. This is coming from the top. Really, the top. We have to deliver."

"Who's we?" asked Blue.

Chapter 61
Let My People Go

"What's happened to him?" Xi's unrecognizable voice wanted to know.

"He self-administered the chip," said Ma-lin. "It wasn't ready, wasn't properly programmed."

"And he's a vegetable?"

"Close enough," said Ma-lin, hating to have to say it. "We had to hook him up to an IV to get any nourishment in him. And a catheter for his outflow. He just sits there."

"Like Hu?"

"Much like Hu."

"Can the chip be removed?"

"Not without severing the connection between the brain and the spine. He'd be brain-dead and paralyzed as well."

"A shame," said Xi. "He was good for as long as he lasted."

"He was brilliant," said Ma-lin, hating the past tense.

"And you think this was all about you?"

"As I told you, I believe it was a factor. I cannot see inside the Colonel's heart."

"We can fix that," said Xi. "You can attend the autopsy."

"No thank you."

All right. What do you think we should do? This project is too far along to put it on hold."

"My suggestion, if you wish me to offer one..."

"I just asked you to."

"My suggestion will sound incredibly naïve."

"The Uyghur, right?" said Xi. You don't get to the top by being stupid.

"It is a last resort, and something I say without pleasure. But as you have said, the project is too far along to let it stall out."

"Do you trust him?" Xi asked.

"Absolutely not," she said, too quickly. "He is part of a race that has no respect for China's history, culture, or achievements. Most importantly, it has no respect for the Party."

"Well," said Xi, "if we're going to judge everyone like that, I would have to clean house in every one of my ministries."

"I understand," said Ma-lin. "No, I do not trust him. For some reason the Colonel did, at least partly. I believe he respected the Uyghur's intelligence."

"He's intelligent?"

"Oh, most certainly. Though I dislike saying it, he is very intelligent."

"How do we know he'll follow orders, do what we want him to do?"

"There are several pressure-points you could use. The fact that most of the people dear to him are in Lop, for instance."

"Where we could make their lives unpleasant, you mean?"

"Let us say, 'even more unpleasant.'"

"I see. What else?"

Ma-lin could tell that Xi was not yet convinced. It was a tremendous risk on her part to suggest such a thing to the General Secretary of the Party. Their entire relationship was on the line.

"I believe he wants to win. With the American gone ..."

"This is the famous Henry?"

"With ... Henry gone to America, he will probably be forced to work for our enemies, to recreate the work he ... and Nur ... have done here. They will be in competition. I believe Nur wants to win any such competition."

"So," said the ultimate ruler of China. "How do we proceed?"

"Comrade General Secretary..."

"Oh, stop," said Xi, like a favorite uncle might protest forced formality.

"I would ask you to do two things. The first is to allow him to speak to you directly."

"Me? Speak to a Uyghur? Do you know what..."

"Yes, I know what I am saying. Not to you. To your hologram, in the Colonel's office.

"But that's just a ... toy."

"Sir, we both know that you can inhabit the hologram anytime you wish to. I have been in the Colonel's office on occasions when you, too, were there. I have seen your eyes blink involuntarily. I have seen your face twitch in humor or disagreement. I know you are there, even if others think it a ... toy."

"How would that work?"

"I will interrogate the Uyghur," Ma-lin said, "in the Colonel's office, with the hologram active. You will inhabit the hologram and listen to what the Uyghur says. Then you can make a decision."

"What kind of decision?"

"About whether to put him in charge of the Institute."

"A Uyghur? In charge of the AI Institute?"

"You would prefer, for example, General Deng-tal to come back?" They both knew that Tanteeth had been a disaster when she temporarily took over for Hui.

Xi's answer was silence. "It might just work," he said finally. "And it might have some advantages. Perhaps the United States and United Nations would stop whining about our treatment of the Uyghurs. Calling us racists. It's the only word every American seems to know. We could show them real live evidence that we hold no grudge against that race. That we even reward the ones who are ... deserving."

"I think your idea is brilliant."

The hologram was green when Nur entered Hui's office. Ma-lin was in a hardback guest chair halfway across the room. She motioned for Nur to take a seat directly in front of the hologram.

Xi peered down from a height of ten feet. He was neither smiling nor frowning. But his eyes were moving, from Ma-lin, to Nur, and back to the lovely lieutenant.

"Comrade Nur," Ma-lin began. "Please describe the state of readiness of the metaverse project you have been working on."

Dwarfed by the hologram, intimidated by the beautiful lieutenant who he knew disliked him, Nur rallied his brain and said, "At the command of the General Secretary of the Party, Xi Jinping, and, until recently, under the supervision of Colonel Hui Jen-Sho, our team is close to perfecting a miniaturized chip that can reach the bloodstream, attach itself to the brain, and control all visits to the metaverse. If the chip is widely enough distributed, we can determine what humans see on their virtual visits."

"How was this accomplished?"

"Again, under the steady supervision of the Party and its leading experts, the chips were created in Xinjiang province to meet the specifications of Colonel Hui, who was of course, following the wise guidance of Comrade General Secretary Xi."

"And what did you find out about the chips when they were coded in a certain way?"

"If they are coded in a certain way, once attached to the medulla oblongata, the chips became the connection between the brain and the spinal cord. Which meant that they could not be removed. Which meant that once in the metaverse, visitors could not leave it."

"And if they are coded differently?"

"Then the process is reversible. You can leave the metaverse."

"How close to total completion are you?"

"Given the continuing support of Comrade Xi, our team can complete the project in a month."

"Comrade Nur, it is said that you, more than anyone, are responsible for the coding, the modeling, and the production of this chip you have described."

"I am merely a cog in the machinery devised by Comrade Xi and realized by Colonel Hui."

"With Colonel Hui otherwise ... occupied ... would you be willing to accept new and heavier responsibility at the Institute for Artificial Intelligence?"

Nur's brain was prepared for the question. His tongue was not. "I, I, I ... live to serve the Party."

The hologram blinked, turned its gaze on Ma-lin, nodded once.

"Thank you, Comrade Nur," Ma-lin said, "we will get back...."

"I have a request!" Nur said, far too loudly for a two- or really, three-way conversation.

"A request?" Ma-lin, startled, said. The hologram's eyes narrowed.

"Well, a condition." Nur turned away from Ma-lin, faced the hologram. "Comrade Xi, please excuse my impertinence. I know that I have no right to speak directly to you, let alone ask you for something. But I must.

"Comrade, the Uyghur people, especially those in Xinjiang province, have suffered ... no, are suffering greatly. If some of them in the past have not understood that the Party is the source of all wisdom, and have used violence against the Party, then they deserve to be punished.

"But Comrade, most Uyghurs are peaceful people. They know they can never be Han, but they are content to live in this great country, which you lead with such skill and dedication. Many Uyghurs are being punished for the actions of other people. And I know that the Party does not condone such

treatment of its citizens. For we, we Uyghurs, *are* citizens, Comrade. Even if we do not look like Han, and speak a different language, we reside on Chinese soil, and serve under your wise leadership.

"Comrade, by fortune or fate, I have been gifted with skills that enable me to work on Artificial Intelligence, and cross it with the metaverse, in a way that will serve the Party's wishes. With the completion of this project, you, or rather the Party, will be able to control billions of people who long to escape from this dreary world and seek solace in the metaverse. If we can inject them with this chip – which is being produced by Uyghurs, you know – we will gain complete control over their visits. They will stay in the metaverse, live in the metaverse, realize their secret wishes and longings in the metaverse, and, when you wish, die in the metaverse. Let them die happily, in the metaverse. The real world will be yours to control, Comrade.

"The Americans, especially, Comrade, are ripe fruit to be harvested now. Despite their wealth, their privileges, their freedoms, they hate the life they live in this real world. They are jealous, greedy, self-absorbed children in a world that should be guided by adults. Like you, Comrade. They will flock to the ... to your metaverse to escape what they consider injustice, inequality, repression. These are what Americans concentrate on now, Comrade. Let them be freed from these horrors. In your metaverse.

"If you wish it, Comrade, I will do more for the Institute than I have already been privileged to do. I will be a trustworthy steward of Colonel Hui's legacy and achievements. I am young, and I am Uyghur, but under Colonel Hui's careful eye, and with his confidence in me, I have learned some important lessons.

"A century ago, there was a song popular with Western religions like Christianity. It recalled the exodus from Egypt of the Jewish people, then called Israelites. The pharaoh of Egypt had behaved harshly to the Israelites, thinking them unworthy, and subhuman. The song was a cry from the Israelites to their God to help them. The song was called *Let My People Go*. Comrade Xi, in order for me to assume the tasks you have offered me, in order to concentrate on my work and to complete your domination of the metaverse, I am respectfully asking you:

"Let my people go."

Ma-lin was openly gawking. She expected soldiers to burst into the office and gun her and Nur down. Or to be led to a prison, never to be released. She knew that Xi had agreed to see Nur only at her suggestion. She would be blamed in equal measure for this outburst of audacity. And so, when she dared to, she looked up at the hologram, now a glowing green. And she saw without believing what she saw, the hologram blink once, and slowly, as if just now reaching a decision how to respond, nod its head, once.

A second later, the hologram vaporized into clear air.

Chapter 62
Divided States Of America II

The interrogations were over. All except one.

Despite some scars that could not be erased with plastic surgery, and knowing that his lacerated kidney would give him trouble for the rest of his life, Henry was on the road to recovery. The medical treatment at the secret hospital at Langley was first-rate. Diet, exercise, careful progression of activity and interchange with visitors – all these things were nudging him toward something like a normal life.

When, after he was drugged and kidnapped at the Chinese Embassy, and was briefly held in a room in Lop, it was the day he was given new clothes that he knew his captivity was coming to an end. So, when a brown box arrived containing a suit, shirt, underwear, socks and shoes – all in the right size – he knew what to expect.

DICK's office was furnished in such an understated manner that it was impressive. DICK himself was equally remarkable, in a pearl-gray suit, pink tie and (really?) rope sandals.

"I've read the transcript of your interrogations," he began. "You're a snotty little shit, aren't you?"

"Those two things come from different orifices," Henry said. He had resolved that no behavior would be beneath him. He might shout, cry, throw food. In other words, act like a real dick.

"Look, Henry, do you know who I report to? Directly?"

"I know who you serve. Or is it service?"

DICK shot up out of his chair. "Where'd you see that? That was a long time ago."

"Everything on the internet is eternal."

"All right, Henry. You want to play tough. So can we. We're in it to win it." DICK puffed up with pride.

"You've already lost," Henry said. "You just won't admit it."

DICK looked deflated. "Let's have a conversation, ok? Man to man."

"As long as you stay behind your desk, fine," said Henry. If this was going to be a chess match, he would wait for DICK to make the first mistake.

"When did you realize what the Chinese were trying to do with the metaverse? To control it?"

"When Colonel Hui first told me about it," Henry answered. Actually, it was when Nur first explained it so he could understand the enormity of the project. But those were minor details.

"Do you think it can be done?" DICK asked.

It's already been done, Henry thought, but didn't say. Just look at Vice Minister Hu, or what's left of him. "There is a laboratory in California that has already created, and is going to market, a pin-sized robot, injected into a vein, controlled by AI, which will guide it through the body's bloodstream and into the brain. The goal of this device is to use electromagnets in the tiny robot – or call it a chip – to treat brain disorders. That is being done now. You think it's impossible to do the same with a chip that takes you to the metaverse?"

"Look, Henry," said DICK, "let me lay it out for you."

"Please don't."

"Huh? Anyway, this billionaire, who, between us, has more money than morals, wants to use the metaverse as his own personal playground. He created a website that has billions of users. Now he wants to send them all to his own little metaverse, where they'll spend real money on imaginary things, and think they're happy while they're doing it. Of course, when they come back to the real world, they're no happier than before, and they're broke. And so, they'll go back to this guy's metaverse to drown their sorrows, so to speak."

"Why are you telling me this?" Henry asked.

"We, my boss really, but others as well, we want to make sure that the government can regulate whatever this guy is cooking up. That we can put a sales tax on anything that gets bought on the metaverse. And that whatever world he's cooking up is fairer, more inclusive, more diverse, more equal in wealth, more of everything that's good for people."

"*Dahuangyan,*" said Henry.

"Huh?" said DICK.

"A Chinese expression. It means 'the big lie.'"

"We wouldn't lie! We want what's best for people."

"And you'll decide what that is, right?" said Henry. He'd had enough already. "The crap you people try to put out as 'what's best.' Your mouths are full of cotton balls and fabrication."

"Not cotton," said DICK.

"Excuse me?"

"My boss doesn't let us use the word cotton. In fact, we're working on some bills to ban cotton from being grown or used in clothes. The boss says it stirs up memories of slaves picking cotton for white people. We're even thinking of having that word removed from the dictionary."

Henry looked down, shook his head.

"In fact, we're going to erect ... build is probably a better word ... a statue to all the people who had to pick cotton. But we're not going to use that word. We'll just say that they were forced to work unjustly. And that Donald Trump was responsible for it."

"Wasn't that before Trump?" Henry asked, his anger now sharing room in his brain with pity for these pathetic stooges.

"Maybe a little bit before him, yeah. But people like us want to hear what a bad guy Trump was. Is. It's a win-win. Anyway, Henry, we need your help to force our way in ... 'enter' sounds better, doesn't it? ... the metaverse competition. It can't be just about business and profit."

"You're a sad bunch of smug hypocrites, aren't you?" Henry said. "You used Rose to worm your way into my world. And Hui's world. Then, when I got away from you, you sent her to get me back. And now you're using patriotism as an argument for me to help you?" Abruptly, Henry stood up. DICK pulled himself back in his leather chair, as if he feared being attacked.

"Your, and America's, priorities are so fucked up it's too late to save you," Henry said. "You use words like *justice* and *equality* like bumper stickers from Disney World. Which, by the way, is going to ruin itself by getting involved in politics. A kid's park, screaming about not being able to tell a six-year-old that fellatio is good. You've made America every bit as repressive as China. You just cover it up by saying you want to help minorities and poor people. That means hurting the majority and rich people, doesn't it? But you don't care about that."

DICK was open-mouthed in horror about what Henry was saying.

"I got caught up in your stinking world because I know a little bit about AI," Henry said. "Yes, I worked for China, and then you, and then China again. And you know what? You both suck. But at least China doesn't pretend to be saving the world. It just wants to control it, same as you do. But without so much bullshit."

"Henry," said DICK. "You don't have to agree with us. But we need your help. We need you to replicate that chip you programmed. You did it for Hui. Now do it for us."

And right then, right there, Henry saw what he had to do.

"All right," he said. "I'll do it. But on my terms. It must be clear that I'm in charge of the project. I'm not going to kiss anyone's ass. What I say, goes."

For a moment, DICK was overcome. "Well, that's great, Henry. Just great. My boss will be so happy, so at one with peace and karma."

"By the way," Henry said, trying unsuccessfully to hide his disgust. "When I thought Hui was sending me on a plane to Beijing to meet with Chairman Xi, I brought along a sample of the chip that we'd been working on. I wanted him to see what it was, and even try it out if he wanted to. It was hidden, so your goons never saw it when they kidnapped me. If you want one, you can give it to your boss. See what it's all about."

DICK vibrated with excitement. "Givittame," he said, all pretense of office dignity abandoned. "I'll present it. Me-me-me." He could already imagine how his status would change when he showed up with a ready-to-use metaverse chip. He'd be famous.

Henry handed him a chip in a plastic container, with red ink on the outside.

"Hope you know what you're getting into," Henry said neutrally.

"Yeah," said DICK. "Me too. Haha. That's what launched her career. That's my favorite expression."

Chapter 63
A World Without Words

They communicated wordlessly but with far deeper meaning than the drivel that filled most emails, texts, letters, advertisements, and Zoom calls. Nur now occupied the office that had once belonged to Hui Jen-Sho, the former Colonel whose swift cognitive decline had resulted in his – unknown to him – retirement from the PLA without public acknowledgement. Nur was canny enough to keep the hologram of Xi Jinping on at all times, when he was working. When he left the office, which was seldom and always late, it was only to descend several flights of stairs to the small habitation that had once been assigned to his workmate, Henry. Nur found it psychologically comforting to know that it was here Henry had slept, here he had made love to Ma-lin Cho, here that he had stored his secret thoughts that, since he had never allowed their chip to be fastened to his brain, were still secret.

There was broad outrage at the Institute for Artificial Intelligence about a Uyghur being named to lead it. Outrage that is, until Xi Jinping made the announcement official in a speech to the Party Politburo, with instructions that it should be treated as a rebuttal to the many lies about Uyghurs being mistreated in China. Xi had identified the new director only as "Nur," which was the equivalent of referring to him as "Joe."

Xi kept his word. The Lop re-education camp was closed without official acknowledgment. Week after week, a handful of inmates – "students" rather – were rousted from their cells, given a set of clothes that seldom fit them, a pocketful of yuan, and told they were free to go and to always obey and be grateful to the Party from now on. Most tried to get as far away as the money and their health would take them. But some, whose work in the chip-loaded Fentanyl factories and flag manufactories, the cheap clothing mills, the plastic toy shops, opted to stay on. Their cells were converted into affordable living spaces, overseen by the Evergrande Real Estate empire. Their salaries, while minimal, were sufficient to live on. Especially since they were living in freedom, some for the first time in their lives.

Some whispered that the boy genius who had been plucked from an assembly line and swept to Wuhan was responsible for the change. This was quickly shush-shushed by their elders, who insisted, with a wink and a nod, that their good fortune was due to the wisdom of Xi Jinping.

They were both right.

Nur took encrypted calls from Xi, naturally, to answer any questions and give updates on progress to the ultimate leader. Neither ever raised the topic of Lop, or indeed used the word Uyghur. What was the point? A youth from an inferior race had connived the top authority of China to change policy for one small batch of lucky savages. The other Uyghur camps in Xinjiang remained operational. More than a million of his people were still enslaved and tortured. Nur told himself, Rome wasn't built in a day. It would have been built in a few minutes in the metaverse, but that was an unnecessary digression.

Nur hired a new coder to fill in the gap left by Henry's departure. His choice was a recommendation of Ma-lin's. It was a young woman, extremely bright, attractive, who, best of all, like Ma-lin, had fluent English.
They never spoke of this, but Nur was certain Ma-lin wanted him – Nur – to have a quick channel of communication with Henry, should the need ever arise.

In all other things, Nur and Henry spoke in code. Literally. Though each worked with highly classified coding, Nur had found a way to route encrypted code language through North Korea, from there to Brazil, from Brazil to Belize, and then onto Washington. There was no doubt that it *could* be traced. But until it was, they enjoyed reading insights into what each was doing.

Coding is its own language as much as French or Sanskrit. Each coder has identifiable foibles, habits, giveaways. Nur, for instance, knew which of the Geeks had produced what part of each day's work just from the way it was formulated. He and Henry had worked long enough that they could recognize and translate each other's work, like a long-married couple can read each other's facial tics, sighs or headshakes.

Nur had lived long enough without a social or sexual life that he had not missed it. Until now. With the burden of working for Hui lifted, and the sense of satisfaction that he had liberated at least some of his people, Nur now felt the itch for companionship. He made sure to be kind to the new coder. She was pretty. She was smart. She made him feel... human.

Chapter 64
The Other Side
Of The World Without Words

In Langley, Henry finally had an office of his own, a receptionist and a cadre of coders who knew that their new boss had lived an interesting life, but who were too intimidated by him to ask about it.

Henry did not try to be popular. He wanted only to be obeyed. His coding abilities were so far above those who worked for him that he knew he could give orders, without accompanying explanations, and that what he wanted would be done.

He read lots of websites, scanning for news from China, from Wuhan, from the AI Institute. He knew that Nur was now in charge. There was no mention of Hui. Henry thought he knew where Hui was.

The topic that had Americans' attention now was a reported spate of cases in which people visiting the metaverse to play action games or pretend they were in jungles, on beaches, in Paris, or in Pittsburgh became disconnected from reality and could not bring themselves out of their fantasy world. This new phenomenon went unnoticed by the media until a famous movie star was found at her Los Angeles mansion, critically dehydrated and malnourished, unable to speak, and oblivious to all that was going on around her in the real world. The Fox News website, always in search of catchy headlines, dubbed the syndrome "Meta-curse." Twitter exploded. The billionaire who had predicted that one day everyone would live their lives in the metaverse said none of this was his fault. Congress scheduled hearings.

A month later, it was reported that drug abusers, especially Fentanyl tweakers, were falling unconscious after smoking, injecting or licking the Fentanyl from medical pain patches imported from China. A New York congressperson who insisted on being addressed in non-binary fashion said that mentioning where the patches were made was clearly evidence of racism. She was invited onto every network Sunday talk show, where she was unable to explain her accusation.

The other story getting millions of online hits was about LOFW. It was reported that she had not been seen for eight days now. When reporters inquired about her, they were told she was dealing with important matters and that she was unavailable for comment. Henry thought that she wouldn't comment because she couldn't comment. The chip he had given to the careerist DICK, he was pretty sure, was now lodged securely in LOFW's brain. Henry hoped it would not be too lonely there.

Rose made good on her longstanding threat to resign, and had disappeared, to the best of Henry's knowledge, to a ranch in Wyoming, a state that she had always said fascinated her. There was no communication between them.

There *was* communication with his parents, who after a few puzzled attempts to find out just *what the fuck* had happened to their wayward son, had agreed to a compromise: Henry would visit them occasionally, and they would perform the Kabuki dance of pretending they were a normal American family. Since everyone knew that was untrue, the lie seemed acceptable to everyone. They accepted the story that Henry was a desk jockey at some obscure branch of U.S. Space and Defense Inc., a government-affiliated company in Northern Virginia that provides security and technology advice for space expeditions.

On one trip home, Henry's Mother said she would like to introduce him to the daughter of a neighbor friend of hers, who had just gotten divorced and moved back in with her mother. When Henry declined, his mother invited the young woman to their house unannounced. She was cute as hell, and Henry reluctantly resigned himself to conversing with her. Whereupon she began to enumerate the many faults of her ex, in embarrassing detail, and seemed unaware that Henry had completely tuned out and was listening to music in his head.

"So?" she said.

"So what?" Henry answered.

"What do you think about the way Gerald tried to chisel me in our settlement?"

Without meaning to, Henry began a tuneless recitation of *You Can't Always Get What You Want*.

Which is what he had been telling himself since his latest return to America. He told his parents he would not be seeing them again for some time.

The next week, on a Wednesday night to be exact, he was looking on his home laptop to a string of code sent through the hop-skip-and-jump mail system he and Nur had established. To his amazement, he saw that Nur had made two identical typos in several consecutive lines of code. Garishly inappropriate and without any coding value, Nur had inserted *c-ur* and *Lnsede*. Since Nur never made errors and since the three letters and the dash had no business being in this coding page, Henry wondered if his former workmate was going a little soft in the head.

Still without answers, he was preparing to go to bed when he got a text message on his civilian —which is to say years-old, unencrypted – cell phone.

"CVS. Clarendon. R."

He felt chilly. Clarendon was where Rose had lived. Was she back? Why would she want him to go to the CVS there? Certainly, his airborne torture at her hands had evened the score between them. I don't want her, he told himself.

Single men of a certain age can ignore all sorts of wisdom in their pursuit of those few special moments which is the reason the human race continues to exist. He ordered an Uber, threw on jeans and a T-shirt, put on his jacket and headed out.

There was no one in front of the CVS so he went in. The store looked empty. He tried the cosmetics aisle. The candy aisle. The birth control aisle. In the row that sold computer and phone accessories he saw Rav, looking puzzled, trying to attach her phone to various power cords. She looked at, then away from, him.

"Nothing that I have tried seems to work," she said, and her voice, its frozen, perfect British English and clean phrasing, hollowed his stomach.

He thought he would not be able to speak. Too many urges and emotions competed inside him. And so, he chose the obvious. he said, "You have a Huawei phone."

Duh. What other brand would a Chinese soldier carry? "It'll work with a Nokia power cord," he said. He reached to the top shelf – she would have been too short, even if she knew which brand to look for – pulled one down, and handed it to her.

"Anything else? Is Hui waiting for you back at some hotel?"

She said nothing, only shook her head no.

"At least you kept my cell number in your directory. I should be flattered."

She began to speak, held her tongue.

"How did you get here? Again? Another wedding?"

Head shake. No.

"Are you actually married to that Embassy baboon?"

"Of course not!" It was the first time she showed any emotion. A spark of indignation in those mesmerizing eyes.

He gestured toward the power cord. "You have to pay for things in America. I hope you know that."

"I will pay. For everything."

"Second and last time I ask, Lieutenant. How did you get here?"

"I was given permission."

"By who?"

She smiled. "We both know Hu can no longer give permissions. Or anything else." When Henry's face did not change expression, she added, "Inside joke."

He remembered Nur's silly coding error: c-ur. See her. "Uyghurs aren't as dumb as you thought, are they?"

She understood. "Nur is very intelligent. Like you."

"What do you want, Rav?" The name just popped out, as though nothing had ever happened between them.

"To be with you."

"The last time you said that, I woke up in Lop."

"I didn't know."

288

"It doesn't matter," he said. Yes, it matters, he thought.

"Henry, I thought the Embassy was going to request that you spy for China. Not that you would be kidnapped."

"How long have you been in love with Hui, Rav?"

"I am in love with us, not Hui."

"I love you, Rav. But I don't trust you."

"I know you have seen a recording of the metaverse session in which the Colonel believes he is with me. And in which I say intimate things to him. But Henry, you of all people know, the metaverse is not real. At least it is not *yet* real.

"What you heard was only what Colonel Hui *wished* to be real. It was he who wanted to hear those words, and so he heard them. I was not there with him. Not physically, not mentally, not spiritually. You saw a recording of the world he wished to be in."

Henry looked around. "Talking about love in the middle of a CVS is pretty silly, isn't it?

She didn't know what to say.

"Come on. I'll call an Uber."

Back at his place, they made love, and talked some more and made love some more.

"Is there not some way we can be together, Henry? I will earn your trust."

He tensed, remembering what Rose had said to him their first time together. *"I'll have to earn it, won't I?"* Is this what all women say? Is this how it will be with every woman I am with?

No. A voice inside – perhaps from the metaverse told him – there will be no other women. You are together now. Stay that way. Forever.

"We can't stay here," Henry said. "If I disappear they'll track me and us down very quickly. And I have no passport. I can't get out of America. And before you ask, I'm never going back to China."

"Neither am I," she said.

"At least you have a passport."

"No," she said. "Part of the agreement is that I would leave my passport at the Embassy. I must return in forty-eight hours or they will destroy my passport, then find and kill me."

Henry was silent for a long time. His life flashed by, as they say. Home. School. College. Khadija, Hui, Rav, Tanteeth, Wuhan, Fang, Qi

Qi, FBI, CIA, Rose, the Embassy, Lop, Hui again, Wuhan again. And Nur's typographical errors in his code.

"What does *Lnsede*, mean?" he asked Rav.

"What?"

"*Lnsede.*"

"It doesn't mean anything," she said. "Unless you're trying to say *Lan se de.*"

That was what Nur had written. "Ok. What does that mean?"

"It means 'blue.' The color blue. "

And before he thought too much more, or too much, he got up, went out to the kitchen, poured two glasses of mineral water, dumped two blue chips in, one in each, and came back in.

He gave one glass to her.

"Do your trust me, Rav?" he said.

"No," she said. "But I love you."

"I don't trust you either. But I love you. Drink this."

Epilogue
Together, Forever, Until

They were found, days later, dehydrated and emaciated, with their arms wrapped around each other. They were naked, and there was evidence that the bed on which they lay had been hard-used.

Their lips moved constantly, and sounds that could not be distinguished came from deep within. When one sleep-spoke, the other smiled. If one's burbling ended on a high note, the other nodded. They spoke a language that involved all sorts of nuance, too complex for lesser beings, like the experts who studied their every move.

One thing was obvious:

They trust each other.

There was no fooling these experts.

The Company sent a team to transport them to the same hospital where Henry had recovered from his beating.

Another team tried in vain to identify the woman who was found with Henry.

"No passport. No ID," said one. "Probably some whore he picked up on the street." He pronounced the word "hoor."

"Our guy has no passport either. And there's no record of when he arrived in the country. How's that possible?"

When they reported this, they were told to keep it to themselves. Another team, this time of so-called scientists, arrived an hour later, bearing a grisly array of syringes, scalpels, saws and plastic tubing. Their assignment was to find out what had happened to this pair, since the same thing was happening to thousands of Americans who visited the metaverse and seemed unable to get out. Those who did escape were ruled to be brain-dead. And since neither had any identification, it was assumed no one would miss them. These men of science, these experts, trooped out of the hospital room to let headquarters know what should be done. They were, after all, experts.

These two would be perfect for experimentation.

On the other side of reality, Henry heard the words being spoken. He knew that they were talking about him. And that when they returned, they were going to do beastly things to his body, until they cut into the back of his head and found the chip attached there. Mystery solved. The experts win again.

He could live – die, actually – with that. But he didn't want them to mar Rav. As Victor Frankenstein wished that he had never created his Monster, Henry felt pangs of regret for what he had helped bring into the world. And just as the Monster's creator knew it more intimately than anyone, Henry found hidden strength, enough to pull himself partly out of the somnambulant state he had co-authored.

Please, Mora, let me talk to Nur. And the Uyghur appeared before him in the metaverse, his sly smile somehow even more welcome in this nightmarish dreamworld.

Nur, Henry tried to say, but could not. He could only think it, only send what he hoped was a telepathic message to the one true friend he had. Please, Nur, feel me, please feel me. Please flip the switch on our blue chips. Let us out of the metaverse.

That had been Nur's secret. He had written two codes. The blue chips could detach themselves and allow the user to return to the real world. The red ones could not. Meta-Nur nodded.

He felt Rav jerk violently. Then he too experienced something like an electric shock to the back of his neck, just above his spine. Nur had felt him.

And the bright colors and ever-open doors and senseless shapes and endless possibilities of the metaverse began to fade away, slowly at first, then more rapidly. And he opened his real-world, imperfect eyes and saw Rav, she already looking at him with her extraordinary eyes. Eyes to die for.

"This world is not so bad," Rav said.

They would be back soon. But for how long?

Seven thousand five hundred and eighty miles away, on the other side of the real world, Xi's hologram nodded. He knew it too.

—August 2021-April 2022

For sales, editorial information, subsidiary rights information
or a catalog, please write or phone or e-mail
Brick Tower Press
Manhanset House
Shelter Island Hts., New York 11965, US
Tel: 212-427-7139
www.BrickTowerPress.com
bricktower@aol.com
www.IngramContent.com

For sales in the UK and Europe please contact our distributor,
Gazelle Book Services
White Cross Mills
Lancaster, LA1 4XS, UK
Tel: (01524) 68765 Fax: (01524) 63232
email: jacky@gazellebooks.co.uk